STARFALL

Books by Michael Griffo

The Archangel Academy Trilogy

UNNATURAL

UNWELCOME

UNAFRAID

The Darkborn Legacy

MOONGLOW

SUNBLIND

STARFALL

Published by Kensington Publishing Corporation

STARFALL

THE DARKBORN LEGACY

MICHAEL GRIFFO

KENSINGTON PUBLISHING CORP.
www.kensingtonbooks.com

K TEEN BOOKS are published by

Kensington Publishing Corp.
119 West 40th Street
New York, NY 10018

ISBN-13: 978-0-7582-8076-3
ISBN-10: 0-7582-8076-9
First Kensington Trade Paperback Printing: May 2014

eISBN-13: 978-0-7582-8077-0
eISBN-10: 0-7582-8077-7
First Kensington Electronic Edition: May 2014

10 9 8 7 6 5 4 3 2 1

Printed in the United States of America

For my friends—
Allen, Jeff, and Dennis

Acknowledgments

Once again a big thank-you to Evan, John,
and the entire Kensington team

Part 1

Star light,
Star bright
Three stars invade my night.

I wish so hard
with all my might,
But a wish alone
will not win this fight.

Prologue

Something is coming.

I know it. I feel it. I feel it as strongly as I feel the transformation that is beginning to take over me. The knowledge is in my bones and in my thoughts and in my soul. It doesn't have a name, but I know that something is coming that will change all the rules yet again. Everything that I've learned, everything that I've grown to accept and understand and hate about myself is going to be erased, because the world around me is on the verge of an evolution. Whatever this thing is, when it comes I'm going to have to forget everything and learn how to be something new, learn how to be something else. But all that will have to wait because right now I have to give in to the full moon looming over my head, the full moon that is ripe and silver and commanding. The time has come for Dominy to disappear and for the wolf to take her place.

After all this time, after all these countless transformations, I'm still fascinated with the moon. In these last moments right before the change, I'm still compelled to look up, marvel at how something so ignored, so common, so insignificant in the sky can cause such frenzy down here on the ground. The moon is so far away and yet it's so close; it's buried underneath my skin, tethered to my soul, joined to me with a lock that has no key. I am the moon and the moon is me. And after all this time I'm still finding out new things about myself just by lifting up my head.

My breath catches in my throat instead of releasing itself into the warm night air because it doesn't want to leave me. It knows that despite everything I say and everything that I tell my friends, I'm still afraid of these transformations, and now when I look up at the moon, I'm more frightened than I've ever been before because I can see my true self.

Looking into the face of the moon, I see a face that is cold and empty and filled with darkness, and I feel as if I'm looking into a mirror. I shudder because I don't want to be like the moon and yet I know that's the truth; that is what I am. The only reason I can be seen now is because I reflect the light; I'm being shined on by other forces. The moon and I have no light of our own; we are both born of darkness.

Was my life before turning into a werewolf nothing more than an illusion? Was it something that was only mine to borrow, to be returned when the moonclock started ticking? Was my goodness before the curse kicked in just on loan? If that's the truth, then that's the cruelest trick of all, crueler than anything Luba could ever conjure up, because now that it's gone, now that the goodness and the light have been ripped from me, the only thing I'm left with is the memory of how precious they really are. And the realization that sin, like Luba, will never be that far from me.

All I have to do to find proof is look to the left. It's there floating in the sky next to the moon, Orion's three stars staring down at me like three angry eyes. Luba, Nadine, and her unborn child. The first two stars shine bright, their light overpowering, overwhelming, while the third star—the one that used to belong to Napoleon before Nadine killed him— is dim. For the moment this third star is as empty as I am, but it won't stay that way for long; soon it will be filled, brimming with evil, and together the three stars, and the three witches, will be more powerful than ever before.

Maybe that's what's coming. The arrival of Nadine's baby will change everything, make my life even more miserable than it's already become. Is that even possible? Could things actually get worse? My laughter decimates the sounds of the night until it's all that I can hear, and I know that the answer is yes; things can always get worse.

In response to my laughter that ripples through the darkness the third star twinkles; its already faint light trembles, then disappears quietly, the same way Napoleon died. I can't stop my laughter even though I know it's incredibly inappropriate, even though my body is burning and breaking and barely recognizable. I just hope that Napoleon understands I'm not laughing at him or at his death, I'm laughing because I'm aware that, no matter where I turn, death is a heartbeat away, and I don't have the strength to cry. I don't have any strength at all at the moment because the wolf is taking it from me. Along with my voice.

A familiar howl escapes from my still-human lips that is part groan, part shriek, a sound that I've grown accustomed to because, as unnatural as it is, it's mine. The echo rams into my ears even as I begin to shrink inward, even as I'm being pulled from the world so the wolf can emerge victorious, and the echoing howl stays with me long after the girl has ceased to exist. Underneath the thick mane of fur, inside the belly of this ferocious animal whose claws and fangs crave destruction and domination, I can still hear my voice, because no matter how hard I try, no matter how hard I want to, I cannot fully disappear. I'm still here.

The wolf and I are no longer separate entities; we're fusing together to become something new like when water and dirt combine to form mud. It didn't happen immediately; for a long time one controlled while the other waited, a stagnant pool of water resting within a mound of dirt. But slowly both sides began to shift, to weaken; water flowed into dirt and dirt burrowed into water to create something new, something that could only be born from the two original elements.

When the transformations first started to take place, the wolf took over completely because the girl was frightened and the beast was stronger. Then as the girl understood what was happening and realized she couldn't stop it, she bartered for her salvation; she agreed to swap places with the wolf, allow him to come alive to feed and hunt, and the wolf agreed to retreat once his primitive hunger was satisfied. But now the wolf and the girl are entering a new phase where boundaries are blurred, and they're being molded together to create a new being, a creature who shares qualities of them both. It's not what I want; I want there to be a clear separation, but I don't have a choice. Like I have no choice now but to feed.

The thing that we've become spies the raccoon, just a few hundred yards away, sleeping or resting or waiting to be devoured. The urge to feed can't be resisted because if I do I'll bring this unstoppable hunger with me to my human self when the full moon fades away. But strangely I have no desire to resist, to stomp out this all-consuming hunger; I only want to give in to it. The new me wants to pierce the raccoon's flesh with my fangs that are wet with saliva; the new me wants to taste this inferior animal's raw flesh. The new me wants to feed. And so the new me does.

Leaping into the silent air, this new thing that I've become invades the tranquility of the night and lands inches from the petrified prey. Before it can move or cry out, my front paws have grabbed it by its neck and back and my fangs have snuggled deep into its stomach. The raccoon writhes valiantly, but since my paw has crushed its throat it isn't making a sound; to an unsuspecting eye it could appear that the raccoon is being tickled instead of eaten. The world is so easily fooled. The world maybe, but not a mother.

I look up, a thick string of blood connecting me to my feast, and see the raccoon's mother staring at me. Her eyes are vacant; they aren't judging me; they aren't pleading with me; they have been ripped of all feeling because she knows no emotion will change the fact that her child is lost to her forever. Her quiet acceptance makes me think of my own parents.

Crouched on all fours, my snout stained with the remnants of my kill, I pause as human memories fill my mind. I think of my father, who knew from a very young age that he would ultimately lose his firstborn to the clutches of this preordained curse. I think of my mother, who knows that she has lost her children forever, but is still dreaming of a reunion that will never take place. Deep in their hearts burns the agonizing acceptance of their fate. I've placed the same fate on the head of this raccoon staring at me. Despite everything that I know, I'm letting the cycle continue.

Resigned, the dead raccoon's mother bows her head—perhaps in prayer? Do animals pray?—and slinks into the night, swallowed up by the shadows, and I want to follow her. I want to peel back that curtain of darkness and let it envelop me so I can remain there until the sun returns. But this new me won't allow it. The wolf can't take over or let me borrow its strength. The girl can't retreat into nothingness until the dawn breaks no matter how desperately she wants to, no matter how desperately afraid she is. And there is so much to be afraid of; there is so much to fear. Especially now that the something I've been waiting for is getting closer.

Instinctively, I crouch lower, my belly pressing into the earth, and growl. The wolf may have abandoned me, but its skills are now mine; I know how to act when I may have to strike back and defend myself. I know how to kill.

My neck swings heavily to the left, then the right, looking for an intruder, a visitor, a new arrival, but I don't see anything. I hear a noise, and for a second I think that I'll see

Louis and Barnaby leading the rest of the town vigilantes coming to hunt me down. But could that be? I thought they had both given up their quest and realized their zealousness was nothing more than panic and they were behaving like members of a foolish mob. How could the killer be linked to the full moon? It's insanity. At least that's what Luba and Melinda want the two of them to think. But perhaps Louis is coming out of the fog that he was under just as Barnaby has and they have come to the only logical conclusion, regardless of how absurd it sounds: The Full Moon Killer is real and worthy of its name.

And then I see it. So small, so inconsequential that I almost miss it. A spark of light, nothing more, demands my attention, and instantly I realize that the danger isn't coming from the earth, but from the sky. Orion's constellation has shifted, and where there were three stars, there are now only two. But the third star hasn't disappeared; it hasn't imploded or faded into the black landscape of the night; it's falling.

I don't know if Orion has released its grip on the star or if the star has turned its back on its creator; I only know that it's about to plummet to the earth. And even this new me, this fusion of wolf and girl, knows that can't possibly be a good thing.

Backing up, my paws dig into the ground and gouge the earth, restlessness turning quickly to anger. This cannot be it! This cannot be how I'm going to die! Not after everything that I've overcome, not after everything that my friends and I have confronted and defeated and survived. I refuse to believe that I'll be destroyed by a falling star! When I hear the buzzing, I know that I'm right. It was a trick; a star hasn't fallen to the earth; a swarm of bees has come alive.

I hear the bees before I can see them. The buzz, buzz, buzzing sound is soft, comforting, like a mother's lullaby, but quickly it turns violent. The gentle mother is gone and replaced with something vicious, something that wants to destroy, something wolf-like.

"Jess!"

Her name slams against the buzzing, part-growl, part-yell, and splinters in every direction. Jess will come; she will save me like she always does; I know she will.

Then where is she?!

"Jess!!!"

The noise sounds nothing like her name, but I know Jess will recognize it anyway because it's coming from me. But why is the night not interrupted by a golden light? Why isn't the hot August breeze laced with the smell of cherry blossoms? Why isn't she coming?!

"JESS!!!"

All I see is the black funnel flying toward me, its sound now deafening and filled with murderous determination. I can't wait for Jess any longer, I can't wait to be saved, I have to save myself so instinctively my body whips around and I run blindly into the darkness. I picked this place to transform because it was hidden, tucked away in the bowels of the forest and populated with a large cluster of thick trees, perfect for camouflage, but difficult for escape.

This isn't like the last time I was chased by a swarm of bees. That was a dream; this is real. Then, salvation came when I woke up; now, with my eyes wide open, salvation is nowhere to be found. Running wildly I can feel my body scrape against the trunks of the trees, causing pieces of their bark to be ripped off and fly into the air. I run for a few feet in one direction, but then have to veer off into the other to avoid crashing into a massive rock, and then back to my original direction to avoid getting tangled within the gnarled roots that have grown so immense that the ground can no longer cover them completely. No matter which way I run, there are obstacles preventing me from sprinting to safety, but is there such a place? What place can possibly offer a wolf-girl protection that a bee can't penetrate?

The buzzing is getting louder and it sounds like someone is pulling the cord on a chainsaw directly behind me. My thick red fur billows from a combination of wind and fear, and I honestly don't know which is stronger. Why *hadn't* a star fallen to earth? At least then I wouldn't be the only one in danger; I'd have company. When I run through a puddle, the water so cool against the burning, calloused flesh of my paw, I know that although I am alone, salvation has finally arrived.

Inhaling deeply I can smell the scent of fresh water on the breeze, and I turn sharply to the right. I hope I'm going in the right direction, but I don't have time to contemplate; body trumps mind, and I must keep moving.

The trees finally give way to a clearing, and I can see Weeping Water River less than a mile away beyond a stretch of flat, open land. I fight the urge to turn around and see how close my enemy is, but before temptation grows too strong I see out of the corner of my eye that several bees are flying ahead of the swarm. They may be leaders who have moved forward, waiting for the precise moment to give the order to strike, or they may be rogue bees so anxious to taste wolf flesh that they've broken free from the swarm, but whatever they are my response has to be the same; I need to run faster. Need to reach the river now!

The buzzing is so relentless and strong it feels as if it's taking up residence inside my brain. Involuntarily, I shake my head to loosen its hold, but it's a stupid thing to do because it only slows me down and gets me off balance so I collide right into the stinger of one of the wayward bees.

The pain is slight and oddly comforting because it's confirmation that this isn't a normal bee. I see a stream of silver light trailing from my body, and I know these bees are connected to Orion, his constellation and his intention. A star might not have fallen, but these bees have come from the heavens to kill me.

I have no choice. I have no other chance, so I take one deep breath and plunge into the river. The cold water is shocking and heavy and divisive; it's making the wolf come back alive and the girl drown. Wrestling with each other, the wolf and the girl struggle to get control, but what does it matter? If the wolf wins he and the girl will break through the surface of the water and into the waiting, angry swarm. If the girl wins she'll force them both to stay underneath the water until their breath abandons their body and they drown. Either way the outcome is the same: They're going to die.

Looking up through the opaque, gurgling surface of the water, I see that the swarm is relentless; it isn't moving, but something about its shape has changed. It's parted; it's created an opening in its center to make way for something, the queen bee perhaps? The true leader of the swarm, the bee that will wait until the thing below can no longer hold its breath and gives in to the natural desire to breathe? No, the swarm has separated because something stronger has entered the pulsating crowd—a butterfly.

Less than an inch below the water, I can see the black mass of the swarm, but it's as if they're miles away; there's only one thing taking up my vision: this beautiful butterfly. Its delicate wings are golden yellow, a flutter of sunlight amidst the dark night, and I know that this butterfly isn't real; it's a sign. A combination of Jess and Napoleon, my best friend and the grandson of my enemy, come together to offer me a way out. No! That isn't it! They've come together to remind me that I can get out of this on my own.

I may not have my own light, my own spirit may have been ripped from me, but I have Jess's light within me. She cut open my human flesh and poured some of her own golden magic into me so I would always carry her within me, so no matter where the journey of my life would bring me, I would never have to travel—or fight—alone.

Following pure instinct I open my mouth under the water, but the wolf is frightened; the wolf doesn't understand that Jess is going to help us, and he shuts his mouth tight. I can feel the water around me ripple and undulate, and it takes me a moment to realize that I'm causing the movement. My body is shaking violently because my paws are clutching at my snout, trying to open my mouth, and the wolf is fighting me.

A knife-sharp fingernail separates my lips and cuts my tongue. Blood seeps out of my mouth, and I watch the water around me change; streams of crimson liquid loop and dance and swirl around me as if firelight has ignited underwater. My eyes are entertained, so my body can take action.

Finally my paws rip open my mouth with such force I think I may see my severed snout floating amidst the blood-stained water. Instead I see a golden light, a light that emanates from deep within me, from my soul, impale the water. It cuts jaggedly through the swarm of bees, causing them to scatter, and then the light bursts open triumphantly, like the first light of a newborn star, to blind the bees. They don't know what's happening; they don't know if the yellow light is friend or foe, but they don't wait around to find out. Immediately, cowardly, they retreat back into the sky where they came from.

On the banks of the river I pant and gasp while air swirls around and inside me and I am grateful that my paws are touching dry land. The butterfly's wing flaps next to my ear, its gentle breeze like a tidal wave of love. I bow my head to it in an offering of thanks, and when I look up it's gone; the only remnant of its existence is a cluster of leaves still fluttering on a branch high above me and the vision of its beauty engraved onto my memory. Turning to the right I see the last of the black swarm disappear and fold into the dark, bleak sky, but when it vanishes completely, I don't celebrate; instead I beg God to bring it back because in its place is something even more frightening: Nadine.

The werewolf and the witch stare at each other, two cursed creatures forever joined at the soul. Similar and yet so very different. I know that with my wet, matted fur and shaking limbs I must look bedraggled and weak, while Nadine with her curved belly filled with both promise and danger looks commanding and strong. Roughly I shake the water that's still clinging to me off of my body in an attempt to appear aggressive, but Nadine only smiles. Until she opens her mouth to scream.

"It's here!"

Her voice is voluminous, and just like the roar of thunder, it produces silence. It takes the earth a moment to respond, but when it does, even though the reply is soft, it is even more dangerous. The snap of a branch, the click of metal. Slowly, I crane my neck around and see Officer Gallegos staring at me, a thick stream of sweat dripping down the left side of his face, introducing a pungent, musky scent into the humid August night. Louis and Barnaby may have given up the quest to find the Full Moon Killer—I really can't be certain—but there's no doubt that Gallegos is still on the prowl. He may be acting alone or within a larger group, whatever it is I can't speculate about that now because I'm under attack. His one knee is bent and pressing into the ground; his right arm is extended straight out so that the gun in his hand, pointing at my body, can be as close to me as possible. I don't know if he's under Nadine's spell, if he's a witch, or if he's just a cop hunting down a killer, but I don't have time to figure it out, because without blinking, without his body flinching, he pulls the trigger.

Springing low and to the right into empty space, I feel the bullet whip past the crown of my head. It feels the same as the butterfly's wings did; how amazing that beauty and death are so alike, almost as if they are one and the same. If Gallegos has his way, they will be.

I don't have to turn around to know that he is up and running toward me; I can hear the grass bending underneath his pounding feet. He shoots again, once more. Both bullets are wild shots and don't land anywhere near me, but he isn't giving up, and once he controls the adrenalin racing through his veins, he'll shoot with more accuracy. I can't wait for that to happen. Unfortunately, I may not have the chance to prevent it.

Just as I see that the ground is about to dip, I extend my front paws, but instead of slamming into dirt, I slam into air. For a few seconds I'm flying, graceful and disconnected from everything around me, but without warning I'm tumbling down an unexpected hill, rocks and twigs and unruly mounds of earth assaulting my body, making me twist and turn in all directions. The sharp edge of a protruding rock slashes into my back, and I look up to see Gallegos lying facedown on the wind, falling a few inches above me. His face is not contorted by surprise, but by a serene mask of hate.

Even in midair his gun is pointed at me; he might have lost his footing, but not his determination. I watch his finger pull back on the trigger once again. I hear the click of the gun, and I brace myself for impact.

My mind races, the mind that's being shared by both the wolf and the girl, and I realize that in the morning my secret will finally be out; everyone will know that Dominy Robineau is the Full Moon Killer; everyone will know that monsters are real. I don't know if I feel more sorry for myself or for them. But there is no bullet; there is no invasion into my body; the gun barrel is empty. The only impact is when my back crashes into the rocky earth and Gallegos's body smashes on top of mine.

When the blurred image comes into focus, it isn't Gallegos's face I see inches from my own, but Nadine's triumphant smile peering down at me from the top of the hill. One hand rubbing the orb that is her belly, the other waving at me in a perfect imitation of a friendly greeting, her actions proof that she is a sick, twisted girl. Growling and shrieking at the same time, I want to jump up and strike her with my claws, slice the smile off of her face with my fangs, but I can't move because the dead weight of Gallegos's body is pinning me to the ground.

Just as I begin to shove him off of me, his eyes flicker. Recognition gives way to terror, but in seconds both are overcome by purpose. Glaring into my blue-gray eyes, Gallegos raises the gun over his head; it may be empty, but it's still a deadly weapon. Good thing that so am I.

His blood tastes like mercy, a gift for the agony I've lived through tonight and these past few years, and I want the sweet, red liquid to fill me up until it spills out of me. If Nadine weren't staring down at me, gleeful at the prospect that I could so easily and so joyfully kill, I might do just that, but I can't let her win. She and Luba have already taken too much from me.

Howling madly I shove Gallegos's writhing body off of me and watch him roll several times before stopping. I can hear his heart beating and his panting breath from where I am, so I know that he's bruised, but alive. Just like me.

I look up expecting to see Nadine watching the scene with disgust, but she's gone. Makes sense since the entertainment is over; why should she stay any longer? And what would I do if she were there anyway? Now that my mind is free from the bloodlust, I know that I can't kill her while she's carrying a child; I can't be that much of a savage. Can I?

Gallegos's body starts to move, and I know that in a few moments he'll be awake, consumed with conviction, and ready to strike again, ready to win this fight against me. But

I've had enough fighting and adventure and surprise for one night. It's time for me to return to the safety of the woods, back to the shadows where I belong. Where I can be alone in the darkness to wait for this thing that I know is coming. This thing that I know will change not only my world forever, but the world of everyone around me.

Chapter 1

Where is the sun?

Lying in my bed it's like I'm still shrouded in the bushes, still blanketed in a smooth sheet of blackness; I still feel like the wolf. Glancing at my arms I see skin and not fur, so I know I've changed back, but why do I feel like a full moon continues to hang in the night sky? Outside the wind gets a little rowdy, and in response the window rattles just enough to get my attention. On the other side of the glass the sun is shining; I can see its rays, a collection of yellows, reaching out in every direction except in mine. It reminds me of Jess.

Where was she last night when I needed her? I cried out for her, and she ignored me, and it isn't like she even has to hear me shout her name for her to know that I'm in trouble; she can read my mind. That is if she wants to. Maybe she has better things to do than always rush to my side when I'm in trouble and need her help, which I have to admit is starting to become more and more often. Maybe I'm wrong; maybe something isn't coming; maybe something is ending.

No! I can't imagine a world without Jess. I know that most everyone else has accepted that she's gone, including her family. Why should I think I'm so special that I should be able to keep her around long after she died?

Because remember, Dominy, you are special.

Possibly. Not better than anyone, but I guess this thing I become once a month does make me special. Then again continuing to see Jess after her death could be my penance. Maybe she's remained in my life because I'm the one who killed her. Let me get used to feeling I defied the odds and that our friendship, our connection will last for eternity, so our inevitable separation will be that much harder to handle. Because when I desperately needed my friend, she stood me up.

I fling the covers off of me and jump out of bed. Of course, when I try to shove my feet into my fluffy fake-fur red slippers (a fun and very unsubtle Christmas gift from Arla), my feet flatten out the heels, so I have to bend down to run my finger along the length of the inside of the slippers so it doesn't feel like I'm wearing clogs, which for some stupid reason totally annoys me. Oh yes it's going to be one of those mornings when everything gets on my nerves. Like looking outside to find out that it's going to be a beautiful, sunny day.

The sun wants to pour into my bedroom; it's aching to cover me in its golden glow, but the curtains are drawn, and the thin pink cloth is a barrier against the majestic star's yearning. Reaching up I grab the curtains and then stop myself from ripping them from the rod, because I'm reminded of my parents. These are the curtains I had in my old bedroom, almost the same shade as the color of the paint on the old walls, This Little Piggy. When I moved here into Louis's house, I needed something reminiscent of my old home and my past so I put up these curtains as a reminder. Since then I've conjured up a fantasy that my mother had picked them out special for me and my father watched her string the curtain rod into the hole at the top of the material while he painted my room. Who knows? It could be an accurate recollection of the past, my parents as a young couple setting up their firstborn's nursery. Their firstborn child who bore the brunt of Luba's curse.

Well, even though that child has grown up, and may still need to be comforted by things from her past, she also knows how to live in the present. Pushing the curtains to the side, I brace myself for the onslaught of sunshine, and I'm not disappointed. The light and heat and smell of the sun wrap themselves around me like an old friend. I close my eyes and get lost in the embrace, allowing myself to give in to the familiarity and accept its goodness. This is what an old truck must feel like when it pulls up to a gas station; it knows it's going to be rejuvenated. But, unfortunately, the feeling doesn't last very long.

The central air conditioning in the house is doing its job against the oppressive August heat. So while the sunlight remains in the room, its rays reaching out to dance on the ceiling, lounge on my unmade bed, and stretch to the far side of the room to shine some light onto my collection of stuffed animals, the heat and smell of the sun are quickly overtaken by the man-made power of the AC. Even here in my bedroom, sunshine cannot win.

I shake my head and feel the material of the curtains become twisted in my clenched fists because everything in my life really does venture back to Luba. I'm reminded that my natural goodness can only last so long before the curse kicks in and I'm on the hunt to kill some innocent animal to quench my hunger. Or kill my best friend.

My thoughts race back to Jess, not to the night that she died, but to last night. I know that in the end she sort of came to my rescue anyway—her light within me saved me—but it wasn't the same. A solo victory can feel hollow; it's so much better to win or defeat your opponent with your friend by your side. But Jess has constantly told me that although she has morphed into a powerful Amaterasu Omikami, she has limitations, so, no matter how painful it is to believe, I better start accepting the fact that her appearances may also start to become limited. Not everything can last forever. Or can it?

What's that sound? I hold on to the curtains tighter as if that's going to shush the world so I can hear more clearly and listen with my wolf ears. I was right! I can hear humming, a low vibration, just like a swarm of buzzing bees. I let go of the curtains and they fall silently against the window, my frustration still living within the fabwrinkles of the material, and following my wolf-sense I walk toward the sound.

The girl takes over and grabs my bathrobe from the hook on the wall. Just because I may have to defend the house and everyone in it from an assembly of angry, vicious bees doesn't mean Louis has to suffer a heart attack watching me do battle in a flimsy T-shirt and short-shorts. I can conquer evil just as easily wearing a soft pink fleece bathrobe decorated with rows and rows of smiling Hello Kitty faces. I suppress a gigglaugh when I realize that, even if I must fight on my own, I do have Jess underneath and on top of my flesh. I'm armed and ready.

The noise is louder in the hallway and coming from the left. I don't see anything; there's no black cloud floating in the air, but the sound definitely has a rhythm. Listening to the buzzing I can hear the volume grow, then hush, as if the dark mass is moving in one direction and then the next, not ready to strike, but too anxious for my arrival to remain still.

Could this be true? Could the bees have followed me home? Have they been waiting all night long to attack me again after I made them flee and retreat back to Orion or wherever they really came from with my faux light display? How did they track me again? The answer comes before I even finish my thought. Nadine. Maybe the bees weren't under Orion's command, but hers? If that's the case, then of course they know where I live, and it sounds as if they've been using the bathroom as their rendezvous point.

I stop outside the bathroom door and can hear the

Nadinibees on the other side. With only the thin door sepa-rating us now, I hear their buzzing like a cluster of overeager heartbeats, and I know they can hear me because their move-ment has increased. Up and down, left and right, circling wildly, they can sense me; they can sense that the time to at-tack is imminent. They know that in just a few seconds they'll be given the command to zoom underneath the cracks in the door and douse me with so much fear that I'll run blindly in search of safety that doesn't exist. Forget it, Na-dine! If I can fight off a bunch of bees as a wolf when I'm am-bushed, there's no way I'm going to run in terror as a girl when I know what to expect.

Flinging open the door I realize my expectations have to be lowered.

"Barnaby?"

"Dude," my brother replies. "Didn't they teach you how to knock at Stupid Girls' Academy?"

As insulting as that comment is, I must admit that it's war-ranted, and I do feel as if I graduated last in my class at SGA. My brother is standing before me at the bathroom sink, half naked, wearing only his pajama bottoms, shaving. He's hold-ing an electric razor in his hand, and the three little wheels are spinning maddeningly against the air instead of the hairs on his face. The whizzing rhythm of the razor mimics the angry sound of the bees' buzzdance so perfectly I'm once again reminded that the wolf and the girl are linked together on so many levels, more levels than I probably have yet dis-covered. As are my brother and I.

"You can borrow it when I'm done," he offers. "You know, if you need to take care of another outbreak of hirsuteness."

Sometimes it's easier to strike down a foe of supernatural proportions than it is your brother, mainly because the for-mer wants to kill you while the latter just wants to maim you with a lifetime of insults.

"It was a *phase!*" I scream idiotically.

"I know," Barnaby replies, rubbing the razor lazily against his chin. "In our history textbooks it's known as The Doggirl Era, a fascinating time in our culture."

It's so hard to argue with the truth. Before my very first transformation, the wolf spirit must have known the curse was about to begin, and it was trying to rush things, escape and break free from the invisible constraints a few months earlier than Luba had originally planned. The result was that I got a little hairy and grew a full-on mustache. Vernita, owner of the Hair Hut and beautician extraordinaire, restored my upper lip, my arms, and my legs to their silky smooth glory less than twenty-four hours after the outbreak, but when you're pushing sixteen and look like the cop from the Village People or some unshaven South American dictator, word gets out. Thankfully that part of the curse is behind me, and I'm girl enough to admit that becoming hirsute even for such a short period of time was one of the most devastating parts of this whole experience.

With no way to defend myself without revealing to Barnaby the details of the spell Luba cast on me before I was even born, I react the way any big sister would: by zeroing in on the attribute her little brother is most self-conscious about.

"That's all in the past," I declare. "Unlike your huge nose."

Examining his face in the mirror, Barnaby turns to the left and then to the right. When he's done he looks directly at his reflection, and his smile is filled with teen narcissism. "I like my nose."

Whatever happened to teenage angst and self-criticism?

"You do not!" I pout.

He keeps his face pointed straight ahead so I can get a good look at his profile, but turns his eyes toward me. "It's got character," he states. "And unlike most of your features, it's not hidden behind a bush of unruly hair."

Where are the bees? Where are the deadly, Nadinepropelled bees so I can be engaged in a fair fight? Give me thousands of poisonous stingers instead of my brother's zingers that are admittedly kind of witty, but, worse than that, steeped in truth. Because against his comments I really have no defense and feel that I, in fact, didn't graduate last in my class at SGA, but graduated with honors.

"So tell me, manboy," I start, hands literally on my hips in a bad imitation of a bad tween actress from some bad Disney Channel sitcom. "Does Louis know you stole his razor so you could play grown-up?"

Smirking, Barnaby shoves the electric razor in my face, and I have to step back for fear that one of the three rotating wheels will cut off my eyelashes. Big-sister stance is ruined when I bang into the door behind me, lose my balance, and my left hand has to fly out to press into the wall to steady myself from falling. When I see what's engraved on the razor, my big-sister bad attitude is ruined too.

BMR. My brother's initials, which stand for Barnaby Mason Robineau. Just as I have Jess inside of me, my brother will always have my father. And if he doesn't have our father in the physical sense to teach him how to be a man and guide him through the complicated rites of manhood, at least he has Louis.

"Louis gave it to me for my birthday," Barnaby beams. "Man to man."

Staring at my brother, I'm conflicted. Part of me wants to crack up in his face in response to his silly, melodramatic comment, but the other part of me wants to hug him tightly and tell him how grateful I am that he has Louis in his life now that our father's gone. I opt to straddle both sentiments with a response that can be construed as either sarcastic or sugary, depending upon how Barnaby chooses to hear it.

"Well, it's nice to know that one of you is finally growing up," I say.

It's also nice to know that our little makeshift family is getting more familial all the time. Downstairs my slippers make scuff-scuffing sounds on the hardwood floor that I'm sure announce my arrival before I enter the kitchen, but Arla doesn't look up; she's too interested in whatever she's reading on her cell phone and too busy eating her breakfast. It's her usual ultra health food cereal, a concoction of soy milk, fruit, oatmeal, and granola. Normally it looks like inedible gruel to me, but this morning it looks appetizing.

"Yum, that looks scrumdillyishesque," I gush. "What's a girl gotta do to get a bowlful?"

"Step one, open the fridge," Arla replies, her mouth full of gushy froatola. "Step two, figure the rest out for yourself."

When Barnaby and I first moved in with the Bergerons, even though we've known them our whole lives, we felt more like guests, completely wanted, but with an expiration date. I kept having the feeling that Louis was going to greet us at the door one day after school with all our bags packed, announcing that we were going to be shipped off to some Dickensian locale like the Weeping Water Orphanage. Unwarranted thought, because he and Arla have shown us nothing but kindness and patience and support during our transition from someone's child to someone else's ward. Now that Barnaby and I have been living here for well over a year, we've matured into someone's family, which is an incredibly comforting feeling. Just as comforting as Arla's borderline snarky comment.

Sitting next to her at the kitchen table, my own health-soaked cereal in a bowl in front of me, I take advantage of our alone time and start to tell her about last night's escapade.

"Sounds buzzworthy," Arla jokes without smiling.

"More buzz than worthy," I add. "Especially since Jess didn't show up."

Scrunching up her forehead, Arla tilts her head and looks at me. Even first thing in the morning, even with no makeup on to cover the faint scar over her left eye, even with a super-short, close-cropped Afro, Arla is beautiful. Her words, however, are not as pretty.

"Maybe your relationship with Jess is changing," she suggests. "Just like ours."

So she senses it too! The problem is while my relationship with Arla is changing in a good way—we're moving closer to being sisters than being just friends—my relationship with Jess is moving in the opposite direction.

"But I don't want things to change with Jess," I say.

"Dominy, haven't you realized by now that there is very little in this world that we can control," Arla replies. "And since Jess is technically part of another world, the chances of your being in control of anything that includes her are automatically cut in half."

Hmm, that's quite profound so early on a Saturday morning.

"Hence the reason I wear my wigs," she adds.

Hmm, from profound to perplexing.

"I may not be able to control my future," Arla says, "but I can control my futylesensiny."

"Your *what?*"

"Sorry, my future style sense," she clarifies. "I'm not good at making up new words like you are."

"We all have our strengths," I say. "You should've gone with something like fufashionista."

"*Subarashi!*" she cries.

Jess may not be around, but her Japanese slang remains.

Slurping up the last bits of her breakfast, Arla asks me if last night's transformation held any more surprises, other than it turning into a remake of *Attack of the Killer Bees*. Before I can elaborate on how the evening ended, the front door slams. Either Barnaby's finished shaving and has gone out to partake in some manly Saturday morning activity or Louis really has finally come home after partaking in his all-night hunt for the Full Moon Killer. Four seconds later when Louis bounds into the kitchen we know Barnaby is still preening and Louis is pissed.

Grunting something that resembles a "good morning," Louis yanks open the refrigerator door, grabs the container of orange juice, and bangs the fridge shut. Next, he opens up the cupboard over the sink and slams that shut too, only to open another cabinet door that houses what he's looking for, a glass. He pours it full of OJ and takes a huge swig, swallows, and repeats.

The refrigerator door is abused once more as Louis opens it, rummages around inside for a few seconds, grabs some yogurt, and slams the door shut yet again. A kitchen drawer is pulled open, its metal contents jostling against each other, making more noise as Louis searches for a spoon, and is clanged shut, the noise of wood hitting wood making the harshest sound of all.

Since this is uncharacteristic behavior, Arla and I are stunned into silence. We don't know how to respond to Louis's aggressive actions. His back to us, Louis is shoving spoonfuls of yogurt into his mouth and making really gross swallowing noises that are so loud he probably wouldn't hear us if we spoke, but we don't risk it; we mouth our words.

"Melinda?" Arla silently asks.

My eyebrows arch in shock-guilt at the non-sound of her name. Arla and I may not be psychically connected like she is with Napoleon's spirit, but the same uneasy thought is ricocheting in our brains. Maybe Louis ran into Melinda Jaffe, his ex-girlfriend, last night or early this morning and was reminded of his very public breakup, which I just happened to orchestrate, and that's what has put him in this obviously foul mood.

"Ask him," Arla voicelessly instructs.

I am not going to ask my sort-of stepfather if he stumbled

upon his homicidal maniac ex-girlfriend! That is so not appropriate breakfast conversation.

Shaking my head wildly from side to side, I hope to convey to Arla that her instruction is absurd and will not be followed. The girl, however, won't take a silent no for an answer.

"Ask him what's wrong," she silently over-annunciates.

Different question, same response. Arla's become so desperate she resorts to whispeaking. "He won't yell at you."

Arla may be smart, but she has terrible short-term memory. "He yelled at me the other day," I remind her.

Waving her hand in the air, she now whisscoffs. "You ruined his best white shirt."

If it was his best white shirt, it should've been protected underneath one of those plastic dry-cleaner-covering things and not laid out on the couch just asking to be drenched in somebody's midmorning blueberry shake. I had to spend most of the day using every stain-remover product known to mankind to try and get it out, and I have to admit I was quite successful. No one will notice the stain as long as Louis wears a really big tie and leans to the right so the tie can dangle a bit.

Just as I start to explain this to Arla in a voice that I know will more closely resemble a yell than a whisper, Barnaby's voice cuts me off.

"What's wrong with you?"

I can tell by the way Arla is looking at Barnaby that once again we're sharing the same thought: Unlike us, he's not afraid to go to the source. I'm a bit annoyed that my brother has guts that I lack, but again it's nice to know that he and Louis have a friendly, open relationship.

Louis drops the spoon into the sink, and once more metal clinks against metal. Avoiding all our gazes, he crosses to the garbage can and tosses the empty yogurt container into it.

Unable to think of any other way to stall for time, he finally speaks.

"There was another attack last night," he announces.

Shocked by this statement, Arla actually turns to face me, wearing a classic "Was there something you forgot to tell me?" expression. Luckily, Louis is staring straight at the kitchen floor and Barnaby is staring directly at Louis, so neither of them witnesses Arla's faux pas.

"Who?" Barnaby asks.

"Officer Gallegos," Louis answers.

"So the whole full moon thing is more than just a joke," Barnaby states, his voice sounding deeper and so much more masculine than I ever realized.

Shrugging his weary shoulders, Louis throws his hands up before he replies. "I don't know, but maybe, yeah," he stammers. "Things have been quiet for the past few months, so I was hoping it had just been a stupid coincidence, but now this." He stops talking to focus once more on the floor. We know there's nothing interesting about the linoleum; he's just choosing his next words carefully. "The town is going to go crazy again."

I want to keep my mouth shut; I want to let this be the last word, but I must know.

"How is Gallegos?" I ask. "Was he hurt, you know, really bad?"

It feels like forever before Louis replies.

"He's incredibly lucky," he confirms. "The doctors said he'll make a full recovery."

I keep my relief to myself, but Arla senses it. She also knows that I had something to do with Gallegos's accident.

As Louis starts to leave the room, he says, "I have to take a quick shower and get back to the station."

"Can I hitch a ride with you into town?" Barnaby asks.

"Sure," Louis says. "But you can't play with the siren."

Good to know he hasn't lost his sense of humor even though he's about to lose control of the entire town.

The moment Barnaby and Louis leave the room, I start to ramble on about how cute they are and how happy I am that they seem to be developing a deep bond and a sweet relationship despite all the heartache they've both been through. I mean every word I say, but it's only filler talk and Arla knows it.

"Bees," she says.

"What?"

"All you tell me that happened last night is that you were chased by a bunch of bees and you leave out the part about attacking a cop," Arla lays out.

"Deadly . . . um, *killer* bees," I reply.

Based upon her reaction, Arla doesn't get my sense of humor. But the truth is she does get me.

"Dominy! Haven't you figured out that our relationship is changing?" she says. "Friends, sisters, whatever we are, you know that you can tell me anything. I'm not going to judge you; I just want to know what's going on so I can help you."

She's right. Maybe it's human nature to want to keep secrets, but now that I'm only part human, I should really try mastering the art of disclosure.

"I attacked Gallegos last night because he was going to kill me," I admit.

Unfazed, Arla seems greatly satisfied. "Now was that so hard?"

Actually, it wasn't.

"You defended yourself, totally understandable," she says, fully supportive of my actions. "And the doctors said Gallegos is going to be okay, so obviously you restrained yourself. The girl didn't let the wolf have copfood."

Vulgar and blunt, but at the same time reassuring.

"That's right! That's exactly what I did," I cry. "I defended myself against Nadine and her insectisidekicks with the help of my inner-Jess, *and* I fought off Gallegos without doing any permanent damage."

"You should feel really proud of yourself," Arla says, shoving one last spoonful of cereal into her mouth.

It's a feeling that proves fleeting.

"Gallegos has slipped into a coma," Louis announces after bursting back into the kitchen and grabbing his car keys. "He might not make it."

Louis rushes out of the house with Barnaby and my pride right behind him.

Chapter 2

Two days later, and my victim is still in a coma. Me? I'm in a bikini.

While my attire might be appropriate for an end-of-summer party on the banks of the Weeping Water River, which looks incredibly ordinary in the daylight, my attitude is completely inappropriate for someone who is responsible for assaulting a police officer.

"That's because it was self-defense," Arla declares for I think the forty-second time, though I can't be certain because I've stopped counting.

"That's right, Dom," Archie agrees. "You did what any self-respecting wrrgrrl would have done in the same situation."

"Did you just call Dominy a wrrgrrl?" Arla asks.

"Yes, I took out the vowels like a fast-talking sassy urban youth would," Archie replies. "Do you approve?"

Arla thinks for a moment and smiles before she answers. "I guess Dom isn't the only one with a way with words."

Archie and Arla are sitting next to each other on a huge, silver-gray king-sized bed sheet that Archie swiped from his house. Typically, the sheet covers an ultra-firm mattress or the sleeping bodies of Mr. and Mrs. Angevene and not the grassy landscape leading down to a river, so it probably feels as uncomfortable being here as I do. My friends look perfectly at ease, and their encouraging attitude toward me and my involvement in this latest development engulfing our hometown should make me feel the same way, but it doesn't. Maybe it's their appearance that I find a little off-putting.

After Napoleon's death, Archie withdrew, kept to himself for a while, which was to be expected once the shock wore off and he had to accept the fact that he was a teenage widower and his Winter Wonderland had lost one of its cofounders. When he reemerged from his self-imposed isolation, I was grateful for two things: His eyes, although not as vibrant, were still violet, and he had not lost his sense of adventure; he shaved almost all his hair off. So now instead of white hair he has white fuzz.

Alone, he looks great, as if he's a clean blank slate from head to toe, a guy about to embark on a serious do-over. Lounging on the sheet next to Arla, he looks eerie. Her close-cropped hair is undyed and back to its natural color, the same shade as her skin, so it's a kind of dark mocha and a stark contrast to Archie, who's all albino-white. Together they look like the negative and positive resolutions of the same photo. To me they look like twins, except that one is good and one is evil. Just like Napoleon and Nadine.

"And if you hadn't fought back," Archie adds. "Gallegos might've killed you."

"Wrong," Caleb announces.

I thought my boyfriend had dozed off, but it seems that he's been listening to every word we've said. He doesn't open his eyes or lift his head from our supersized beach towel, which makes his proclamation that much more intense. No need to back up his statement with any extraneous movement to make his point.

"What do you mean I'm wrong?" Archie asks. His body

language mimics Caleb's; he's similarly relaxed. It's just that
the tone of his voice is now much more agitated.

"Not might've," Caleb corrects, finally opening his eyes
and rolling over. Boy, does he look beautiful when the sunshine blends in with his blond curls. "If you hadn't fought
back, Domgirl, Gallegos would definitely have killed you."

How quickly beauty dies.

I wish I could disagree with him, but he's right; they're all
right. During our confrontation Officer Gallegos had bloodlust in his eyes. Even without my ESP—enhanced sensory
proficiency—I would've been able to see his rage. But he only
wanted me dead because he didn't know it was me. I know
they're all coming to my defense and trying to make me feel
better for putting a man in a coma, but why can't they see
that I acted harshly? I'm the one who's wrong.

"Of course he wanted to kill me; he thought I was a killer
wolf," I say. "But if he had known it was me underneath all
that fur, he would have acted differently."

"No way," Caleb says, now sitting up, suddenly energized.
"He still would've wanted you dead."

I am wrong. They're not trying to defend or protect me;
they're trying to educate me. I feel as stupid as I do in any
class that falls under the math-o-sphere. The only difference
is that in class I feel dumb because the left side of my brain
somehow got left back a few years while my right side continued to matriculate. Now I feel dumb because I'm avoiding
reality.

"You really think so, Caleb?" I ask.

Hesitation is never a good sign. Caleb looks over to watch
some kids roughhousing in the river, squinting at them as
they try to dunk each other, their splashing adding waves to
the slow, lazy current. He's not interested in their antics; he's
merely contemplating how to tell his girlfriend what she
should already know: that she's got a target on her back
whether or not her back is covered in a mane of red fur.

Looks like Archie and Arla know exactly what Caleb wants to tell me, and they must agree with him, because they avoid conversation as well. Their bodies are carbon copies of each other, both languidly lying on the sheet, legs stretched out in front of them, ankles crossed. Their upper bodies resting on their elbows, heads leaning back so their faces are pointed toward the sun that looks like a ball of bright yellow flame in a cloudless blue sky. Their eyes and voices are closed to give Caleb as much time as he needs to find the right words to make me understand. Well, I can't wait.

"Should I repeat my question in sign language?" I snap. "I only know the individual letters of the alphabet and not complete words, so it could take a while."

Slowly, Caleb turns to face me. His blond curls have gotten so light this summer; some strands of his hair are almost as white as Archie's, and there are golden flecks in his brown eyes. The sunlight that I feel is avoiding me is drenching Caleb in its glory. A few beads of sweat are starting to form on his tanned forehead, somehow making him look even more incredibly handsome. And he still sounds incredibly honest.

"Chances are that even if Gallegos knew it was you trapped within the body of the wolf," Caleb starts, "he still would've killed you, because he would consider you the source of this town's nightmare."

"There's also the possibility that he was only acting cop crazy 'cuz Nadine was lurking over us pulling his strings," I add.

The twins suddenly get a sibling. Archie, Arla, and now Caleb all look alike thanks to their sharing the same shocked expression: jaws dropped, mouths open, staring at me like traumatized triplets.

"I guess, um, that I forgot to tell you Nadine was also there during the night in question?" I rhetoric-ask.

Archie speaks first: "Nadine was there?!"

Then Caleb: "When you transformed?!"

And finally Arla: "When Gallegos tried to kill you so he could mount your taxidermy-ized body on the wall of my father's office?!"

So many questions, only one answer.

"Yes," I reply. And before they can start ricoshouting again, I continue. "I'm sorry! I wasn't deliberately trying to conceal information from you guys. I mean it! I've just been a little preoccupied knowing that some innocent man's life is in limbo because of my actions."

"So once again it's all Nadine's fault." Archie states what his non-biological siblings are both also starting to believe. "She probably lured Gallegos to the woods and worked her mumbo jumbo to get him to try and kill you."

Half-right. "I'm sure she gave him a push," I say. "But cops are like lemmings and criminals to them are like cliffs; they have to take that leap no matter what unseen danger lies on the other side."

"Nicely said, Dom," Arla replies. "The not-so-nice translation is that Nadine's just a bitch."

"No, she's a bitchjaffe!"

I don't know what's more surprising, my boyfriend's self-satisfied smile at coming up with a new word or the fact that the atmosphere can change so abruptly. From effed-up to effervescent in less than sixty seconds. And it appears that our new bubbly take on life is contagious.

"Holy transformation, Batman!"

Archie isn't making a sly comment about my monthly conversion; he's voicing an opinion we all share. About the brand-spanking-new Gwenevere Schültzenhoggen.

Even if I hadn't already buried "The Hog" last year when I realized it was a hateful nickname, Gwen herself could do the honors without a shovel or an ounce of dirt just by emerging from the river like she's doing right now. It's the boys' turn to act like pigs.

"When did *that* happen?" Caleb asks.

"While I was in mourning, I guess," Archie replies, shrugging his shoulders. "This is the first I'm noticing, but I'm gay, so heterific changes sometimes fly over my head. What's your excuse?"

"I only have eyes for Domgirl," Caleb replies instantly, if not sincerely.

My boyfriend knows what I want to hear. "Good answer."

"But when-the-vere did that miracle happen?" he adds.

On both sides of Caleb, Arla and I playfully slap him in the arm, but we can't blame him for thinking he's witnessing yet another miraculous transformation. At some point between the last day of school and today, Gwen has become U.S.-certified babelicious.

The basic architecture is the same. Gwen is still tall, 5'11", with long limbs and, as expected, less-than-petite hands and feet. But her shape has changed drastically. Broad shoulders have rounded, thick neck has become slender, her once-soft stomach is hard and flat, and her legs no longer resemble tree trunks, but elongated branches. Her German-Korean ancestry no longer plays out like a multicultural mishmash on her face, but like an exotic smorgasbord. High cheekbones, slightly slanted eyes, square chin all add up to serious beauty. And serious attention.

Male, female, gay, straight, all eyes are on Gwen, soaking in her new body like the river water is soaking into the material of her emerald green bikini. Arla and I catch each other's eye, and I know we're thinking the same exact thing: If Gwen weren't so oblivious to the commotion she's causing, we'd be jealous. We both fall into the category of pretty, and when we pull out all of the stops cosmetically we can barge our way into borderline stunning, but we made our ascent gradually, so no one's ever really made much of a fuss. Somehow Gwen went from harsh to heart-stopping in roughly two months. Such a feat shouldn't inspire jealousy, only admiration. As well as the occasional proposal.

"Gwen!" Archie shouts. "You look *subarashi!*"

"Thanks," Gwen replies. "I think."

The girl obviously doesn't speak Jess.

"It's Japanese for above and beyond amazing!" Archie explains.

Blushing and awkwardly trying to cover her body with her beach towel to dry herself, Gwen obviously isn't used to hearing such accolades.

"Thanks, Archie," she starts. Then she proves that the old Gwen is still alive and living in nuGwen's body, by rambling. "My whole family went on a crash diet, and we started doing step aerobics together because my mother was going through the attic to find things to sell at the annual town-wide yard sale and she found an old videotape of Jane Fonda, do you know her? She was this actress, then became like this physical fitness guru, kind of started the craze. Anyway, my dad had to go back up to the attic to find his old VHS player, have you ever seen one of those things? It's like a DVD player, but humongous and really clunky. Anyway, we all started doing step aerobics and eating super healthy and in no time at all we all started losing weight. Except my sister, she was skinny to begin with, so she would just watch us, but last week I think she noticed an improvement in all of us, and she's joined in, so now it's all four of us. The family that aerobicizes together, stays together!"

I stifle a gigglaugh because I'm so happy to hear that while Gwen's physical appearance has improved, her personality has remained the same. She's as quirky and sweet and good-natured as ever. But since I don't want her to think I'm laughing at her when I'm really proud of her achievement, I keep quiet. Truth is, Gwen knows exactly who she is, and she has no desire to change. Just like Archie.

Then again, maybe not.

"If I were straight, Gwen, I would totally ask you out."

"Archibald Angevene, that is so super sweet!" Gwen yelps. "But I'd have to turn you down."

I can stifle no longer. And neither can Arla and Caleb. Our raucous laughter almost drowns out Archie's reply.

"You would turn me down?" Archie cries, his question rife with disbelief. "Is it my new hair? I know it's radical, but it grows in really fast."

Now Gwen joins in and laughs so fully at Archie's comment that she bends over and clutches her stomach, letting her towel fall to the ground to expose her bouncing boobs. If I didn't know her better, I'd think she was aiming for slutty and not just giving in to the hilarity of the sentiment. If her body doesn't silence everyone, her explanation does.

"I can't go out with you or anyone, Archie," Gwen says. "I already have a boyfriend."

"What?!"

The sound of our collective cry is so loud I swear it startles a family of birds nestled in the crook of a branch of a nearby tree. Before Gwen can take offense to the fact that we're all stunned to find out she's someone's girlfriend, she's pummeled with more questions.

"Who?!"

"Do we know him?!"

"How long have you two been together?!"

Regaining her composure, Gwen wraps her towel around her like a little girl donning a superhero cape. She's all grown up and childish at the same time.

"None of your business, yes, and five and a half weeks," she replies, answering all three of our questions.

Archie is about to protest and demand a more detailed response, but I throw a bottle of suntan lotion that lands right in the little dip in the middle of his chest and shuts him up. "A girl's entitled to her secrets, Arch," I declare.

His mouth opens up, and he gasps a little, but he hears the words I haven't spoken. *Leave the girl alone because we*

*wouldn't want someone pestering us to share our secrets
with the world. Let Gwen have her privacy.*

"Thanks, Dom," she says. Then she adds with a wink, "I
knew you would understand."

When she whips around, her towel-cape skipping in the air
behind her, I wonder if Gwen is smarter than she appears.
Does she know the truth about me? Does she know my secrets? No, that's impossible; she can't know that I'm cursed
and once a month play werewolf underneath the full moon.
Watching her plop onto the ground in between my brother
and his friend, Jody, the three of them cackling about some
unheard, inside joke, I realize I'm wrong. Not everyone's secrets are deadly or supernatural or unexplainable; some are
just personal and silly and girlie. And if I know one thing, I
know girlie. At least I think I do.

"She has got to be dating a band geek," I state firmly and
according to Caleb, pompously.

"Domgirl! Don't be so superficial," he chastises. "Gwen
could be going out with someone as hot as me."

My boyfriend's ego is huge, yet correct.

" 'Cause remember, Caleb is a geek without even being in
the band," Arla snaps.

And now bruised. Which of course makes us laugh even
harder than before. Soon, however, our laughter turns to crying, at least for one of us.

"Winter?" Caleb asks. "What the hell? Are you all right?"

Archie buries his face in his hands, and for a few seconds
his shoulders shake, indicating that his outburst may quickly
get out of control. But just as suddenly as it took control of
him, it's released. Roughly wiping away his tears, Archie
composes himself, but he's obviously upset by something. Or
someone.

"Sorry," he says. "It's just that . . . well, this is the first time
I've laughed since Nap died."

Softly, Arla rubs his back, just so he knows he isn't alone. Unfortunately, it only reminds him that he is.

"I guess I didn't know how lonely I was," Archie says quietly. "Until I was no longer alone."

Now it's my time to turn away and remain silent. I know exactly how Archie feels. I have my friends, my brother, Louis, Jess, this wolf-spirit, all living inside of me or next to me, and sometimes I catch myself feeling desperately lonely, unreasonably so, but still it's powerful and consistent and hypnotic. Despite the fact that I have my Wolf Pack and so many other people in my life standing by me, not judging me, it's hard to shake off the feeling that I'm completely and utterly alone. Without Napoleon, that's how Archie feels.

The way Caleb and Arla are bowing their heads, I can tell they feel as stupid and selfish as I do. Sure, time ticks on, and life resumes no matter what happens—I know that better than anyone—but pain clings onto a heart and a memory and refuses to let go. Even when the source of pain is unwanted.

"Oh my God!"

Okay, now Archie is about to turn left onto Embarrassed Boulevard and make a fool out of himself in front of everyone and not just the three of us. I don't care how superficial that makes me sound, but the rest of the kids are not going to be as sympathetic toward Archie or understand that his emotional outburst is because he misses his boyfriend, because not everybody knows that he and Napoleon were a couple. It's time to pack up and move this party to a location without an audience. Turns out we don't need to flee our audience, just our nemesis.

"I cannot believe she has the guts to show up looking like that!" Archie exclaims.

Turning around, we all see that Archie isn't getting excited because a Jaffe twin has died; it's because the other Jaffe twin is still alive and walking this way.

I don't know if there was a sale on some magical Kool-Aid at the Price Chopper, but Nadine, like Gwen, has undergone a makeover. In Nadine's case, however, it isn't that she's lost weight, but that she's gained. And pregnancy becomes this witch.

She looks completely different from Gwen, but just as surreal. As she walks toward us, a breeze stirs around her as if the air is parting so it doesn't have to touch her flesh. The result is that she looks like she's floating instead of walking.

Her brown hair is longer than I last remember, falling to her shoulders, and it's curling at the edges—not sure if that's natural or from spending the morning with a curling iron, but it frames her face nicely and softens her appearance. She's not wearing any makeup, but her complexion isn't as pale and gray as it used to be; there's color in her cheeks, and her forehead and nose are a bit sunburnt. Thankfully, she's had the decency not to wear a bikini, but her sundress is just as flattering. It's sleeveless with elastic just underneath the bustline, so the cotton fabric that falls to about two inches above her knee has enough room to billow and bounce as she walks. It's plain white with just a few yellow daisies decorating the neckline and the hem. Seriously, I don't know what's worse: the fact that she looks good in it, or the fact that I would totally wear it myself.

Regardless of how cute her dress looks, it can't conceal the fact that she's a few months pregnant and her belly's already showing. The wind picks up, and she instinctively clutches the sides of her dress, doing that girl-thing that I've done thousands of times before so you don't give a free show to the rest of the world. I feel my heart beat a little bit faster. I'm not nervous that the enemy is approaching; I'm angry because the enemy is more like me than I care to admit.

"If she keeps expanding at that rate," Arla observes, "she's going to look like the *Hindenburg* before her second trimester's over."

At least she gets the chance to look bloated and fat and about to explode. It's something that, thanks to Luba and her psychotic clan, I'm never going to get to experience. I've decided I'm not going to have any children. As much as I would love to know what it feels like emotionally and physically to give birth, I just can't risk the possibility that I may pass this curse along to my child. My fear may be groundless—Luba did place the curse on my father's firstborn only—but we don't know the extent of Luba's abilities, and now that the curse is in my blood, my DNA may have acquired power of its own. Getting pregnant isn't worth the risk of ruining another innocent child's life. There are other ways to experience motherhood.

I've already thought about adopting someday. Way too soon to make such a lifelong commitment, I know, but when I'm older, maybe married to Caleb or someone who's just as good and kind and strong as he is, we'll adopt a child and raise it as our own. I'll do everything for my son or daughter that my father did for me, and everything my mother would've wanted to do for me if she had had the chance.

I'm so lost in thought I don't realize that my breathing has sped up and is dangerously close to sounding like a wild animal's panting. Not much I can do about it, not when I'm in the presence of a hunter who I know wants me dead.

"Hi, guys," Nadine says cheerfully.

No one responds, not from our little group anyway. In the distance, however, Gwen waves to Nadine, as do a few others, and Nadine's eyes brighten and she waves enthusiastically to them as if she truly cared about their acknowledgment and friendship. But she doesn't care about anyone except herself. Well, maybe that baby she's carrying. The baby who has an unnamed father out there somewhere.

I take several deep breaths to try and remain calm as I look from Caleb to Archie, wondering if one of them could possibly be Nadine's baby daddy. Please no; please don't make that the case; please spare them that fate! Looking around I scour the area for other potential suspects. Could be Jody Buell; he was quite a vocal participant of the vigilante squad. Or The Dandruff King. No, Nadine's gross, but not even she could be that gross. Then my eyes fall onto Barnaby. I know that Nadine said he wasn't the father, but she could've been trying to steer me off course, away from the bull's-eye. With so much uncertainty in my life and surrounding Luba's great-grandchild, I'm going to opt to believe Nadine. I don't know if it's the wisest decision, but I do know that it will destressify my life and help me focus on more important things than the horror that I could be about to become an aunt to the Antichrist.

And even if I'm terribly wrong and Barnaby is the father, it doesn't look like he wants anything to do with Nadine either. He's staring at her with pure disgust. For a time I thought that Barnaby was under Nadine's spell, but that time has obviously passed. Either he's grown strong enough to break free of her charms or Nadine has moved on, tired of trying to overpower an unwilling recruit. Whatever the reason, I'm thankful Barnaby can see her for what she really is. I wish Archie could do the same.

"Hi, Nadine," he says. "You look great."

What?! Wasn't he just shocked to see her outside strutting her impregnated stuff? What's going on? The silver light isn't emanating from Nadine's body; it's not reaching out to twist Archie's mind and thoughts and words, but could she be doing it telepathically?

"Thanks, Archie, you too," Nadine replies. "Love your hair."

Absentmindedly Archie rubs the top of his head; he really looks like he's mesmerized by the vision and voice of Nadine. I don't know what's going on, but the tears burn my cheeks even before they start to fall. I can feel them from the inside out, where all my secrets and pain and anger live. I don't know why they're springing to life; maybe because I hate what Nadine and her family have done to my friends and me, or because I know that the Jaffe family's vendetta isn't finished. All I do know is that I don't want to cry in Nadine's presence. But I have less control of girl-cries than I do wolf-howls. Sometimes the body just takes over when it knows the mind is too overwhelmed. Which is why I find myself running toward the river.

The water feels cool and invigorating and very familiar. A few nights ago I reluctantly sought refuge in this same river, but now there isn't any struggle; I don't have to fight the wolf to stay under water; I know this is where I belong.

Letting my body relax, I feel myself start to float. I see my red hair spreading out around me like freshly drawn blood, and for an instant I think that I'm dying, that my life is being pulled out of me so only the wolf can remain, and remarkably in that instant I'm consumed by a sense of peace more radiant and jubilant than any I've ever known.

I look up, and I'm lost in a glow of sunshine so strong that it penetrates the surface of the water to brighten what lies beneath. The light is like Jess's friendship, amazing and cherished and pure, and I marvel at how a thin layer of water bewitched by the sun separates me from the chaos on the other side. Is this feeling warranted, manufactured, a premonition? I don't know and I don't care; I just want to stay in this tranquility forever. But I have to breathe.

Breaking the surface of the water my body stiffens because I'm leaving peace behind and entering enemy territory. When I open my eyes, however, I'm startled to see that I've brought some of that peace with me. Nadine is nowhere to be found.

I race over to my friends and am filled with such glee that I practically pounce on top of Caleb. He recoils from my touch; my boyfriend is not in the mood for playtime. Matching dour expressions are clamped to Archie's and Arla's faces as well. I offer my friends the gift of peace and this is how I'm repaid? Ingrates!

"What's going on?!" I shout, standing over them. They suddenly look far, far away. "The wicked witch may not be dead, but she's disappeared, which is almost as good."

"Nadine wasn't looking for an invite to stay," Caleb informs me.

"As if anyone was going to pony up an invitation," I reply. "Right?"

I can't help myself, and my eyes linger for a few seconds on Archie's face. He doesn't answer my question, but he does provide some insight as to why my friends look like the end-of-summer bash has turned into a pity party.

"She, um, just stopped by to show you . . . this," Archie says, handing me a rolled up newspaper.

I open it up to see that it's this week's edition of *The Weeping Water Weekly,* and immediately I know that their impromptu party is being held in my honor and that Nadine, despite her softened appearance, is still made of barbed wire. One touch and she can wound.

The headline of the *Three W* is one word, but it only takes one word to destroy my world: WEREWOLF.

Chapter 3

I feel like I'm still under water. I know that I'm standing. I know that my bare feet are pushing down into the grass. I know that my arms are pressed against the sides of my body. I know that I'm completely stiff and immobile and stationary, and yet I feel like I'm floating.

A wind gust travels past me, and my hair is lifted; for a second it's horizontal, and I'm reminded of how it looked while I was submerged within the body of the river, separated from my friends and from the rest of the world, while I was at peace. I want to be there now. I want to be on the better side of the water's surface, where words have no sound and headlines have no meaning.

"Dominy?"

The wind is gone, and my hair falls to my shoulders. Its landing is gentle, but it feels as if a huge boulder has crashed onto me, making my knees buckle and my arms shake.

"Dominy!"

Finally, I gasp, and the warm air rushes into my lungs, revitalizing me, bringing me up from the water's depths and back to the present, to where I don't want to be.

"Domgirl, sit down."

Caleb is speaking, but I can't see him clearly just yet. My vision is lagging behind my breath. I feel his hand on my left arm. Someone else's hand takes hold of my right arm, and together they help me descend, not to the bottom of the river, but to the safety of my towel.

My legs stretch out listlessly in front of me, so the heels of my feet glide across the soft fabric, while my hands press down at my sides and my fingers grip the thick cloth tightly. Peace and destruction, living together simultaneously; my body is in perfect balance. My mind is in perfect chaos.

"They know," I say. My voice is soft, barely a whisper, but it's made of fear, so it sounds to me like I'm shouting.

"No, they don't," Caleb replies. His voice is just as quiet, but it's different, it's confident. "It's just a stupid headline."

Archie holds the paper up again so I can see the word— WEREWOLF—and it's like someone has pressed a white-hot branding knife into my eyes. The burning sensation is so ridiculously painful and it penetrates so deeply into the core of my brain that at first I don't feel a thing; for a moment the meaning of the word escapes me. But then my mind kicks in, and it remembers the word's definition and origin and implication, and pain roars throughout my body.

Thankfully, when my mouth opens, no sound rushes out, so no one else knows that my world has officially collapsed. No one else hears the girl screaming and the wolf howling and all the other sounds blasting inside my body; it's my own silent symphony, my own unheard expression of fear and panic and sorrow. And worst of all, my own inevitable capture.

"Caleb," I say, my voice so much calmer than my thoughts, "I've been found out."

Lines appear on his forehead as it scrunches up and his eyebrows come closer together. For some insane reason his lips elongate into a smile. "No, you haven't," he replies.

I grab his wrist tightly, too tightly, more like an animal and less like a girl, but I can't help myself. "Read the headline," I seethe.

"No," he says, his voice getting louder, braver. "You read it." He grabs the newspaper from Archie's hands and shoves it into mine; it feels like lava. "Read it carefully."

It's only one word; how carefully do I have to read it?

"I don't know how, Caleb, but they've found out what I am," I declare.

"No, Dom," Archie interjects. "They have no idea what you are. It's only speculation."

It isn't speculation; it's discovery! God, I hate when people act like idiots! When they can't see the truth or when they deliberately avoid the truth when it's right in front of their eyes. Like I'm clearly doing right now.

"That's why they added a question mark," Archie says.

I reread the headline, this time seeing it for exactly what it is, and it's like I'm seeing a sliver of hope. Lars Svenson hasn't presented fact to our town, not at all; the editor of the *Three W* is simply playing a guessing game. Gigglaughs rip out of my mouth when I realize that grammar really does save lives. Plug a question mark after the word *werewolf,* and it takes on a whole new meaning, one that's rife with doubt. And even though doubt is just fact without the certainty, it has to come from somewhere; there has to be a reason that compelled Lars to plaster his paper with superstition. All I have to do is skim the opening paragraph to find it.

> While initial laboratory tests confirm that officer Pablo Gallegos was mauled by a wolf during Thursday night's attack, they also indicate something far more disturbing. Evidence of human saliva was found in the officer's wounds.

That word sounds so foreign to me—*human*—like it doesn't have any place in the sentence or in my world. What's it doing there? That's the same question Lars seems to be asking.

> No one else was admitted to the emergency room and no other person is believed to be involved in the assault, but, until Gallegos awakens from his coma, we can only speculate as to why both human and wolf DNA were found in the victim's blood sample. It could be simple human error, or it could be something much more unholy.

Unholy? Really, Lars? Talk about trying to incite a riot. Then again, when I realize this curse began thanks to Luba's unholy alliance with Orion, Lars's choice of adjective is less sensational than it is accurate. But is it believable?

"Do you think the question mark really makes that big of a difference?" I ask.

"Totally!" Archie cries.

"Absolutely!" Arla shouts.

"You know it does!" Caleb yells.

Lots of noise, but is it just noise to cover their lack of conviction? My friends know, just as I do, that there are three groups of people in this town. The first group will read this article and laugh at Lars's attempt to mix fiction with fact, forgiving him for letting his creative juices overflow onto the newsprint. The second group, the one that nurses a less favorable view of the man because of the editorial monopoly he holds over Weeping Water's readers, will believe they have proof that Lars has once again succumbed to his paranoia and memorialized one of his conspiracy theories. They'll feel they have written confirmation that he's a quack. That leaves the third group, and while this might be the smallest, it's also the most dangerous. This group is comprised of the people who willingly accept superstition as truth and myth as fact; they're the ones who passionately argue that aliens are being bred in a huge hangar in the Nevadan desert for secret scientific study and that man didn't walk across the face of the moon, but across an elaborately designed Hollywood soundstage. These are the people I'm afraid of, because this headline is all the proof they need that someone like me really does exist.

"Liars!" I reply. "You all know what this means."

Three blank stares. Has Stupid Girl Academy gone coed?

"The people in this town with vigilante tendencies are going to throw a party," I explain. "Attacks that only take place when there's a full moon, human and wolf DNA swimming together in the same petri dish—this is like the grassy knoll suddenly developed a mouth and the power of speech and said 'Hell yeah, there was another gunman!' "

"Even if some people do latch onto Lars's outlandish theory," Arla begins.

"Which we all know is unoutlandish," I clarify.

"Even if they do, who is really going to believe him? It's ludicrous," she finishes.

"Them's there are some big words, Arla," Archie says. "But people are scared, and trust me, scared people will grab hold of possibility like a life preserver. It's human nature."

There's that word again. Well, this girl is only part-human, so my flesh tingles and my fur stands up on end when I feel the outside world closing in tighter and tighter around me. My nature is to fight against the inevitable. But how?

"What do we do?" I ask.

"Nothing."

And it's official: Caleb is SGA's valedictorian.

"I can't just do nothing," I protest. "This is like a public relations nightmare."

Caleb rubs some sunscreen onto his arms, the white cream making his muscles look like a snow-topped mountain range;

he's obviously more interested in protecting his pale skin from sunburn than in protecting my life from ruin. "There's nothing you *can* do, Domgirl," he says, his eyes focused on his task and not his girlfriend. "Without exposing yourself to everyone and sabotaging yourself by making your own worst nightmare come true."

"Bells is right, Dom," Archie adds. "If people are that susceptible and that willing to believe that Comic Con is a cover-up so supernatural creatures can safely show their ugly heads in public, there's nothing you can do to stop that."

"Are you saying that when I'm a wolf I'm ugly?" I ask.

"I so knew she was going to go there," Arla chimes in. "Riddle me this, Dominy, does the wolf ever wonder if she's a pretty girl when she transforms back?"

"Bite me," I joke. Grateful that I still have friends who make me smile, when all I really want to do is cry.

"If you would learn not to bite first," Arla replies, "you wouldn't be in this situation."

Friends who also make me question why they're my friends in the first place. "Arla!"

"I'm sorry, Dom, but it has to be said," she continues, not backing down. "I know that Nadine probably had something to do with Gallegos's going all bounty hunter on you, but you have got to learn how to take control when you find yourself in these out-of-control situations. Otherwise . . ."

The next headline is going to replace the question mark after the word *werewolf* with an exclamation point, and my photo is going to be directly underneath. Grammar can save, but it can also kill.

Sighing heavily, I lie back on the beach towel and look up at the sky. I can only see an immense stretch of blue; no sun, no golden light is anywhere to be seen. It reminds me of the absence of Jess. If only she had shown up when Gallegos was pointing his gun at me, she could've created a distraction, some illusion like an abrupt fire or yellow lightning to make

Gallegos pause and give me time to flee into the night. But Jess never came. I know it's not her fault. Well, that's a complete lie; it's at least sort of her fault, but how can I blame her? She was my first victim and my first savior; she doesn't owe me anything. I've just come to think that whenever I'm in danger, Jess will rescue me. Time to start rethinking my options.

But why do I have to think about survival techniques on such a beautiful day? Why do I have to do anything other than look at my hot boyfriend's bathing suit ride up the length of his thigh? Because I'm cursed, that's why. Cursed by a psychotic old Native American Indian woman and her pregnant granddaughter. Which reminds me.

"Shouldn't Nadine be staying home at night taking prenatal vitamins instead of hiking through Robin's Park and hypnotizing cops?" I ask, absentmindedly tugging on the little hairs just above Caleb's ankle.

"She was probably foraging through the woods looking for some root herbs to make a potion so her baby won't grow up to be as vile as she is," Arla replies.

I smile because my friend knows exactly the right button to push to make me feel like I'm nothing more than a superficial, gossipy girl. And Archie knows exactly which button to push to make me tumble back to reality.

"Unless her baby daddy is some unbelievably smokin' Abercrombie & Fitch flip-flop-wearing dude," he ponders.

It's as if Caleb's invisible string is pulling at me to look at him, but I refuse; there is no way that he's the father of Nadine's baby. I won't accept it, and I can't believe for a second that it could be true.

Turning my head in the other direction is just as bad because I see Barnaby hanging in midair, about to plunge into the river. Stay under, Barnaby; stay where it's peaceful; don't ever come back up. My wish is ignored, and seconds later he pops up, shaking his head from side to side and spraying

Gwen and Jody with water. The three of them quickly engage in a splash fight, and I wish I could watch them forever, but there's something nagging at me in the pit of my stomach, the same something that's growing inside of Nadine's. The next generation of evil has got to have a father. Then again maybe not.

"You are not going to believe this!"

In one quick motion Caleb, Archie, and I are surrounding Arla, looking at the screen of her iPhone.

"And just why are we looking at a jellyfish?" Caleb asks.

"This isn't an ordinary jellyfish," she replies. "It may also be a jaffefish."

A what?

"This type of jellyfish reproduces asexually."

I'm only mildly better at science than I am at math, so I can't follow Arla's lecture. Luckily, Caleb is a left-side brain person, and he gets it instantly.

"You think Nadine could've impregnated herself?" he asks.

Archie and I make the same face, as if we just realized we bit into a booger burger; we are beyond disgusted to think that Nadine did the nasty to herself. Teenagers, however, are incredibly fickle, and grossed out quickly turns into engrossed.

"And you will never ever guess what this type of jellyfish is named," Arla taunts. "And by never ever I mean never to the infinite power."

Well then, why should we even try to guess?

"It's called a *moon* jellyfish!"

The three of us gasp so loudly that the cluster of kids near us looks over to investigate. Luckily their interest is only mild, and they soon continue with their own conversations, and we follow suit.

"Let me see that!" I demand, ripping Arla's phone out of her hands. She's right! The only type of jellyfish that can reproduce without any help from another jellyfish is called the moon jellyfish. That can't be a coincidence because I've already proven that there are no coincidences. No, this is a sign; the universe is telling us that just as the moon controls me, it's controlling Nadine. My boyfriend's thoughts are less sophisticated.

"Do you think Nadine hooked up with herself again after the dirty deed?" Caleb asks. "Or do you think she's been avoiding all her texts?"

Seconds later out bursts his trademark high-pitched laughter, and soon we all join in, our laughter so loud that we attract even more attention. What does it matter? There's no way that they can know what we're laughing about; there's no way that they can know we've stumbled upon another possible truth that defies explanation. Because if I can turn into a werewolf and Luba can draw upon Orion for her unnatural powers, why can't Nadine get pregnant on her own without having sex? And even if the concept of an indecent conception doesn't entirely compute, it at least allows me to have a few worry-free hours hanging out with my friends.

Until I get home and have to face Louis.

"Gallegos woke up."

This news should thrill me; it should relieve me of the guilt I've been feeling these past few days, but there's something in Louis's expression that gives me pause. He has more to say.

"He's going to be fine," he adds.

That can't be all. Louis looks the way my father used to, when right behind his words lay the truth, but it was a truth he didn't fully understand. Barnaby senses it too. I watch my brother from across the kitchen table, waiting for him to swallow his food, because I've learned that my brother's natural tendency is not to hide, so I know he's going to ask the question I'm dying to ask.

"What's wrong, Louis?"

Turning his back to us to wash his hands at the kitchen sink, Louis shakes his head and mumbles an almost incoherent *nothing*. We know he's lying, but Arla and I are too afraid to push him any further. Barnaby isn't.

"Then why do you look like Gallegos died instead of woke up from his coma?"

Louis takes his time. He turns off the water faucet, pulls the kitchen towel from its magnetic ring on the refrigerator door, wipes his hands dry, and then slowly folds the towel and puts it back in its holding place. Deliberate actions that no one interrupts because we all know Louis is searching for the best words to answer Barnaby's question. And those words appear to be foreign to him.

"Because he woke up afraid," Louis finally says.

I feel my chest heave, and I put my hand up to my mouth for no other reason than to quiet the sound of my breathing.

"What do you mean he woke up afraid?" Barnaby asks. "That doesn't make sense."

It does if you know the last thing he saw before he passed out and slipped into unconsciousness, the eyes of a girl on the face of a wolf.

"I know, Barn. It really doesn't," Louis replies, grabbing a plate from the cabinet above the sink and sitting down at the table. "Some disorientation I can understand, but not fear. He's trained for hand-to-hand combat and dangerous situations. He's a cop after all, and I don't know why he isn't acting like one."

The snarktastic teenager in me wants to say, "That's ironic, Louis, since it took my father's death to make you start acting like a cop." But the inquisitive wolf inside of me wins out.

"Has he said anything?" I ask. "Has he explained why he's so afraid?"

Shoveling a huge chunk of leftover meatloaf into his mouth, Louis half-chews and half-swallows the meat. A wolf-memory is triggered, and a sea of saliva rises up like waves against my teeth. In my mind's eye I see the saliva dripping from my lips and over my chin to hang in the air, and I drink almost the whole glass of my iced tea before I transform into an unsightly mess right here at the table. It almost prevents me from seeing that Louis is trying desperately to avoid my question.

"Daddy," Arla says. "What did Gallegos say?"

Resting his forehead in the palm of his left hand, Louis repeats Gallegos's words without looking at us. "He said he was afraid of the eyes."

"What's that supposed to mean?" Arla prods.

Louis looks at Arla, and it's clear that he doesn't want to share this information, but it's burdensome and making him weary. He needs to lighten his load by letting some of it roll off his tongue. "He said the eyes didn't look like they belonged to an animal," he relays. "He said they looked like they were the eyes of a girl."

Louis shrugs his shoulders and then exhales loudly with his lips shut tight; he has nothing more to say. When he leaves the table I finally look over to my brother and see that he's rereading the cover of the *Three W*. He pores over the headline one last time before he lifts his head and stares directly into my eyes.

Chapter 4

Maybe I should've killed Barnaby when Jess told me to.

I know that's a terrible thought, and I would never do it—
I couldn't do it when I was instructed to—but that's all I've
been thinking about since I caught him staring at me. My
brother knows that I was with Jess the night that she was
killed, the night the so-called Full Moon Killer first appeared,
and he's always suspected that I know more than what my
father told him about what happened that night and what I
admitted to. Now that the W word and this news about Gallegos is spreading through town like rats running from a
flood, maybe it's triggered something; maybe he's remembering things he didn't know he knew. Who knows, maybe
Luba's filled him in on the parts of the curstory that I never
want him to learn.

"That's a lot of maybes."

My bedroom suddenly resembles the inside of a honey jar.
It's been a while since I've had such a beautiful view, so I let
the golden sunshine seep into my pores and warm me from
the inside out. It floats through me like sundrenched blood
until I feel as if my entire body is glowing from within, like

the little piece of Jess that I carry inside of me suddenly exploded. Along with my anger.

"Well, it's about time you showed up!" I yell.

Ignoring my outburst, but not my statement, Jess replies, "I've been put on a short leash these days."

Ignoring her excuse, I keep yelling. "Like you ever listen to what Mr. Dice has to say."

"Respect, Dominysan," she says. "The man you call Mr. Dice is my mentor, my Sarutahiko, and he is in control of my free will."

Sometimes even I have trouble speaking supernatural.

"Free will is immune to outside forces," I explain. "That's why it's called free."

"For mortals perhaps," she states. "But not Omikami."

I peer deeper into the sunlight, and I see the change. Instead of hanging horizontally in the air or floating in her favorite yoga position, Jess is sitting at my desk looking at her reflection in the mirror. But before, when she would inspect her face in the mirror while she was alive, she'd look unhappy or frustrated or as if she were searching for a way to fix things; now she looks as if she's staring at a stranger. As if the girl in the mirror is a recurring character in a dream she had when she was very young, and she's trying to recall it.

"Jess," I say. "What's wrong?"

It takes her a few moments before she can move; she doesn't want to lose the connection to the girl staring back at her. Or the one that she's now facing.

"I'm sorry, Dom," Jess says softly.

"For what?" I reply, even though I know exactly what she's talking about. She's sorry for abandoning me lately; she's sorry for leaving me on my own instead of coming to help me when I called out for her, when she should've known that I needed her help. She's sorry for not being a real friend. When she speaks, I realize that I'm completely off base.

"For telling you to kill Barnaby."

Oh, that.

"I got a little too Omicocky and allowed myself to be tricked," she says. "By Nadine."

I don't know why, but I grab hold of Jess's hand. I'm not sure if I need to touch her or if I need to reassure her that I don't blame her for what she said or what she told me to do. I didn't act on it; there was no way I could. Barnaby wasn't hurt in any way; he was never really in any danger, so there's nothing to be sorry about. Jess sees it differently.

"Saruta . . . Mister Dice warned me to be careful," she shares. "But I didn't listen. I didn't think I had to listen to anyone."

Be careful of Nadine? Why would Jess have to be careful of Nadine?

Like water rippling through my fingers, Jess lets go of my hand; she's gone before I can squeeze tighter to make her stay. Fondly, she holds the Hello Kitty stuffed animal lying on my bed, cradling it as if it were a newborn. She rocks it slowly from side to side, and it's almost as if I can see Jess's youth and humanness spill out of her with every movement.

"Because when I'm with you or when I'm near Nadine, whenever I'm here on earth, really, I'm Jess," my friend tells me. "But that's not who I am anymore."

Wrong! I search my brain for the pieces of Japanese vocabulary Jess forced me to learn so I can speak to her in her favorite language. What's the Japanese word for wrong? *"Machigatta!"*

Jess smiles, wistfully, but not as my friend, more like an adult amused by the naïveté of a child. She's sitting right next to me, and yet she feels so far away.

"I'm an Amaterasu Omikami; you know that," she says. "Jess is who I used to be."

Jess is who you will always be! For some reason those words get caught in my throat, and I remain silent.

"The time is coming, Dom," Jess says.

No! Something is not coming! I was wrong, everything is staying exactly the same.

"The time is coming for me to fully embrace this new person I've become," Jess states.

Instantly my mind and my heart do battle; they're engaged in warfare because even though my mind understands what Jess is saying, understands its implications, my heart refuses to accept the meaning of these words. Not yet. Please not just yet! I need to shift the conversation back to something other than Jess and me; someone else needs to take center stage. "What does any of this have to do with Nadine?"

Clutching Hello Kitty in front of her, her arms wrapped around her protectively, Jess looks directly at me. When she speaks she sounds eerie, almost robotic, as if she's struggling to maintain her own voice, her own personality.

"Nadine tricked me into thinking that she was going to use Barnaby to father her child," she says. "And because I was listening to her thoughts and watching her actions as Jess, I wasn't looking beyond the surface, so I didn't see her true motive."

I'm almost afraid to ask. "Which was?"

"To wrongfully convince me that Barnaby would help her create evil, knowing that I'd urge you to kill your brother." The words slide out of Jess's mouth like rain, effortless and comforting and natural, as if they should somehow help me, as if they should somehow ease the pain I went through and still go through whenever I think that I could've ended my brother's life had I grown weak, had I given in and followed Jess's obscene instruction. The words that gush out of my mouth are like an angry flood.

"That's supposed to make it all better, Jess?!" I scream. "You were *tricked,* so you ordered me to kill my brother without really thinking it through?!"

"I know it's hard for you to understand because no matter

how much you've changed, Dom, you're still the same girl you always were," she says. "I'm not."

"I know you're not, Jess, and I know that I'm responsible for that!" I shout. "But Barnaby could be dead because of you!"

I'm so angry with Jess that I miss the most important part of this revelation: that Barnaby is definitely not the father of Nadine's baby.

"Wait a second. . . ." I start.

Smiling genuinely for the first time since she's arrived, Jess says, "With all your wolf-smarts, you're still always a few beats behind."

"So he isn't?"

"No," she replies.

"Is there a father?" I ask.

Her smile turns into uproarious laughter. "Of course there's a father, Dominysan!" Jess squeals. "Are you so caught up with the bee and the butterfly that you've forgotten all about the birds and the bees?"

Through my own gigglaughs I explain the revelation of the moon jellyfish's unique ability and our thought that maybe Nadine's baby is biologically fatherless. Jess is amused, but her opinion isn't swayed.

"That would have made a clever coincidence," Jess admits. "But it's wrong. Some coincidences are really just that, Dom, fun and interesting but completely devoid of any truth."

"How can you tell the difference?" I ask.

"Sometimes you're not meant to know the difference," Jess replies cryptically. Then with a mischievous gleam in her eye she adds, "How else would the supernatural powers that be laugh at your mistakes?"

We really are just laughter for the gods.

Anticipating my next question, she continues talking before I can even open my mouth. "And I cannot tell you who the baby's father is."

"Limitations?" I ask.

Another wistful smile and another change. Jess looks exactly the same as she always has, since the day she died, a fifteen-year-old girl, not a child and not a woman, stuck in that frustrating in-between world. But now she appears to be older. She looks as if she's outgrowing her shell, as if the outside and the inside are no longer a match. The more I contemplate what this could mean, the more frightened I start to get.

Suddenly Jess spins around, and strips of golden light encircle her body with each turn, like she's one of those rhythmic gymnasts who jump and twirl and flip around while carrying a wand with a long ribbon on the end of it. It's a gold-medal performance, but it's all for my benefit; Jess isn't feeling any of the joy she's creating.

"So then why are you here?" I ask. My voice makes her come to an abrupt stop, but her golden light continues to wrap itself around her unmoving body for a few seconds longer until it fades away and disappears into the air. "Did you come to crash the party?"

"What party?"

Now I know something's wrong. In less than an hour our house is going to be filled with our friends for Caleb's going-off-to-college party, his final blast before heading off to Big Red, the University of Nebraska. It's one shindig I know Jess wouldn't want to miss.

"You know exactly what I'm talking about!" I protest. "Caleb's party! Don't try to act as if you're not interested."

But Jess isn't acting; she really isn't interested.

"I think I've outgrown my party-girl phase," Jess replies.

I sit in my desk chair. It's still warm with Jess's golden light, and I realize Jess isn't any type of girl at all anymore. "Then . . . why did Dice let you off your leash to come here?"

"I have to warn you," she says, standing in front of me, but once again she's more interested in her reflection than my response.

"About what?" I demand. "And before you say anything, make sure that what you're going to tell me is accurate; no more misguided commands to kill."

"Something's coming," she says firmly.

I don't question her further, not because I know there's little more that she can tell me, but because I've sensed the same thing for weeks now, since my last transformation. I've tried to ignore it, but it's always been there, in the back of my head, right behind my eyes. Not a feeling, more like an expectation.

"Something's coming, Dominy, that will change everything," Jess states. "And you need to be prepared."

The message isn't as scary as the tone of Jess's voice, which is abrupt and distant and final. Who is this person standing in front of me? I have no idea who she is! Before I get any more answers, Jess disappears, taking all of her warm, golden sunshine with her.

Just as the last flecks of gold leave my bedroom, I hear her call out to me.

"Enjoy the party!"

It takes me a little over an hour to feel relaxed enough so I can fulfill Jess's wish and actually feel any enjoyment. But when I catch my reflection in the mirror that joy is tested. Just like Jess, I feel as if I'm confronting a stranger.

The young woman staring back at me looks intriguing, like someone I've met, but whom I don't fully know yet. She's a curious creature. I'm not embarrassed to admit that I find it strange that someone who is cursed could look so beautiful.

My hair is fuller and thicker and curlier than ever before, with a definite wild-like quality. Sometimes it's hard to manage, so when that happens, like tonight, I let it fall freely. Right now it hangs several inches below my shoulders, and since it's freshly washed it blooms with the smell of honeysuckle.

From the neck down there's been a change as well. All remnants of the little girl I once was are gone; in their place are naturally sculpted curves that I know are perfectly proportioned because Caleb can't take his eyes off of me lately.

The only parts of my body that give me hesitation, that I'm ambivalent about are my eyes. I love their shape, more oval than round, and especially their color, because my mother shares the same blue-gray. But now that Gallegos has risen from his coma proclaiming that he's being haunted by a pair of eyes that belong to a girl instead of a wolf, some of their beauty has been tainted. I know it's a long shot, and I know that most people don't take Gallegos seriously, but I'm worried that if he sees me he'll make the connection.

Luckily I have another, more important connection to occupy my thoughts.

"Is this seat taken?" Caleb whispers in my ear, while placing his hand on my butt. It's a crude comment, but it also makes me feel sexified, so I let him get away with it.

"Sounds like somebody's rethinking his decision to move away to college," I say, after Caleb takes a pause from kissing me.

"You know I'm gonna miss you like crazy," he replies, his fingers interlocking and resting on the base of my back.

"I'm gonna miss you too." I sigh. "But we, um, still have a few more hours left before you leave."

Smiling impishly, Caleb tries to read my thoughts, but I detect doubt along with the passion in his smile, so I press my body against him even harder. Instantly, he understands the meaning of my words and my gesture. There's no need to speak, so I kiss him deeply and feel his hard muscles flex underneath his T-shirt as his hands go in search of other parts of my body. I've thought about it thoroughly, I've talked about it with Arla incessantly, and I've decided that I'm ready to give myself to him, and I want him to know that. I want Caleb to be my first, and I know that he feels the same way.

It may be a bit inappropriate, however, to let our body language announce our true feelings to everyone else in the room.

"Do you have to?"

Archie's voice is like a vise that comes in between Caleb and me and pries us apart. I self-consciously try to tuck my shirt into my jeans until I realize I deliberately chose this top because it just skims my low-rise jeans. Caleb acts in a similar way, but he's got reason; he's trying to wipe my lip gloss from his lips with the back of his hand. Of course he just smears the glossy stuff all around his puffed-up lips, so he looks even sexier than he did when he was holding me a few seconds ago. Not that any of our post-make-out tidying up makes any difference. Archie isn't repulsed by our canoodling; he's upset that he and Caleb won't get to platonicanoodle like they used to. This is the third time this week that Archie's been moved to tears thinking about Caleb's move to a higher educational plateau.

"Bells, I know this is a party, and I don't want to bring you down," Archie rambles. "But I don't know if I can take another breakup."

We all know that he and Napoleon didn't break up, but there's no way that I'm going to correct him. When Caleb wraps Archie in a bear hug, I know Caleb's not going to reinvent himself as a linguistics tutor either.

"Winter, I'm only an hour away," Caleb says. "You can visit me any time."

Wrestling free of Caleb's stronghold, Archie continues to whine. I know that he's being serious, but I'm finding it hard not to laugh at his dramatics. "But you're premed," Archie whines. "You're not going to have time for me."

Caleb got a scholarship, which is paying most of his first-year tuition, which will be renewed the following year, as long as he maintains a 3.5 grade average. It's like a scholastic Band-Aid, apply pressure and repeat. Archie's right; Caleb is going to be quite a busy freshman and probably won't have time for his friends. Or his girlfriend. Thanks a lot, Archie! I didn't think depression was contagious. Or incurable.

"Again?!"

We all turn around, expecting to find Arla mocking Archie's most recent mini-breakdown like a good friend should, but then I see that she's trying to prevent the most recent mini-break-in.

"You are like Cirque du So What!" she says. "Seriously, Nadine, when are you going to learn that you're not wanted around here?"

When perhaps the rest of the crowd learns it.

"Hi, Nadine," Archie says. His voice is quiet, but not shy. He's not trying to make a statement, but he also doesn't care who hears him.

"Hi, Archie," Nadine replies sweetly. "It's good to see you again."

Then she does something so natural, yet so abhorrent that I grab Caleb's arm just for support so I don't topple over. She rubs her protruding stomach with her hand without taking her gaze off of Archie.

I don't need to look into a mirror to know that my face is almost as white as Archie's. Digging my fingers deeper into Caleb's flesh, I make a very selfish choice: If Nadine's baby's father has to be either Archie or Caleb, I pray that it's Archie. I don't know what type of person that makes me, perhaps merely an honest one, but thinking of my boyfriend being seduced by Nadine's disgusting spirit makes me sick. When she walks toward us, her actions make me feel violent.

Involuntarily, I look down at my arm, and I expect to see fur and claws and bones pointing in the wrong direction; that's how consumed with rage I am. But nothing has changed, at least not with me. When Nadine presents Caleb with a gift, beautifully wrapped in red, shiny paper and topped with a silver bow, all the venom racing through my body does some transmutation thing to pierce Caleb's flesh and make him speak to Nadine in a way I've never heard before. He doesn't raise his voice; very few people in the room can really hear what he's saying. But his words sound like the first cracklings of an uncontrollable inferno.

"You listen to me, Nadine, and you listen good," Caleb starts. "I do not accept your gift, nor do I accept your friendship. In fact, I don't want anything from you except your promise that you will stay out of our lives forever."

He doesn't wait for a reply, but leans in a little bit closer to her. The unruly curls on his forehead dangle in the air as they usually do, but instead of appearing harmless, they look like coiled daggers ready to expand and strike when their master gives the order.

"I would say that you're a despicable human being," Caleb seethes. "But we all know that you're not even human."

If Caleb's words sting, Nadine doesn't show it; her expression is impenetrable until her lips slither to the sides as if someone is forcing them apart, and she smiles. She tilts her head toward Caleb and finally speaks. "Neither is your girlfriend."

Caleb takes a step forward, and I increase the pressure on his arm. I don't want him to start a fight here that could get someone killed.

"Only because of you and your psychotic grandmother!"

Nadine's smile remains, but her eyes are filled with hatred. Oh how I wish my body could change at will; one slice against her flesh and I would rip open her stomach and let the baby she's carrying tumble to the floor like garbage. Oh my God! What the hell am I thinking? Could I possibly be capable of such a heinous act? Are these my thoughts or is it just because I'm in Nadine's presence that I'm becoming as vicious as she is? But how can someone be vicious while she's laughing?

"Well, you have that right," Nadine cackles. "My grand-mother has been known to go a little psycho from time to time."

Now laughter and the smile are gone, and only the real Nadine is left behind.

"Then again," she adds, "so have I."

Silver light rushes out of Nadine's body like a sudden fog, but seconds after it hits the air it changes color. Gone is the silver starlight born millions of miles overhead within the constellation Orion, and in its place are beams of black energy, just like the ones that pour out of Luba's diseased flesh. I don't know if Nadine has chosen this change or if the choices she's made lately—working with her family to kill Rayna, going witch-rogue and killing Napoleon herself—have made the light turn on its own, but it's clear that any goodness that was within her has fled.

No one else seems to bear witness to this energy display, but it definitely has a target: Archie. Why does she want to hurt Archie? He's the only one who's been borderline nice to her for weeks. It doesn't make sense. Neither do Caleb's actions.

In one graceful move, Caleb breaks free from my hold and stands in front of Archie just before Nadine's determined black light can wrap itself around Archie's body. Caleb isn't flinching, he isn't acting surprised in any way, but can he possibly see what I see?

Catching Nadine's stunned expression, I realize that she's as shocked as I am. I always knew that my boyfriend was gifted, but I didn't know he might possess talents of the unexplainable nature. So far he's the only one of us who hasn't been physically changed by Luba's curse in some way, but maybe his innate goodness is all that's needed to protect him from such evil. And all he needs to protect the people he loves.

"Like I said, Nadine," Caleb repeats. "No one wants you

in this town, so why don't you and your demented family just leave?".

This time when Nadine speaks, her face is devoid of emotion and sentiment and feeling. Her flat tone of voice suggests that she makes no attempt to be funny or witty or cruel. She's only being honest. And when you're dealing with a witch, honesty can be terrifying.

"Because, Prince Caleb," Nadine replies. "We haven't finished what we came to this town to do."

Chapter 5

I've never loved my boyfriend more than I do right now. And if we weren't surrounded by a group of our friends, I'd show him. He'll have to settle for being told.

"I can't believe how you stood up to the unwed witch," I say. "You really are my prince."

"And since I do not have a bf," Arla adds. "You're my prince too. If that's okay with you, Dominy?"

I love a friend who asks permission to borrow my boyfriend.

"Since you asked so nicely," I say. "We can do a time-share."

"What about you, Winter?" Caleb asks. "Do you want a piece of the prince too?"

The way Archie is glaring at Caleb, it looks like he wants a piece of him, but not so he can worship or praise or offer thanks that Caleb's turned the party into a Nadine-free zone. It looks like Archie wants to tear off a piece of Caleb's body and let the bloodied remnants rot in the sun. Immediately, I look at his eyes and expect to see that at least one has changed color and turned black, but all I see is beautiful violet; his eyes look the way they should; it's his face that appears to being wearing a mask of evil. And the mask, unfortunately, seems to fit him really, really well.

Nadine may have left the party, but her presence is still here; she's alive and well and living inside my best friend's body. I don't know if anyone else is picking up on the signs, but Archie's changing; he's acting the same way I did before the curse kicked in. Small, barely there changes that alone don't amount to much, but when placed side by side, spell danger with a capital O—for Orion.

How the hell can I rip Nadine's blackened spirit out of Archie? How do I even make him aware of the truth, that he could have Nadinevil running through his veins, without completely destroying his life? Why am I suddenly holding a shot glass filled with blood?

"To my new roommate!" Jeremy howls. "And to Big Red! She's never gonna be the same!"

I look around the room, and, while I was contemplating Archie's relationship with the pregnut, my friends have formed a circle. They're all holding shot glasses like the one that someone must have placed in my hand, and I'm guessing the red liquid is some kind of alcohol laced with tomato juice in honor of the school that will become Caleb's next alma mater. Everyone is laughing and shouting, and stomping their feet in and out of rhythm—Caleb, Arla, Gwen, Jody, my brother, The Worm, The Dandruff King; the only ones not participating in this spontaneous ritual are Archie and me. We're the only unwilling members of this teenage coven.

"And to its newest victim, Caleb!"

Jeremy tosses his head back and practically throws the red liquid into his mouth. When the drink slams into the back of his throat, he shakes his head like some wild animal and grimaces; he's either enjoying the taste or he's repulsed by the sting, I can't tell which. I look around and one by one all my friends imitate Jeremy's actions. Whatever they're drinking it seems to be both foul and potent, but they're not swallowing the contents of the shot glass for its taste, but for what it represents. Rebellion, freedom, adulthood—ideals that are just out of our reach. They remind me of Archie.

I look at my friend from across the circle. He's only a few feet from me, but he might as well be a hologram; his real self could be thousands of miles away. Honestly, I don't know if I'm looking at Archie or Archie 2.0, the version that's been injected with Nadine's special brand of bee venom. His next actions only make me more confused.

Mechanically, Archie raises his glass to his waiting, parted lips. He tips his hand, and the liquid trickles onto his tongue slowly, the complete opposite of the rest of the group's violent motion. I realize I was wrong. Archie isn't like me; he isn't a reluctant participant; he's made a conscious decision to join the frenzy. What's frightening is that he isn't entering the hysteria with wild abandon, but with a quiet calm.

Some of the drink detours and slides down the side of his mouth like blood escaping the site of a wound. The rich red color against Archie's milky white complexion shines like a beacon; it's commanding and beautiful and frightening. Just like my friend.

Stopping the stray liquid with his thumb to thwart its attempt at escape, Archie pushes it back into his mouth and swallows the offering. I watch his Adam's apple expand grotesquely as the fluid travels from his gullet to his gut, and it looks like a snake gorging on a rodent. I don't know if I'm witnessing this with my own eyes or the wolf's, so I'm not sure if Archie's physical deformity is the result of his drinking a funky-looking alcohol-laced concoction or of his symbolic induction into Nadine's evil star worshipping club. But clearly Archie's salvation is not on the top of everyone's minds. My boyfriend, for instance, is preoccupied with more selfish concerns.

"What's wrong, Domgirl?" he asks. "You're not going to toast me?"

Caleb clinks his empty shot glass against my full one, and I see that I'm the only one who hasn't taken a drink in his name. Sliding my arm around his waist, I smile, and in a movement that lies somewhere in between Jeremy's delirium and Archie's deliberation, I empty the contents into my mouth. I was right; it's tomato juice spiked with something alcoholic. I've consumed less than a six-pack of beer in my lifetime, hardly a liquonnoisseur, so I have no idea what's been added to the juice, could be vodka, could be gin; but whatever the secret ingredient is, it's causing a warm sensation to spread throughout my body, and I'm terrified because it feels like I'm going to transform.

I squeeze Caleb's waist harder, my fingers digging deep into his muscular flesh, and I hear the glass shatter at my feet. The echo sounds as if it's coming from somewhere in the distance, somewhere far away and not right here. This can't be happening! I will not allow it to happen!

Instinctively I clutch onto flesh, someone's nearby arm, and when I hear a scream, I force myself to loosen my grip. I need support, not sustenance. I turn to my right, and I see Gwen looking at me nervously. Her mouth opens and closes, forming words, a question, but I can't hear her, so I don't respond. Instead I take action.

Deep within my body I tell the wolf to stop playing games. It is not his time to emerge. Could he be waking up? Has the alcohol nudged him from his slumber or am I simply reminded of what it's like to turn? It doesn't matter; I'm freaking out, and I can't let the wolf grow stronger and take over. I tear the plastic bag off of my head and with one swift slice rip it into shreds with my claw.

"I'm okay."

The words cut through the air louder than I hoped they would, but at least they're my words, human words, not a wolf's howl. I'm just a girl who had a drink that made her feel weird. And a girl who's suddenly become a punch line.

"Talk about a cheap date!"

"What would you know about a date, Worm?" Jeremy shouts, not so much in my defense, but as a chance to mock someone else.

The laughter camouflages the concern that lingers in Caleb's eyes, but it doesn't wipe it away. Even after the party's over, after everyone else has left, it's still there.

"You kind of scared me back there," Caleb whispers.

We're up in my bedroom sitting on the floor, our backs pressed into the footboard, our bodies snuggled together. Downstairs, Arla and Barnaby are cleaning up to make the house presentable before Louis gets home. He knew we were having a little party, and after much D2D—daughter-to-daddy—cajoling, he gave in to Arla's request and allowed us to have it unchaperoned if we promised it wouldn't get out of hand and that the house would be cleaned and back to normal by the time he came home. At least two out of three of his kids are holding up their end of the bargain.

Arla sweetly told us that we could have thirty minutes of private time while she and my brother turned into a teenage Hazmat squad to clean up the mess. Arla must have bribed Barnaby into cooperating; he's matured these past few months, but he's hardly Peace Corps–volunteer material. Especially while his big sister is upstairs behind closed doors with her boyfriend. I'm sure whatever Barnaby thinks we're doing is way more X-rated than what's actually happening.

"I scared myself more than anything," I reply. "The alcohol reminded me of my transformation, and I didn't think my brand of show 'n' tell would be an appropriate party game."

As he raises his eyebrows and smiles devilishly, Caleb's voice grows even huskier. "We could play my brand of show 'n' tell."

His lips feel incredibly soft against mine, and when our tongues touch it's hot and wet and exciting. His hand grabs the back of my neck and heat jumps from his body to mine, but this time the feeling is different. I'm not scared, I'm not frightened by what's going to happen next, because I know the wolf is buried deep inside of me. It's just my boyfriend and me.

I push forward and lean into Caleb, pressing my hand on top of his chest, and I can feel his heart beat underneath his flesh; it's like someone is trapped underneath stone and trying to burst free. I smile when I feel his fingers travel up the inside of my shirt and fumble with the clasp of my bra. Gigglaughs slip out of my mouth even though I try to keep them silent, but I can't help thinking that for all Caleb's bravado he's had no practice trying to undo a girl's bra. My gigglaughs get louder when I think that I even wore my slut bra, the one with the super simple clasp in the front for easy access, and he's still having trouble.

Oh, spoke too soon.

Our eyes open at the same time, both of us surprised that Caleb's claimed victory and both hesitant to move forward. I look deep into Caleb's brown eyes, the color of rich earth, and kiss him. It isn't a deep kiss; I wouldn't classify it as a sexikiss, but more of an invitation. I'm giving him my permission to go further. He accepts.

We've done this before, touched each other, but never like this, never as a prelude to something that will become a shared memory. And usually I take charge and take off my bra or my bikini top; this is the first time I let Caleb lead the way. I sigh, and I'm not sure if it's because of the sensation of Caleb's hand moving timidly across my breast or if it's because it's so exhilarating to let someone else have control of my body. For the past two years I've been fiercely protective of maintaining control; it's liberating to be able to let go. And there's no one in this world I trust more than Caleb to give that power to.

"I love you."

Finally, I accept his words as truth. I don't worry that he's only trying to make me feel loved because I've spent so much time feeling cursed and ugly and alone. I don't wonder if he's going to stop loving me when he goes to college and meets other girls who don't come with wolf-lined baggage. I don't debase his sentiment thinking he's only horny and giving in to lust. I believe what he says, because I feel the same way about him.

"I love you too, Caleb," I whisper. "I always have, but I was too scared to admit it."

My confession leaves me overwhelmed, and I have to admit that this feeling is more powerful than anything I've ever experienced. It's stronger than transforming, more frightening than facing Luba, more mind-blowing than finding out the bee and the butterfly are offspring of a distant star, because it's so simple. Only me and Caleb, nothing else. Except, of course, the occupants downstairs.

"Barnaby!"

Arla's voice invades my bedroom like a sledgehammer swatting a fly. It's inappropriate, but it does the trick.

She's quieter now, but with my ESP I can still hear her berating Barnaby for almost dropping her grandmother's crystal bowl on the kitchen floor. Defending himself in a loud whisper, Barnaby tells her that if she was worried about the punch bowl getting broken she should've washed it herself or used the dishwasher to clean it. My brother does have a point, but he's forgetting that Arla has inherited her mother's domestic skills and has no idea how to use a dishwasher. She does, however, have other skills.

"Keep up the sass and I won't cover your ass," she says.

"You promised!" Barnaby barks.

"You want me to write your history paper on what happened in the world over summer vacation?" she bellows. "Then keep cleaning and make sure you don't break any of my family's heirlooms!"

So that's how she persuaded my brother to act all gentlemanly, with a scholarbribe. It isn't going to help Barnaby learn, but if it gives me some alone time with Caleb, I'm all for it. Problem is we're not alone, and now we both know it.

"Maybe this was a mistake." Caleb says out loud what I'm thinking.

"But you leave tomorrow!" I say. It's a testament to the honesty of my feeling that I don't cringe at all when I hear how whiny I sound. "Like at eight a.m. to drive to college. This is our last chance."

Why is Caleb laughing at me when I'm wearing poutface and an unclasped bra?

"It's hardly our last chance, Domgirl," he states. "Plus, I really don't want sex as a parting gift."

"I was, um, thinking of it as more of a going away present," I reply.

Kissing me softly, he leans his forehead against mine. The warm sensation has now been replaced by a calm coolness. Slowly, Caleb reclasps my bra, and I don't know how, but it's an even sexier move than when he finally undid it.

"And I guess I don't want to do it with an audience downstairs," I add.

Caleb sits up straight and takes my hands in his. "Let's wait until Christmas break," he suggests. "That way we won't have to rush, and we won't have to worry about disturbing the cleaning staff."

The anticipation makes a bit of the warm feeling return. "It's a date," I say.

"Speaking of dates," Caleb says. "We have an early one tomorrow. I should really be getting home."

A few more sweet kisses, and Caleb leaves. From my window I watch him get in his car and drive away. A crescent moon hangs in the sky, and I breathe in deeply to smell his scent lingering in the air. If only each night could be this perfect. And if only the morning didn't have to come so soon.

* * *

Sitting on Caleb's front porch, I'm hit with the undeniable truth that he's leaving. He's going off to college, and although I know he's only going to be an hour car ride away, he's not going to be in my life day-to-day. I know senior year of high school will keep me busy, but I'm going to miss him terribly. *Don't think about the separation; no, think about the connection, the connection he and I have and the ones he has with our friends.*

Arla and Archie have joined us for this last farewell, so Caleb's front porch is a bit crowded. In honor of Big Red, Arla is wearing a big red wig that makes her look a little bit like a grown-up Little Orphan Annie. Archie looks the same as he did last night. His eyes are still the color of violets, so physically things seem to be normal; mentally I can't tell. I can't worry about him right now though; this morning is all about Caleb and gift-giving. As a group, we agreed that we would give Caleb our going-away presents now instead of at the party so they would be more personal. And if necessary, kept private.

It's obvious that Arla is still a resident of academia, but at least she isn't one of its most wanted offenders. She doesn't promise to do Caleb's freshman-year homework, but she does give him a biology app for his smart phone so he can be up-to-date on the latest bio breakthroughs and developments.

"You are now one step closer to becoming Prince Caleb, MD," Arla announces.

"Excellent!" Caleb beams. "Thank you so much."

"Me next!" Archie cries, shoving a wrapped present into Caleb's hands. Its slim size means that it can only be one thing, a DVD. And I'm right. It's the old Christmas special starring the white-haired Winter Warlock who reminds Caleb of Archie.

"Just in case, you know, you miss me while you're becoming collegiastic," Archie says, trying to sound more sarcastic than sentimental, but failing.

Caleb hugs Archie tightly and whispers in his ear loud enough so we can all hear. "Winter, don't tell Domgirl, but I may miss you most of all."

When the boys release each other from their bromantic embrace, my turn arrives. Like Archie, I wanted to give Caleb something that would remind him of me, and since subtle is not my forte, I decided to go with the obvious.

"A calendar with all of the full moons highlighted so I can keep track of your transformations," Caleb says.

"And think good thoughts," I add.

"When I think of you there are no other kind."

Clearing her throat loudly, Arla jokes, "Based on last night's nontivity, thoughts are all you got."

Slapping Arla in the shoulder for her comment and Archie in his for his lewd expression, I change the subject. "I made one for myself too so I don't get blindsided by another blue moon like I did last year."

Yes, this is Dominy Robineau taking control of her life.

"And this is something for you," Caleb says, handing me a small gold box.

And this is Dominy Robineau losing control once again.

The tears running down my face feel almost as soft as Caleb's touch, and the beauty of his gift is as sweet and natural and honest as his feelings. Two bracelets made of string, one for me and one for Caleb. They represent the invisible string from *Jane Eyre*, our favorite novel, come to life. When Caleb ties my bracelet around my wrist, he leans in close, and this time when he whispers it's soft enough so I'm the only one who hears.

"Until Christmas."

Standing in between Arla and Archie, I watch Caleb drive away with his parents toward his new life. Selfishly, I'm grateful that it isn't that far away and I'll see him again in a few months. But even while I can't see him, I'll still feel his presence. Just like Jess.

"Dominy."

I hear her voice, but I don't see her golden sunshine. She hasn't come to visit, just to issue a warning.

"You need to protect him," she declares.

What?!

"How can I protect Caleb?" I silently ask. *"He just left for college! You couldn't tell me this yesterday when I still had a chance to stop him?!"*

"Not Caleb," she corrects. "Archie."

I can feel my breathing quicken. I can feel fear spreading throughout my veins, but I don't want to frighten my friends standing next to me. Let them think I'm just reacting to my boyfriend's leaving town and not because I'm being issued a telepathic warning by an Omikami.

"Why do I have to protect Archie?"

I silently ask Jess the question even though I know the answer before she tells me. I have known it ever since Nadine's black energy ripped through his body and contaminated him.

"Because his soul is in danger."

Chapter 6

"From now on your only reason for living is to be a protector."

It's heartwarming to hear my father's voice again. It sounds the way I prefer to remember it: strong and unafraid and certain—not the broken, pitiful way he sounded when he told me about the curse. Doesn't matter that it's just a tape of a speech my father gave addressing the Omaha Police Academy and that he isn't talking directly to me, standing next to the open back door that leads into the police station; my father's words sound heaven-sent and not prerecorded. For a moment I get so lost in the sound that I forget why I came here, but then my father says something that pulls me out of the past and back into the present.

"In your new role as a police officer you will see things that you may wish to forget," my father says, "but those are the very things that you must force yourself to remember if you want to protect your community."

I came here to the police station to have a private talk with Louis to find out if Gallegos has remembered anything more about the attack, if he's recalled Nadine's being nearby, or if he's mentioned anything else about the unnatural eyes peering back at him from the wolf's body. I never expected to catch Louis in a private moment.

"Dammit, Mason," Louis whispers. "I need your help, my friend."

Quietly, I inch closer to the door, and see Louis is sitting at his desk, his back to me. I'm unseen, but I can see that he's reading the already-infamous issue of the *Three W*. Perhaps reading is too physical a description, since Louis is just holding the paper in front of him, looking at the one-word headline—WEREWOLF?—and glancing up to look at my father on the TV screen.

Seeing my father's moving image for the first time in almost two years I'm struck with an odd combination of grief and joy. How wonderful to see him alive and talking, but how sad to know that it's fake. I wish I could jump into the TV and be with him just for a few minutes, just to talk things over with him. Louis feels the same way.

"Could this possibly be true?" he asks.

I knew it. Whenever there's a hint of corroborating evidence to back up an idea, no matter how preposterous, the absurd suddenly appears logical. I don't know if Louis believes in lycanthropy, that someone in town is truly turning into a wolf when there's a full moon, or if he thinks that the lunar activity is somehow having a baneful effect on the wolf population, but he's getting closer to believing what really is happening. Which means he's getting as dangerous as Luba. When he speaks again I realize a part of him already believes what most people consider unbelievable.

"Is this why you died?"

Yes! I want to scream. That's exactly why my father died!! Maybe if I explain everything to Louis he would be able to help; maybe he could put an end to this nightmare. Maybe he'd be able to help me protect Archie from Nadine before she causes even more damage. Maybe I should be more careful.

Not paying attention, I take a step closer to the door and

accidentally kick a beer can with my foot. Looks like someone's been drinking on the job, and someone else is disturbing the peace. Me.

"Who's there?"

I'm out of Louis's view before he even turns around, and
as quietly as possible I walk around the corner to the other
side of the building, but it isn't far enough. I can hear Louis's
chair squeak against the floor, and I know he's about to come
outside to investigate. If I start to sprint I know Louis will
never catch up to me, but the police station is in the center of
town, hardly an isolated area, so there's a very good chance
he'll see me before I can make it to Robin's Park and the shelter
of the woods. Nope, the only safe direction for me to go is up.

I've never scaled a building before, but how much different
can it be from scaling The Weeping Lady? Turns out, for me,
it's just as easy.

Jumping as high as I can to grab on to the top of the window ledge, I hoist myself up until my feet are on the ledge
along with my hands. Can't stay in this crouched position for
too long, not when I hear Louis exiting the building, his feet
grinding into the dirt underneath him. Luckily the police station is only a two-story building, so in one swift move I leap
up to grab hold of one of the gutters. It creaks loudly, buck-
ling under my weight, but the sound gets derailed by the
wind and doesn't connect with Louis's ears. Not wanting
Louis to see me hanging off the side of the building, I call
upon my animal instincts and swing my body to the right
with such force that I land on the roof. I lift up my hands off
of the gutter just as Louis rounds the corner of the building.

"Anybody there?" Louis asks.

We're both still as he waits for a reply. I cover my mouth
to hide my panting and don't move until I hear Louis retreat
back to his office, this time closing the door behind him.
Enough with spending time in a place where I don't belong;

time to make a visit to the one place I know I'm always welcome.

Admittedly The Retreat hasn't put out a welcome mat
with my name on it, but Room 19 has. Unfortunately, to get
to my mother's room I have to walk past the receptionist's
desk. The last few times I was here, either Nadine was filling
in or one of the custodians was sitting behind the desk, looking more out of place than I would at a national math competition. As annoying as it was to have to deal with Nadine
or some man who grunted at me while clutching a wet mop
in order to visit my mother, it was a comforting feeling to
know that Essie had not yet been permanently replaced.
Today, all comfort is decimated by shock.

"Hello, Dominy."

Essie?!

I shut my eyes and count to ten, but when I open them,
nothing has changed; I'm still staring at Essie's face. The face
attached to the body of the person I watched die in the park-
ing lot out front. The same body I saw lying in a casket that
was then locked and buried underground. This can't be real!
Not even Dominyreal! Essie cannot be back from the dead.
What the hell am I thinking? She was buried in Weeping
Water soil; anything is possible.

"Essie?" I whispask.

My confusion is laced with a heaping amount of hope that
Essie has somehow been resurrected.

"Oh no, dear," the woman replies. "I'm Elkie, Essie's twin
sister."

And with that announcement, hope, like comfort, is shat-
tered. And replaced with suspicion.

"Essie never told me she had a twin," I state.

"My sister was a very private woman," Elkie replies. "And
she told me that you never asked her about her family."

I think I liked this woman better when I thought she was a

zombreceptionist and not a well-informed sibling. I can't argue with Elkie's comment, so I stare at her and meet her unwavering gaze. Physically she's an identical blueprint of my dead friend, but she possesses a quality I never detected in Essie—natural courage. It takes me only a few seconds to determine that I'd be a fool to treat this woman like a foe instead of an ally. I also get the sense that unlike Essie, Elkie will have no problem calling me out if I try to rewrite history and sugarcoat it, so I opt for honesty.

"I regret not taking the time to get to know Essie better," I admit. "Chalk it up to being a self-absorbed teenager."

"And how would you describe yourself now?" Elkie asks.

"Let's just say I've grown up a lot in the past few years," I reply.

"Essie told me that too."

Okay, now I'm curious. "What else did Essie tell you?"

"My sister was very fond of you," Elkie continues. "And she was right about your transformation."

My what?!

"You are definitely becoming a beautiful young woman."

Suddenly I feel terrible. Essie cared enough about me to make me the center of conversation with her twin when I barely made time to have conversations with Essie throughout her life. It's never too late to make up for being self-centered and inconsiderate and disinterested, as long as you mean what you say. And I do.

"Essie was a wonderful friend," I say honestly. "I miss her more than I can say."

"I can tell," Elkie replies. "I can see it in your eyes."

Again with my eyes! What is everybody seeing in my eyes?! I hope not nearly as much as what I see in Elkie's eyes when The Cell Keeper comes out of his crypt.

The way Elkie glares at Winston Lundgarden, it's as if she's locked eyes with the devil. I'm sure Elkie knows every ugly detail about Essie and Winston's brief affair and hates the man who dumped her sister, but Winston doesn't appear to be very fond of Elkie either. However, his reaction could have more to do with her uncanny resemblance to the woman his lover's mother-in-law killed and less with the evil eye she's brandishing in his direction.

Winston turns around to scamper back into his den, but his scampering lacks its usual finesse, and he slams right into the wall. Trying to collect himself, Winston tugs on his suit jacket, but when he stares at me I trace my finger along my cheek. In response, he touches the scar that is still prominently displayed on his cheek, but the second his finger feels the gnarled flesh, he regrets it. I guess not every man wants to be reminded that his girlfriend slashed his face in a fit of boredom. Melinda Jaffe might not be a card-carrying witch, but she's sandwiched between two demons—Luba and Nadine—so she's had a lot of training. Winston must be an idiot if he thought he wouldn't become a victim to one of them if he hung around long enough.

Still nervously touching his scar with one hand, he blindly searches for the doorknob with the other. Once he makes contact, it still takes several tries for him to turn the knob and push so he can flee to the safety of his office. Looks like the once dashing and debonair Winston Lundgarden is playing a new role that showcases his true cowardly nature.

I suppress my laugh out of some warped desire to respect my elders, but as an elder herself, Elkie isn't hampered by such guilt, and soon the hallway is consumed with her deep, throaty laughter. I think I've found a worthy replacement for Essie.

"Elkie," I say. "You and I are going to get along just fine."

Still laughing, she replies, "I knew we would, dear."

I suddenly feel like skipping down The Hallway to Nowhere. It's rare that I'm so happy at The Retreat, and unfortunately the feeling turns out to be not only rare but short-lived. Mixed in with Elkie's laughter that's still wafting through the air, I hear voices coming from my mother's room.

Outside her door, I listen, but nothing, only silence. Perhaps my wolf ears are picking up voices in another room? I don't typically get confused or bombarded by different sounds, as I can easily tune them out, so when a noise breaks through, it's usually trying to capture my attention. Or I'm just hearing things that aren't there.

Inside, my mother is alone, the same way she's been for the past decade. I pull the bottle of Guerlinade, her favorite perfume, out of my bag, and spritz some into the air. We're in a field of lilacs, the tiled floor replaced with grass and the walls torn down to make way for sprawling oak trees.

"Hi, Mom, how are you?" I ask like I've asked her every time I've seen her since I was a little girl. Sometimes I've actually gotten a response; most of the times, like today, my greeting is met with silence. That's okay because that's why I came here, for silence and peace and just to look at my mother's unnaturally beautiful face.

Unless I get close to her to see some lines around her mouth and the corners of her eyes, she looks like she's in her twenties. My mother wasn't vain about showing her age— she's French after all—and I know it's way too early for me to worry about my own wrinkles, but it's nice to know I probably won't have that problem for many decades to come. I have enough problems as it is. Like why is there a silver light in the corner of the room? I blink, and the light is gone.

First I'm hearing voices that aren't there, and now I'm seeing things that don't exist. No, things don't happen to me without good reason. Jess may be right; not all coincidences turn into bombshells. But this isn't a coincidence; this is a premonition, and my premonitions come true. Plus, my senses are excellent, so someone or something was here.

Gently I tap my mother's hand as I walk toward the corner

where I saw the light. Just in case she's aware of my presence, I want her to know that I'll be right back. Stepping into the corner of the room is like stepping into a meat locker: It's ice-cold. When I breathe I see a cloud of cold air emerge from my mouth and float up to the ceiling. Shivering violently, I cross my arms, and I swear icicles are forming on my body. I hear something hit the ground. My first thought is that I'll see ice cubes scattered on the floor. What I see frightens me even more. My mother's compact.

I bend down, and I'm amazed to see my mother's Little Bo Peep compact, the one her mother gave her, my grand-mère. What is this doing here? I locked it away with the few other family heirlooms I have in my box, which is now in the back of my closet. I bend down to pick up the compact, but it's so cold that, when I touch it, it burns my fingers. I kick it with my foot so it slides near my mother's bed and hopefully out of the Arctic Circle.

Gingerly I touch it again and as expected it's warmed up; its temperature is perfectly normal, and so is mine for that matter. Wherever the cold zone came from, it's relegated to only a small portion of the room. It has to be a gateway, some sort of time tunnel or dimensional port, to be able to reach out to my bedroom, grab the compact, and bring it here. But why?

It's definitely the same one that my mother gave me. Silver border, Little Bo Peep's worried profile against a shimmering purple night sky that's filled with three stars.

Three stars! What? Were there always three stars on the cover or is that new? Think, think, Dominy!!

"Yes, Dominy, think."

Luba.

"Get out of here!" I shout.

I don't know if it's because I haven't seen Luba in a few months or because of her close proximity to my mother, but I'm not afraid to be in her presence. In the past, there was always a sense of dread and fear when she stood before me, despite how courageous and defiant and powerful I tried to appear. Or maybe I'm garnering strength from my mother, because this is what it must feel like to be a parent; you'll calmly stare evil in the eye in order to protect your child.

"Is that how your mother taught you to treat a guest?" she asks.

"You are many things, Luba," I reply. "A *guest* of mine or my mother's is definitely not one of them. Now get out!"

Ignoring me, Luba floats toward me, her feet several inches from the ground. She doesn't bother to land when she reaches me; she hovers in the air so she's taller than me, and I have to tilt my head if I want to look her in the eyes when I speak with her. Not sure if it's a tactic to make herself feel superior or if she simply has more energy now that she's taken over Rayna's spirit. Sadly, she looks like she's taken over the poor girl's wardrobe too.

Luba's sporting a pair of green cotton capri pants and a pink tank top trimmed in matching green lace. Hand-me-downs from Rayna's preppy whoredrobe when she was dating Jeremy that was designed to look innocent while exposing the maximum amount of flesh possible. If you knew Luba's real age, you'd think she looked ridiculous, but if you saw her for the first time, you'd think she looked amazing.

Her skin is still pale, but gone are the bluish veins and bruises that were visible underneath her flesh; her hair is deep black and vibrant, still parted simply in the center and falling way past her shoulders, to the middle of her back. Her face, however, has made the most prominent and disturbing transformation, because now her smooth, wrinkle-free complexion reminds me of my mother. Both their looks are death defying.

"Three stars," Luba hisses. "I wonder where I've seen that before?"

Her laughter begins slowly, a mere chuckle, but soon she's

laughing maniacally with her fingertips pressed against her lips. This gesture looks even more sinister and grotesque and indecent than it did before when she was emaciated and withering, because it's now out of place. Luckily I know exactly where I am, and even though I'm literally standing in Luba's shadow, my defenseless mother at my side, holding a trinket that may be a message to warn me about what's going to happen next in my life, I'm still not afraid. It's not foolhardy; it's learned. I know that I'm not the one who should be afraid; Luba is.

"You don't frighten me anymore," I announce.

My proclamation only makes Luba laugh harder.

"Don't confuse being arrogant with being courageous, child," she warns.

"And don't confuse me with a child," I reply. "I've grown up quite a bit, thanks to you."

Her laughter stops, and she bends toward me, her body arching so she can gaze into my face and get a better look at the young woman she's helped create. Her hair falls forward to create two black walls on either side of my face that hinder my vision. All I can see are Luba's preternaturally youthful features, and all I can hear is her voice.

"You're welcome."

She breathes such hatred into each word that I wince. The smell and touch and sound of her words cut right through me; it's a disgusting sensation, but not nearly enough to make me back down. I don't know where I'm getting my strength from—maybe it's this silly compact; maybe it's being next to my mother—but whatever the source, I'm well-armed.

"So don't make the same mistake your granddaughter's made and underestimate me," I say. "You and what remains of your family may live to regret it."

Suddenly, the freezing cold travels and consumes the entire room. At first, I think that I'm the only one who senses it, but Luba feels it too; whatever it is, she isn't immune to its power. Landing on the ground with a thud, Luba jerks her head to the left, to the right, searching for the origin, desperately trying to find out why she feels the deep freeze that's taken over the room, what's making her react like a mere mortal. All she has to do is look at my mother.

"Something is coming."

Those are the same words Jess said to me, the same words I used before my last transformation, and it's the same feeling that's been haunting me for weeks.

"Something is coming," my mother repeats, "that will change everything."

My mother's voice is soft, her body is calm, she's unaffected by the cold, but it's clear that Luba is terrified by her words. When my mother speaks again, Luba's artificially youthful face turns even whiter.

"And Luba," my mother says, opening her eyes and turning her head to face my enemy. "It's getting closer."

Chapter 7

First day of senior year to-do list:

1. Rule the school.

2. Pass calculus!

3. Try not to miss Caleb too much.

4. Protect my best friend's soul.

5. Wait for something to come to help me defeat Psycho Squaw.

Items one through three are doable. I'm a cheerleader, I've got a boyfriend in college, and I've got gorgeous hair; that's enough to garner an underclassman's respect. If I maintain focus in calculus and beg Mr. Dice for a little Omikami intervention, I'm guaranteed at least a B minus. And as long as I don't lose my smart phone, I can keep texting and FaceTiming Caleb until he comes home for the holidays, when he and I will finally share some much anticipated private time. Numbers four and five are a bit trickier.

I don't know what scares me more: the fact that Archie's soul needs protecting, or that something is coming to town that frightens Luba. Neither thought fills me with the warm fuzzies or even the lukewarm fuzzies, but maybe I should stop dwelling on the fear factor that these commands ignite and look at the flipside of what they mean—both of them offer hope.

If Archie's soul needs to be protected, it means that Nadine hasn't completely destroyed it yet. She might have stained it, she might have tarnished the edges, but there's still more white than black, still more good than evil, still a chance for Archie to remain the person he was before he was touched by Nadine's spirit.

An even better thing is that I may soon have a weapon to topple Luba from her bloodstained pedestal. What that thing is, I have no idea, but I've had a premonition that something is coming to help me in my fight against the Cursemaker and her tribe, a feeling that has been seconded by Jess and now my mother, who really only speaks when she has something super-vitally important to say, so I'm convinced that whatever is on its way is definitely something good. I'm not ready to do the paperwork and change my name from Dominy to Pollyanna, but maybe that something will serve a dual purpose and help me fight Luba *and* protect Archie's soul at the same time. Personally, I don't think that's too much to ask for after everything my friends and I have been put through. I just hope it gets here soon, like before Nadine gives birth. The problem is, I have no idea when to calendar doomsday. Neither do my friends.

"Any idea how to convert Nadine's baby bump into a due date?" I ask Archie and Arla over lunch.

"Any idea why she's wearing her pregnancy like a badge of honor?" Arla retorts. "Instead of being embarrassed by her quote unquote 'situation.' "

"Why should she be embarrassed?" Archie replies.

What?! I'm not sure if I scream that out loud or if my inner voice bounces off the insides of my skull. Why is Archie once again meandering over to Team Nadine? Sounds like I'm not the only one who's mega-confused.

"Don't take this the wrong way, Archie," Arla begins, "but what the ef are you talking about?"

Speaking with a mouthful of mashed potatoes, Archie doesn't sound like he's upset by either spoken or silent questioning.

"Nadine shouldn't be ashamed," Archie states calmly. "She got pregnant, and now she's doing the right thing by taking responsibility for her actions."

If Nadine were to take responsibility for her actions, she'd excuse herself from school, visit Louis at the police station, and confess to committing murder. Then again, what's good for the bee is good for the wolf, so I'd have to be the next in line. Maybe I should adopt Archie's nonjudgmental stance and not judge Nadine.

"Well...I guess when you put it that way, you're sorta maybe kinda right," I verbally fidget.

"You two are missing the point," Arla says. "Nadine isn't some normal teenager who's found herself on the receiving end of a broken condom and accidentally wound up with a bun in the oven, as they said back in the day. She deliberately planned this pregnancy."

"We don't know that for sure," Archie replies, a bit less calmly.

Looking at me with bugged-out eyes before speaking, Arla is having an even harder time staying calm than Archie is.

"I do," she states. "Nothing Nadine does is accidental. The only thing we don't know is if she's going to be a single mother or a single mother slash father."

I grab hold of this chance to veer the topic onto safer territory and share with them Jess's comment that not all coincidences turn into fact. It does the trick.

"Really?" Arla pouts. "But it's the *moon* jellyfish; it's so perfect."

"I know! I was very disappointed to find out that Nadine isn't asexual," I reply. "But then again, despite her pregnancy glow I still find her unattractive, so I guess she still is."

And I should have known, if we kept talking about Nadine, it would only be a matter of time before Archie would steer the conversation back into the danger zone.

"Regardless, it makes me sad to see her sitting all by herself."

It's a powerful comment, because within the absurdity of his words lies some truth. If I didn't know that Nadine was a psychopath, I'd think she deserved pity. She's sitting alone in a corner of the lunchroom eating a sandwich, every once in a while placing her hand on her belly and rubbing it, as if to make sure that her unborn child is still there, afraid that it'll abandon her like everyone else has. As long as she isn't alone, she has the strength to ignore the judgmental stares and hushed commentary. Archie and Arla can't hear the nasty whispremarks, but I can.

"Can you believe she came back to school looking like that?"

"She could've left town over the summer, and no one would've known she got herself pregnant."

"One kid dies, the other gets knocked up—her mother must be flipping out."

"It's like the Jaffes are cursed or something."

Damned is more like it. *Yes, keep reminding yourself of that, Dominy. Don't forget that Nadine Jaffe and the rest of her relatives aren't the hunted; they're the hunters. Don't let Archie's soft heart cloud your thinking, because you can't protect your friend if you go soft too.*

After Archie leaves for a football meeting to discuss very important football matters, Arla proves that nothing Archie says could make her soften her opinion of Nadine. Even when it's not her voice doing the talking.

"There's something wrong with him."

I haven't heard Napoleon's voice in a while, but it's instantly recognizable, even when his words tumble out of Arla's mouth.

"Nap?" I whisper-ask. "Can you maybe be a little more specific?"

"He's changing."

Yes, into a Nadine sympathizer.

"This is only the beginning," Nap adds. "There are many more changes to come."

Glancing around quickly to make sure that no one is listening to our conversation, especially the dead speaker's sister, I grab Arla's hand. She feels the same, not too warm nor cold, hard nor soft. Yet it's so incredibly off-putting, even for me; there's a supernatural being inside of her, taking control of her body, and Arla still looks and feels exactly the same. It's not like she goes all zombie and her eyes roll back in her head; she's staring right at me and talking to me, only she's using another person's voice. Or more accurately another person is using her voice.

"What do you mean the *beginning?*" I ask. I stare directly into Arla's eyes, amazed that Napoleon is looking at me from the other end.

"The arrival," he replies.

Old news. I've received the warning and the confirmation. I know that something's coming, but tell me what it is so I can greet it when it drives into town!

"I need more than that, Nap," I say. "Stop being like Jess and give me details."

Be careful what you wish for.

"You're going to do things you never dreamed you could do," he replies. "Things you never thought you were capable of doing."

I asked for details, not some kind of cryptic omen!

"What are you talking about?" I demand.

"Ow! Why are you squeezing my hand?"

Dammit! It's Arla's voice; Nap's gone. And so is any chance of finding out what or who is about to arrive. Or what I'm about to do.

"Sorry," I say. "I was trying to get Nap to tell me what he was talking about."

"You were talking to Nap?" Arla asks.

I don't know why I'm surprised that Arla's surprised, but I am. I know that Arla's transformations are different than mine. She doesn't get a warning. When Nap takes over, he does it instantly, and Arla kind of blacks out without the embarrassing slump to the ground. But I thought that while Nap was in control she knew she was losing time. Guess not.

"Where exactly do you go when Nap takes over?" I ask.

"I call it the Quiet Place," she replies. "I can't hear or feel a thing, but it isn't frightening in the least, very peaceful, almost womb-like, I imagine."

"So you know when Nap takes over?" I question.

"Of course," Arla answers. "Just like you do when the big, bad wolf wants to be, you know, all big and bad. But you're sure it was Napoleon's voice?"

Okay, now I'm more confused than before. Even if Arla doesn't get a warning, she knows when Nap is taking over her body, so why does she look so shocked? This isn't the first time she's been Nappossessed.

"I thought the whole Nap-talking-through-me thing was over with," she admits. "I figured he was too busy doing heavenly things to bother with me anymore."

My friend has so much to learn about how otherworldly creatures operate. "Well, heaven must have recess, because he was just here," I convey. "Loud and clear."

"What did he say?" Arla asks in a voice that doesn't conceal how much she really isn't sure that she wants to hear Napoleon's message.

Holding her hand again, this time not to reconnect with

Nap, but to make my bond with Arla even stronger, I answer, "There's something wrong with Archie."

Breathing deeply, Arla replies, "I don't need Napoleon to tell me that."

Before I can tell her that Jess has also told me that I need to protect Archie's soul, she continues. "But as much as it's painful to hear," she says, "I get why he's pro-Nadine."

"What?!" I cry. "What possible reason could he have for defending Nadine and feeling sorry for her? She's the enemy."

"She's also his ex-boyfriend's sister," Arla reminds me. "I think Archie feels sorry for Nadine because he misses Nap."

"You think Archie is displacing his feelings for Nap onto Nadine, the same way Jess did in her diary?" I ask.

"It's a possibility," Arla replies.

"But Jess didn't know all the facts," I state. "Archie *knows* that Nadine is evil."

"And so is Archie."

Not only does Arla's voice disappear when she speaks, but this time so does her face; in fact her entire body dissolves in front of me, and in her place is sitting the dearly departed Napoleon Jaffe.

His hand feels warmer than Arla's. Has he been lurking around Jess's golden shadows? Who knows?! The only thing I'm sure about is that Nap obviously felt he didn't convey his message clearly enough the first go-around, so now he's decided to use a visual aid. Since I don't hear any shrieks of shock around me, I'm pretty positive that I'm the only one witnessing the dead twin's return from the grave.

"You're wrong, Nap," I declare. "Archie is not evil."

"Because you don't want to see it," he replies just as firmly. "Look harder, and you'll find it."

How dare he call my friend evil! Not when Napoleon comes from a family of sin and corruption himself.

"You should talk!" I seethe. "You're not much better than the rest of the filth in your family!"

I'm not sure if it's because I let go of Nap's hand or because of my unedited analysis, but Napoleon's image vanishes. Unfortunately, the memory of it remains. I hear Arla asking me what's wrong, but all I can see are Archie's eyes, one gold and the other black. No! I don't care what you say, Nap. I refuse to believe that my friend is evil simply because he's sympathetic toward your murderous sister.

"I blanked out again, didn't I?" Arla accurately deduces.

"Just for a few seconds," I reply, shrugging my shoulders as if it were a completely forgettable few seconds. "C'mon, let's go."

"What else did Nap say?" she asks, stealing a quick glance at Nadine as we walk out of the lunchroom.

As usual when it comes to speaking the truth, I trust my gut instinct, so I lie. I pray that my words aren't a complete fallacy. "He said that he misses Archie too."

The rest of the first day of school is just like Archie and Napoleon's relationship: bittersweet. Every day, every hour that ticks by brings me closer to leaving one of the only places that has given me continuity and rescue and normalcy these past few years. I know that most high school seniors cannot wait for graduation to say good-bye to their alma mater and move forward in their life and never look back, but I'm really going to miss Two W. Even the lame assemblies.

Looks like Principal Dumbleavy took a page out of Archie's style book. Dumbleavy has always kept his hair short in that simple, nondescript, middle-aged professional man style. This year he's sporting a weird hybrid combo of state trooper meets 1950s businessman. His hair, now more salt than pepper, has been buzzcut so the top is as flat as a textbook. It looks like freshly mowed grass after an unexpected snowfall. I wonder if he went to Vernita's Hair Hut during her Men Only Monday special—first Monday of every month—for his new 'do. Jess's mother once told me Vernita loves the military look.

On top of his redone hairdo, he must've altered his diet to include meat and potatoes, hold the vegetables, because his face seems to have expanded about an inch on both sides, and his neck and belly are both spilling out over the sides of his collar and belt. Apparently, his clothes cannot contain his new girth. When he speaks, I feel bad that I've silently criticized him so harshly, because it's obvious that stress is the main reason for his makeover.

"We are living in troubling times," he begins. "And we—as a school and as a community—need to be careful."

His voice isn't quivering; it doesn't break. But it is overflowing with terror. This man is frightened, and for the first time in my life I look at him with respect. The only reason he's standing in front of the entire student body is that he feels a responsibility, an obligation, morally or otherwise, to lead us out of this dark period in our town's history and into the light. He could easily have quit his job and moved far away from the unexplained, from the murders, from the disappearances, but he stayed. He looks worse for wear, but he's still here.

He continues speaking about how we must be more diligent, more cautious, more aware that there is danger out there. I look over at Nadine sitting among unsuspecting students, her back rigid, her lips forming an informed smile, and I want to grab Dumbleavy by the arm and whisper in his ear that danger is right inside these walls. But Miss Rolenski beats me to it.

"Oh yes," Dumbleavy mumbles before clearing his throat. "Thank you for reminding me."

Hold on a second. Did Miss Ro really tell our principal that danger is sitting right in the bleachers?

"I almost forgot to announce that we have a new student," he says.

Nope, just another potential victim.

"And she comes all the way from Cos Cob, Connecticut."

Cos Cob! Arla and I look at each other and then at Nadine, whose face has just gone pale, and since it's the afternoon it can't be because of morning sickness. Cos Cob is the quirky name of the town where Nadine and Napoleon grew up.

"Please give a warm welcome to the newest member of Two W's senior class," Principal Dumbleavy announces. "Vera Bailey-Clarke."

Once I hear her name, I know that the something I've been waiting for has finally arrived.

Chapter 8

I hear the girl approaching before I see her, and already she frightens me.

Squeak, squeak, squeak. That's the only sound I hear echoing through the gym. It's Nadine's signature sound, the one I hear when she walks down The Hallway to Nowhere at The Retreat, but Nadine isn't making any sound; she's barely breathing. She's sitting in the bleachers, her body and face like white stone, one hand gripping the metal seat, the other placed on her belly as protection from this intruder. But why does she need protection? And who is this Vera? Is she the fulfillment of some sort of prophecy, or is she just the next phase of this curse? When I finally see her, I feel like an idiot; she isn't either.

The squeaking is gone; I'm not entirely sure it was ever there in the first place. Could've just been my imagination because I'm like a Pavlovian Girl; I've been trained that whenever I'm frightened my thoughts immediately go to Luba and Nadine. Now that I'm a little less scared, a little more in control of my emotions, I can only hear the sound of strong, confident strides. Nadine-squeaks are a memory.

The heels of Vera's simple, sensible shoes click against the floor with each step, and while the sound fills up the entire gym, it isn't overbearing, hardly a thunderous roar, more like a sudden gust of wind that is massive in size, but in no way threatening. This stranger's presence sweeps over our heads and hangs there not to crush us, but to demand our attention even before she reaches the podium. I look around, and I swear the entire Two W population is in a trance.

When Vera turns to face her audience, I'm stunned, because she looks incredibly ordinary. Where is her power coming from? Examining her with a wolf's eyes and a girl's mind, I see she looks like she's stepped out of a painting of a New England landscape; she looks beautiful and clean-lined and artificial. Her blond hair is silky and straight, parted on the right and cut in a no-nonsense bob that curls inward just below her chin. Her nose is slightly upturned, not enough to look like a deformity, but enough to make her appear as if she's always critiquing her surroundings. Icy blue eyes that are inviting though guarded and unblemished skin that is smooth but veil-like complete her facial features.

Her body is thin in a healthy way and not as the result of some diet pill laced with dubious FDA-unapproved ingredients. Long arms fall naturally at her sides, and even longer legs give her the appearance of being taller than she is. Naturally she's wearing the Two W uniform like every other student in the building, but her khakis are spotless and freshly ironed, and her navy blue polo shirt is tucked neatly into her pants, so she looks like she's wearing a costume instead of clothing. Under such wolf-girl scrutiny, she's really a bunch of jumbled contradictions, like a painting with interesting visual elements that when combined create, perhaps not a masterpiece, but something pretty to look at.

Glancing at Arla, Archie, and some of the kids near me, I realize that *pretty* appears to be downright mesmerizing. They're staring at Vera Bailey-Clarke as if her real name is Mona Lisa. Nadine, however, is gaping at her as if she were the model for the Venus de Milo right at the moment when some machete-wielding maniac sliced off her arms and made her a statistic before she was turned into a statue. For her part, Vera appears to be very comfortable in the role of Dumbleavy's latest exhibit piece, the most recent acquisition to his collection of students. But unlike our principal, she doesn't take her position as seriously.

"Welcome, Vera," he announces solemnly. "*Our* school is *your* school."

First an obedient, almost coquettish smile forms on Vera's lips that makes Dumbleavy blush. Subtle patches of red appear on his cheeks, as if his face has become a canvas and Vera is swirling a paintbrush in little circles on his skin. Then, unbeknownst to her subject, she peers out into the crowd and rolls her eyes. When the students laugh and applaud, Dumbleavy is so startled he shivers like Vera's taken her brush and flicked red paint all over his face. He no longer looks demure, but devastated, sort of like Carrie did the second after she discovered she was wearing a layer of pig's blood and not a red pashmina over her prom dress. Quickly reclaiming his self-anointed noble stance, he smiles at us approvingly, but I can tell that something about Vera has unsettled him. Not as much as her presence has terrified Nadine though. And it isn't just the witch who's frightened, but the witch's light as well.

Framing her body is a coating of her light, now black with no trace of silver, about two inches thick, but instead of the light floating and undulating and moving freely around her, it's frozen. Encasing Nadine like a force field, the light is preparing for an onslaught. Unfortunately, it's a futile weapon; Nadine knows it, I know it, and from the self-assured smile on Vera's lips, she knows it too.

When Vera raises her hand and waves in Nadine's direction, I know that war has been declared. And when the witch's ebony armor melts into her toxiskin, retreating from this new opponent, I know it's a war Nadine isn't sure she can win. My mother was wrong—*something* hasn't come to Weeping Water to help us defeat the psycho clan; *someone* has.

Calculus is difficult enough during those rare moments when my mind is ready and willing and able to concentrate on math. It's indecipherable when I'm thinking of so many other more important things.

Tugging on my string bracelet, all I can think of is Caleb. Funny how much you miss someone the moment he or she is gone. Jess, my parents, and now my boyfriend. The mathematical gobbledygook on the SMART Board in front of the class morphs into Caleb's face. Plus signs become eyes, parentheses become ears, an equal sign his kissable lips, and a series of eights become his beautiful blond curls. He's right there, in front of the classroom, once again my own private tutor who I can talk to and make out with and tell all my secrets and fears. Until his face is erased and replaced with someone even more powerful than my boyfriend.

"Finding my lesson a little boring today, Dominy?"

Mr. Dice is standing in front of me, no longer looking like Mr. Dice, but like the Sarutahiko Okami that he truly is. Japanese master, supernatural deity, and Jess's mentor all rolled up into one. Which means that right now he's rolled up in golden sunshine looking translucent and not at all humanesque. Which means the rest of the class is going to have a joint heart attack and make Nurse Nelson file for overtime for having to revive a classroom full of unconscious students. But why are the only screams coming from inside my head? Why is the rest of the class quiet and attentive and mathinterested?

"Because you're the only one who can see me like this," Dice replies.

Glancing quickly to my left, I see Gwen and a few others not even paying attention to the change in the scenery. In fact, they're all facing front watching Mr. Dice teach today's lesson. The teacher and the Okami have temporarily parted ways, so Human Dice is still teaching, while Spirit Dice is gloating.

"My students really do enjoy my class," he says. "You're the only one who has trouble concentrating."

"Because I'm the only one who knows your secret identity!" I silently shout. "I'm like Lois Lane when she finally sees through Clark Kent's lame disguise."

Way to go, Dom. You've just insulted a god.

"I think my disguise is pretty clever," Dice sulks. "Everybody on this side of the great wall thinks so."

Obviously an immortal adult is still an adult when it comes to understanding teenagers.

"Not your disguise, Superman's," I explain. "And what are you talking about? The Great Wall is in China. You're Japanese."

Now it's my turn to be on the other side of the generation gap.

"The figurative wall, not the literal one," Dice replies. "There's an invisible wall that separates earthly life from everything else in the universe, a necessary barrier that protects the living until it enters its next phase."

Why is this existential and philosophical and intangible stuff so much easier for me to understand than mathematical formulae?

Reading my questioning mind, Dice answers, "Because you're one of the lucky ones, Dominy; you straddle both worlds."

"That makes me lucky?"

Even silent, I can hear the sarcasm in my voice.

"Incredibly," he replies in a voice that isn't necessarily human, but is definitely teacherly. "And it's time you realized that."

Honestly, I am so sick and tired of hearing that I'm blessed and lucky and should be grateful for this tremendous gift that's been bestowed upon me. I'm cursed! I'm a werewolf! I've been drafted into a war against a bitter, vindictive woman and her pregnant granddaughter! That may be the definition of lucky in the Omidictionary, but here on earth, a.k.a. the only world that really matters to me right now, that's the definition of royally screwed!

"Ignore her. She always gets like this when she's frustrated, and calculus is three steps beyond frustrating," Jess explains. "Super-mega-ultra frustrating, to be exact."

Now Jess is sitting on my desk, perched there like some overgrown golden bird. I'm so ticked off I don't even look around to see if Gwen or anyone else can see her. But I wish they could see her and Okami Dice, then everyone could be as lucky as me!

"I don't even know why you took this class, Dominysan," Jess continues. "Without me to help you study, you know you're going to fail."

"I am not failing!"

Jess has gotten me so annoyed, I didn't even notice that I flipped the switch from inner to outer voice; I spoke out loud. But if I did, why isn't anyone staring at me like I'm a GWT—Girl With Tourette's?

"Think of it as being in a world within a world," Dice suggests.

"Kind of like when you're trapped within the body of the wolf," Jess adds, ever-so-helpfully. "You know, when it feels like you're in a little, red fur-lined cage."

"Enough, Jess," Dice chastises.

Not feeling the slightest bit embarrassed or contrite, Jess defends herself. "Oh, Dominysan knows I love her red fur. It's so soft and pretty and exotic," she says. "Can I turn her into a wolf right now so I can pet her?"

I know Jess has been out of school for a couple years, but she should remember that there's no petting allowed in the classroom. Teaching, however, is encouraged, though it appears as if Mr. Dice didn't get that e-mail.

"How am I supposed to learn anything if you two keep interrupting me?" I ask.

"Never fear, Dominy," Dice replies. "When we're done I'll turn back time and start the class over from the beginning so you can hear every word of my lecture."

Yes, I am a very lucky girl.

"And when I do, promise me you'll remain focused on the lesson," he adds. "All those other thoughts running through your mind about Caleb and Nadine and Vera are intrusions and can be dealt with after class."

Jess loses a little of her sunshine.

"So . . . you finally met Vera?" she asks.

She hasn't moved, but she looks like she's a bit farther away, like she's standing in the shade. "We haven't been officially introduced," I start. "But I saw her at yesterday's assembly."

"That's good," Jess replies curtly.

I wait a moment for Jess to continue to speak, but the only sound I hear comes from the distance, Human Dice's voice earnestly educating my classmates. I know better than to ask Jess who Vera is, because I know she's going to pull out the *L* card and cry limitations. I also know better than to ask for her opinion about Weeping Water's latest resident, because I can hear in her voice that she doesn't want to talk about the girl. Not sure if she's acting like an Omikami and being evasive or if she's acting like my best friend and being jealous. All I know is that she feels as if she's overstayed her welcome.

"Looks like Dice is all set to call for a do-over," she states, "which is my cue to leave."

Before I can beg Jess to stay to keep me company, share my seat with me, and shower me with sunshine, whisper the correct answers in my ear, she's gone. Okami Dice has disappeared, and all around me students are shuffling into class and plopping into their seats. Time really has been turned back, and it is now the start of class. If only I had that power, I'd turn back time to the day of my father's sixteenth birthday and make him stay home. I'd break his legs, I'd strap him to his bed, anything to keep him home so he wouldn't go out hunting alone and accidently kill Luba's husband. Make all of the bad stuff go away.

Shaking my head I realize I'm being stupid and unfocused and wasting time. I can't move backward, only forward.

Walking down the hallway after class I feel like I'm walking toward my future when I see Vera coming toward me from the other direction. A jumble of words bang against the inside of my head like rocks, each one hitting the bone inside harder, trying to make its way into the world. What do I say to this girl? What can I possibly say to the person who may be my salvation, the person I've dreamt about, the person my comatose mother warned Luba would change our world? Are there even any words that can possibly communicate how excited and nervous and unsettled I'm feeling?

"Hello."

Instinct has taken over. I'm not sure if the girl is in charge or the wolf, but whichever one it was, it's taken the simple, most direct route. Treat Vera like what she appears to be, the new girl in school.

"I'm Dominy," I hear myself say. "Welcome to Two W."

In response, Vera stares at me. From her expression I can't tell if she thinks I'm one of Dumbleavy's disciples, a sycophantic senior looking to make good with the administration instead of someone who just wants to be her friend. Lie alert! I don't really want to be her friend; I just want to know who the hell she is, why she's come here, and why I was given advance warning of her arrival. Her reply offers no insight.

"Hi," she says, smiling. "I'm Vera, but you already know that."

That's about all I know.

"Having any trouble finding your way around?" I ask.

Excellent! Now I sound like the hall monitor, exactly the type of person whom a newbie is going to want to befriend in order to be able to hobnob with the A-listers.

"No," she replies. "I know exactly where I'm going."

If I weren't so desperate to find out who Vera is, I'd be put off by her haughtiness. She's got that same air of superiority that Nadine has. I used to think it was merely an East Coast thing, but now I know it's much more than that. It's an indication that Vera is something other than what she presents herself to be. She may look prim and conservative and reserved, but I know she's something else. I know something completely different lies just underneath the surface. Knowledge that Nadine and I share.

"Oh, hi, Nadine," Vera says.

Just after turning the corner into the hallway, Nadine stops short. She's so startled by Vera's presence that she can't even stifle her gasp. When she hears Vera's voice, she loses her balance and practically teeters over and slams into the lockers.

"It's nice to see you again," Vera adds.

Again?! So these two do know each other. I knew they came from the same town, but there was always the possibility that they ran in different circles, went to different schools, but now I know they share a past. I've got to find out what else they share. Nadine has other ideas.

Mouth wide open, but unable to make any sound, Nadine looks as if she's gazing at her soul and finally understands what she's looking at, as if she might finally take ownership of the horror she's caused. Looking at Vera, Nadine is afraid. And like the coward she is when confronted with something that is frightening, she turns and runs. The sound of her shoes squeaking lingers in the hallway long after she's gone.

Vera shrugs her shoulders and smiles at me clandestinely, as if I'm supposed to understand the depth of what has just taken place. There's only one reason Nadine would react so obviously: She must perceive Vera to be a threat. But that doesn't necessarily translate to a good thing for me and my friends, because while it could mean that Vera is a very good person and has come to help put an end to Nadine's reign of terror, it could also mean that Vera is even more dangerous than Nadine and Luba, with powers that make even evil cower and run away.

The excitement I felt upon Vera's arrival is short-lived. Now I'm not sure if this is the beginning of something good or just the beginning of the end.

Chapter 9

If you can't find someone online, do they even exist? That's the question I've been pondering all week. I've kept the meager bit that I know about Vera to myself, lest I be labeled the girl who cried wolf in addition to the girl who became a wolf. I wanted to find solid evidence to prove that the mysterious newcomer is a threat before alerting the troops. After a week of research online and off—I actually did some old-fashioned sleuthing and called Cos Cob High School—I still can't find any proof that Vera Bailey-Clarke, Vera Bailey, or even Vera Clarke existed before coming to town. I was encouraged, however, to discover that Cos Cob High School's nickname is the Two C.

"So it's like she just magically appeared one day and waltzed into town?" Arla surmises. "Stranger things have happened within our borders, you know."

I do know that, which is why I'm scared. But not as scared as I get when we enter the lunchroom and I see Archie sitting with Nadine.

"This has got to stop!" I cry.

I don't even get to take one step before Arla stops me.

"He misses me," she says.

Well, not Árla, but Napoleon doing their ventrilospiritualist thing again.

"He needs time," he orders. "But you must watch him."

That's what I've been trying to do, but it's been difficult with everything else going on lately. Nadine's pregnancy, Caleb's leaving for college, Vera's arrival, not to mention trying to, oh I don't know, enjoy a moment of senior year before it's all history.

As if reading my mind, Nap as Arla replies, "Try harder."

And on top of everything else I have to deal with ghostude!

Shaking her head, Arla grabs onto my arm to steady herself. Looks like she's back from Napville. "I blacked out again, didn't I?"

"Yes," I confirm, steering her to a table as far away from Archie and Nadine as possible. "And the next time you talk to Napoleon, tell him to cut the attitude."

"I can't be held responsible for anything Napoleon says when he uses my vocal chords," Arla replies, flicking the bangs of her blond wig out of her eyes. "But that doesn't mean I don't want to know every word that he said."

"Same old 'watch Archie,' " I offer, without offering up the part about watching out for Archie's soul.

"That's it?" Arla asks, plopping into a seat across from me.

Ignoring her, I go off on a little tirade.

"What good is it to have supernatural connections if we can't get any answers?" I whine. "Between not knowing what Archie's going to do next, not knowing who fathered Nadine's baby, and not knowing where Vera came from, I feel one hundred percent human."

Unsnapping the lid off of a Tupperware container, Arla grabs a raw carrot and bites into it. Chewing with gusto, she sums up what I'm feeling. "And being human is so last century."

Being a friend, thankfully, is not.

Having resisted the urge to drag Archie from Nadine's lunch table, I take Napoleon's advice and keep an eye on him while we're both on the football field, him during practice as a starting running back of this year's varsity football team, and me as cheerleading co-captain. I almost quit the squad this year; I didn't think I had enough oomph left in me to keep rah-rahing. But then I found out we were getting new uniforms. I do have my priorities. We swapped our traditional skirts for navy blue boy shorts topped with long-sleeved, white-collared shirts that have our new logo on the back in blue sequins—W^2. Thanks to the school uniform policy, my daily style is restricted, so I couldn't pass up this opportunity to expand my wardrobe.

Even though I get to wear a more fashion-forward outfit, my heart isn't into cheerleading, so I usually let Deeanne Ulrich, the other co-captain, run the practices. Her rahs still have capital R's, so she's a much better leader than I am. Plus, she doesn't have a friend who needs an intervention.

Because of my heightened senses, I see Archie throw the punch from across the field before Sully does, which is unfortunate for Sully, because he's the guy on the receiving end of Archie's fist. By the time I sprint over to them, Archie's sucker punch has escalated into an all-out brawl between the two guys, and their teammates are screaming and shoving and debating whether to join in.

Despite the fact that Coach Emerson has grabbed Archie around the waist and is holding his right arm behind his back, Archie continues to hit Sully with his left. It's horrifying to see Archie lifted off the ground, horizontal, and still so filled with rage that he can't stop his arm from swinging into Sully's body. One of the assistant coaches finally drags Sully far enough away that Archie can no longer make contact. Once his fist isn't ramming into flesh, Archie calms down, as if his fury without a target has finally escaped him.

Immediately, I look at his eyes, certain that I'll see they're two different colors, but I'm wrong; they're both their normal shade of violet. Maybe Archie wasn't consumed by some demon; maybe he doesn't need protection; maybe this was just a guy thing? Unfortunately, it's now turned into a disciplinary thing.

Outside Dumbleavy's office, Archie is sitting by himself for a moment, hunched over in his chair, his face covered in his bruised hands, scraped and bloodied knuckles exposed. Inside, Emerson is filling in our illustrious leader on the latest on-campus act of violence. I'm sure I'm not supposed to be here, but I'm only following Nap's orders.

But before Archie raises his head and sees me, before I can even try to console him, I see something that breaks my heart. Underneath his stark white hair are dark roots. It looks like an oil spill on a snowdrift, one natural occurrence destroying another. At least one mystery is solved. Archie is definitely changing because of what Nadine did to him in the cabin. He's been changing emotionally, and now he's changing physically. I'm staring at the proof.

When Archie looks up and sees me standing in front of him, I keep staring. I will not abandon my friend, no matter how difficult it is for me to keep looking at him. Or how painful it is for me to listen.

"What's wrong with me?" Archie asks.

His voice is thick with fear and confusion and something else that I can't describe. I pray that it isn't knowledge. I pray that he doesn't know what's happening to him. Let him stay in the dark for a little bit longer, because I had to learn the hard way that once the truth is learned, innocence can never be retrieved.

The truth, however, is that innocence is merely something that's borrowed. We have it for such a short time, some longer than others, but eventually we're stripped of it. It's taken away from us either by age or circumstance or incident. I went through agony not knowing what was going on with me after I was initially cursed, and I know that Archie is struggling with the same frustrations. Perhaps I owe it to him; perhaps I'm the only one who can explain what's happening to his mind and his body and his soul.

"It started that night in the cabin," I say.

But before I can explain further, Dumbleavy calls Archie into his office. Their talk is going to come first, so ours will have to wait.

On my way home I feel so tired that I have to rest. It isn't physical weariness, but the weight of an emotional burden. Leaning into The Weeping Lady I let her absorb some of my feelings, let my frustrations seep into her bark, let my anxiety intertwine with her branches so I can have a bit of peace, so I can breathe easier.

I close my eyes and wait for the comfort to wash over my body, but it doesn't come. When a tree grows tired of your intrusions, you know you're pathetic! I mean really, what else does The Weeping Lady have to do? My cell phone vibrates, and I see Caleb's name pop up on my phone. At least he hasn't abandoned me. When I look at his text message, I wish he had.

What is he talking about?! Sometimes if you want to communicate, you have to use your mouth and not your fingers. As I hear his phone ringing, I can feel my heart starting to beat faster. He must be mistaken; there's no way he could be right.

"That's impossible!" I scream the second the phone clicks and I know he's on the other end.

"I wish it were, Domgirl, but I just saw her," he replies. "Nadine is here."

Stupidly I look around as if Nadine is going to pop out from behind The Weeping Lady or I'm going to see her staring at me from across the open field. "I just saw her at school. There's no way she could be at Big Red!"

The moment the words fly out of my mouth, I realize that

I'm the one not making sense. Nadine is a witch; normal modes of transportation are unnecessary for her if she wants to travel. She may not have a broomstick, but she doesn't need a car to travel. But why? Why did she make the trip? The answer is obvious.

"Stay away from her, Caleb!" I cry. "She's going to try to trick you or cast a spell on you or do something to you that she's going to regret."

"I don't think so," he replies. "She didn't come here to see me."

What?! "Then who did she travel all that way to see?"

"My roommate."

What?!

"What does Nadine want with Jeremy?" I ask.

Actually, that doesn't matter. The real problem is that if Jess ever finds out that Nadine is visiting Jess's brother at college, she'll ignore the fact that she's bound by spiritual limitations and make a very mortal decision to kill Nadine.

"Caleb, don't do anything that could get you into trouble," I instruct, "but you've got to find out why she's there."

"I think that, um, I'll be able to do that."

Why is my boyfriend stuttering? "Why are you stuttering?!"

"You'll never guess who just walked into my room."

Nadine!

"And she, um, wants to speak to you," Caleb announces.

"Hi, Domgirl."

That word sounds disgusting when it comes out of her mouth.

"I figured I'd save you from death by curiosity," she starts, chattering into Caleb's cell phone. "I'm here because Jeremy is doing a paper on physical therapy, and he asked me for some information about The Retreat's policies and procedures."

Kudos for the kinda-believable lie, but I totally don't believe her.

"And you just had to hand deliver the info yourself? You couldn't e-mail?" I ask. "Don't they have Wi-Fi in the fiery pit of hell that you come from?"

I have to pull my ear away from the phone or else go deaf from crazy mother-to-be's cackle. "Your girlfriend is so funny, Caleb! You really are a lucky guy," Nadine says. "And, Dom-girl, contrary to popular belief, I have lots of friends, and I made the trip up here to see one of them."

Jeremy Wyatt can't possibly be her friend. Could he? He does make poor choices when it comes to women; I mean he did date Rayna Delgado.

"Hey, Domgirl, it's me," Caleb announces. "Nadine just left."

Thank God! "Lock the door! Maybe you should call security in case she comes back."

"I'll be fine," he assures me, even though we both know we can't guarantee anyone's safety as long as Nadine is alive.

I'm so disoriented that I don't even flirt with my boyfriend; I just say good-bye and rush home. This uncomfortable feeling doesn't leave me, and when I get inside I'm dizzy, but oddly the problem isn't coming from inside of me; it's the light. I feel as if I'm standing directly underneath a spotlight, cranked up to megawatt power; it's so blinding my vision is all blurred. When I see Vera sitting at my kitchen table, I know I'm hallucinating.

"Hey, Dom. I think you already know my new science tutor."

Barnaby's explanation does nothing but confuse me even further, so much so that I have to grip the back of a chair because I feel like I'm going to faint. I hear voices and words forming sentences, but I can only splice a few bits of information together, because the voices are talking too quickly and my head is spinning too fast. Guidance counselor, AP classes, science major. Finally, the room stops circling around my head at about the same time Barnaby wraps up his monologue. After a moment of silence, Vera continues.

"I've already taken some classes in scientific research, biology, and physics, so our counselor . . . Sorry, I forgot her name."

"Miss Martinez," Barnaby offers.

"Yes, thank you," Vera says. "Miss Martinez suggested that I tutor Barnaby, share some of my knowledge and make a new friend. You know, the old win-win."

Great! My brother finally severs ties with one supernatural creature and he is already cuddling up to someone else of equally mysterious heritage. There should be some code inhuman beings could use to identify one another; then I'd know if Vera was like me, more than just a girl. I can't even get a feeling from her; it's like she's put up a wall so no one can find out what she is. Well, if I can't use my superpowers, I'll have to go old school once again.

"So what brings you to our little town?" I ask, pulling out a chair and sitting down. I even fold my hands and place them on the table to make myself appear more like an inquisitor at the start of an interrogation.

"My father's company transferred to the area," Vera replies. "He tried to find a job back home, but they were willing to help us move, and when he dragged his feet they offered him a raise, so we really had no choice."

"Ah, the old offer-you-can't-refuse," I say.

There's no need to glance over at my brother to know that he's giving me the "shut up, you sound like an absolute idiot" look. I've heard my own voice, so I know how dumb I sound. It doesn't prevent me from continuing. "You must've known the Jaffes, right?"

I'm staring right at Vera, not even blinking, waiting for her reaction, waiting to see a flicker of something flash across her eyes that will give me a clue as to what she's really doing in town.

"Vaguely," Vera says. "We went to different schools, so we never hung out or anything."

School! Okay, now I have something I can latch onto. "What school did you go to?"

Finally a reaction. Just a smile, but it's a smile that works alone, without her eyes. She's pausing. She knows she can't avoid answering my very simple question, but she doesn't know how to reply.

"A small private school. I'm sure you never heard of it."

That's because you've never heard of it either!

"Are you done with your questioning, officer?" Barnaby asks snidely. "I'd like to get back to my tutoring so I can pass my first test tomorrow."

Sure, now that I know Vera failed hers.

"Well, this is a much smaller town than Cos Cob, so I'm sure we'll get to know each other really well," I warn.

"I think you can count on that, Dominy."

Without looking back at me, Vera turns to Barnaby and starts rattling off some scientific jargon that sounds more complex than anything Caleb ever said to me while he was tutoring me in math. I really do miss my boyfriend. It was wonderful to hear his voice earlier; I can't believe I wasted it by talking so much about Nadine. Ah well, I know we'll talk again very soon, and I won't waste time doing anything else but flirting.

Through the kitchen window I see that it's already dusk, and the three-quarter moon is on its upward journey in the sky. Another transformation will be here before I know it. Turning around I look over at Vera, her head practically touching my brother's, and I wonder what type of thing she's going to turn out to be.

Because as sure as I know that I'm going to become a wolf in a few more days, I know that girl in my kitchen isn't human.

Chapter 10

Sometimes it feels more natural to be underneath a cloak of red fur.

I barely felt the transformation this time, barely felt my blood turn to flames or my bones snap and change shape. This time it felt like I was turning into what I'm supposed to be, what I was born to be, what I should be all the time. The thing that most people in this town want dead, the thing that makes brave men act frightened and foolish men act wise, the thing Luba created.

A rough breeze rips through me, lifting my fur, glorious and lush and defiant, and I feel strong. My time in this form is short, so I move quickly to make the most of it.

The night dirt is cool underneath my paws, and, with every step I take, it's as if little pieces of the world are bending to my command, to my strength, to my power. The earth knows that something with more authority is roaming loose, something with the potential to destroy everything that crosses its path, but something that also knows when to show mercy.

A short distance in front of me a doe has just given birth. She's alone with her calf, licking the blood and placenta and mucus off her child's newborn skin, wiping it clean of impurities, washing away any reminder of the violent passage the calf just underwent. But when the doe sees me staring at her, it's clear that their emotional connection will never be severed.

The doe's tongue continues to graze over the calf's face, continues to cleanse the child, but the rest of her body is immobile. Eyes, ears, legs, all unmoving, because she knows the only way to save her own life is to offer the life of her child to me. And such a thought is inconceivable for this animal.

A memory tugs at my mind of a woman with golden hair lying in a bed, covered in a white sheet, the smell of lilac and powder clinging to the air around her. I don't know who this woman is, but I know she's as important to me as the doe is to her calf. I corral my instinct to lunge forward and plunge my fangs into the fresh, minutes-old body of the calf. My front paws dig farther into the dirt, bury themselves so as to anchor my body to the ground, keep me from moving forward to do what I was born to do: hunt and destroy.

But there's another part of me, hidden deep underneath the flame-red fur, that was born to do something entirely different: protect and save. For some reason that's the part that I listen to now; that's the part that comes to the surface and takes control, allowing the doe and her child to live or at least not to die tonight because of me.

As I walk away from my would-be meal, I see the doe bow her head to me in gratitude. In response I let out a fierce howl that makes her child stir, nuzzle closer to the warmth of its mother's belly. I mimic the newborn's movement, twisting my neck, and push against the cool air, and the smell of lilac intensifies. The scent slams into my snout with such force that I stumble backward and have to shake my head to prevent myself from falling into unconsciousness. It's as if the smell is trying to tell me something, remind me of something or someone from my past or another life.

When the next wave of hunger threatens to consume me, I abandon all thoughts of mercy and allow my primitive character to take over. The groundhog is plump and juicy and weak; if he has any will to escape the grip of my fangs, it must be bludgeoned by fear and never shows itself. He lies underneath me, his body rising slowly up and down as I feast on his innards, his blood staining my red fur to create one unbroken line of death to life. Licking my fangs to savor the sweet, ripe taste of this animal's blood, I feel proud; I've served a dual purpose tonight—I've hunted life, but I've also spared life. I've maintained balance.

Walking into the center of a rocky plain, an area I've overheard humans call Dry Land, I'm paralyzed by another memory. Screams of a girl, sounds of terror silenced only by my claws and my teeth, then the utterly glorious taste of first blood. This is where it all started; right in this spot is where my hunger was unleashed; this is where I was reborn. I look up into the sky and I see the same thing that I saw that night, the blazing moon. It's more of an instinct than a memory, but I know that I stood here drenched in the silver glow of the moon, stood here on a precipice, on the edge of my existence, and this is where I remain. Sometimes I teeter toward the moon; sometimes I retreat in fear from it, but I will never fall too far from its pull. The energy of the moonglow will always pulse through my veins.

Whether I'm a werewolf resting after a meal or a girl waking up from a dream.

"Arla?"

She's standing at the foot of my bed, her light brown skin glowing in the first light of dawn that is streaking in through the open window. Looking like a statue carved out of rosewood, Arla stands there motionless, the only movement coming from her cotton nightgown rippling slightly in the breeze. Her eyes are open, but vacant; her voice is soothing, but not hers.

"Remember, Dominy, you are blessed."

That's what my mother used to tell me, and now Napoleon's repeating her words.

"You're blessed," Nap says, "because she has finally come."

Nap has got to be talking about Vera.

"And she's brought with her an ending."

An ending? To the curse? To my life? To what?

"Arla . . . Nap . . . an ending to what?"

My voice is rough, like I've spent the night screaming or howling. I try to speak again, but my mouth is dry and parched and I have to swallow hard. By that time Arla has turned and left the room. Leaving me alone with the sunlight and my memories and my questions.

And the unsettling feeling that the wolf now buried deep within me is trying to speak to me through my dreams.

"At least you know when the wolf is going to take over your body," Arla states, walking down the hallway in between classes a few days later. "I never know when Nap is going to swoop in and do the body-swap thing."

She's wearing her black pageboy wig today, so she reminds me of a Japanese schoolgirl, and naturally whenever I think of anything Japanese I think of Jess, that country's number one fan, human or otherwise.

"Isn't it ironic that despite how hard Jess tried, she and Nap were never really connected when they were alive," I say. "But now that they're both spirits, they're so much alike, coming and going whenever they want, on a whim."

Scrunching up her face so her eyes squint and she looks even more Asian than ever, Arla shakes her head. "I don't think they have any control over when they visit," she declares. "They never come just to say hello; they've always got a message."

She's right about that. And Jess's messages have been very infrequent lately.

"As long as Nap doesn't take over my mind while I'm driving or trying to win a track meet, I'm okay," Arla announces. "Guess this is my new normal."

"Welcome to Dominyland," I shout.

A land where anything can happen, where dead spirits and live humans can converse, and where every ounce of beauty is doused by a rainstorm of ugliness.

"Nap was a faggot! He probably got killed trying to get some straight guy to be a faggot too!"

The hate etched into every word Jody Buell shouts hovers in the air like dense fog. It's sudden, it's unexpected, and it's impossible to see beyond. The entire hallway is plunged into immediate silence by the shock of hearing Jody, usually quiet and reserved, utter such a malicious comment, and before anyone can protest, Archie reacts.

He's standing at the other end of the hallway, facing Jody, who's in front of us. Barnaby, Gwen, and a few others are next to Jody, all of them stunned by the ferocity of his statement and so preoccupied with their friend's outburst that they don't see Archie's evolution; they don't see him change from human into something else.

I don't even think Arla can see it from this distance, but it's as if I'm looking through a magnifying glass, and I can clearly see his left eye turn black and his right eye turn gold. Even though my view is perfect, I'm still shocked to see his right eye flicker several times before changing once more to match the same dark color as his left. All goodness has left his body.

Leaping through the air, Archie is horizontal for a few seconds before making contact with Jody. It's not until both boys are on the ground that Jody even knows he's being attacked. That's how quietly and quickly Archie pounced on his prey.

In a series of deft movements, Archie straddles Jody's stomach, pins his arms under his knees, and starts punching Jody in the face. Once, twice, three times. I lose count, and my head begins to swim because I'm no longer looking at my friend in a brawl, but at an animal unleashing its fury. This is what I must look like when I'm consuming my prey, elegance and precision and rage all coming together to create an action that feels incredibly natural because of its very inhuman nature. I know exactly what Archie's feeling, so I know I'm the only one who can stop him.

Barnaby, Gwen, and some others are trying to pull Archie off of Jody, but they have no idea that his body no longer belongs to him; it's stronger and more vicious than they can imagine. Glancing to my left, I see Arla holding onto an open locker door to keep from falling onto her knees; she understands as well as I do that Archie is being possessed. The problem is that, just like on the football field, he's doing nothing to fight off the attack; he's reveling in his newfound power.

I know my actions are going to appear suspicious, but I hope that the frenzy of activity surrounding Archie and the screams ripping down the hallway will act as a buffer, and my movements won't appear as incredible as they'll probably look. Running behind Archie, I wait until he raises his arm in preparation to strike another blow against Jody's battered face, and I hook my arm around his so our elbows lock. Then I grab Archie's other arm, the one pressing down on Jody's forehead to keep him immobile, and yank it behind his back, so I have him in a makeshift wrestling hold. I hear some gasps behind me, but I ignore them. I'll attribute my strength to a rush of adrenalin. Right now my friend needs protection.

"Archie, I know you can hear me," I whisper into his ear. "I know you're in there. You have to fight this."

The only thing Archie wants to fight is me. His body twists

from side to side, and it feels like our skin is burning against each other.

"This is not the person you want to be," I urge. "This is not the person Napoleon wants you to be."

At the sound of his former boyfriend's name, Archie's body stiffens. Finally, I get the sense that he's fighting the evil coursing through his veins. He stops moving long enough for me to pull him off of Jody and to a standing position at the same time that Mr. Lamatina hoists Jody up and over his shoulders in a fireman's lift. Luckily, our diminutive teacher's surprising action trumps mine, so most of the kids are amazed that little Mr. Lamatina, school hypochondriac, is playing the hero.

"I'm taking him to Nurse Nelson," he cries to Dumbleavy as they race past each other.

"What the . . ."

I'm not sure who looks more surprised by Archie's actions, our principal or Archie himself.

"Seriously, Dom," Archie starts as he grabs onto my wrist with a hand that's shaking and bruised. "What is happening to me?"

His eyes are back to their normal violet color, but they're no longer beautiful because they're soaked with fear.

"Don't worry," I say. "I'll explain everything later."

I'm so distraught, so focused on watching my friend walk down the hall as if he's walking to the electric chair, I don't realize Nadine is standing next to me until she speaks.

"Are you going to tell Archibald that he's going through the changes?" Nadine asks.

I'm so infuriated by Nadine's comment that I hesitate. Barnaby doesn't.

"You think this is funny, don't you?" my brother asks.

Smirking slightly, Nadine replies, "I'm not laughing, am I?"

"I don't know what the hell your problem is, Nadine, but

Archie was defending your brother!" Barnaby shouts. "Something you've never done."

I'm filled with pride and fright at the same time. Pride because my brother is confronting Nadine, clearly no longer under her spell, and fright because her blackened light has extended from her pores and is curling around Barnaby's neck. Just as I'm about to reach out and grab hold of the light, wrench it from my brother's body, it retreats on its own, buries itself back inside its source like one of those retractable cords on a vacuum cleaner. Thanks to Vera.

"Hi, Nadine."

Nadine actually shivers. I don't know why Nadine is afraid of Vera, but she is. She looks like she wants to hide, but here in the hallway she has nowhere to go, so she's forced to speak.

"Hello, Vera," Nadine finally says.

"We really have to get together soon so we can catch up," Vera suggests. "It's been a long time."

Maybe that's it! Maybe Nadine isn't afraid of Vera, but of what she represents—her past. They come from the same town, so maybe Nadine thinks that Vera knows all about her. As blatant as Nadine and Luba are about their powers with the Wolf Pack and me, they haven't exactly shouted their true nature from the rooftops. Better to maintain anonymity while on a supernatural crime spree, I suppose. And better to keep your enemies quiet until you figure out how to quiet them permanently.

"That sounds great," Nadine replies, her voice sounding forced and thin. "I'd like that."

Without waiting for a response, Nadine hurries down the hall, the squeaking of her sneaker shoes echoing off the walls.

Vera watches her scurry away, and I can't tell if she's pleased to have reconnected with an old friend or thrilled to have made an old enemy squirm. Until she speaks.

"Obviously Nadine hasn't changed a bit," she says. "She's still able to bend the truth while wearing a straight face."

Maybe Nadine can truthbend, but I can't any longer. Archie needs to know what's happening to him; it's only fair. Sitting underneath The Weeping Lady, covered in shade and shadow, Archie sits between Arla and me.

"Well, I'm not expelled," he announces. "Thanks to Barnaby."

First my brother stands up to Nadine, then he saves Archie's hide? Could little brother have more superpowers than all of us combined?

"How?" I ask.

"He told Dumbleavy what Jody said," Archie explains. "Barged right into the principal's office while I was getting screamed at."

"Barnaby officially rocks!" Arla cries.

"We're both suspended for a week, Jody and I, and we have to do some formal apology thing in front of counselor folk," Archie adds. "But I'll still graduate."

"That's great news," I start.

"And now why don't you tell me the not-so-great news," Archie finishes.

A low-hanging branch sways in the wind, and some leaves scrape against the crown of my head. It's as if The Weeping Lady is giving me encouragement to speak. Guess she hasn't abandoned me after all. I reach out to grab Archie's hand, and I can feel his rapid pulse. He knows what I'm about to tell him will change his life. I pray it can change it for the better.

"That night in the cabin, Nadine tried to kill both you and Napoleon," I state, forcing my voice to remain calm and flat. "And Jess could only save one of you; she had to make a choice."

"She chose me?" Archie asks.

I nod my head and squeeze his hand tighter; it's practically twitching because his pulse is beating even quicker.

"She chose me over Nap?"

"You were her friend, Archie," Arla interjects. "She might have dreamt of a life with Napoleon, but she already had one with you, so you were the one she chose to protect."

"But she couldn't protect you completely," I add.

"What . . . exactly do you mean?" Archie questions.

Be simple, Dominy; be straightforward. Talk to Archie the way you wish your father would have talked to you before the curse kicked in. Give him information so he can arm himself against these forces that are trying to take over his soul.

"Jess infused you with her golden light," I say, "but . . ."

"But?" Archie says. "Nothing good ever comes after a *but.*"

"But Nadine also infused you with her black energy."

He doesn't say a word, but I know that he gets it. I can see it in his face.

"So I'm Jessine," he deduces.

Maybe he doesn't get it.

"I'm part Jess and part Nadine."

Nope, he gets it. Just trying to be clever in the face of a personal crisis.

"I'm half good and half evil; that's why I'm changing," he continues. "That's why I'm fighting all the time and why my hair is changing. I'm just like you, Dom, aren't I? I'm turning into something else, right?!"

There is absolutely nothing I can say to Archie except the truth.

"Yes."

Abruptly, Archie rips his hand from mine and stands up. Fists clenched, he starts to pace. My words are rippling throughout his body, bubbling just underneath the surface of his skin. He swipes at the air involuntarily as two lines of tears descend from his eyes, staining his reddened cheeks. He starts to mumble something that I can't quite make out, but he repeats it over and over, so I finally understand.

"Make it stop!"

Oh how I wish I could, Archie, how I wish I could make all of this stop. But wait—he doesn't want me to take action; he's talking to someone else.

"Make it stop!"

He grabs Arla by the shoulders and shakes her violently. She looks like a rag doll in his hands, and once again I have to pull Archie off of someone before he inflicts permanent damage.

"Why don't you talk to *me*, Napoleon?!" Archie cries. "Why don't you make this go away?!"

Now Archie's kneeling, having slumped to the ground because he can no longer stand, and his fingers are clawing at the grass, pulling up blades and root and dirt. He's crying and begging Nap to intervene and change things, give him his life back. I can't blame him for what he's doing; I did the same thing when I understood what was happening to me. I begged God and Jess and anyone who would listen to lift this curse from my head. It took me a while to realize that no one has that power. Archie has to come to that realization on his own. Right now he simply has to understand that he has to fight.

"You have to make a choice, Archie," I instruct.

"What do you mean?" he asks. "What kind of a choice?"

"Whose side do you want to be on, ours or Nadine's?" I ask him.

"You know whose side I want to be on!" he screams.

"No, Archie, I don't," I say. "From the way you've been acting lately, you could go either way. Starting right here and now, you have to make a conscious choice before you do something that you'll regret for the rest of your life."

Archie turns away from me to lock eyes with Arla. He

looks so innocent, and yet I know he's aged drastically in the last few minutes.

"So what's it gonna be, Arch?" I ask. "You want to be on Team Gold or Team Black?"

Archie hesitates before answering.

"Team Gold of course," he finally says.

I want to bury myself underneath the wolf's red fur so I can hide, because Archie's hesitation has told me everything I need to know about my friend's fate.

Chapter 11

To the girl my bedroom feels like a prison cell; to the wolf it's a waiting room to freedom.

It feels like only yesterday that I transformed, but tonight the full moon returns. Sometimes it takes forever to arrive; other times it shows up in the blink of an eye. No matter how hard I try to keep track of the moontide, I'm often surprised by its appearance. Thank God I made his and hers moon charts for Caleb and me.

The sky is already darkening. It isn't a sheet of navy yet, but a blend of blues, deep indigo and softer cornflower, as if the sky can't make up its mind if it wants to be day or night. Standing in front of the open window, I feel the same confusion. The girl wants to shut the window, crawl under the covers, and fall into an uninterrupted sleep. The wolf is anxiously waiting for its clue so it can escape. They both know whose dream will come true in a few short minutes.

Too hyper to stand still and wait, I pull out my father's green metal box from the top shelf of my closet and place it on my bed. Kneeling before it like it's some ancient altar, I open the lock with the key that I hide in my underwear drawer, trying to make as little sound as possible. I've come to treat the box as if it contains precious cargo, which is the truth, because it contains my last remaining links to my parents.

Inside is all my father's wolf paraphernalia, his lunar maps, his notes, all his werewolf mania research. I've since added some photos of the two of us and the few rare ones that I found of our entire family. My mother's immortalized face stubbornly peeks out from underneath my old Timber-wolves banner, and I pull out the faded picture to gaze at a past I don't quite remember. My parents are standing behind Barnaby and me at some country fair. My dad is holding a huge teddy bear that has long since moved away and been re-claimed by a needier child or is simply living in a trash heap somewhere; my mother is holding a stick of cotton candy, the gentle swirls of blue no match for the beauty of her eyes; and Barnaby and me, five and six years old, are smiling, each missing a few teeth, holding hands, happy. We're a family. No, we *were* a family.

I love and hate this photo for the same reason: It's a re-minder of what we had and what we'll never have again. No matter how hard I try, no matter what the future brings, the four of us can never again be a family, thanks to Luba and the moon that's starting to take control over the sky.

Moving quickly, I take off the string bracelet Caleb gave me and place it in the box to keep it safe until daybreak. I'm startled when my cell phone vibrates on the other side of my bed, and when I reach over to grab it, I hit the box, so it tilts over and some of my family's memories spill out onto the bedspread. So much for maintaining an air of respect and re-ligiosity.

It's a text from Caleb—

Be careful, Jane. The moon is bright tonight.

My boyfriend has perfect timing. He knows exactly what to say to coax a gigglaugh out of me. Even if I'm gigglaughing at him. He's taking a poetry interpretation class at Big Red as an English requirement, so his texts are becoming a bit fancified lately. But I guess if he's going to be my Mr. Rochester, he should adopt flowery speech, and I do love twisted wordplay.

After typing a quick thank-you, followed by a stream of *x*'s and *o*'s, I shut my phone off completely and start to gather the spilled contents of the box and put them back in their sacred tomb. I know I don't have that much time left, but I'm drawn to my mother's Little Bo Peep compact. There has to be a reason that it was airlifted to her room at The Retreat: It must contain some sort of a message if it made the cross-dimensional trip on its own; but what exactly was Little Bo trying to tell me? Maybe nothing. She is a wayward shepherdess, so perhaps she was just antsy being cooped up in a box for so long and wanted to explore? Opening up the compact, I try to do the same.

It takes a second for my eyes to focus. I'm not sure if it's because I'm afraid of what I'm going to see or if it's because I know I'm going to transform at any moment. I don't get a ten-second countdown, T minus ten to wolfdom, Ms. Robineau. God forbid the curse would be that accommodating.

Once my reflection comes into view, I stare at it. Red mane, check. Gray-blue eyes, check. Pale skin, check. My father's nose, check. A few random, scattered freckles, thankfully no pimples, I'm all there, and yet it looks like something's missing. Where's the spark? Where's the inner light? Where are the smile and the happiness and the joy that I saw in the little girl in the photo with my family? All I see is me. But maybe I'm not being fair; maybe I should check my reflection when I'm not about to have my inner light snatched by a predatory creature, one who devours, one who thrives in the darkness.

Snapping the compact shut I toss it back into the box, turn the lock, and because I'm running out of time I shove the box underneath my bed with the key still in it. It's not the smartest thing to do, but I've locked my bedroom door; if for some reason Louis has to break it down, I doubt he's going to check underneath my bed when he sees the window wide open. He'll simply assume I've run away. Which is basically what I do once a month.

Just as I'm about to crawl out the window, the voices from downstairs distract me.

"You can't join us tonight, Barnaby," Louis informs him. "It's getting too dangerous."

Thanks for the warning, Louis, but that's news even Lars Svenson would consider old. I've already hidden a spare set of clothes deep in the woods, in a part that I usually don't roam, because I need to start exploring different areas in order to throw my pursuers off track. Funny, the closer they get to me, the closer I get to acting on my own primal instincts. Jess told me once that I have two sets of guts, and it looks like I'm finally listening to both of them.

I fall to the ground, making only the smallest noise, the earth seemingly bending at my touch, and for a moment I'm in between my house and the moon. I can feel both tugging at me, each trying to claim victory, but right now there's no competition; the moon will win. Not because the wolf is growing stronger by the second, but because the moon's lure is growing more attractive to the girl.

As I stand in the backyard, the moon shines over me and creates a light all around me like reverse shadow. The moon has returned fire and spirit and energy to my body, so the only way to repay its gift is with total surrender.

I feel the transformation take over while I'm in mid-stride, as I'm running as far from my house as I can, and it's like I've slammed into an invisible wall. Amazing how expected and unexpected the change still is. I know what's going to happen, I know how my body's going to react, and yet it shocks me every single time. The exquisite pain, the demoralizing feeling of being overcome, the futile attempt to fight against the inevitable, always come back to me, always rise to the surface of what's left of the girl. I should be used to these feelings and these responses by now, but I'm not, and suddenly I'm hit with the most beautiful thought, a message of peace coming to me amid all this violence and pain and chaos.

Maybe the change is still shocking to me because it is truly unnatural; the wolf is a foreign visitor inside the body of the girl and not the other way around like I was starting to think. And maybe the reason I never remember turning back, doing the wolf-to-girl trip, is because that's the natural order of things. I'm returning to the person I was born to be, the person I'm supposed to be despite cruel attempts to make me think otherwise.

For the second time tonight I burst into gigglaughs. But this time they're silent and only in my head because the wolf is already licking its fangs with its saliva-drenched tongue. Good-bye, Dominy; hello, dinner.

Oddly, even after feeding, I'm still not entirely satisfied. Even though my stomach is full, the smell of the coyote's flesh still clinging to my fur, I'm restless. Could be because I'm in new territory, deep within Robin's Park, that neither wolf nor girl has ever explored before. It's dense and cold and suffocating; the landscape is claustrophobic, perfect for hiding, and even though that's what I should be doing in case Louis and his makeshift army become brave enough to expand their normal route, I don't want to blend into the scenery. I don't want to become part of my surroundings; I want to stand out; I want to be seen and heard.

I'm not the only one.

The voices travel to me as both a warning and a promise: *Listen, and you will learn. You may not want to know what you're about to be told, but the information is being offered to you; use it wisely.* But first I must act wisely and let this new creature I've become, this wolf-girl, act freely.

I crouch low, my bloated belly dragging against the twigs and the rocks and the rough grass so I can ground my body, camouflage it from the intruders. At the same time, I listen. And what better way to hear two girls talking than to listen with a girl's ears.

"I want you to leave."

The statement is simple and clear and direct; the tone of Nadine's voice is anything but. She's doing her best imitation of lethal Nadine, but sounding more like a little girl lost, frightened because she's trying to find her way home and there's something standing in her way—Vera.

"But, Nadine, I've just arrived."

The contrast between the two girls is striking, both physically and emotionally, and Nadine is taking a position I've never seen her take before, that of victim. Standing a few inches taller than Nadine, Vera now looks like she's towering over Nadine's frame. That might have more to do with the fact that Nadine is cowering than it does with Vera's height, but the image is still impressive and telling. Whatever Vera knows about the Jaffes, Nadine wants it to remain secret. Unfortunately, her tactics at overpowering her frenemy don't seem to be working.

"You never should have come here," Nadine whines. "We all know it was a mistake."

A smile slithers across Vera's face, causing her eyes to semi-close and lengthen as well. Her face takes on the characteristics of a snake.

"So now you're speaking for all of us?" Vera asks.

I have no idea what she's talking about, but even I know her question is rhetorical. Nadine, however, is so startled by the comment and its unknown implications that she tries to respond.

"No, no, I . . . I . . . You know I would never do that." Nadine stumbles.

"But, Nadine," Vera interrupts, "you just said 'we'; you said 'We all know it was a mistake.' "

Taking a step toward Nadine, Vera lengthens her body so she seems to grow an inch taller. "You shouldn't say such things when you know others are listening."

Instinctively, I retreat into the brush, hide deeper in the mouth of the woods, but my action is unnecessary. Vera isn't talking about me. Nadine doesn't look around; she doesn't scour the area for an intruder; whoever else may be eavesdropping on their conversation can't be seen. Its presence, however, is still being felt. And it's not a presence that's entirely welcomed.

Placing her hand on her stomach, Nadine doesn't absentmindedly rub the protruding mound; she doesn't lovingly caress the dome that underneath houses her unborn child; she keeps her hand there unmoving and protective and strong. Despite the fear that's clinging to her voice, her body is still defiant. She knows that whatever thing or person is listening to her words, she may have to defend herself and her child, and she's ready to strike back if necessary. And despite what I know, it's an action that is maternal and beautiful and admirable.

"Don't twist my words," Nadine replies. "You and I both know that you don't belong here."

Throwing her shoulders back imperiously, Vera smiles down at Nadine. "Luba may belong here; she is a product of this environment, She who came unto the Land so to speak," Vera haughtily replies. "But what about you, Nadine? You may have been born here as well, but now you're nothing more than a visitor, a passerby."

Courage climbs slowly, but steadily up Nadine's spine. She doesn't tilt her head back to look up into Vera's steely gaze, but lifts her eyes to prove that they are equals.

"You're wrong, Vera. This is my home, and I do belong here," Nadine affirms, her voice sounding more like the harsh noise I've grown accustomed to. "My whole family belongs here."

Pursing her lips, her eyes smiling brightly and lighting up the shadows, Vera waves her index finger at Nadine; she's a schoolmarm chastising a student for coming late to class. "Now, now, Nadine, you know that's a lie. Napoleon definitely didn't belong here, and you saw to it that he went away."

Wind sweeps across Nadine's face, taking with it any lingering strength, and I catch in her expression something new. Not remorse—no, Nadine isn't human enough to experience that feeling; something closer to dismay. She wonders just for a split second if the murder she committed will be met with anything less than approval. In an instant the wind is gone and so is the questioning thought. It doesn't matter what anyone else may believe; Nadine is convinced she did the right thing when she took her brother's life.

"My brother was never a true part of our family," Nadine states. "He was always looking for an escape route, and so I gave it to him."

"Such sisterly devotion," Vera says, clasping her hands together. "I wonder if the rest of the world would applaud if word got out about your noble deed? What do you think, Nadine? Is siblingcide celebrated these days?"

This time there's no wind that takes away Nadine's expression, only the wickedness that thrives just beneath her flesh. Her face contorts into a mask of hatred, gnarled and grotesque and honest.

"Don't you dare judge me! Don't act as if you're horrified by what I've done! And don't act as if you want to expose me and avenge my brother's death, because if that were your intent, you would've done so already!" she reels off. "So tell me, Vera, why have you come here?!"

Vera's whisper pierces the night more decisively than Nadine's wild screaming. "We've become curious."

We? Who is Vera working with?

"We've become terribly, *terribly* curious."

Now, all bravado is gone. "About what?" Nadine asks timidly.

"About where all this is going to lead."

Before Nadine can reply, Vera grabs the sides of Nadine's stomach tenderly, but tenderness shifts into something maniacal, and Vera lifts Nadine in the air, holding her overhead like an offering.

"Let go of me!" Nadine shrieks.

Her cries twist into the night, wrapping around the coarse black light emanating from Nadine, frantically searching for a way to break free, but Nadine and her light know they are no match for Vera. Perhaps if she weren't pregnant Nadine would fight back, but now she doesn't risk it.

Summoning up courage she hasn't had to call upon in quite a while, Nadine places her hands on top of Vera's and seethes. "You leave . . . *this* out of it!"

Undaunted and so very unafraid, Vera raises her head to look Nadine in the face. Her features have now lost their patrician beauty, and she has gained a much more menacing countenance.

"But, Nadine . . . *this* . . . is the reason I've come to visit," Vera replies, slowly placing Nadine back down onto the ground. "It's difficult being an unwed mother without any friends," Vera taunts. "I thought I could help out."

"I don't need your help," Nadine spits. "I have my mother and Luba."

The noise that echoes throughout the woods is so loud and unexpected and feral I'm surprised it doesn't result in Louis and his gang's immediately arriving onto the scene. When the shock of the sound wears off, I realize it's only Vera's uncontrollable laughter.

"Despite each having gone through labor, Melinda and

Luba are the two least maternal women I know!" she laugh-speaks. "I'd rather have Medea as a midwife."

Ignoring or failing to understand the implications of Vera's statement, Nadine praises her female relatives. "They have done everything to help me!" Nadine shouts. "Because they both understand the importance of my pregnancy, and they both approve of the destiny I've created for our family."

"But does Orion approve?"

I feel my paws digging deeper into the damp, quiet earth. I need to stabilize my body because my mind is spinning. Why did Vera just say that name? How could she know of the link between the Jaffes and the star god? Unless . . . unless she's part of them; unless she's like them too. Which means she's another witch, another enemy, another thing that I have to fear and fight and defeat.

I thought something was coming to help me, not make matters worse! I thought Vera was a sign that the tide was turning in my favor, that I was going to be given help, not more obstacles!

The growl escapes my lips before I know I'm making any sound, and Vera's head turns in my direction. We're separated by a great distance, bent trees obstructing her view, but I know that she sees me; I know that she's looking at the wolf and that she can see the girl caged up inside. I don't know exactly what Vera is, but I'm right; she isn't human, and she has powers. Why doesn't she use them against Nadine to end this? Why doesn't she strike out and kill her with the same amount of mercy Nadine showed her brother?

"Remember, Dominy, you are blessed."

Lifting my snout to see above the bushes I search for my mother. It's a stupid gesture, but uncontrollable; she's the one who originally spoke those words to me, so every time I hear them I think they come from her mouth. But her mouth is closed, and she's lying on a bed in a hospital miles away. And

I'm here with a pregnant witch and a stranger who refuses to reveal her true intentions.

"Orion understands and supports my actions," Nadine says, her voice quivering like the string of a bow that's just released a poisonous arrow.

The arrow becomes a boomerang when Vera replies.

"Because He knows exactly how evil you've become," she replies. "And He knows you must be stopped."

Glancing up toward the sky, I can tell that Nadine is desperately trying to see Orion's constellation. She's trying to connect with her life-source; she's trying to reach him to make him thwart Vera's words, but the sky is empty except for the full moon. Nothing else exists except the thing that keeps me cursed. Looks like it's doing the same thing to Nadine tonight.

"He would never try to stop my destiny!" Nadine bellows. "He has given my family the power of the Original Hunter, and He expects us to use it! He expects us to help Him reach His full potential!"

"He also expects you to use His power wisely," Vera declares. "Which you have proven you are incapable of doing."

I can hear Nadine's shoes squeak as she shifts nervously from side to side, her body and her black light trying to remain stationary despite the obvious need to strike and maim and kill. "I am the *only* one capable of leading! The *only* one who is willing to do what's necessary to lead this family to unprecedented victory and power!" she roars. "Now I will tell you for the last time, Vera, leave this town at once!!"

"Oh sweet...stupid...Nadine," Vera mocks. "I'm not leaving Weeping Water until my job is done."

Unable to control her anger, Nadine swipes at the air, her black energy mimicking her actions, so she looks like a multi-armed creature doing battle against an unseen foe. It's a movement created by fury, but met with equally ferocious laughter.

Holding her hand up to her mouth in an attempt this time to stifle her unnaturally loud howls, Vera is greatly amused by her opponent's lack of restraint. "Please, Nadine, watch your temper," she orders. "It's not good for a girl in your condition to get overexcited. You don't want to give birth out here all alone in such a hostile environment."

Reclaiming some of her dignity, Nadine scoffs at Vera's remark. "That's absurd. I'm not due for months."

Her comment makes Vera laugh even louder, and I shrink closer into the shrubbery to hide myself, because her noise has got to attract anyone within a mile of us. But again no one comes. It's as if Vera's words are only to be heard by Nadine and me.

"Are you sure about that?" Vera asks. "Because I think you're going to deliver sooner than you think."

Before Nadine can protest, before she can point out that Vera's prediction is medically impossible, Vera does something that proves to us both that she is a witch and that impossibilities are the norm where she comes from. Staring at Nadine, Vera raises her arm over her head, and just like Luba does she presses her thumb and her pinky finger together so the three remaining fingers point toward the sky. Suddenly, the blank, black sky that housed only the full moon moments ago is changed as it welcomes three new visitors. One, two, three blindingly bright stars forming a line, unconnected and connected at the same time, Orion's constellation created by Vera's command.

Nadine gasps, and I don't know if it's because of Vera's power—Vera altered nature by herself with one cavalier movement when it took Nadine, Napoleon, and Luba's joint effort to create a full moon in the sky where one didn't exist. Just how powerful is this newcomer? And just how afraid is Nadine of her? When Nadine starts to respond to Vera's action and comment as if she were a stuttering child, I get my answer.

"I d-don't care what you th-think," Nadine stammers. "You d-don't know everything!"

"Oh, but I do, Nadine, and I know that your improbable pregnancy will come to an end sooner than you think. If you don't believe me, just look up," Vera replies. "The truth is right above us for it's all written in the stars."

Chapter 12

According to Lycanthropy.com, which has interestingly grown in popularity since last year, the only other girl to suffer from wolfnesia is Viktoria K. from Perm, Russia, but that's because she blacks out during a full moon from fear because she *thinks* she's going to turn into a werewolf. I black out because I mutate. As a result it's been three weeks since my last confession.

I cannot believe I've kept this secret for so long. The first week really doesn't count, because during that time I was struggling with a bout of the aforementioned wolfnesia and could only remember a vague encounter between two partially human girls as seen by a wolf, just a regular, every-day occurrence in this part of Nebraska and nothing really shareworthy. When my memory sharpened and I recalled the whole discussion, I became a bit selfish; I wanted to unravel this latest wrinkle in the ongoing mystery surrounding the Jaffe clan on my own. How refreshing would it be if I gathered my Wolf Pack and served up some bona fide concrete info instead of platefuls of suspicion and intuition and conjecture? Refreshing, but unrealistic. The one thing wolves and girls have in common is that they're not solitary creatures; they need company. And what could be better company than hosting your boyfriend, home for his Thanksgiving break, in the soundproof closet off of the music room. Turns out I need to register for a course in how to be a good hostess.

"Vera's a witch."

"Could you lead with something more enticing, Domgirl?" Caleb asks. "Like, say, a kiss?"

And a refresher class in girlfriendiquette. My boyfriend wants some lip action, and I'm annoyed. Note to self: *Reorganize your priorities.*

Dutifully, I press my lips against Caleb's, but luckily the moment we touch I lose my memory again. I have no idea what I was about to tell him; I'm more interested in kissing his soft, kissable lips. I place my hands on his shoulders and let them glide down the length of his arms to his elbows, and I can tell he's been squeezing in some extra workout time in between studying; his body is harder than ever before. I let my hands meet behind his back and rest on the slope right above his butt. Caleb's closed-eyed, wide smile tells me that he approves.

"Now that's more like it," he whispers. "I've missed you."

"Me too," I say, all sweet and girl-like. Then I follow up my words with a wolf-like attack. "But this Vera mystery has filled up most of my time."

Simultaneously rolling his eyes and shaking his head, Caleb replies, "So glad I've been replaced by a mysterious stranger."

With an accent on strange.

"The problem is I don't know if Vera's a good witch or a bad witch," I ramble. "But if she's cavorting with Nadine, the Four W, my money's on the latter."

"The Four W?"

"Wicked Witch of Weeping Water," I say as if it's the no-brainer question on the SATs. "If Vera's hanging out with Nadine in the middle of the night and in the middle of the woods, Vera's got to be up to no good."

"Domgirl," Caleb says, in a voice oh-so-close to patronizing. "Why don't you start from the very beginning and fill me in on all things Vera?"

We sit on the floor, lean into the cushioned walls, intertwine our legs and arms, and I proceed to tell my bf about the latest member of our community and all the details that I finally remember of our moonlit encounter.

"I thought Barnaby was doing well in science," Caleb says. "I didn't think he needed a tutor."

Someone has education on the brain. I'm glad my boyfriend's very scholasti-focused, but seriously, I tell him about two witches squaring off in the forest and his takeaway involves my brother's academic regimen? I guess once a tutor, always a tutor.

"Miss Martinez suggested Barnaby get some extra help in science since he wants to major in something that requires he wear a lab coat," I explain. "And she put him and Vera together, which bothers me only slightly less than when she paired him off with Luba."

"Interesting that Barnaby's always getting wedged in between these women," Caleb muses, more to himself than to me. "Almost like he's a pawn."

I've long since known that Luba and Nadine tried to use my brother in their plot against me and my father, but now Vera? That's too much to deal with right now. First things first, we have to determine what she is, and her secret meeting with Nadine holds the key.

"Forget about Barnaby for now," I instruct. "Let's concentrate on the covenites."

Frowning, Caleb clearly doesn't agree with my mandate, but he gives in.

"So Vera actually said Orion?" Caleb asks.

"Yes!" I squeal. "*But does Orion approve,* those were her exact words."

"Well, if she isn't in cahoots with Nadine, she knows enough about her herstory," he surmises.

"You mean her *history*," I correct.

"No, *herstory*," Caleb recorrects. "Jeremy's taking some women's issues class, and according to his professor *history* is gender-hateful. But Professor Doyle has way too much testosterone for a woman, so I think she's just lashing out at a gender that doesn't find her attractive."

"How is Jeremy?"

Caleb doesn't answer the question because he doesn't hear it. I don't answer the question immediately because I don't understand it. Why is Jess asking Caleb about her brother?

"You don't know?" I finally ask.

"I'm only guessing," Caleb replies, defensively thinking I'm referring to Professor Doyle. "I'm trying not to judge, but she's stocky and does have this hairy mole thing on her cheek, so chances are men have shied away from becoming romantically involved with her."

I can't concentrate on what my boyfriend's speaking about, not that he's making much sense anyway. I'm more concerned by Jess's words.

"Not you," I say. "Jess."

Stunned, Caleb looks around the room.

"Jess is here?"

"She's sitting right between us," I inform him.

"No way!" Caleb jumps up like he's bouncing on one of those hippity hop things, and shifts his position to give Jess more room. "Tell her 'hi' for me."

"Tell her yourself; she can hear you," I say. "But actually she wants to know how Jeremy's doing."

"Can't she find that out herself?"

My thought exactly.

"I've, um, I've been busy," Jess replies.

Jess is many things, but she's not one to stammer. Something's wrong.

"Jess, what's going on?" I ask. "You're not your usual bright-goldy self."

It's true. She's still bathed in golden sunshine, but her glow isn't as bright; it's softer, like she's standing behind a big piece of yellow gauze.

"I'm fine, Dom, totally *subarashi!*" she cries, complete with a faux smile.

If I knew the Japanese word for the opposite of *subarashi*, I would say it, but I don't, so I simply speak my native tongue. And harshly. "You're a liar, Jess," I state. "Something isn't right. Does it have to do with Vera?"

Wrong witch.

"Maybe she's upset because Nadine visited her brother again," Caleb suggests.

Bingo!

"She's going to pay for what she's done," Jess hisses, her golden sheen illuminating brightly for just a second when she speaks.

Nadine's going to pay for a few random visits? I get the feeling that Jess the girl is talking and not Jess the Omikami. From previous experience I've learned that otherworldly creatures primarily warn and advise and guide; they don't participate in this-worldly matters unless the circumstances are dire and immediate and personal. I didn't think vengeance was an Omikami trait.

"It isn't," Jess replies in answer to my unspoken thought.

"Then why do you sound like some vengeful spirit?" I ask out loud. "Oh I get it!! Jess, are you trying to act like one of those vindictaghosts from those Japanese horror movies you used to make me watch? The ones that attack people through their TVs and cell phones and laptops? I mean, isn't it enough that you're a Japanese deity? What more do you want?"

"To restore balance," Jess replies, her voice flat and filled with importance. She *is* more Omikami than girl, which

means I should listen to what she has to say. "Nadine is trying to tip the scales; she has to be stopped."

She isn't telling me anything I don't already know, but how?

"What's she saying, Domgirl?" Caleb asks.

"Nadine is doing something that's making her even more
evil than before."

"Impossible," Caleb declares.

"Tell Prince Caleb that he's pretty, but stupid," Jess instructs.

"I will not!"

"You won't what?" Caleb asks.

"Jess said you're stupid." Guess I did. "But she also said
you're pretty."

"Thanks, Jess," Caleb says, obviously focusing on Jess's
positive comment only. "How can Nadine possibly be more
sinister? That would make her soar past Luba."

"Exactly," Jess says.

No, not exactly! Vague and cryptic and ambiguous as
usual. I need specifics; I need information; I need to know
what Nadine is up to and why Vera's come to town and what
type of witch Vera is exactly.

"Vera isn't a witch."

Once again I pause in responding because I'm surprised by
the speaker. It's always startling to hear Napoleon's voice
come out of Arla's mouth, but even more so now because I
was so enraged by Jess's crypticomment that I didn't hear
Arla and Archie come into what I ridiculously thought could
be Caleb's and my temporary private sanctuary. Now that
they're here, maybe we'll finally get some answers.

"Then what exactly is she?" I demand.

"She's hope," Nap replies.

Okay, maybe not. Nap's statement is lofty, but it lacks that
certain something I'm looking for, like say, a detail.

"Could one of the dead people in the room please talk in a
language the living will understand?" My words are harsh,

yes, but also necessary. And words that embody a sentiment shared by at least one other person in the room.

"Please, Nap, you have to tell us more," Archie pleads. "That's great that she offers us hope, but why and how and where'd she really come from?"

I know what Caleb feels like when he watches me speak to Jess, but only sees me conversing with airspace. Archie appears to be begging Arla for facts, when he's really trying to reach his dead boyfriend. It's a fact that hits Archie a few moments later.

He clasps his hands around Arla's neck in an attempt to strengthen his physical bond to Napoleon. "We need your help, Nap," he whispers. "Bad stuff is brewing; I can feel it. . . . I can feel it inside of me. Please help us make it stop."

Archie knows. He knows not only that Nadine is conspiring to bring a whole new brand of evil to town, but that he is also capable of unleashing a diabolical force. From the way that he's peering into Arla's eyes, desperately trying to reach Nap's spirit, it's clear that Archie has come to understand what I already know, that he isn't in complete control of choosing which side of the moral ground to play on. Until he notices Jess.

Ever since Archie, Arla, and Nap entered the room, Jess's light started to grow brighter. I'm not sure why. Could be because she was excited to see old friends or because there were more old friends who could actually see her.

"Jess!" Archie suddenly shouts. He's so excited to see his old friend that he lets go of Arla. "It's so good to see you again."

Breakthrough! If Archie can see Jess, that must mean that he's choosing light over dark. Maybe he's finally made the right choice.

Not so fast.

"Nothing is as simple as it appears."

I don't see Arla lean in to me, so all I hear is Nap's voice speaking softly in my ear, calling out to me from beyond the grave, from some fringe world, from some place that's as far away as Jess's new hometown, but also just a whisper away. He's not telling me anything I don't already know; he's just telling me something I don't want to believe.

I don't want to accept the fact that Archie may be going down a path that only leads to destruction and pain and horror and from which there's no way to return. He's already started walking, that I know, but he can turn around; he can come back; he can be saved. He just has to be! When will I learn that I don't know everything?

"Not everyone can be saved, Dom," Jess adds. "Not everyone can make the right choice."

"Shut up!"

Archie's words slam into our ears, the cushion on the walls doing nothing to soften the sound.

"You have no idea what you're talking about!" he continues. "Neither do you, Nap!"

He pushes Arla so hard that she stumbles back, right through Jess and right into Caleb's arms.

"Winter!" Caleb shouts. "Take it easy."

I want to look away, but I can't. I have to stare at Archie standing at a crossroads, one foot on either side of a very thin line. I think Archie can see it too, because he looks down at his feet, fascinated by the floor. Then again he might just be bending his head so I can see the dark roots that still litter his scalp, roots that have their origin at the tips of his soul. When he looks up I gasp, not out of terror, but relief, because his eyes are still violet; they haven't changed. That's one thing to be thankful for. More company in our cramped space is not.

"My, my, this closet is very crowded."

Surrounded by my friends, I have obviously become more girl than wolf, because my predatory senses should have picked up another intruder, yet I'm as surprised as everyone else to see Vera standing in front of the closed door. Is she like Jess? Can she walk through walls? Is she like Archie and just really good at picking a lock?

"The string on my violin broke," she announces. "I need a new one."

Or am I letting my imagination run wild?

"A violin playing scientist," Caleb remarks. "That's quite a combination."

Slowly, Vera raises her hand and with her index finger brushes her hair aside and then over and behind her ear. Her silky blond hair is tucked neatly away to expose a glittering earring that shines like starlight. Her blue eyes are shimmering, and her lips have lengthened to form a sly smile. Individually, these acts are simple and innocent and natural; together they create a message.

"You must be Caleb," Vera purrs.

"He's my boyfriend," I say as if I'm claiming ownership.

"Oh I know who he is," Vera replies.

"Well, that makes one of us," my boyfriend says brazenly.

"There's so much more to me than music and lab reports, Caleb," Vera responds. "One day I'll have to fill you in on all things Vera."

Make that a warning. Instinctively, I know that Vera's as musical as I am. She came here to let us know that she knows that we're discussing her, but she doesn't seem upset about it; in fact she seems thrilled that she's the center of our conversation. It's, unfortunately, a conversation that has become repetitive. We still don't know anything more about Vera, other than the fact that she's connected to Nadine. Until she's about to leave.

As she turns back around, Vera's hair whips around and slices the air like a blond knife. "And even though yellow is such a hard color to wear, Jess, you pull it off really well."

Smirking more than smiling, Vera opens the door and leaves us speechless. Whatever she is—human, witch, spirit—she's rendered us mute and shocked and confused. Jess, Arla,

Archie, and I—the Omikami, the possessed, the evil-good hybrid, and the werewolf—defenseless against the snickering ice princess. Four supernatural creations stunned into inaction by Vera's unexpected presence and calculated words. Prince Caleb is the only one not affected by Vera's mystery.

"I've got a plan."

Chapter 13

Leave it to the human to save the day.

My boyfriend's plan is sheer brilliance, combining the mundane with the mysterious, science with the supernatural, and the outcome of his clever scheme will hopefully shed light on some dark matter, namely Vera's origin and her true connection to Luba and the family Jaffe. The only problem is that a key element to making his plan work is involving every member of the family Robineau, the living, the dead, and the in-between.

"I'm not a hundred percent comfortable using Barnaby," I state.

I take a deep breath of Caleb's new cologne, citrusy and breezy and soft; this must be his college smell. Luckily, he feels the complete opposite. He's strong and grounded and secure.

"I know you want to keep Barnaby safe," Caleb says. "But we're not doing anything that he wouldn't be doing on his own."

"Just placing him closer to the danger zone," I remind him.

"Where his actions can be more closely monitored," my prince replies.

Exhaling slowly, I realize that Caleb has a point. My

brother is going to be seventeen soon. I can always treat him like my little brother, but it's time I stopped treating him like a child. Even when he acts like one.

"That's feeb."

My brother scored points this morning for being perceptive when I set out to put Caleb's plan into action, but lost just as many for being uncooperative.

"So I'm Feeb Girl," I replied. "But it doesn't change things. It's still their anniversary."

My parents would have been married twenty years today, a milestone anniversary, and one that shouldn't go unrecognized simply because neither of them are in any condition to celebrate. Their children can raise a nonalcoholic glass of champagne in their honor at their mother's bedside, right before one of them has to be tutored by a possibly paranormal professor-in-training. Caleb's plan is to get Vera to come to The Retreat so she can have a session with Luba before she has a session with Barnaby. When I told Vera earlier about the change of venue, she was fine with it; Barnaby's the one giving me a hard time.

"We can go to The Retreat tomorrow," he offered. "It's Saturday. We can party all day if you want to. It isn't like Mom's going to know the difference."

Usually I'm a big fan of irreverence, but not when it screws up the master plan.

"You know she'll know," I say, securing my newly appointed position as Feeb Girl. "Family occasions and especially anniversaries were very special to her; she loved throwing parties whether it was for really special days or just lame events. Dad said she would always bake a pineapple upside-down cake to commemorate their first date because Dad had promised to take her to Hawaii one day and they have pineapples in Hawaii. He never took her, but every year she reminded him that he broke his promise to her, which is what married couples and family members do—they remind each other of their shortcomings."

Sometimes when I ramble I actually listen to myself and hear the kernels of inspiration.

"Which is what you and Vera can have," I teased.

"I don't like pineapple."

Obviously, Barnaby zoned out during my rambling.

"No!" I shout. "It'll give you and Vera a chance to spend time in a different setting, get to know each other, you know, on a more personal level. Kind of like a date."

What?!

Barnaby shouted that word at the same time it echoed throughout the inner lining of my brain. I've proposed to set up my brother with a girl who could turn out to be a she-devil, and the thought was just as disturbing to him as it was to me. But why? Despite the fact that she could be hiding hooves under her Mary Janes, Vera's really pretty in that so-phisticated, borderline snobby, unapproachable way that is thoroughly enticing to boys Barnaby's age.

"My relationship with Vera is strictly professional!" Barnaby railed.

I've learned to read the subtext of my brother's dialogue, so his comment can mean only one thing. Barnaby may be a red-blooded American boy, but one whose hormones are pointed in the direction of other red-blooded American boys. How did I not see this before? He's just like Archie. He has no desire to go on a date with Vera because he's gay.

"Besides, I already have a girlfriend," he added.

Or because I'm a complete idiot who not only doesn't know that her brother is straight, but that he's already acting on his straightness.

"You do not!" I shouted.

"I do too!" Barnaby shouted back.

"Since when?!"

"Since the summer!"

Barnaby's had a girlfriend since the summer and this is the first time I'm finding out about it? Baby brother definitely is no longer a baby, but somebody else is calling him "baby," and I need to know who that person is, pronto!

"You what?! When? How?" I stammered and then finally added, "Who?!"

"Gwen," he replied proudly.

"Gwenevere Schültzenhoggen?" I say. "You're dating Gwenevere Schültzenhoggen?"

Barnaby, clearly not thrilled with my shocked, high-pitched tone, crossed his arms and pursed his lips. "Yes, Gwen is my girlfriend."

"Gwen is also two inches taller than you are!" I countered.

"Five when she wears high heels," Barnaby said, as if that fact was something to put in the happy column.

"And she's a senior and you're a junior," I said. "Doesn't that bother you?"

"I'm dating up!" he cried. "I don't care how old or tall Gwen is. I really like her, and she really likes me, and really, Dominy, how superficial can you be?"

Very!

I should be thourathrilled that Barnaby is dating a nice human girl like Gwen and not remotely interested in anything Vera can offer him except scientific data, but there's a part of me that isn't. I like Gwen; I just don't think she's right for my brother. Then again, I'm sure Caleb's sisters wouldn't choose me for their girlfriend-in-law if they knew my secret. Actually, this is a much better scenario, because when I stop thinking like a lifelong member of the Shallow Hall of Fame, I'll realize that Barnaby will be nothing but a pawn in Caleb's plan like we originally thought and not a willing participant. Let the manipulation begin!

Now that we're at The Retreat, I expected to feel a pang of guilt or anxiety or nervousness, but nothing. All I feel is eager. It's sort of a foolhardy feeling, since none of my plans ever work out the way I think they will, so gauging by my track record this plan will undoubtedly crash and burn as well. But maybe since this scheme wasn't my brainchild, only the recipient of my stamp of approval, odds are greater that we'll succeed. When I see Elkie I'm reminded that things don't always work out the way you hope they will.

No matter how many times I see her sitting behind Essie's old receptionist's desk, it's always a shock. Although the resemblance is uncanny, the personalities couldn't be further apart. Unable to deal with looking at a woman who looks just like another woman who's buried in a graveyard, Barnaby doesn't even need me to tell him to wait for me in our mother's room. He races right down the Hallway to Nowhere and doesn't stop until he's safely inside Room 19. I have my own agenda to meet.

"Hi, Elkie."

"Your brother knows I'm not one of the living dead, right?" she asks.

"He's at that awkward age," I semi-lie. "Emotionally volatile, but verbally stunted, he's got a lot he wants to say, just doesn't know how to say it."

Tossing her head back, Elkie scrutinizes me for a second before speaking. "Which is not a problem you seem to have. What do you want to know?"

She might look like her twin, but she doesn't act like her. Except for during the early years when I was very young, Essie ignored me, didn't even know I was standing in front of her sometimes unless I ripped the celebgazine out of her hands. Maybe it's because during their embryonic stage Elkie sucked out all the insight and inquiry from their parents' DNA and left Essie with just enough curiosity to focus on pretty pictures of starlets. Whatever the reason, Elkie knows I've come here today to do more than commemorate a special anniversary.

"Is Luba in her room?" I ask.

"She hasn't left since you called here this morning," Elkie replies.

There goes my career as an impressionist!

"You knew that was me on the phone asking for Luba?" I ask dejectedly.

"Excuse me, madam, but could I trouble you for information regarding one of your patients?" Elkie replies, repeating my earlier phone dialogue.

If my British accent were as good as Elkie's, there's no way she would have known it was me! Ah well, I had to make sure Luba was here, otherwise there would've been no plan to plan. When I see Vera walk through the front door, it's time to set the plan into motion.

Another one of Elkie's traits that Essie didn't possess is her ability to remain calm even when she knows danger is a breath away. Like now.

"Hi, Vera," I say.

"Hi, Dominy," she replies. Clearly Vera changed after school because she's wearing a tight-fitting emerald green cashmere sweater, tight-fitting corduroy capris, the color of a dandelion, and brown shoe-boots with a thick, but high heel. Buh-bye, Mary Janes; hello, va-va-va-Vera.

Without missing a beat or breaking her stride, she walks right up to Elkie and extends her hand. "I'm Vera, but you already know that."

I almost miss her comment because I'm so in awe of her surprisingly fashionable fashion sense, but then it dawns on me: Why would Vera think that?! Does she suspect that we were talking about her? Does she know she's about to walk into a trap?

Reacting to my deer-in-the-headlights expression, Vera clarifies. "You just mentioned my name."

Oh right! Clearly I'm more nervous than I thought. Unlike Elkie.

"Very nice to meet you, Vera," Essie's twin replies. "We've been waiting for you."

Before Elkie guesses my intent and says anything that might warn Vera to turn right around and leave, I grab Vera's arm and practically pull her away from the desk. "Let's go find Barnaby."

"See you later, Elkie," Vera says as we turn the corner.

It isn't until we're standing in front of Room 48, Luba's room, that I realize no one mentioned Elkie's name in Vera's presence. Add psychic to her growing list of talents. Along with Lubattacker. Because the moment Luba sets eyes on Vera, it's as if she's been assaulted.

"Luba," Vera says. "It's about time that we met face-to-face."

Vera isn't at all surprised. It's as if she expected to be brought to see Luba instead of my brother. Either she's very good at reading minds or predicting the future or a little bit of both.

"Thank you, Dominy, for making the arrangements," Vera adds. "I knew you would be so helpful to me. Isn't she helpful, Luba?"

Looking at Luba is like looking at the polar opposite of Vera. Where one is calm and cordial and controlled, the other is stunned and sickened and scared. The woman who cursed me, the woman who has the power to turn into a mangy beast and fly through the air and harness a star's power, is frightened. Most of her body is rigid except for her left hand; the three fingers from which I've seen angry, black smoke rocket out are shaking, quivering slightly, not as a result of some physical malady, but out of fear of being in Vera's presence. And when Vera speaks, Luba's condition gets worse, no matter how hard she tries to retain her strength.

"You look like you've lost twenty years, Luba," Vera remarks. "Or acquired the spirit of a seventeen-year-old."

I don't know who's more astounded by that statement:

Luba or me. How does Vera know about Rayna? If she knows that the triumvirate sucked the life out of Rayna and funneled it into Luba's then-decrepit shell of a body, restoring her youth and vigor and beauty, what else does Vera know? Or more accurately, what else does she know that Luba doesn't?

"Did Nadine tell you I came to town?" Vera asks, knowing full well that the answer is a big fat no.

When Luba opens her mouth, I expect a trail of black ooze to fly out and wrap itself around Vera's throat or splatter into her eyes, viciously blinding her, but the only thing that emerges is a weak sound, the slightest intake of breath, that makes an even more powerful impact because it's so unexpected. I have never seen Luba this meek.

And I've never seen Vera more masterful.

Hands clasped behind her back, she starts walking toward Luba. Who needs fists for fighting when you have words and attitude? As youthful and fit as Luba is now, she's no match for the real thing; next to Luba, Vera looks vibrant and glowing with health. She's also brimming with more verbalicious weapons.

"Well, you must be very proud then," Vera continues. "Because if Nadine is keeping secrets from you, that must mean the student has learned from the master."

Once again Luba tries to speak, but her body refuses to comply to her wishes and she only succeeds in coughing roughly. Finally, she finds her voice, but it's strained. "My granddaughter and I have no secrets."

Inches from Luba, Vera laughs heartily in her face, and Luba reacts as if she's scalded by the sound, turning her face from Vera and holding a hand to her cheek, only letting go when she's convinced flesh still clings to the bone.

"Oh, Luba," Vera sighs. "You always did make me laugh."

From my position I can see Vera and Luba staring at each other. Vera's eyes are unflinching; Luba's are searching, constantly in motion, wary of her opponent's next move and even more wary that she'll be unable to defend herself against Vera's actions. This is a scenario I would have thought was impossible, Luba practically cowering in Vera's presence. I thought I would learn more about Vera by pitting her up against Luba, but just the opposite has happened; I'm learning more about Luba than I ever could have imagined.

And just when I think I've seen it all, Luba lives up to the name I've given her, because only a psycho would want to try to attack someone who clearly frightens her.

Luba raises her hand and points the three fingers at Vera that only moments ago were shaking. Three streams of black smoke jut out from her fingertips, but before they can pick up speed, Vera blows lightly on the smoke streams, and they disappear.

"Now isn't the time or the place for us to put on a show, Luba," Vera declares. "You should know better than anyone that timing is everything."

Turning around, Vera walks to the door steadily, her heels noisily digging into the tiled floor, and never once does the smile leave her face, because she's won this battle. Luba will make no attempt to stop her.

"Now if you'll excuse me, ladies, I have to tutor Dominy's brother in the fine arts of science," Vera announces, poised in the open doorway. "But let's get together again real soon. This was fun."

It only takes about ten seconds after the door slams shut for me to realize that I'm alone in the room with Luba. Correction, I'm alone in the room with the woman who was just put in her place by a teenaged girl. Whatever Vera is, Luba knows Vera's more powerful than she is, and while that fact should frighten me, it fills me with nothing but joy. And it fills Luba with nothing but rage.

Flying through the air at tremendous speed, Luba reaches out her arms until her hands wrap around my throat. All the rage she was prevented from unleashing at Vera is now being directed against me. In the next instant I'm being hurtled up off the ground. Luba's back is flat against the ceiling, her hands still tightly gripping my neck, and I'm dangling from her hold. It's not by choice but necessity that I'm looking into her face, which appears to be less a product of nature than a grotesque shape symbolizing fury. My body shifts furiously underneath Luba, my legs stupidly kicking in search of ground that refuses to help.

"Do not think that you've outsmarted me, changeling!"

Luba's words and breath bang into my face like a scorching pain. Despite all the things she's done to me, I've never seen her this enraged, and I know why: because I've seen her defeated. Now she's doing everything she possibly can to erase the incident from my memory. She's going to have to try a lot harder if she wants me to forget what I've just seen, because it's valuable ammunition. Luba's attempt is admirable.

"Remember, Dominy," she begins, "LUBA ALWAYS WINS!!"

I only know I've fallen when my back slams into the hard tiles of the floor, and I don't know if Luba let go of me or if her screech ripped us apart. Not that it matters; the outcome is the same: Luba's reminded me that she may not be an alpha creature in the universe, but she is still a vessel of enormous power.

The ache in my body is too great for me to move, but out of the corner of my eye I can see Winston and Elkie standing in the doorway. They must have responded to the commotion and burst in to investigate. Lifting my eyes, I see that they missed the main attraction, because Luba is no longer plastered to the ceiling, but sitting quietly in a chair in the corner of the room. She looks like a patient in a mental hospital instead of a nursing home, giggling softly, her long, thin fingers pressing against her lips. A truly sinister sight, but one that doesn't deter the intruders from entering the room. Elkie because she isn't frightened by Luba, and Winston because he is.

I feel my body being lifted, the pain weighing on me like an iron weight trying to keep me pinned to the floor. Calling upon all my wolf-strength, I finally get up and see Elkie on one side of me and Winston on the other.

"Are you all right?" Elkie asks.

Nodding my head in contrast to how I feel, I reply, "I will be."

My voice sounds as wounded as my body, and I'm more out of breath than I thought I was. Winston sounds worse than I do.

"You have no idea what you're starting, Dominy," he whispers. "You don't want to get Luba mad."

Shrugging off Winston's clammy, cowardly hands from my body, I apply extra pressure to Elkie's arm so I don't topple over.

"Oh, Mister Cell Keeper," I say, smiling broadly. "That's exactly what I want to do."

Chapter 14

Something feels wrong because things are starting to feel right.

Ever since Vera's arrival, even before she burst into town, I've had this sense that something was coming, something was being sent to me to help in this fight. Now that I've had a ringside seat to Luba versus Vera, Round 1 and witnessed Vera treat her opponent like a silly puppy instead of, well, instead of the deranged lunatic that she is, it's yet more confirmation that I should listen to my bodies and trust my instincts. Don't know if it's wolf-gut or girl intuition, but my premonitions seriously rock. And finally so does calculus.

Luba's fear of Vera is greater than my fear of Luba. We're like the practical application of some mathematical equation, Dice's lecture come to life. By making math personal, I've made it less scary. Same thing with Luba. I know she's still dangerous—I'm not a total idiot—but having seen her very personal reaction to the visitor with the capital *V* has made Luba less frightening to me.

The correlation of my life to the world of compleximath makes even more sense when I open up my textbook—which is of course clad in a Hello Kitty book cover, with Arithmakitty wearing a cute plaid school uniform, sitting at a desk surrounded by thought bubbles containing plus and minus signs—to a random page that pronounces that calculus is the mathematical study of change. Signs don't get clearer than that.

As with most things in my life, I don't know how long this oh-I-get-it phase is going to last, so I'm going to enjoy it. It's taken me quite a while to get here, it's definitely been a struggle, but I feel more peaceful than I have in months. I still don't know exactly what Vera is, but I'm certain she's an ally, an unexpected force that's changed things for me, just as I know that in calculuspeak, the rate of change of momentum of a body is equal to the resultant force acting on the body. Loosely translated it means that Vera is the unexpected force that's going to help me get my life back on track, even though Luba and Nadine will continue to try and push me off course. And sometimes my enemies will call in reinforcements.

"Psst."

Ignore her.

"Psssst."

It takes me a few seconds to realize that it isn't Jess who's pestering me with her *pssts,* but Gwen. Ironically, this is the first time in my math-room history that I'm annoyed about being interrupted, because I understand what my teacher is saying. I completely get this thing about the integral derivative. Or was that the antiderivative? Damn you, Gwenevere!

I look over at her in the seat next to me and mouth the word "what." Immediately, I feel bad, because that silent communication contained way more attitude than I had intended. Why should I be ticked off at her? She can't possibly know that I'm in the middle of an academic breakthrough. She probably thinks my startled expression means that I have no idea what Dice is talking about, which is usually the case, instead of the truth, that I finally get it; I finally understand the principles he's been blabbering on about all semester. Most likely her *psst* means she's trying to help me understand, save me from my own stupidity, which only makes me feel worse for my snipitude.

Gwen's always been sweet to me; she's sweet to everyone in fact, which is probably the reason my brother has fallen for her. To him she's like this cuddly, almost six-feet-tall, teddy bear. A mental picture invades my brain, and suddenly all thoughts of high-level mathematical concepts are vying for space with an image of my brother wrapping his arms around a towering stuffed animal whose face bears a striking resemblance to the girl sitting next to me. The girl desperately trying to get my attention. The girl tossing a folded up piece of paper at me that lands squarely in the middle of my notebook.

Trying to soften my nasty face I smile in Gwen's direction, but she doesn't smile back. Was my initial expression that uglyesque? Have I lost the little bit of charm I still possess?

Looking like the mayor of Somberville, Gwen juts her chin in the direction of the note lying on my notebook, willing me to open up the missive. Not wanting to risk unleashing the wrath of this sitting Goliath, I do as I'm silently told, but when her words meet my eyes, I want a do-over.

Meet me in the music room closet after class.

Direct and demanding and dangerous.

I can already feel the walls of my inner sanctum closing in on me. That small closet off of the music room is my safe haven, where my friends and I can go and hide from the world to have some very private moments. It's the place I can go to that allows me to escape from the Lubossibilities that threaten me at every moment and the Nadinophobia that wants to cripple me and turn me into a frightened little wolf-girl. I know Gwen has entered our hallowed space before, but it was as an intruder, not a party planner. As much as I like Gwen and as much as she's about to become part of my life via her status as my brother's girlfriend, I want to keep her at a distance, and the close quarters of the music room closet don't allow for that.

Besides, I know exactly why she wants to meet me in private; she wants to ask for my brother's hand in boyfriendom. Her German-Korean heritage means she's all about procedure and policy and protocol, and since my father's not around, I'm next in line to offer the Robineau blessing. She really is *very* sweet. But wait a second, how stupid am I? Barnaby and Gwen have been dating since the summer. Why would she just be asking me for permission now? Could they want to go steady? Get married? Did Dice just say something about the slope of a secant line? What the hell is a secant line? Why is it sloping? Why have I let Gwen take over the reins from Luba and Nadine and drive me back off course?

I nod my head furiously in her direction, and finally the girl smiles. *Glad you're happy, Gwen.* I'm back at point zero, feeling academically stupid and royally arithmeticked off. *You better make a strong case to be Barnaby's girlfriend, because right now I consider you a very unsuitable suitor.*

She's proving to be an even worse speaker.

Normally, communication spews out of Gwen like curlicues. Rivulets of words interrupted by asides and encumbered by tidbits of TMI tangential thoughts. But now Gwen can hardly get the words out. She's stuttering and stammering and stopping herself just when I think she's about to tell me the reason that we're here, alone in what I've come to consider one of my homes away from home. Her words are like undelivered letters, lost, misplaced, never read. Finally, I can't take it anymore, and if Gwen won't speak, I'll speak for her. Even if I don't fully believe in what I say.

"You don't have to worry that I'm going to ship Barnaby

off to some boys-only boarding school," I blurt. "You two officially have my approval to date."

I've unlocked the key to Gwen's word library.

"Oh I know that you know about us!" she squeals. "And Barn's told me that you're okay with Gwenaby."

What exactly am I okay with?

"Gwenaby?"

"Our smooshed up name," she says. She also scrunches up her brow and shrugs her shoulders in that annoying way people do when they can't believe you don't already understand what they've just said. I can't be too harsh on Gwen though. I am a wordsmith; I love to portmanteau, make up new words to add to my fauxlexicon, and Gwenaby sounds like it could be a perfect addition. I think for a second, and it is perfect, even if it's based on an imperfect pairing.

"Like the name the paparazzi would give you and my brother if you two were celebrities from two different mediums who suddenly started dating one another," I explain, getting more excited about Barnaby and Gwen's relationship now that I've distilled it down to its literary implications.

"Exactly!!"

Her voice sounds incredibly shrill in the close confines of the closet, and I'm sure that Gwen sings superdiva soprano in all those choirs she belongs to. From the way she keeps talking, I'm also sure she has every solo that's ever performed.

"I know that you were surprised to hear that your brother and I are a couple, at least that's what your brother said, which is why we didn't want to say anything at first. We wanted to wait until we knew we wanted to be boyfriend and girlfriend, because I'm a year older and a few inches taller and he's a year younger and a few inches shorter," Gwen says, wandering in the land of verbal redundancy. "But I think we make a super-cute couple, don't you?"

Before I can answer in the negative, Gwen continues.

"Well, that isn't an entirely fair question. You have to say yes," she states. "You're family, well, Barnaby's family, not my family, not yet anyway!"

The only reason Gwen stops talking is because her laughter overtakes her and erupts out of her like some benign volcano spewing a high-pitched sound instead of high-intensity lava. She doesn't care that she's making me semi-deaf; she's reveling in the fact that we're semi-family!

"Don't worry. Barn and I have decided to take things slow," she consoles. "We have to graduate high school first and then college before we even start thinking about anything more permanent and long lasting. But I have a feeling, and my feelings are usually very accurate, that one day me and Barn and you and Caleb might be spending the holidays together! Wouldn't that be beyond fantastic?!"

If ear-shattering and heart-stopping and soul-crushing are the next steps beyond fantastic, then yes, I agree completely.

"I'm so glad that you and my brother are thinking things through sensibly," I say with a remarkably straight face.

"Which is so incredibly hard to do 'cause your brother is so sexy!"

Not surprisingly my insides twist and turn uncomfortably.

"I mean he's smart, he's a track star, and such a great kisser!"

Once again I'm assaulted by Gwen's high-pitched squeal, and I have to grip the sides of my khakis so I don't accidentally unleash my wolf-fury in an attempt to shut her up. But why do I need a wolf's strength when I have a girl's words?

"That is so gross, Gwen!" I shout. "I don't want to hear about my brother's rank as a kisser. I don't even want to think about my brother kissing. Some things should be kept private."

"You're absolutely right," Gwen replies. "Sorry!"

She nods her head and raises her hands, palms toward me, to signify a truce and an end to this awkward topic. Only to enter into even more awkward territory.

"That's why I asked you to meet me here," she continues. "I needed privacy to talk to you about my father."

What?! An opening sentence like that cannot lead to a happy conclusion. I flash back to the only time I ever had to talk to my friends in private about my father, and those conversations led to the revelations about my curse, undisputedly unhappy times. Logic tells me that Gwen isn't going to disclose that she too has a curse hovering over her head, but I get the sense that we're headed into equally icky territory. A path I really don't want to travel down.

"Shouldn't you maybe talk to Miss Martinez?" I suggest.

Excellent solution, Dominy! Who better to offer guidance than our guidance counselor?

"This is way too personal a matter to bring in an expert," Gwen replies. "I need a friend."

When did I become Gwen's friend?! Did I sign up for the role and forget? And I can't possibly be Gwen's closest friend. There must be someone else whom she can lure to a desolate area of the school to talk about a very private matter involving her and her father. Suddenly my knees feel weak, and I actually hope that a transformation is starting. Snap my legs so they break and invert—I'd take that over listening to whatever Gwen wants to share with me.

"Are you okay, Dom?" Gwen asks, grabbing my arm. "Maybe you should sit down."

Maybe we should leave!

Ignoring my unspoken plea for escape, Gwen leads me to the corner of the room, kicks away a stray clarinet, and helps me to sit down. She sits across from me, her hand releasing its grip on my arm only to take hold of my hand. Her skin is incredibly smooth, her touch warm, and her connection strong. Being superficial sure can get in the way of seeing a person's true worth. Gwenevere Schültzenhoggen has more than my approval to be my brother's girlfriend; she has my blessing.

When I take a deeper look at her, I forget about my own discomfort and realize she's troubled. She doesn't need my blessing; she needs my friendship. I don't know what's going on between her and her father, but even though I am reluctant to learn all the details, I know that Gwen needs to talk to someone about them. I take a deep breath and prepare to listen. It only gets worse.

"It's about my father and Nadine."

Gwen's face disappears, and suddenly all I see sitting before me is the shriveled, near-dead body of Rayna, seconds before she begged me to end her life. Heat pours through my body, and a vise slips around my neck, making it difficult to breathe. Stay calm; don't show your fear; let Gwen think that the mention of Nadine's name doesn't affect you. But unfortunately it does. Because I know where it can all lead.

I squeeze Gwen's hand, strengthening our connection. I will not let her suffer the same fate; I will not let Nadine take yet another victim; I will not let Gwen continue this conversation.

"Tell your father to stay away from Nadine," I command.

"How can he?" Gwen asks. "He's her doctor."

So their relationship is professional and not personal. I guess that's better than what I thought Gwen might possibly say when she linked the two names together, but still they're connected, and that's not entirely good. Even if Nadine needs Gwen's father's services and expertise and doctor-patient confidentiality. Well, two out of three ain't bad.

"My dad is Nadine's OB/GYN, and I overheard him telling my mother that there's something unusual about her pregnancy," Gwen explains.

What could be so unusual about a witch's pregnancy? Maybe Gwen's found out who the father is? Or maybe Gwen double-crossed her own father?

"I got curious, and so I hacked into my father's computer and swiped the ultrasound," she confesses.

You did what?! Suddenly the cuddly teddy bear has turned into a barracuda!

"Isn't it kind of illegal to steal confidential medical files?" I rhetoric-ask. "And by 'kind of' I mean 'definitely'!"

"Yes! My father would kill me if he found out what I did, but the way he and my mother were talking about the 'unwed Jaffe girl with the dead twin,' which is how my mother refers to Nadine, I just had to find out why her pregnancy's so unusual," she admits. "And I just had to share it with you."

Like a timid temptress, Gwen pulls out the ultrasound from the inside of her bra. It's a move that is more comical than slick. Just like her pronouncement.

"Unfortunately, Barnaby's a gentleman," she declares. "So it was really, really, *really* safe in there."

Good to know. Now could you please fill me in on the reason we're here in the first place?!

Bending to my silent command, Gwen shows me the ultrasound photo, and I do my best to conceal my horror.

"Isn't that strange?" she asks.

Adopting my father's tried and tested tactic, I don't answer Gwen's question, which only forces her to keep talking.

"That silver-black light isn't supposed to be there," she adds. "My father has no idea what it is. He doesn't think it's harmful, most likely a problem with the photo itself."

So that's what has the good doctor and his daughter concerned.

"Once I saw it I couldn't keep it to myself," Gwen explains. "I figured since you're friendly with Nadine, you know, especially after Napoleon died, maybe you could talk to her and make sure she's okay and that she isn't under too much stress. An unwed pregnant teen mother is more likely to confide in a friend than her doctor. At least that's what my father says."

Disregarding the fact that I am the opposite of Nadine's

friend, I quell Gwen's fears and agree to have a follow-up visit with Nadine.

"Absolutely, Gwen. You did the right thing sharing this with me," I say.

Gwen must not notice the sarcasm in my voice. I'm not sure if it's because she's too sweet or just relieved that she won't have to confront Nadine to find out about the latter's prenatal health, thereby breaking the code of patient–doctor's daughter confidentiality.

"Don't worry about Nadine," I state. "I'll take care of her."

Beaming, Gwen leans over and gives me a great big teddy bear hug. I squirm a little because I now know how Barnaby feels. Yes, I want a closer relationship with my brother, but not this close. Then again, having his girlfriend as my friend could have unexpected perks.

"Barnaby's right," Gwen says with a smile. "Beneath your hard exterior, you really are a softie."

Thanks for the, um, compliment. But I'd much rather have a parting gift.

"May I keep this picture?" I ask.

Standing up, Gwen looks down at me, and I seriously feel like Jack just before he climbed his way up to become a fairy tale legend.

"Sure," she says. "If I want to take a closer look at it, I'll just hack into my dad's PC again."

Yup, such a sweet girl.

When I'm finally alone in the music room closet, everything sweet turns sour. I look at the ultrasound again, and yes, the silver-black light is odd and to the untrained eye unexplainable, but I know what it is; I know that it's Nadine's life-force that exists within her; I'm not surprised that it's showed up in the photo. What's frightening to me is what the light is surrounding: Nadine's children. She's not just having a baby; she's having twins!

It's far from a natural occurrence—one twin pregnant with

her own set; it's a calculated plan. Because once Nadine gives birth, she and her children will be the triumvirate, and Luba will have outlived her purpose. I've seen Nadine in action, and I know that she'll cast Luba aside with the same indifference she displayed when she killed her brother. And without Luba around there will be no stopping Nadine or the horrors she and her children, with her as their mentor, will create.

Never in my life did I think I would say this, but I have to save Luba.

Chapter 15

"Sounds like one plus two minus one equals three."

My boyfriend is so smart.

Caleb really is learning so much in college, how to distinguish a DNA from an RNA, how to make a gene mutate properly, how to differentiate between a bad witch and a badder witch. He totally understands that right after Nadine gives birth to her twins she'll kill her grandmother before she starts breastfeeding. It's right there in the *Pregnancy Handbook: Vindictive Witch Edition*. And as terrible and cruel and heartless as Luba is, she's predictable. She only began her psychotic crusade in response to something my father did. I'm not justifying her actions, but in her own crazy mind she had a reason, which is more than her granddaughter has. Nadine is evil because she can be. She's like wildfire, destroying whatever stands in her way, simply because it's in her path. I know without a doubt that Nadine will pass down her immoral compass to her children, and when they grow up they'll be deadlier than their great-grandmother could ever hope to be. No, Nadine needs to be stopped, which means Luba needs to be spared.

"It's time for you to make your enemy your ally."

My boyfriend is so stupid.

"You can't be serious?!" I shout-ask.

"I'm completely serious," Caleb replies in a much calmer tone. "It's the only thing you can do."

The only thing I can do is work alongside the woman whose life's work has been to destroy my family and me? That's what he proposes I should do?

His dorm room suddenly feels smaller than the music room closet, and I glance at myself in the mirror hanging over the closet door to make sure I'm not transforming in the middle of the day. I feel my fingers itch as if claws want to rip through my flesh and my teeth throb as if fangs want to pierce my gums; the wolf wants to break free and take control to teach Caleb a lesson.

"There is no way that I could ever work on the same team as Luba!"

Looks like I'm the one who's about to learn something.

"Then you don't know Dominy Robineau like I know her."

Caleb's voice is its usual blend of quiet strength, not overly forceful, but powerful enough to command attention. He has mine.

I sit next to him on his bed, not because he's pulled me toward him, but because I want to sit next to him. Yes, I want to hear what he has to say, but more than that I just want to be close to him. I didn't come here for any other reason than to talk this latest discovery through with him, but now that I'm in his presence, I'm feeling the animal urges; those primal instincts that belong to both the wolf and the girl slowly rise from the depths of my stomach and spread throughout my body like a resolute virus that will not settle for less than total possession. I'm ready to give in, but Caleb just won't shut up.

"The Dominy I know is stronger than anyone I've ever met in my entire life, anyone I've ever read about," Caleb states.

"She is more courageous and resourceful and smarter than anyone could ever hope to be. Not to mention more beautiful."

His compliments are extraordinary not because I deserve them—on the contrary, I don't believe I do—but because he believes every word he's just said. They started in his heart, flew out of his mouth, then poured all over me. A direct and almost unbearable connection.

I can feel the tears start to well up in my eyes, but I don't dare look away. I may not agree with what Caleb's just told me, but I have to respect him enough to accept that this is how he feels. It's just that after all I've done, after all of the bad things that I've done and that have occurred because of me, I can't believe that someone would say something so exquisitely simple to me.

My body responds to Caleb's kindness before I can contemplate how to verbally reply. It's not the reaction he wants.

"Don't shake your head," he orders tenderly. "Don't disagree with me, and don't dwell on the bad stuff."

"But there's so much of it, Caleb," I say, panting more than speaking.

"There's bad stuff everywhere, Domgirl. We're all surrounded by it."

And that's the difference. He's surrounded by badness and corruption and ugliness. So are Arla and Archie; so was Jess. But I'm not like all of them; all of that darkness exists because of me.

"Most of it is inside of me, Caleb," I reply. "I was literally born into darkness, thanks to Luba, and because I'm a slave to the moon, there's no true light inside of me. The only light I have is borrowed . . . from you and Archie, Arla, and especially Jess! She's given me her light even though I'm the last person on earth who deserves her forgiveness. I'm the reason she's dead! I'm the reason that Arla almost went blind and Archie's battling his demons and you . . ."

"What about me, Dominy?"

Caleb's words hit me hard, and I feel like I've been slapped in the face. What about my boyfriend? So far he's untouched, physically anyway, but emotionally, there must be scars, even if he's unwilling to look at them. Leave it to the girlfriend to expose them for him.

"You've changed because of me!" I cry. "You're not the same person!"

"No, I'm not."

Finally we can agree on something!

"I'm a better person for loving you!"

Not so fast! I jump off the bed, because being near Caleb has suddenly turned suffocating where a few moments ago it was invigorating. His words are still piercing my flesh, but instead of joining in with the rhythm of my heart, becoming part of the flow of my blood, they feel toxic. I know he's said those words to me before, we both have, but that was in the heat of passion, not in the boring light of day. Now that he's had time to think things over, think about our relationship rationally, he must be lying. How could he mean what he's saying?

"How can you possibly love me?"

My whisper is so soft, the only way Caleb can hear it is because it latches onto our invisible string and glides from my mouth to his ears, from my heart to his, and when my words reach their target I can feel my boyfriend's pain because it's my pain. We share the same agony, the same heartache, the same love.

Then it hits me. I don't know how it's possible, but Caleb truly loves me. And despite my conflicted feelings when we first started dating, despite the reservations I had when I realized my life would be forever cursed, despite my reluctance to bring Caleb along as a partner into my uncertain future, I love him too.

"Don't let your fear do the talking for you, Domgirl; speak with your heart," Caleb urges. "It doesn't matter why I love you. It only matters that I do, and I know you believe me when I say that."

I do, because I know my boyfriend wouldn't lie to me.

"So the only other important thing that we need to know is do you love me?"

And my boyfriend knows that I can't lie to him.

"Yes, Caleb, I do love you."

He smiles like he's looking at me for the first time, and in a way he is, because we both know that we're about to change our relationship forever. All the other times we stood on the edge were just practice. No more false starts; we're ready to jump.

"Then there's nothing left for us to say, is there?"

Caleb's words are filled with such joy and love and anticipation that he can hardly get them out before he kisses me, softer and harder than he's ever kissed me before. I push all thoughts of Luba and Nadine and her twins out of my mind. Thoughts of darkness are replaced with a blinding, passionate light that consumes the both of us, and willingly we surrender.

Only when Caleb starts to unbutton my shirt with fingers that are more nervous than eager do I fully realize what's going to happen.

"But it isn't Christmas yet," I remind him.

Smiling at me, half boy, half man, he can't stop himself from kissing me while he replies. "When I'm with you, Domgirl, every day is like Christmas."

Caleb is right. There are no more words to say, and so I don't waste time searching for them. I just give myself to my boyfriend, the person I trust more than any other living person I've ever met, the person I want to give myself to, body and heart and soul, the person I want to make love to.

Afterward, lying in his arms, naked underneath the covers, I start to gigglaugh, because there's really only one word to describe how it felt—*subarashi*.

*   *   *

And only one word to describe how it feels the next morning when Jeremy bursts into the room—*kimazui* a.k.a. Japanese for awkward.

"Hi, Dom, didn't think you'd still be here," Jeremy says cheerfully. "Thought you were going to head back home yesterday."

Ever the gentleman, Caleb takes the verbal lead. "We had a change of plans."

Although I'm fully dressed and Caleb's bed is made, I know that Jeremy knows what those plans entailed. Oddly, I'm not embarrassed; I really have no reason to be, because I haven't done anything wrong. All I feel is happy, and it seems like Jeremy feels the same way.

"I'm really glad to hear it," he says. "Life is too short, and you guys make the perfect couple."

So much for being an obnoxious college dude. Obviously, I'm not the only one who's changed; Jeremy's acting much different than the last time I saw him. Could it possibly have anything to do with Nadine's visits?

"How've you been, Jeremy?" I ask. "After . . . well, after everything."

The unspoken everything includes his sister's death, Rayna's unexplained disappearance, and the weird connection he has with Nadine.

"Honestly, I've never felt better," he declares. "You know better than anyone that Jess's death hit us all really hard. I wasn't sure how I'd get over that."

I squirm a bit in Caleb's desk chair. This is the first time I'm hearing Jeremy talk about how his sister's death affected him. As usual I have to tuck away the guilt and remorse and sorrow that I feel as the cause of that event. The feelings just never get any easier to control.

"Then when Rayna ran away . . . I still don't understand

that. . . . I mean I know she wasn't perfect, but I never once got the impression that she wanted to run away."

While Jeremy gazes at the rug, I glance over at Caleb and meet his gaze. We're both thinking the same thing: We'd love to tell Jeremy the truth, let him know that he's right, Rayna would never have run away from him or Weeping Water, but what's the alternative? Tell him the truth? Impossible. Luckily, Jeremy provides us with an out, so we don't have to offer any explanation.

"Guess you never know what's going on inside someone's mind, no matter how close you think you are to them."

Very true.

"Sometimes you don't even know what's going on in your own mind."

Very strange.

"What are you talking about, Jer?" Caleb asks for both of us.

Shrugging his shoulders, Jeremy seems more interested in putting away his freshly laundered clothes, courtesy of the washing machine back home at his family's house. "I don't know really," he starts. "Except that I feel like I'm coming out of a fog. Ever feel that way?"

No, but Barnaby said exactly the same thing to me once.

It's funny how one casual comment can fill in the blanks and shed light on a mystery that's been plaguing us all for months. And it's sad that the same act, making love, could end up with two totally different scenarios. For Caleb and me, it's brought us closer; even with Jeremy in the room I can feel the tug on our invisible string. I know that Caleb is right next to me, thinking about me, thinking about the wonderful experience we just shared and the beautiful memory that we'll carry with us for the rest of our lives. No matter if we stay together or if we drift apart, we will always remember that we were each other's first.

But Jeremy will never know that Nadine is carrying his

twins. At least I hope he never finds out. I hope he never connects the dots like I just did: the lifting fog; Nadine's visits; her previous pronouncements to me that neither Barnaby nor Caleb could be the father; Jess's anger at Nadine for doing something she won't get away with. If Nadine didn't use my brother or my boyfriend as a sperm donor, why not choose the brother of my best friend? In her warped mind, it's perfectly logical. My instincts are telling me that Nadine used Jeremy to get pregnant, and my instincts haven't failed me yet.

After Jeremy leaves to give us some going-away privacy, I concentrate on how gorgeous Caleb looks and how perfect he makes me feel, so he won't suspect that anything is happening to his roommate other than emerging from a period of depression. I must be doing a good job because Caleb's having a hard time letting me go.

"Have I told you how beautiful you are?"

"You have."

"And how wonderful you were?"

"You did."

"I knew it would be amazing, but . . . wow!"

"It was everything I dreamed it would be, Caleb," I tell him. "And more than I could ever have imagined."

Once again words fail us, so we just hold each other and kiss. Our bodies melt into one another, muscle and flesh and lips, all connecting, all desperate to remain united, until I open my eyes and look over at the clock on his nightstand.

"Sorry, Caleb," I say. "If I don't leave now I won't make it home before Louis gets back from his cop conference."

"They have cop conferences?" Caleb asks.

"In Nebraska they do."

"You don't think they have them all over?"

"I have no idea," I reply. "But why are we bantering about police business?"

"I just like to banter with you," Caleb says, smiling devilishly. "Among other things."

My gigglaughs and Caleb's high-pitched laughter fill up the room, the crumby little dorm room that will always hold a special place in my heart.

"Tell me everything!"

Jess's voice startles me. It's not accompanied by her golden light, and it literally blares at me the second I walk through my bedroom door.

"Where are you?" I ask the uncolored air.

"Right here!" she squeals.

Finally her body joins her voice, but once again it's a body that isn't shining as brightly as I've grown to expect. She's shimmering like she's somewhere off in the distance.

"Why do you look different?" I ask.

"I don't have much time left," she announces.

Her voice is flat and final, and just like with Jeremy I instinctively understand what she's trying to tell me even though she hasn't the strength to utter the words. Her time here on earth is coming to an end. For some reason she isn't going to be able to straddle both worlds much longer.

When I look at Jess, she looks away, so I know I'm right. How can this be happening? How can something so heartbreaking follow something so magical? I've just connected with Caleb on such a deep level, in a way that has left me feeling euphoric, and now my best friend and I are about to be ripped apart. How is that possible?

"It isn't like it's going to happen in the next second, Dominy," Jess corrects me. "But it will happen soon."

I don't want it to be soon; I don't want it to be ever! I want to stay connected to Jess for the rest of my life! I don't care how selfish that sounds; that's what I want! *Oh, will you listen to yourself, Dominy! Stop thinking about yourself and think about Jess! Think about what she's going through, a spirit, some kind of ghost, all by herself.*

"Are you happy, Jess?" I ask.

"I am," she replies without hesitation. "It's truly astonishing here, Dom, I think it'll take me a few eternities to explore it in its entirety."

Her words should make me feel better, and they do partly, but I really just wish she could stay.

"Remember, Dominy, you have a part of me inside of you," Jess says. "So it's kind of like I do get to stay."

Regardless of that fact, our time is still running out, so I don't want to waste time thinking and worrying about the future. I want to gossip about the present.

"It was everything I dreamed it would be, Jess," I share. "Just beautiful."

Lying next to me on my bedroom floor, Jess grabs my hand, and it's covered in sunlight. "I'm so happy for you," she says. "For both of you."

Then why do I detect such sadness in her voice? It doesn't take me long to figure it out.

"I'm sorry it's something you never got to experience," I say.

"Don't be silly," Jess replies. "As crazy as it sounds, sex doesn't matter over here."

What?! That is crazy. But not as crazy as Jess's next comment.

"If you want to defeat Nadine, you have to listen to Caleb," she says. "You and Luba have to work together."

"That's crazier!" I shout.

"It's your only chance."

It can't be! I was planning on using Luba like she used me, but work with her? Cozy up to the psycho? I don't think I could do that even if I were all wolf all the time.

"Don't fight me on this, Dom," Jess says. "There isn't enough time. You have to prove to Luba that you and she can be allies."

"How can I possibly do that?!" I ask. "Luba knows that I despise her."

"Let Vera help you."

Vera?

"Can she really help me defeat Nadine?"

Jess turns to look at me, and I see my best friend's face, but when she speaks I know I'm once again hearing a message from an Omikami. I know I have to trust what she says even if I don't understand the true meaning of her words.

"Why do you think Orion sent her?"

Chapter 16

If Vera has Orion's blessing, how in the world can that be good? And why in the world would I want to learn from someone who's in cahoots with Luba's idol? Sometimes Jess really doesn't make any sense; it's like she's in her own private world and has her own set of rules and has completely lost touch with reality.

Sometimes I can be such an idiot. That's exactly where Jess is, in her own world or at least in Omikamiworld, a place that has a different set of rules than we have down here on earth, and her grasp on reality is loosening; she's being pulled farther and farther away from me and closer to *her* new reality.

I don't even realize I'm holding on to the thick trunk of The Weeping Lady's oak for support until I press my hand so hard into the tree I can practically feel its rough flesh through my gloves. I can't lose Jess, not yet, not now! I don't care how selfish that sounds; I don't care that our relationship has continued long after it should have been severed; I don't care if there are other people in my life willing to step into the best friend role. Jess is irreplaceable.

Closing my eyes to welcome the blackness, I swim in that sea of nothing, pushing all thoughts out of my head. The feeling lasts for about three seconds. After that the deep black void bursts into golden sunshine, and I see Jess floating, lazily twirling her hand in the air, making sparkly circles of yellow light. Bringing light where there was darkness, bringing a smile where there was sadness, bringing peace where there was only havoc. Bringing into focus that other side of me that sometimes I can't reach. If Jess leaves for good, will she take that piece of me with her?

Remember, Dominy, who you really are.

The cryptic comment wraps around my eyes like a cold compress. I try to let the words sink in so that they can be interpreted by my brain, but the sensation just remains on my skin, enveloping me, but not penetrating. They're just words with no meaning, coming from some unknown voice. Until I listen without my ears.

The gasp that escapes my throat is loud and sudden and revitalizing; it brings me back to life, back to my own reality, even if I would rather burrow through the cold earth and live among The Weeping Lady's tangled roots for the rest of my life. Still leaning on the tree for support, I look up to the sky and watch an innocent cloud be stretched apart like an unfortunate piece of cotton candy that's being mutilated by several pairs of greedy hands. When the cloud is ripped into puffy shreds, I can see what it had been hiding; I can see what was lying behind it, just out of reach, just beyond this reality. I can see the faintest trace of Orion's constellation.

As is often the case, I don't know if I'm looking through my own eyes or the wolf's, but I have to stop thinking in dualities; I have to stop categorizing. I am a girl, and I am a wolf, not either-or, but one and the same. It's time I accepted that concept, because it isn't going to change. Regardless of the reason, I can see the murky outline of three stars in one line, not touching, but connected. Their light is dim, but their presence is overwhelming.

Remember, Dominy, who you really are.

I've never heard this voice before, and yet I know exactly whom it belongs to. Orion. The Original Hunter. Luba's god. The demon who gave her the power to curse my father and me, now trying to offer advice. *I don't want any advice from you! I just want you to leave my family and me alone!*

Remember, Dominy, I am your family now.

NO!

The third time I ram my fist into the tree, the few leaves remaining on The Weeping Lady's branches rustle loudly in the wind, as if to compel me to stop. Hurting someone else never eases your own pain, no matter how good it may feel in the moment of release. I whisper "I'm sorry" to The Weeping Lady, and she replies by relinquishing one leaf as a sacrifice. It falls slowly, sliding bumpily down the unruly waves of my hair, then spiraling horizontally like a roasted pig on a skewer until freefalling to the frosty grass. Bending down to examine the leaf, I see that we have a lot in common. While it's still mainly green, there are blotches of brown on its surface, and its center is starting to become brittle and worn. It's still intact from its journey, but it's beginning to show signs of becoming weary.

Orion's voice is clinging to my memory. I don't know if the sound is still alive and echoing or if I'm mentally playing it over and over and over again in my mind. I detest the way it sounds, because it's not at all the way it should be; he sounds kind and reassuring and fatherly. He should sound unnatural, as if words are uncommon to him and have to be yanked out of his throat by a clawing hand. Instead, his words demand attention.

But as sickening as his words may sound, they're true. My knees crash into the ground, and I hear the leaf crunch underneath the weight of my body. The Weeping Lady's offering is gone, severed into many tiny pieces like the cloud thousands of miles above. Destruction is rampant because I am part of Orion and a part of Luba and Nadine as well. A cold wind showers down on me and pushes me to the earth, and I realize I'm the same as Nadine's unborn children. All three of us are children of darkness.

The same way my innocence was tainted by Luba's curse, Nadine's innocent twins are going to be tainted by her sins. They'll have no say in their future, just like I had no say in mine. They'll inherit a legacy of evil, and with Nadine as their mother and mentor and guide, they'll embrace their darkborn legacy just as I've had to embrace my curse. Even if they accept it with reluctance, with Nadine at the helm of their lives, they will accept it as their fate.

Slowly I feel my body stand up, and I finally regain my balance so I don't have to lean into the tree for support to stand. But I'm still not comfortable. I feel a gnawing at my knee, not a pain, more like an itch, and I look down to see that the remnants of the leaf are stuck against my jeans, three separate pieces of what was once one leaf pressed against me. One by one the pieces fall to the ground, landing in one straight line until it's as if the wind rises from inside the cold blades of grass and the pieces are torn from each other and scatter. Even with my wolf vision I can't see where they go; they're lost to me and to each other.

This time when revelation consumes me, I don't let out a gasp, probably because I'm too shocked that such a horrid thought could voluntarily enter my brain, but sometimes the world is a horrid place. The best way to stop Nadine from creating her own bloodline of evil is to stop her children from ever being born. Kill her spawn before they're hatched.

The girl is appalled by such a thought; the wolf just licks its fangs.

Once again I'm reminded that I'm not two things any longer; I'm one. Part of me might be disgusted by the idea of killing innocent children, but the other part of me understands that it's necessary. But could I actually do such a thing? Could I actually listen to the wolf voice, the hunter, Orion's descendant, and destroy two lives before they can take their first breath, simply because they will grow up determined to destroy everything in their path? Wipe out the source of misery and evil and violence before it has a chance to begin? Is that what Jess means when she says I have to learn from Vera?

No! Absolutely not! Jess may be in another realm, forces may be pulling us apart like a cloud, but she could not condone such a heinous act. Especially after she was duped into believing that killing Barnaby was a solution. She might still be impulsive and carefree and brazen, but she wouldn't be so reckless. There may be a lot Vera can teach me, a lot that I need to learn, but twinicide is not part of it.

I look up at the sky, and Orion's constellation is twinkling in the midday sun, as if anointing me with three gold stars, agreeing with me. I think I just passed my first test.

Louis is about to take his own personalized exam.

"Melinda?"

Arla and I are thrilled to hear the question mark firmly nailed at the end of her name when Louis opens the front door. He's as surprised to see her standing on the other side of the doorway as we are; her sudden appearance is unexpected. Hopefully it's also unwanted. I mean what the hell is she doing here? Ringing the front bell as if the welcome mat's message extended to everyone including homicidal housewives, two-timing tramps, and unmotherly mothers. Okay, I'm done. But Louis isn't.

"I told you not to show up like this," he announces, his voice emotionless and flat. "I don't want to see you anymore."

Burabō! Which is Japanese for bravo! The Jaffog has truly lifted, and Louis is able to see and think and react clearly. And he clearly doesn't want Melinda in his life.

"And I told you that I'm not giving you up without a fight," she replies. "Merry Christmas."

"Christmas isn't for another week," Louis reminds her.

"I thought I'd give you your present early," she replies, walking right into the living room and revealing a large red ribbon from behind her back. "Me."

Būinguhisu! Which is Japanese for boo hiss! Clearly Melinda doesn't like to take no for an answer. Nor does this gift-giver like an audience.

"Why don't you two be good little girls and give the grown-ups some privacy?" she asks.

Neither Arla nor I budge from the couch where we're co-reading a fashion magazine. Sadly, I have to admit that Melinda looks like she belongs right on the front cover. Wearing form-fitting Lycra-infused pants the color of Louis's mocha-tinted skin, tucked into chocolate-brown cowboy boots, and topped with an espresso-colored double-breasted suede bolero jacket, Melinda certainly dressed for the occasion. Too bad her occasion was to try and seduce her ex-boyfriend fully clothed and Arla's occasion is to save her father from becoming an ex ex-boyfriend fully committed.

"As a good girl, I know what's best for my father," Arla starts. "And that isn't to be alone in a room with you or accept gifts from strange women."

While Melinda scowls, Louis laughs at his daughter's comment, which only makes Melinda scowl deeper. If the look weren't so frightening, it would be interesting, like some avant-garde fashion shoot, but the problem is Melinda Jaffe isn't a model; she's a murderer. I can tell by Arla's nervous stare that she's remembered that Louis, the only professional detective in the room, hasn't got a clue to that fact.

"What's the problem, Melinda?" he asks. "Winston dump you too?"

At least Louis has his moxie back and he isn't falling for his ex's pathetic attempt to reunite. Unfortunately, his ex may have more than just a reunion on her mind.

"You haven't seen the last of me, Louis," she declares.

"Because when a Jaffe woman wants something, a Jaffe woman gets it."

Her reply doesn't have its desired effect, and Louis merely laughs louder and heartier than I've ever heard him before. Like a desperate out-of-work actor auditioning to be a street-corner Santa.

"Did you practice that line in front of a mirror?!" he asks, the words barely identifiable among his cackles.

Louis is too busy howling with laughter to see Melinda crush the red ribbon in her hand, destroying any semblance of holiday cheer or goodwill that she might have brought with her and unveiling her true malicious nature. She may not be a supernatural power like the rest of the women in her family, but she's something almost as deadly, a sociopath who will stop at nothing to get what she thinks is rightfully hers.

"Merry Christmas, Melinda," Louis says, practically pushing her out the door. "Thanks for the laugh. I needed that."

Slamming the door in front of her face, Louis is consumed with another round of guffaws. "All right, girls, there's going to be a full moon tonight, so I have to gather up the troops to go track a killer."

Louis has no idea he's just insulted one.

"Did you see her face?" Arla asks me when her father is upstairs and out of earshot.

"She was Jaffurious!" I reply.

"In the grips of a Jaffrenzy!" Arla adds.

"Like the Bride of Jaffrankenstein!" I double add.

Oops.

"Dom, you realize that the only thing that a bride wants is a husband," Arla says. "We have to protect my father."

I promise Arla that I'll do everything I can to protect Louis from the clutches of Melindastein, but it's not an easy promise to keep when I'm standing underneath the full moon in the bowels of Robin's Park and I know that somewhere nearby Louis is rallying his posse to hunt me down and kill me. Before I can be anyone's protector, I have to protect myself.

The hunger is so potent and powerful and pervasive that I welcome the transformation. Let my body be devoured by the curse; I can't wait to feed. The howl that escapes my lips and passes my teeth and then my fangs is much more of a warning to every animal nearby that I am about to hunt than it is an expression of the agonizing pain ripping through my body. The hunter has arrived.

My snout is practically buried inside the deer's body as I ravage its flesh and blood and innards. One large paw is placed on the dying animal's neck, not that it can escape, but because I want it to die knowing that it had no chance against me. Like I have no chance against what's coming.

I've sensed it, I've felt it, and now it's finally here. I look up, expecting to see a sign, some major revelation that will explain everything, give fact to the feeling I've been having these past months, the feeling that help has arrived to aid me in my fight against the dark forces threatening to swallow me up whole—but nothing. Just dark sky, empty, still. The skies may be quiet, but the earth is roaring.

I swallow hard and rest my chin on the unmoving deer carcass. The intoxicating smell wafts up from the beast's body and threatens to distract me, but I must remain focused because I'm about to have company. There are voices in the distance, angry, hushed whispers filled with desperation and loathing and fear, and they're all directed at me. Killers are coming, so I need to move. Now!

Into the darkness I run, faster than ever before. My paws are hitting the hard earth so fiercely that I know I must be bruising my flesh, slamming down on stones and twigs and lone patches of ice in an attempt to outrun my pursuers. I swerve to the right, then a quick turn to the left, racing around and in between clusters of trees, following my gut, not knowing exactly where I'm running to, but certain that I'm running toward something. That feeling of certainty is ripped from me when I feel myself falling in midair.

I didn't see the cliff. I didn't know it existed until it was several yards behind me, and now my legs are scrambling to find land that isn't there. The only thing surrounding me is the cold night breeze. Give in, I tell myself, give in to the feeling of surrender. *You've run as far and as fast as you could; the only thing you can do now is relax and let the wind guide you to your destination.* When I crash into a bevy of rocks, some are rounded, some are jagged, all are painful and unwelcoming to my body, and I know my odyssey is over. I've come to the end.

Or is it just the beginning?

I don't know where I am. This is a new part of the woods, a part I've never been in before as a wolf or a girl, but I feel at home. I'm not afraid even when the light from the night sky is so bright it's blinding and I can't see anything except a silvery-white canvas. The entire landscape, the whole world around me has been erased, and what's left behind is only the truth.

The light begins to recede and swirl, and through the motion I can see slivers of a midnight blue sky, tall, lush pine trees, the glowing, all-knowing moon. And then the motion stops, so all I can see are three shining stars. Orion's constellation looking down at me, demanding my attention. I'm too weak and too curious to deny my rapture, so I relinquish. *Show me; show me your truth.*

I can feel pressure on the left side of my snout, an invisible finger guiding me to turn my head so I can see what's happening in the distance. When I see Vera standing alone in a hollowed-out patch of the woods, I'm not surprised. I always knew that she was not in Weeping Water by coincidence, but for a reason; Jess confirmed that. I'm about to learn why. But something isn't right; no, no, something is terribly wrong.

Vera turns to face me, and it's as if she's standing right in front of me. I can see her so clearly. I don't know if it's my doing or hers, but the result is the same: I see everything she's doing as if she's under a microscope. Her smile is genuine; the rest of her body is a fake.

My belly scrapes against the rocks underneath me when I try to scramble away from the sight, when I try to run and flee and escape from what I'm witnessing, but I can't move. Vera has come a long way and waited for this moment, and she will not let something as irrelevant as my fear stand in the way of her unveiling.

Horrified, I watch as Vera raises her right hand to her face and presses the index and middle fingers into her eye, deep, deep into the socket, to reach behind her eyeball. The smile never fades; the pain that should be rippling through her body as she gouges out her eye never comes, because unlike me, her human form is simply a shell. In fact she is so far from being human, pain is not a concept she can understand or suffer from; she's above such primitive feelings.

Finally she releases her eyeball from her face; she removes it from its socket. Immediately a gust of silver light shoots out from her eye, the same color and texture and brightness as the light that used to encase Nadine's body before it turned black with hate and sin. Vera repeats the actions, and soon she's holding both her eyes in her hand, discarded marbles rolling in her palm, bouncing off of one another, a layer of ooze covering them, making her hands slick.

Now two rays of silver light are shooting out of her eyes like laser beams. She looks up toward the sky, and immediately the stars in Orion's constellation pulse with recognition. I'm not the only one who's come home.

The light from the stars shoots down to the earth and greets the two lines emanating from Vera's body. At impact the world around me is doused in radiant starlight; every tree, every bush, every animal is covered in the warm rays of the constellation. Vera disappears in the star embrace, consumed by the unearthly energy, but she doesn't cry out in pain or fear or agony; shrieks of joy and ecstasy fill the night. She might be from this world, but she isn't of this earth.

I am unable to control myself any longer; a howl disturbs the night. I can see my voice penetrate the starlight, making it ripple like a stone skimming across a pond until it stops when it must reach Vera's body or where her body used to be. It's hard to see clearly within the dense illumination, even for wolf eyes.

"Don't move."

The voice sounds like Vera's, but not quite; same authoritative tone, but deeper, more grounded even though her body or her spirit is flowing freely in the air.

I try to will my body to acquiesce, but I fail and turn to run in the opposite direction. After only a few paces I tumble to the ground, my neck and chin hitting the cold earth hard. Wiggling violently on my side, I desperately try to get upright, but I can't, which makes sense when I see that my legs are tied together with silver light. Instinct takes over, and I'm about to struggle against these ropes until I see Vera standing in front of me. She looks almost the same as she does in school, just a teenaged girl, but with two shining silver orbs instead of eyes.

"I have not come here to hurt you."

I don't believe her, because now I recognize the voice. It's a melding of Orion and Vera, both speaking to me at the same time.

"I have come here to help you."

My rough growl translates into words that Vera can hear.

"You know I speak the truth," she replies. "I cannot lie to a member of my own family."

I am not part of your family!!!

"Don't fight what cannot be changed," Vera/Orion says. "Fight against what should never be."

To hell with these ropes! I rub my body against the dirt to try and break free, and suddenly the light fastenings disappear. I had nothing to do with it; I don't have the power to fight this thing. It just knows I'm not going anywhere even if I'm not tied up.

"What are you?!"

As expected, my silent question is heard. When I hear the answer, I can't believe it, even though it's the most logical thing I've ever heard.

"I'm a fallen star sent by Orion to come to earth."

"Why?!"

"To reset balance to the world."

Vera bends down so her face is only an inch from mine. Her starlight is just as bright, but for some reason it is no longer blinding; it's comforting, and I feel tears well up in my eyes, because I know there's only one reason for that: Her starlight is familiar to me.

"The Original Hunter is not happy with how His power is being abused," she says, now sounding more like Vera, the girl, and not some insane entity. "I've been dispatched here to set things right before the path becomes irreversible."

Her words are mysterious, their message unclear, and yet I understand completely.

"You've come to stop Nadine," I say. "You're going to stop her from carrying out her plans."

Or I know nothing at all.

"No, you are."

What?! I've been waiting for something to come; I've felt it in my guts; I'm never wrong! And now you're telling me that you've come all this way, from the stars in the heavens, and you're not going to help me?! I have to do all the work alone!

"Do as your friend Jess instructed," Vera insists. "And listen to me, Dominy."

How dare this fiend mention Jess's name?!

"You are going to stop Nadine from turning Orion's original plans into her own," Vera states. "You are going to prevent Nadine from turning the Original Hunter into something vile and vicious and vindictive, but you are not going to do it alone."

Well, if you're not going to help me, who is?

"I am."

I know the voice before the starlight fades to reveal the woman standing behind Vera, the woman I couldn't see before, but the woman I know all too well.

Luba.

"It's time we worked together, Dominy," Luba says. She sounds humble, which could be a result of her standing in the shadow of the starwoman. "It's time the werewolf and the witch joined forces to defeat our common enemy."

What? Our common enemy? Who are you talking about?

"Wolf or girl, in whatever state you're in, you really are a fool!" Luba seethes, her voice now void of any humility. "I'm talking about my granddaughter, Nadine. I don't know what her plan is, but I know that she wants to be rid of me; she wants to have all the power for herself!"

You want me to help you defeat her?

"No, you cursed creature," Luba whispers loud enough to fill up the infinite skies above. "I want you to help me destroy her!"

Part 2

First there was the moon
that cursed my name

Then there was the sun
that revealed my shame

Now the stars have joined
to play this deadly game

Will the horrors of this nightmare
depart as quickly as they came?

And when my story is finally over
Will I be revered
or condemned
to suffer the blame?

Chapter 17

Be careful what you wish for, because one day it may come true.

A star may fall to the earth on a mission to restore balance in the world that it watches from a heavenly distance. A witch may extend her skinny arm to reveal an olive branch clutched in her magical fingers. And a girl disguised as a wolf may have to make a choice that could change the course of her life yet again.

What is happening?! Vera wants me to work with Luba in order to destroy Nadine, a pairing that has obviously been given Luba's blessing, even though I thought Vera and Luba were enemies. Maybe they are; maybe this is a way of keeping your friends close and your enemies closer. Luba may consider Vera the devil, but since Luba loves to dabble in black magic, perhaps it's a perfect pairing. Luba and Dominy? Could this also be a match made in the heavens?

The growl that spills out of my mouth is like a release of the anger and confusion and wariness that I'm feeling. I don't like these two women—creatures, things, whatever they are—standing in front of me. I don't trust them, and I want them to understand I will no longer be used. I have been used since before I was born, nothing more than the plaything of a widow's vindictiveness, and I refuse to allow anyone to use me any longer.

Neither of them seem bothered by the guttural sound or even fazed by it, which only makes the sound grow and causes my mouth to open wider and my neck to expand and lengthen. Damn them! Damn them for cursing me and for bringing filth into my life! Damn them for expecting me to work alongside this foul woman to stop this curse from festering and becoming uncontrollable! I don't know if my growls contain words or if these things can read my mind, but they both understand what I'm thinking.

"I didn't curse you, Dominy," Vera states.

Her tone is flat, and it's hard to gauge her expression, because her eyes have been replaced by two shimmering orbs of starlight. Not that she ever had eyes to begin with or a face or a body; she's a complete imposter, fleshless, a husk containing the body of one of Orion's stars.

"Luba cursed me and my family using the power of Orion," I reply. "If you're part of Orion, then you're part of the curse."

Vera bends and lowers her head toward me so I'm bathed in starlight. I should be blinded, but it's as if I can see clearer, like I can see right into the core of her existence.

"Being part of the source does not mean I joined in with Luba to curse you," Vera rationalizes. "The same way that Dominy was part of the wolf that killed Jess, but Dominy can never be considered Jess's murderer."

Don't say her name! Don't spoil Jess's goodness by trying to connect yourself to her!

"We're all connected, you fool!" Luba shrieks. "Have you learned nothing? Have you not yet learned that connection and balance and energy all come from the same source? They cannot be separated."

I refuse to believe that Luba and I come from the same

source! I refuse to believe that Luba and I share any of the same qualities. Luba is a bloodhungry, hateful murderer!

"YES!!"

Luba's confirmation of my scathing assessment of her character is less a word and more a euphoric cry. She revels in the fact of what she is and how she is perceived; she accepts it, which only proves that she's sicker and more revolting than I ever imagined. Or maybe it just makes her more honest.

"And so are you!" she cries. "You are consumed with the desire to kill the moment you transform. You fight your primitive God-given urges to destroy until they consume you and you have no choice but to obey the higher power. We are the same, Dominy, wolf or girl. We are the same!"

My body lurches forward, but stops abruptly, and only the desperate, fearful howl that escapes me continues to move forward. I want to follow that lucky sound; I want to float on its back and soar far away from here so I don't have to deal with this woman, so I don't have to make any choices, so I don't have to accept the fact that she's right! Damn her, but she's right!!

I was born into darkness, I am a descendant of Orion, I am connected to Luba—it's all true, I know that, but I don't have to revel in that darkness; I don't have to destroy and kill and hate.

"That's why you must work with Luba."

Vera's quiet voice is almost lost amongst the shouting going on inside my head.

"Just because you are a child of darkness doesn't mean you have to live a dark life," she explains. "You have a choice. Just as Orion does."

What?! Orion is like a child?

"We're all like children, Dominy," Vera continues. "Orion could shine His light in another direction, ignore how His power is being abused, but He has chosen to become involved. He has sent me here as a messenger of hope, like your friend Napoleon said."

"The Original Hunter is offering hope?"

Starlight glides down my fur tenderly and wraps itself around me, spreading both warmth and coolness throughout my body at the same time.

"Not all angels are good and not all demons are evil," she says. "Orion has immense power that He has offered to some here on earth, but sometimes He feels the need to intervene when that power threatens to cause more chaos than order."

"And he feels Nadine is going to abuse his power?" I ask.

"My granddaughter believes she is more powerful and vital than Orion," Luba interjects. "She believes she can rise higher than the stars and contain more power than the moon, and she *must* be stopped."

I notice that there's a small space in between Vera and Luba that is empty, not touched by starlight or black energy, a void where neither of them can exist. It's where I want to be, in a space where neither of them can reach me. My silent request is accepted.

"Work with me to put Nadine in her place and I will grant you that peace."

I stare at Luba for a long while to make sure that I understand what she's saying. I play the words around in my head several times, but always come back to the same conclusion: She's offering me a truce.

"If I cross the line and become your ally," I say, "you'll leave me and my family and my friends alone?"

Even though I don't speak the words out loud, the sound in my head is still shivering with possibility and disbelief. It feels like an eternity before Luba responds.

"Yes."

"You see, Dominy," Vera starts. "Balance can be restored."

I hear a rustling in a near-barren tree to my right, and I

look up to see a gorgeous, vividly colored butterfly, floating in between the branches. A burst of red and yellow amid faded shadows, a sign of hope beginning to move within the bowels of the darkness.

"Then I agree," I say. "I will help you."

I sense a smile buried within the starlight. "Orion will be pleased," Vera replies. "And Orion never forgets. Luba can attest to that."

Haughtily, Luba raises her chin and then her arm in my direction. She touches her pinky and thumb together and points the remaining three fingers at me, extending her arm until her fingers press against the crown of my skull. Faint pressure, but I can feel the dark heat emanating from her body. She's branding me with her sign.

"We are now bound by the light of Orion," she hisses. "Do not betray me!"

Keep your end of the bargain, and I'll keep mine.

I shake my head free of Luba's touch—she is my partner, not my master—and open my mouth, not to let out a sound or a warning, but as a reminder. I have powers too.

The cloud of red smoke tumbles out of my mouth. I have no idea where it comes from, if it's a tangible rendering of my wolf soul, if it's being given to me by Orion or some other outside force, but in times of attack or incredible focus, I can will it into existence. We all watch as the red energy hovers in the air in front of Luba and then expands and bursts like a blood shower all over Luba's body. There are no remnants, no proof that it ever existed once it is gone except the memory and the knowledge that I have branded Luba as well.

"Now we are bound by my spirit!" I cry. "So do not betray *me!*"

Furious yet impressed, Luba responds by spinning her body around several times until there's no bone or flesh or hair, only black smoke that lingers behind after she disappears into the night. I don't know if she felt the need to put on a more masterful display or if she just grew tired of being in the presence of two people she despises. Whatever the reason it's now only Vera and me in the clearing.

"Go and rest now," Vera instructs. "There is much work to be done."

Vera's starlight gazes deep into my wolf-girl eyes and uncovers what lies inside my heart.

"I know you don't trust Luba, and I know you don't fully trust me either," she says. "So only trust yourself."

A fool could give me the same advice, and I'd be a fool not to take it. Starting right now.

I hear Louis before he speaks. About five hundred yards to my left there's a shift in my surroundings, a new noise, someone taking a step forward, closer to his prey, me.

"I found it!" Louis screams.

With nowhere to hide in the clearing, I flatten myself onto the dusty ground just as I hear the gunshot. Raising my eyes I see the bullet fly straight through Vera's star-glistened body. Vera billows as if she's a breeze, and when the movement stops I see that the bullet has created a hole in her stomach from which rays of blinding starlight shoot out. This light is much more powerful than the light coming out of her eyes, perhaps because it was released violently and not as a result of Vera's own actions; I'm not sure. All I know is that I can now only hear Vera's voice; her body is gone.

"Run!" she commands.

"Where? There isn't any cover!"

"Just run!" Her voice carries an unexpected quality of human desperation. "If Orion's wish is to be fulfilled, you must not be harmed."

A quick calculation tells me that the closest refuge is straight ahead, so I leap through pieces of Vera's starshine and run blindly, wildly forward until I'm outside of the clearing and at the entrance to a more densely covered part of the woods. Before I run too far within the belly of the forest, I crouch low and turn around, my panting banging against my ears, and I have to fight the urge to run right back into the openness.

"Don't hurt him!"

I know Vera can hear me, but she ignores my plea. She's too busy wrapping Louis in her starlight and slamming him into the ground. His eyes are wide not so much with terror, but disbelief. His mind isn't working fast enough; it simply can't fathom what's happening to him. I've had a much longer history of dealing with supernatural occurrences, and I'm still having a hard time believing what I'm seeing. Louis looks like a bull being lassoed by an unseen wrangler. One who is showing absolutely no mercy.

Bang! His shoulder rams onto the ground, only to be buoyed up again several feet into the air. Slam! His back crashes onto the dirt so hard that a brown cloud swirls up, comingling with Vera's light.

"Stop it!!"

My cry drowns out the sound of Louis's final plummet. Vera has either listened to me or she's simply satisfied that Louis will no longer be a nuisance this evening. He is lying on the ground, unmoving. I have to listen with all my wolf-hearing to detect any sign of his breathing. It's shallow, but it's there.

"I would never kill him," Vera claims. "But he had to be stopped before he killed you."

She might have stopped Louis, but his backup is still ready to fight.

"Go!" Vera screams. "Now!"

Certain that I'll follow her command, Vera and her light disintegrate before my eyes, and I'm left alone. Just as I'm about to turn and run I hear Luba's words again—*do not betray me*—and I'm frozen. If I've made a pact not to betray Luba, how can I turn my back on Louis? After all he's done for me, how can I flee and think of my own safety when he could be dying? I know Vera said she wouldn't kill him, but how do I know some other animal won't come out of hiding after I leave and devour Louis like I've devoured so many living creatures before? No, I must stay until I know that Louis will be safe.

When I hear Officer Gallegos's voice, I know that my good deed may end in compromising my own safety.

"Captain!"

Gallegos scours the area quickly before running toward his superior, immediately pressing his fingers against Louis's neck to check for a pulse.

"Hold on, Chief," Gallegos says.

"Gallegos!"

The cry comes from the other side of the clearing, and, without seeing the man's face, I recognize the voice; it's Officer Owenski. Older and wiser than Gallegos, he may not move as quickly as his younger counterpart, but his movements are sharper, developed over years of training and experience, and he has skills the more reckless Gallegos may never master.

"It got him!" Gallegos cries. "The damned thing got him!"

Ignoring his fellow detective's emotional outburst, Owenski pulls out his radio, never taking his eyes off of the surrounding area, and calls in an ambulance request to meet them on the north side of Robin's Park. Two other men rush into the clearing, one a civilian, the other a police officer, and Owenski instructs them to carry Louis's body to the awaiting ambulance.

"Be careful with him," he orders. "We don't know the extent of his injuries, but we have to get him to the hospital."

Dutifully, the two men lift Louis up, one at his feet, the other at his shoulders, and carry him out of the clearing to safety. Gallegos is pacing the clearing, and instinctively I retreat deeper into the brush, even though I know he can't see me from this distance. He isn't even looking; he's found something else that he finds far more interesting.

"Owenski!" he calls out. "Look at this."

The two men stare at the ground that is illuminated by their flashlights as if they're looking into a black hole, as if they've stumbled upon the key that will unlock a profound mystery. They haven't found the key, but they've uncovered the door.

"Look at those prints," Gallegos says.

"Well, I'll be," Owenski replies.

"Human *and* wolf prints," Gallegos states, his voice filled with both shock and excitement. "Maybe Lars was right."

"What?"

"Maybe I was attacked by a werewolf."

Gallegos swirls his flashlight all around, and I practically bury myself into the ground to hide, but there's no way I can leave; I have to hear what else they have to say. What are they going to do with this newfound information?

"Or maybe it's some joker who wants us to think it's a werewolf," Owenski replies. When he speaks again, his voice is no longer calm. "Do you have Louis's gun?"

"No," Gallegos replies. "He must have had it on him."

"He didn't," Owenski confirms. "I checked while you were trying not to freak out."

"I wasn't *freaking out!*" Gallegos says defiantly. "I was saving . . ."

"We can debate it later!" Owenski interrupts. "We have to find that gun, or we just might have an *armed* werewolf on the loose!"

I may not be armed, but if they find me they'll still be satisfied. There's nothing more I can do here to ensure Louis's safety; his team has taken care of that. It's time for me to leave. The wolf has done everything he can; soon it will be the girl's chance to take over.

*   *   *

The next day at school, the last before our Christmas break, I try to convince myself that last night was a dream. I didn't find out Vera was a fallen star, I didn't commit to working with Luba, and I didn't overhear Louis's detectives continue to entertain the idea that not only do werewolves exist, but that one is roaming our woods. I do a pretty good job of it too until I literally bump into Vera on the way to my last class. Racing around the corner of the hallway to grab my French textbook out of my locker, I don't see Vera until we slam into each other.

"I told you Louis wouldn't be harmed," she declares.

And she was right. Louis spent a total of twenty minutes in the hospital, most of the time unconscious, while the doctors performed a battery of tests on him, all of which came back negative. And when he came back to consciousness he arrived with no memory of what had taken place right before he blacked out.

He told us this morning that all he could remember was thinking that he saw a wolf, shooting at it, and passing out. He doesn't even recall being attacked.

Looking at Vera now, I search for a clue that she isn't human, that she really is a piece of Orion's constellation walking on earth, and I can't find one. Her disguise is foolproof. At least she can be taken at her word; she said she wouldn't harm Louis, and she didn't.

"Thank you," I reply. "There's just one thing though. Louis can't find his gun."

Vera smiles conspiratorially and reaches into her schoolbag to reveal Louis's missing gun. "That's because I took it."

"What are you doing?!" I shout, immediately positioning myself in front of her so if anyone passes by they won't see what she's holding. "Do you know what'll happen if you get caught with a gun at school?"

"And do you know what'll happen if you let the hunter keep his gun that's filled with silver bullets?" Vera asks.

Silver bullets?

"Louis may not understand what he's dealing with," Vera replies. "But he harbors enough instinct and superstition to take precautions."

I always knew that Louis's Creole background had empowered him with a different type of knowledge than the typical Nebraskan cop, but I really didn't think he would go so far as to load his gun with silver bullets, the only kind that can kill me. Guess I was wrong. About that and a lot of other things.

Vera places the gun in my locker and then slams the door shut. I make a mental note to bury the stolen item after school in case I forget that it's there and Dumbleavy decides to do a school-wide locker search for drugs and other illegal items when we return after Christmas break. She looks directly into my eyes, and she looks like every other girl in this school, but I know that she's so different she's practically unexplainable. Just as unexplainable is the question of why she's going to such great lengths to protect me. Sure, she needs me to work with Luba to thwart Nadine's plans, but Vera's preternatural, for God's sake. Why does she need me to do her dirty work?

"You really should brush up on your Greek mythology, Dominy," she says, reading my mind.

Random! Before I can ask what her odd comment is supposed to mean, she continues, "I thought that giving you one of the only weapons that can truly kill you might convince you that it's time for you to do the right thing."

Frightened, but curious, I ask, "And what exactly would be the right thing to do?"

"Maybe it's time you told Louis the truth."

Chapter 18

I feel like I'm in limbo. In that space that isn't before or after, that space that's filled with worry and anticipation and excitement, not truly free, not truly a prisoner, and thankfully not alone.

Sitting in our basement I'm surrounded by the Wolf Pack, wasting time during that universal limbo period, the time between Christmas and New Year's Day when the trivialities and regular pulse of life go on hiatus and leave us hanging until their return after the first of the new year. It's usually a time when most of the world slows down to breathe easier and more fully, to indulge in forgotten pleasures, to reconnect with family and friends. Unfortunately, my inner circle is about to expand.

"So now that you and Luba are some sort of supercouple like Gwenaby, I think we should refer to you as Domuba," Arla suggests. "No, wait!! Lubominy!"

I hate it, and yet I love it at the same time.

"I think I'm finally getting the hang of this newmenclature," Arla squeals. "Oh my God I did it again!"

Leave it to Arla to make me laugh. Gigglaughing may be

inappropriate, but despite its implications, Lubominy really is a terrific word.

"So it's kind of like Orion gave you the perfect Christmas gift," Arla states.

And gigglaughs are officially silenced to allow reality to regain control.

"Sure, instead of a thank-you card, I have to join forces with Luba," I snap.

Chugging a glassful of chocolate egg nog, Caleb chimes in, "Sounds like me and the starman have something in common." He's either too enraptured by the thick sweetness of his drink or he's just ignoring my sarcasm. He can't ignore Archie's.

"And what exactly would that be?" Archie asks. "The gift of giving really bad gifts?"

Still swallowing, Caleb swats Archie on the back of his head. "Winter! You're supposed to be on my side," he cries. "I told Domgirl that she should team up with Luba the instant she told me Nadine was having twins."

"Which I'm sure was something Dominy was thrilled to hear," Archie says.

It wasn't. But sometimes the most important things you need to hear are the things you don't ever want or ever expect to be told.

"I wasn't thrilled by Caleb's suggestion," I admit. "But when Vera told me the same thing and why, from Orion's point of view, it was vitally important, it really started to seem like the only logical course of action."

Archie remains silent, but I can tell it's only because he can't find the words to disagree with me. He's come to the same conclusion I have; there's no argument against my joining Team Luba. He isn't happy with it, but like me, he can't fight it any longer. Once again Arla's unruffled approach to all things supernatural lightens the tense atmosphere that is threatening to make our basement inhospitable to life, human or otherwise.

"What does it say about me that I thought it was weirder when Vera was a Connecticutian than now that she's celestial?" she asks. "I mean, I'm actually having an easier time accepting the fact that the new girl in town is a fallen star than thinking of her as a former resident of Nadine's hometown."

"It's because you've been hanging around me for too long," I say.

"And none of us would have it any other way," Caleb replies, giving me a quick kiss. His lips taste deliciously chocolaty, and for a split second I forget that we're pondering life-altering decisions, until Archie bends over to scratch his ankle and I see a stagnant pool of blackness in the center of his sea of white hair.

If Jess is right and if the world is truly one giant balancing act, that means there's good and evil everywhere and in everyone. We're all half-breeds, which I know is an offensive term, but it's fitting in this instance, because all of us except for Caleb can be found in the two-for-one aisle of the Price Chopper. Me, Arla, Archie, Jess, Vera, Orion, and if I'm being fair, maybe even Luba. Is it possible that shrouded under all that darkness and deception and duplicity lies some goodness? Is there an uncontaminated piece of her that I can trust? There has to be; I mean if not, then our truce is nothing but a sham. And if she is infused with Orion's star energy just like Vera is and I trust Vera, then according to the laws of mathematics I should be able to trust Luba too. But can I truly trust Vera?

"Vera told me something else," I say.

Archie lifts his head, and all I can see is his smooth white skin and violet eyes. "She always does this."

"I know," Arla agrees.

Heads practically touching they still look like carbon

copies of each other, even though the crew cuts are gone since Archie's let his hair grow out and Arla's wearing her long black wig that makes her look like Cher from the early days of her career, which thanks to cosmetic surgical enhancements looks exactly like Cher four decades later. Physically, Archie's and Arla's appearances may be different, but emotionally, their attitudes are in sync.

"Dom tosses us only a teeny bit of information like we're lab rats who can only chew on a tiny piece of cheese at one time or else we'll explode," Archie states.

"Have we not proven, Dom, that we're not going to explode if you tell us everything you know all at once?" Arla asks.

"She's right, Domgirl," Caleb adds, pouring himself his third glass of choconog. Clearly, college has increased his appetite.

Well, I'm about to increase my friends' cheese intake. I draw my knees into my chest in preparation for the explosion.

"Vera said it's time for me to tell Louis the truth."

On cue Arla, Archie, and Caleb explode, and I'm showered with thought-shrapnel; their ammunition doesn't pierce my flesh, but it's still as powerful. Not that they're saying anything I haven't already told myself since Vera dropped the bombshell that Louis should be allowed membership to the Wolf Pack. Why should I make Louis more involved than he already is? He's managed to free himself from both Luba's spell and Melinda's mind games. Why tell him the truth about both of them now? And if we tell him about them, we have to tell him about me too. And not just the selected truth, the whole truth. That the serial killer he's searching for is living under his roof.

"I can't imagine Jess would want you to confess," Caleb says. He runs a finger slowly over his bracelet, and I can feel his fingers gliding across my flesh. As always his words, like his presence, are a comfort, even if they stir up the little pellets of fear that live in the center of my soul. "Not after everything she's done to protect you since . . ."

Since I murdered her.

"And you said she doesn't blame you, Dom," Arla adds. "She knows she's dead because of Luba. She wouldn't want you to be punished for something you didn't do."

"And if you tell Louis the truth, you might as well subscribe to *Prison Monthly* to find out how to decorate your cell," Archie quips. "A cell that you're not going to be able to escape from, by the way."

They're right. As much as I would like to think that Louis would understand the truth and protect me like my father did, there's a chance that he'll act like the really good cop he's become and put me away for murder. It's a chance I'm not yet ready to take.

"Maybe I can't trust everything Vera says," I confess. "I mean she also told me that I should brush up on my Greek mythology, as if that would hold a key to unlocking this whole mystery."

"She said that?" Arla asks.

"Yup," I reply. "Right before she dropped the bombshell about telling your father the truth."

"Well, you know what they say about mythology," Caleb says, now chomping on a cookie.

"What?" I ask.

"It's all Greek to me."

And the intellectual portion of our impromptu powwow has officially ended.

The following Sunday at church the mystery that is my life takes me on another unexpected journey.

In most communities a church's congregation expands during the Christmas season, and St. Edmund's is no exception. It's SRO what with everyone vowing to return to their religious roots or trying to atone for their sins or simply wanting to make a good impression with the rest of the town. There isn't room for all of us to sit together, so Arla's forced to sit with her dad in his reserved spot in the front row, Archie's stuck in the back with his family, Barnaby and Gwen are sitting with her parents on the right, and I'm sitting in a pew on the left next to Caleb. I'm positioned near a beautiful stained-glass window depicting Jesus wearing a crown of thorns, dragging the cross through the desert under the blazing sun. He's essentially on trial in the court of public opinion. Just like Nadine.

Amid the murmur and chatter of the restless parishioners, I hear a whisper. It tugs on my ear like a thorn scraping against my forehead. It's Nadine's voice. I look over to the right and see that Nadine is sitting next to her mother. On the other side of Melinda is Luba, as if grandmother and grand-daughter now need to be separated at all costs. Although all three of them share the same space, they ignore one another. It's as if they're sitting on three neighboring islands; they all exist in the same vicinity, but their bodies refuse to touch.

Nadine's voice is soft, and I'm sure without my wolf-hearing it would be undetectable, but lucky for me I can hear every word she's saying to her unborn children.

"Someday everyone will be celebrating your birthday just like they celebrate Jesus's," she sighs. "You'll be known everywhere and by everyone as the special children you are, and everyone will look at me with envy because I'm your mother. But when they see how special and powerful and kind you are, their envy will turn to admiration, because they'll understand you could only be who you are thanks to a mother's love."

I feel like I'm listening in on a conversation between a Swedish mother and her children in her native tongue; I'm finding it difficult to comprehend what I'm hearing.

"Your lives will be glorious," Nadine continues. "Lives

filled with wonder and astonishment and glory, and I will be by your side every step of the way. I will never let you drift on your own like my mother and my grandmother did."

Caleb yawns, and I know he can't hear a word Nadine is saying, no one else can, only me and her kids. But is she speaking to them or to me? Does she know I'm listening? Is she deliberately trying to fool me into thinking a softer, more maternal side of her exists, one that isn't consumed with revenge and destruction and total global domination?

"Someday I'll give you the life I never had," Nadine says, her voice softer than ever. "The kind of life I never thought was possible until now."

Slowly Nadine's finger begins to trace something on her bloated stomach. She's blessing her children with an invisible tattoo, the stars of Orion. A tingling sensation starts to twist around my spine, because I know that the words she just spoke to them were prayer-like, but I get the sense that the intent behind them has nothing at all to do with mercy. Unless it's the mercy of the rest of the world. Sitting with her family, but very much alone, Nadine looks simultaneously impervious and fragile; the world could either destroy her or be destroyed by her, depending upon which way the pendulum swings.

"She's an interesting creature, isn't she?"

I didn't notice Vera squeeze into the seat next to me. I'm not sure if that's because I'm preoccupied with Nadine's monologue or because Vera appeared out of thin air. Her mere proximity has quieted Nadine; there's nothing left to listen to, but there's so much more to see.

"Does she scare you?" Vera asks.

When I realize that Caleb isn't reacting to Vera's presence, it dawns on me that she's a hologram; she's here in spirit, not in body. How fitting for a house of God. Not wanting to make my boyfriend think I'm talking to yet another unseen entity, I nod my head. Yes, Nadine does scare me.

"Let me show you something that will really scare you," Vera says.

What a lovely invitation. Vera grabs my hand, and starlight seems to spill out of her pores. At first it moves slowly like silver blood, like a baby who has just learned how to crawl. When Father Charles approaches the altar, Vera's body ignites and becomes an inferno of starlight. Just as my spirit escapes my flesh, leaving my body behind to remain seated next to Caleb, I notice Father Charles looking in my direction, and a flicker of acknowledgment sparkles in his eyes. Either he's given me permission to leave, or he's just prayed that my soul survives my travels.

We rise up, and just as we're about to crash through the church's vaulted ceiling, I look down and see Nadine, Luba, and even Melinda scowling up at us, finally acting and responding as one. The family that hates together stays together.

"It's time to visit the past to get to know Nadine better," Vera orders.

I feel Vera's star-grip around my body tighten as I try to wrench free. I know everything there is to know about Nadine, and even if that isn't true, I don't want to know anything else, especially if I have to journey into the past to find it out. Sorry, but these backwardventures through time never end up well for me.

"The best way to defeat your enemy," Vera informs me, "is to understand her."

Obviously stargirl is not going to take no for an answer. She is on a hunt, and Nadine is her prey.

With no other choice I give in and feel myself careening through time and space. Perhaps it's because I have a new tour guide, but the ride is smoother than before, so I'm lulled into a false sense of security. Until we suddenly stop moving and I find myself standing inside the Jaffe family cabin.

At first I don't notice Nadine, but that's because no one else in the scene notices her either. Luba and Melinda are sitting on the floor with Napoleon in between them. He's very young, barely a toddler, and he's taking what appear to be his first steps. Melinda and Luba clap their hands and shriek with delight at Nap's accomplishment, causing the boy's face to transform with a beaming smile that literally makes me gasp because I have never seen Napoleon this happy before. Even when he was with Archie his happiness was tempered with the knowledge that it wouldn't last. Here, when he is barely more than an infant, Napoleon's smile is unburdened; he has no idea how quickly happiness can be destroyed. His sister, however, has all the knowledge her brother doesn't possess.

Standing in a corner, Nadine watches her mother and grandmother dote on her brother. Her body is rigid, as if she's leaning against a wall or being propped up by unseen hands. She is, of course, the same age as Napoleon, but where he is having trouble maintaining his balance and remaining upright, Nadine seems to have already mastered these motor skills. Regardless of her accomplishments, she already seems to know that nothing she does will receive the same applause and adoration from her family that her brother's actions do. Lessons learned early are lessons never forgotten.

Quietly, Nadine walks outside and is drenched in sunlight. She shuts her eyes from the onslaught, but when she opens them she sees an area that looks very much the way it does now. Slightly overgrown, completely natural, and able to hide things from a curious eye. Like her father.

About a hundred yards from the cabin, Thorne is standing behind a group of trees. He isn't working the land or cutting low-lying branches; he's simply watching, waiting until someone calls for him, or more realistically until he finds the strength to join the family that doesn't care if he lives or dies.

If Nadine sees or senses that her father is nearby, she doesn't react to him; she appears to be as lost as Thorne. Wandering to the side of the house, Nadine seems to be walking randomly, just following her own footsteps, moving without thought, but when she stops next to a lilac bush I see what she was chasing: a butterfly.

Perched on a pink petal, the butterfly flutters its wings in greeting. Its yellow and black wings are winking hello to Nadine, staring at her as if it's the first time it's seen a little girl. I don't know if that's true, but it will definitely be the butterfly's last.

Nadine extends her hand and offers her finger to the butterfly, which willingly accepts. The two are connected as the butterfly steps onto Nadine's tiny finger, a small stage for the young girl to witness nature's beauty. And destroy it.

With her free hand Nadine grabs hold of one of the butterfly's wings tightly. Sensing a game change, the butterfly's other wing flutters more urgently, but is prohibited from making any further movement when Nadine grabs that one too. Holding the butterfly up by both wings like a fresh, cleaned shirt from the laundry, Nadine smiles at her prey. It's the last vision the butterfly sees before its wings are plucked from its body.

Without looking down Nadine steps on the butterfly's remains with her patent leather shoe and rubs the wings across her cheeks, smiling approvingly at the softness, lolling her head to the side, triumphant in her glory. Her victory is short-lived when she turns around to see Luba standing behind her.

"Next time do not hesitate," Luba says. "Don't be a weak fool like your father and give your prey the chance to escape."

Luba returns to the cabin, leaving father and daughter alone to contemplate her words. Neither of them responds verbally, but when Nadine puts the wings into the pocket of her dress like a well-deserved treasure, Thorne understands that once again his mother has emerged exultant from battle.

I feel the starlight wrap around my body, and I know before I'm airlifted that our trip will continue. Since this isn't my inaugural jaunt as a time-traveling passenger, I know that our next stop will be several years into the future, so I'm not at all surprised when we land to see that Nadine and Napoleon have aged. Now they're teenagers, thirteen or fourteen, and I assume we're in Cos Cob, a few years before they returned to Luba's birthplace. The hazy blue of night reigns, but the sky is still lit up, not by sunlight, but by the first sparks of a fire.

In front of a burning building, Luba stands in between her grandchildren. They're untouched by the flames, but they're standing close enough to the fire that their faces are glowing red. Luba's eyes are closed, an ecstatic smile latched onto her lips. On either side of her, Nadine and Napoleon look unsure as to how to respond. Once they do, their reactions seal their fate.

"We can't just stand here," Napoleon says. "People are still inside."

Annoyed by the intrusion, Luba slowly opens her eyes, and without moving her head looks over at her grandson. "Countless hours I've spent praying to Orion that a boy would take my inferior son's place," Luba seethes. "Hours spent in vain."

"Grandmother," Napoleon protests. "These people are innocent, they haven't done anything to deserve this."

Luba raises her hand. A stream of black energy shoots out of her palm and into Napoleon's chest, and he is tossed up and through the air until he lands on the rocky ground a few hundred yards away, writhing in agony. Luba then turns to Nadine. "Perhaps the girl child shall lead us."

Shaking with excitement and fear, it's as if this is the moment Nadine has waited for her entire life. The same moment she has dreaded and hoped for. Deliberately avoiding looking at her brother's still-twitching body, Nadine gazes at the building, her face sheened with sweat. She raises her hands and closes her eyes so she doesn't see the building suddenly erupt into an inferno. Six-foot-tall flames dance and twirl and engulf the quiet air, transforming the night sky into a blend of colors, red, yellow, orange, mingling with one another, devouring the building and the people within it until there's nothing left but burned flesh, ash, and memory.

The twins look at the destruction, and both their mouths drop, Napoleon's in horror and Nadine's in astonishment; neither can believe what she's accomplished.

Luba's demonic laugh, unchanged after all these years, severs the night with the precision of a surgeon's scalpel directly into the hearts of her grandchildren. She lifts her left hand, and with thumb and pinky finger touching, she points three fingers toward the dark heavens.

"Orion has chosen!" she proclaims.

Frantically I try to shake away this vision as well as Vera's stranglehold on me.

"This is what Orion chooses?" I cry. "Pure evil?!"

Whipping me around, Vera makes me see the vision in its entirety, not just the part I want to focus on, and I see Napoleon kneeling on the ground, tears falling from his eyes, his hands clasped in prayer. I hear his words, much quieter than Luba's rally roar, but equally as intense. He's praying to God to embrace the souls of the people who died in the fire. He's begging God and the angels to take the dead souls into their arms and show them the love and compassion that Luba and Nadine tried to burn out of them. He isn't thinking of himself; not once does he ask for forgiveness or revenge; his only thoughts are with the lives that have just been lost. He knows that his own life is lost as well, but he doesn't feel that he deserves to be spared from whatever fate awaits him. It's just like Jess said; balance can be found everywhere. Goodness and evil are alive and well only a few feet apart.

"Are you trying to tell me that Nadine never stood a chance?" I ask. "That the only way for her to survive and be noticed in her family was to turn to wickedness?"

"I don't mean to tell you anything, Dominy," Vera replies. "Just show you the truth. How you wish to interpret it is your choice."

What's there to interpret?! Nadine was born into a disgusting, sin-drenched family. She could've chosen a different route like her brother and her father, but she chose darkness and power and hasn't looked back ever since.

"And if you let her continue, if you don't stop her, who knows what else she'll do, who knows what else she is capable of doing," Vera states.

Sitting back in the pew listening to Father Charles wrap up his sermon, I glance over to Nadine, and I'm more confused than ever. I've always considered Nadine to be a lost cause, but I've just been given proof that she wasn't born evil. The repercussions of that revelation are astounding.

Because not only does that mean that Nadine's children can be saved, but maybe it means that Nadine can be saved as well. Maybe she doesn't need to be destroyed like Luba wants; maybe her wickedness can be reverted, maybe she can be reformed, salvaged in some way.

When I catch Luba staring at me, her eyes practically penetrating my thoughts, I realize Luba is not at all happy with my change of heart.

And I have to wonder if I've joined forces with the wrong witch after all.

Chapter 19

Last night was my first transformation of the New Year and as far as a GTWT—girl-to-wolf transformation—goes, it was completely uneventful. Snuck out of my room, feasted on an unexpected pair of wild turkeys, explored yet a new part of Robin's Park, lounged around for a bit waiting for someone to show up, but wound up spending the night alone. No Vera, Nadine, Luba, Louis, no one. Before I got to school this morning I took it as a positive omen. Now, I see that I was mistaken.

"Ladies! When I say run, I do not mean jog: I mean run!"

It appears by the way Miss Rolenski is acting that she did not have a relaxing and/or enjoyable holiday break. She's normally on the motivated side of type A, but today she sounds like she's crossed over and is in a zone that cannot be alphabetized, or controlled.

"Deeanne Ulrich!"

Miss Ro's voice is never girlie-girl feminine, but her scream sounds like gravel against sandpaper.

"That might pass for running on the cheerleading squad, but in *my* gym it's called walking!" she bellows. "Now I said run!"

Startled into action, Deeanne runs faster than I've ever

seen her run before. I'm not exactly sure what's gotten into Miss Ro today, but I'm not going to risk her wrath. Today is one of those days that I'm thankful to be blessed with wolf-speed.

My third time around the track I realize that I've passed all the girls in my class, some of them twice, so I slow down and act as if I'm having some trouble breathing so it looks like I'm experiencing normal gym girl fatigue. As a side benefit, I can now overhear Gwen talking to Nadine on the bleachers.

Naturally, Nadine is excused from taking gym because she's pregnant, but because Dumbleavy and the brains behind Two W don't want the other students to claim they're favoring Nadine and giving her any undue advantages by allowing her to take another class or have a study period, she has to sit in the bleachers each day and watch her classmates sweat it out on the gym floor. In some warped adult way I'm sure they think they're showing Nadine everything that she's missing. Luckily, my superhearing doesn't allow me to miss one word of Nadine and Gwen's conversation.

"My father says your pregnancy is coming along fine," Gwen mentions innocently.

"Your father talks to you about my pregnancy?" Nadine asks without a trace of innocence in her voice. It's all accusation.

"Oh no . . . no, no, no! He would never do that," Gwen stutters. "I just asked him over dinner one night because, you know, I'm concerned, and I know that your due date is really, really soon, and he hasn't mentioned your name so I wanted to make sure that you're okay. You and your . . ."

"We're fine," Nadine says curtly. "There's nothing for you or your father for that matter to be concerned with. Women have been having children for centuries without the benefit of modern medical intervention, and they and their children turned out fine."

How Gwen cannot recognize that this is the perfect time to

say "gotcha, Nadine, good luck" and get the hell away from her amazes me. But instead, Gwen continues the conversation and antagonizes Nadine with her subsequent comment.

"But that's just the thing, Nadine," Gwen says, placing her hand on top of Nadine's knee. "You aren't a woman; you're still just a girl."

Oh, Gwen, you are so wrong about that! Nadine may not be an adult in the eyes of the courts, but she has killed any trace of the little girl who used to live inside of her. And the way Nadine is staring at Gwen's hand, if Gwen doesn't remove it from her knee immediately, Nadine may add Gwen to the list of people she has killed.

Before I can intervene and shout Gwen's name to challenge her to a sprint as a way to separate her from the Four W, Miss Ro unwittingly does it for me.

"Gwenevere Schültzenhoggen! Are you taking lessons in how to ruin your life?"

Not only does Miss Ro get Gwen's attention, but she gets the attention of *everyone* in the gym.

"Leave the unwed Miss Jaffe alone so she can witness the life she's letting pass her by," she barks. "And get back on the track!"

Like angry claws, two streams of charcoal black energy emerge from Nadine's body and begin the long trip toward Miss Ro. They move slowly; they're in no rush because their prey has no idea she's being stalked.

"And Gwen," Miss Ro adds. "You may want to choose your friends more wisely."

I have never heard Miss Ro or really any teacher at Two W speak so harshly to or about a student before. Did no one get the memo about being sensitive and politically correct to the student body? Especially when that body is housing another body? Or two! But the way that Nadine's been flaunting her pregnancy this year, it was bound to backfire at some point. I just never thought the insults would cross over from the student population to the teaching staff. As shocked as I am by Miss Ro's outburst, my classmates seem thrilled that an adult has finally given voice to their feelings.

"Serves her right for acting like getting knocked up should win her a blue ribbon," Deeanne whispers to one of the girls on the squad. How quickly she forgets that Miss Ro just chewed her out a few minutes ago. Nadine's memory can't be erased that easily.

Looking over into the bleachers I see Nadine's lips moving quickly and in direct contrast to her black energy that is languidly undulating in the air between her and Miss Ro. Her back straight, her hands clasped in her lap, Nadine is motionless except for the frantic movements of her lips. At first glance she looks like an obedient schoolgirl reciting a memorized poem, but since no sound is coming out of her, she looks downright eerie. Whatever she's saying, whatever spell her lips are forming, she has no intention of sharing the words or their intent. The only thing I know is that Miss Ro is in danger.

But more than two minutes later when the class bell rings, Nadine still hasn't taken any action against Miss Ro. I hold back from the crowd and follow Nadine into the locker room so I can investigate further. The room is empty; most of the girls have done a quick-change and have left or are taking showers at the end of the hall. Seizing the opportunity, I take a seat on the bench next to danger herself. Her black energy is for some reason no longer following Miss Ro but is floating around Nadine's body, either showing off or patiently waiting to strike. I think I'll strike first.

"What are you doing here, Nadine?" I ask. "Break a sweat chanting in the stands?"

Smirking, but silent, Nadine shifts her weight on the bench, and her sneakers let out a loud squeak.

"Sounds like your sneakers are having a tough time handling all that extra weight," I say. "You really have packed on the pounds. Must be one giganto baby you have tucked away in there."

Beaming with pride, Nadine caresses her engorged stomach. She's so preoccupied with showing off her treasure, she has no idea that I know her treasure comes in two parts. "You'd be surprised by how much I have tucked away in here, Dominy."

Hmm, not really. But before I slip and mention that I know she's carrying twins, this is a good time to steer the conversation in a new direction. Watching Miss Ro through her office window, sitting at her desk riffling through some paperwork, I've found the perfect distraction.

"This pregnancy must be siphoning some of your power," I say, staring at Miss Ro. "Looks like you're losing your touch."

"Really?" Nadine replies, turning to look over at Miss Ro. "My pregnancy is hardly taking power away from me. In fact it's helping me to become stronger than you or anyone could ever imagine."

"Even Luba?"

As cunning as I can sometimes be, I can also be just as stupid. And this time my stupidity makes Nadine react more horrifically than ever before.

My comment, meant to give me the upper hand, seems to have given me away. From her intense reaction, Nadine is obviously suspicious of my comment. She knows that I know that she is keeping a secret from Luba. Does Nadine know that I've uncovered the truth that she's carrying twins and is planning to murder her grandmother so she and her children can become Orion's triumvirate and she can be promoted to the apex of their triangle of evil? Not sure. But from my uttering two little words, Nadine is certain that I know she's hiding *something,* and that bit of knowledge has forced Nadine to go into panic mode.

The black light that has been prancing around Nadine's

body without purpose or direction has suddenly found it: me. With laser-beam accuracy the light zeroes in on my mouth, and before I can fight against it, I feel a burning sensation, like electrically charged fingers working frantically to pull my lips apart.

I clamp my mouth shut, but the burning only becomes more intense, and it feels as if my flesh is turning to liquid and splattering to the ground. Reaching up, I grab on to the light, but the temperature is scalding, and I feel my skin on my palms and fingertips sizzle. I have a flashback to when I was in Weeping Water River trying to yank open the wolf's mouth to let out my golden light. Now it's just the opposite. I want to keep my mouth shut. I'm not as lucky this time. Involuntarily, my mouth opens to let out a scream that is automatically silenced when Nadine's blackness rushes into my mouth.

My eyes are pools of tears, frightened and angry and desperate, so I can barely see Nadine in front of me. But I can see enough to witness her smiling at me. Despite any qualms I might have had about her, despite the fact that she might have been led toward evil with a gentle push by her grandmother, she has chosen to live her life there, regardless of the consequences to her soul and any poor fool who gets in her way. Like me.

Struggling against Nadine's attack I glance over and see Miss Ro through her window still focused on her paperwork. She has no idea what's happening outside her door. Good. I've got to keep it that way. The girl understands the need not to cause a disturbance that might attract Miss Ro's attention; the wolf doesn't.

Against my own will I feel it starting in the pit of my stomach, a violent reaction, the only real reaction to the beating my body's taking. Unfortunately, I don't think it will be a reaction that can remain unnoticed.

I feel the red cloud churning inside of me. I don't know if

it's rising on its own power or if Nadine is tearing it from me, but the result is the same: The wolf is being awakened and dragged from its sleep.

"Nooooo!!!!!"

My screams have no voice, thanks to the red cloud filling up my throat. Puffs of it are starting to trickle out of my mouth and swirl around the black light, as if trying to grab hold of it, rip it off of my flesh, separate the good from the evil. But it doesn't matter because now the lines have blurred. Good has meshed with evil; girl has combined with wolf.

The heat from Nadine's light is matched only by the fire coursing through my veins. The pain gripping my flesh disappears when my limbs start to invert and break. This can't be happening! I'm transforming right here in the locker room, in plain sight of Miss Ro, with Gwen and some of the other girls showering down the hall, with Nadine laughing at me! The horror of it is that I know it's not completely Nadine's fault; she's awakened the beast within me, but I've allowed Nadine's fury to latch onto my emotions, and in doing so I've allowed the wolf to break free. Watching the red fur encase my arms, I know there's no turning back. For any of us.

"Dominy!!"

Miss Ro's scream slashes through my eardrums. It's pure terror; it's the sound that is let loose when someone comes face-to-face with unimaginable fear.

"Run!!"

I know that my voice is muffled; I know that it's more growl than scream, but she must have heard me—she must have heard me tell her to run! If she heard me, why is she just standing there? Why is she looking at me and not moving? Why isn't she running for her life?!

Nadine bends over and whispers in my ear, "Because her life is over."

When I transform completely, Nadine lifts her arms, one in front of her and one to her right, and I hear the doors leading to the gym and to the showers slam shut. There's no way out now.

"Dominy!!"

Miss Ro's horrified voice burrows into my brain.

"What . . . the hell . . . is *happening?!*"

Even if I still had Dominy's voice, I couldn't respond to Miss Ro's cries, because I don't have an explanation. Is Nadine now just as powerful as Vera, thanks to the twins growing inside of her? She must be. How else did she force me to transform in the middle of the day? If this is what she can do while the twins are still in her womb, what will she be capable of after they're born? I can't speculate on that now; I have to do everything I can to make sure I protect Miss Ro and that those doors remain closed so Gwen and the others don't have to see what she's already witnessed. But I'm not sure I am strong enough.

"Dear God . . . *Dominy!*" Miss Ro screams. "What's happened to you?!"

Her voice is shaking like a leaf twirling from a branch to its death. Desperately trying to stay afloat, knowing that its life may be prolonged a while longer by a random gust of wind, but inevitably it will fall to the earth and die. I know this is the thought going through Miss Ro's mind not because I can see into her soul, but because I want her dead.

Her smell is so pungent that it fills my nostrils until I think my head may burst. My tongue lifts and sways across my fangs as I watch her thick legs shake and her muscular arm reach out to hold on to the locker to steady her body so it doesn't topple over, so it doesn't collapse onto the floor as an offering to me. Too late. Nadine has already served up my meal, and I'm too hungry to fight it.

"No!!"

I don't know whose voice that is—Miss Ro's, maybe Gwen's coming from behind the shower room door, or mine—but it temporarily breaks the spell. Like a caged animal, I run in circles, banging into the lockers, frantically looking for a way out. The only choice I have is to break down the door and run through the gym, hoping no one gets in my way. I leap into the air, and my front paws crash into the door, but it doesn't budge. My strength is no match for Nadine's spell. Or for her ingenuity.

I hear a scream and then a crash and turn around to see Miss Ro's body, wrapped tightly in Nadine's black light, being dragged toward me. If I won't go to my dinner, Nadine will bring my dinner to me.

"If you think that you and some fallen star can destroy me, Dominy Robineau," Nadine roars, "think again!"

Ripping her hand through the air as a command to her energy, Nadine hurls Miss Ro's body into me. Fighting every primitive urge racing through me, pushing the hunger and thirst from my claws and my fangs, I howl furiously and then scurry away, running blindly until I crash into a bank of lockers. The impact is so powerful that the lockers are wrenched from the floor, towels and gloves and sneakers from the top of the lockers raining down on me as the entire bank teeters precariously from side to side before settling down. Slowly Nadine walks toward me, her eyes wide and mad, and when she gets a foot from me, she crouches down until she is nose to snout.

"My babies and I will be the death of you, Dominy," she says. "But first someone else needs to die."

Without looking at Miss Ro, Nadine extends her arm and once again her light drags Miss Ro across the locker room floor toward us. Backing up I hear my claws click against the floor, and I try to camouflage the ugly sound with a growl, but I only succeed in making something ugly sound even uglier. And then the screams return. Miss Ro's voice, Gwen's, the voices of some other girls, of unknown men coming from the other side of the gym door. The screams are all around me, inside my brain, living on my fur, penetrating my flesh, pouring out of me.

Nadine drops her arm and Miss Ro stops moving, her body resting at my restless claws. Petrified, Miss Ro looks into my eyes, desperately trying to connect with the girl she knows is living underneath this animal's hide.

"Dominy," she says, her voice barely audible. "Help me."

Even buried deep within the wolf I am attached to memory, and I see Rayna's shriveled face staring at me in Nadine's cabin, asking me to help her, begging me to take her life. No! No, I will not kill again!

"Stop this!!!"

The locker room is bombarded with my roar, but Nadine hears my plea.

"As you wish."

Silence engulfs the room, followed by the horrible squeaking of Nadine's sneakers as she takes two steps backwards to the edge of the lockers. Her smile never leaves her face as she flicks her wrist and the entire bank of lockers is ripped from its foundation and begins to fall.

"Noooo!!!!"

Entangled by the black energy, Miss Ro can't move. She locks eyes with me, but doesn't say a word, not that she needs to. I can tell from her solemn expression that she has given up even before everything goes black when the lockers crash down on top of us.

"Move!"

I know the voice is coming from deep inside of me, but I can't obey its command.

"Move . . . now!!!"

Again it comes, from the same place, with the same fiery intent, the same need to get me to move my body out from underneath the lockers that have taken the voice and breath and spirit from Miss Ro, the lockers that are threatening to push me closer and closer toward my own death.

Should I just allow that to happen? I've thought so many times about how peaceful it would be to die, to join my father and Jess and be with them forever. It would mean letting Luba and Nadine win, but I would be able to leave the wolf behind and once again be whole and complete and only Dominy. Now that the opportunity has arisen unexpectedly and as a result of my own carelessness, maybe I should latch onto it.

Then I see the light.

From out of the blackness I see two strands of silver and gold light that I instinctively know belong to Vera and Jess. Neither of them can tell me what to do; they can't force me to decide either way, but what they can do is remind me that I am not alone and that if I give in, if I truly allow Nadine to rise victorious from this, there will be repercussions. Without me on earth my brother will be left alone, for all intents and purposes the last family member standing, and Luba will not have me to help her defeat Nadine. The old witch could probably do it on her own, but without me to offer balance, she will definitely choose the path of destruction over peace. No, I'm needed. My life here is necessary. Ironic that it took my impending death to make me see the truth.

Planting my paws firmly on the ground, I push up and hear the metal of the lockers scrape loudly against the floor. Arching my back I lift the lockers higher and raise my head to steal a glance at Miss Ro. She isn't moving. She asked for my help, and I failed her.

In one furious, connected move, I lower my body, then rise up with even more power so the lockers fly back into a standing position. Scurrying backward I'm able to get to safety before the lockers crash back down onto the floor and Miss Ro's dead body. There's nothing else for me to do except escape.

On the other side of the gym door, I hear an axe slamming into the wood to break through into the locker room. On the other side of the shower door, Gwen and a few girls are screaming to be let in. The only way out for me is up. And the only way out for Nadine is down.

As I take a running leap to break through the frosted window near the ceiling, I see Nadine drop to the floor and position her legs underneath a locker. Just as I crash through the thick pane of glass, I hear the rush of voices flood the room and feel the cold winter air ripple against my face and through my hair. Now out of Nadine's line of vision and her grasp, I transform back. Even though I'm outside naked in January in the middle of the day on school grounds, I feel safe. But my safety is quickly destroyed by Nadine's screams.

"It was Dominy! She attacked us!"

Without wasting time to see if I have any witnesses, I crawl through an open window leading into the girls' shower. Like the one in the locker room, it's frosted, so I can't see if there's anyone on the other side, but I don't have a choice, I have to act quickly and take the chance that I'll be seen. Luckily, there's no one left in the showers, so I wet myself, throw a towel around me, and walk into the locker room as if I had been showering the whole time. I'm not sure who's more surprised to see me—Nadine, Gwen, or Dumbleavy.

"Dominy!" Gwen shouts. "I thought you were still out here with Nadine."

Numbly I shake my head. I can't speak because I see with my own eyes the destruction I left behind. Nadine lying on the floor next to an unmoving and bloodied Miss Ro, both trapped underneath a row of lockers. We all watch in silence as Dumbleavy and Mr. Soto, one of the janitors, lift up the lockers to their rightful position. The entire time they're working, I can't take my eyes off of Miss Ro's face, an expression of horror etched into it.

When the men are finished, Dumbleavy wordlessly kneels down next to his colleague and friend and closes her eyes with trembling fingers. Gwen and the other girls gathered in the room begin to scream and cry as they grasp the finality of the situation and begin to process the hard fact that Miss Ro is dead. Although I've seen death before and even participated in its wrath, this is difficult even for me to take, because I'm partly responsible.

I try to ignore what Dumbleavy's saying, but I can't block out his voice. Every word of the Lord's Prayer feels like someone is throwing scalding hot water in my face.

When Dumbleavy finishes, he is beyond weary, but when he speaks, he demands an answer. "Nadine, why would you say that Dominy attacked you?"

Completely in control, Nadine clutches her swollen belly and commands tears to stream down her face. "No, I didn't say that," she lies. "I said it *looked* like Dominy."

"What did?" he asks. "What are you talking about?"

"The wolf," she states. "The wolf that attacked us. I can't explain it, but it *looked* just like Dominy."

"A wolf?!" Dumbleavy cries. "A wolf did . . . this?"

More screams from Gwen and the girls, and Mr. Soto ushers them into Miss Ro's office, away from the madness. But I can't move; I have to bear witness; I have to watch Nadine show absolutely no remorse for what she's done, because it convinces me that I made the right decision to not give in and to fight to live. And to help Luba.

Because if Nadine is capable of killing an innocent woman just because she feels like it, just to prove that she can commit murder in daylight and get away with it, what the hell is she going to do if I'm not around to stop her?

For better or worse, I have got to work with Luba to put an end to Nadine's reign of terror once and for all.

Chapter 20

Sometimes the wolf and the girl are so different, and sometimes they're exactly the same.

It's been several weeks since Miss Ro's death, but when I walk past the cemetery, I still avoid looking at her grave. I did the same thing last night when I raced past it in search of food. I didn't stop. I didn't want to be reminded that another person had died because of me; I didn't want another grave to be piled on top of my shoulders. But even without looking I can feel the weight of Miss Ro's casket pressing down against me. Doesn't matter if it's pressing against fur or flesh; I can still feel it.

A chilly breeze slaps me in the face, and I look up at The Weeping Lady. I didn't come here for abuse, only silence, but there's no way I'm going to get any quiet, not with all the thoughts running through my head. Remembering back to that day in the gym, I know that Nadine had it in for Miss Ro. I know that she was chanting something, casting a spell. But if I had only kept my mouth shut, if I had not taunted Nadine, maybe Miss Ro would still be alive. Maybe. Or someone else would be dead. Life doesn't matter to Nadine—well, only her life and the lives of her twins.

Another breeze, just as cold, just as sudden, but less explosive. This one caresses my face, soothes it, which makes sense, because I hear my mother's voice in the air.

Remember, Dominy, you are blessed.

Seriously?! Not that again.

Before the cool air has let go of me, my cell phone rings. It's Caleb, and I laugh out loud. Okay, Mom, maybe this time you're right.

"You have no idea how happy I am to hear your voice," I say. "Artemis."

Caleb must have speed-dialed the wrong girl.

"Uh, no, this is Dominy," I reply. "Your girlfriend."

"I know it's you, Domgirl." Caleb sighs. "But you're also Artemis."

"Sorry, Caleb, what are you talking about?"

I can practically see my boyfriend's head tilt to the side and his unruly curls hang in the air; it's always the way he looks when he's annoyed that I don't understand something he's talking about.

"Artemis is the goddess of the moon, she who worships and lives under the power of the moon," he informs me. "I.e. you."

He's learning some fascinating stuff up there at Big Red.

"I.e. okay," I reply. "But I still don't know what you're talking about."

"According to Greek mythology, which Vera instructed you to brush up on," he says, reminding me of Vera's dictate, "Orion was *killed* by Artemis."

Great. I don't merely help get gym teachers murdered; I also murder gods. Why is this something Vera wants me to know?

"Is that for real?!" I ask.

"It is according to myth," he replies. "And although to most people myth is just myth, we've learned that myth can be fact, so, yes, I think this myth is real and not just a mythnomer. Oh hey! How do you like that? I made up a new word too, just like you!"

I'll praise my boyfriend's increased vocabulary later. Right now I need him to get back to the source material.

"But why would Vera want me to kill Orion?" I ask. "She's part of Orion. Is she a suicidal star?"

"Maybe she isn't being literal," Caleb says. "Maybe Vera doesn't want you to kill all of Orion, but only a part of him, so you can maintain the balance."

Not only are my boyfriend's vocabulary skills improving, but his logic is too. But logic can sometimes be frightening.

"Caleb, as much as I hate her, I just don't know if I can kill Nadine," I whisper, even though the only one listening to my conversation is a tree woman with bark for a tongue. "Now that she's carrying twins."

There's a pause on the other end of the phone, and words that follow a pause are never words that you want to hear.

"Maybe . . . Orion only wants you to kill one of the twins."

Caleb's voice is as soft and quiet as mine, but I feel as if thunder has just exploded in my brain. Kill one of Nadine's twins?! I can't do that, can I? Could I murder an innocent child just because it's born to a girl who'll never be innocent again, even if she bathes in holy water for the rest of her life?

"Caleb, I . . . I don't think I can do that," I reply.

Another pause, more words I don't want to hear. "Maybe Vera is reminding you that you have to stop thinking like a girl and start thinking like a goddess."

Why can't I just think like a girlfriend?

"That's a big stretch from one to the other," I state. "Do you actually think this could be a solution?"

This time his answer comes immediately.

"I'm sorry, Dominy. I got so excited when I made the Greek connection, I didn't realize the implications," he says. "But the truth is, this thing is bigger than just me, just you even; it's bigger than all of us. So while I don't condone it, I can't necessarily say that it isn't the right thing to do. Maybe it's just something you have to ponder that will lead you to the real way to solve this thing."

I wish I were in the same room with Caleb so I could hug him tight and kiss him a few hundred times to let him know how grateful I am that he did make the connection and that he never has to be sorry about anything when it comes to me. But the words from a distance will have to suffice.

"Thank you," I say. "Just knowing that I could *potentially* kill Orion is important. Remember, Caleb, knowledge is power. Isn't that what they teach you in that big fancy red school you're going to?"

I can hear Caleb's smile come through the phone.

"That and how much it hurts to miss your girlfriend."

The girl in me would love to stay on the phone and flirt with Caleb for hours, but the goddess in me has work to do.

I'm running so fast I don't even see Elkie sitting behind the receptionist's desk.

"Sorry, Elkie!" I cry. "I'm on a mission."

Before the door to Room 48 closes behind me I'm already speaking.

"Nadine is going to have twins, and once she does, she's going to be queen bee, which means she'll no longer have any need for you."

Luba's youthful façade hardens and loses some of its sheen. I guess that's what happens when someone tells you your granddaughter is planning to dispose of you after she gives birth to the next generation of evil.

Regaining some of her composure, Luba adopts a very human ploy; she asks an unnecessary question. "And how have you stumbled upon such information?"

"The old-fashioned way," I reply. "By accident."

Rising from her chair, Luba is once again wearing an outfit that isn't appropriate for a woman of her age. Her knit sweater clings to her body, and her wool pants look like they've been spray painted on. I stare at her moss-green suede shoe boots in sick fascination. How I'd love to step into Luba's shoes for a few hours. Literally, definitely not figuratively.

"How do I know you're not lying to me?" Luba hisses.

"Because you've known from the beginning that Nadine's pregnancy has made her dangerous; that's why you want me to help you defeat her. And now you know the reason why," I hiss back. "It isn't because Orion will look on her more favorably now that she's presented him with a new descendant, it's because she's presenting him with two. And once she plops out two babies instead of one, you'll be made redundant. The triumvirate will have a new leader."

I thought I was being straightforward, but clearly Luba is having a difficult time accepting what I've told her. She paces across the room, her shoes clicking loudly against the tiles on the floor.

"My granddaughter would not hide such news from me," she says unconvincingly.

Gigglaughs drown out the sound of clicking heels. "Yeah, 'cause Nadine's been brought up to tell the truth and not harbor any secrets," I howl. "You might be a powerful witch, but you're a stupid woman."

Abruptly, the clicking stops, and with eyes half-closed Luba turns to me, her face an abstract portrait of disgust meets respect. As much as she hates me right now, she knows I'm right, so there's only one thing left for her to do: lash out.

"Then one of her spawn must die!"

Once again Prince Caleb has saved the day. If he hadn't already planted the seed in my brain that one or both of Nadine's children should be murdered, Luba's hideous reaction would startle me; it would shock me into silence. Instead, I'm armed with a comeback.

"Which would be the action of an even stupider woman."

Her boots never touching the ground, Luba flies toward me, stopping only when she hovers a few inches above me, hair and anger falling down on top of my head.

"These unborn . . . *things* . . . are my flesh and blood!" she bellows. "I will choose what to do with them!"

I can't believe I'm not frightened by Luba's fury. There isn't even a twinge of anxiety in my heart or my stomach or my brain. Knowledge really is power, and I'm wearing it like invisible armor.

"And what do you think Nadine would do if she ever found out that you had killed one of her children?" I ask calmly. "She would hate you for the rest of her life."

Slowly Luba descends, her movement stopping only when her boots click onto the floor. A faint odor fills the room, pungent and sweet and rotted, and I realize it's the smell of Luba's fear. Her eyes are looking straight at me, but I know they're not focusing on me; they're looking through me in search of an answer, some truth, some thing she can hold on to so she can once again feel in control. Luba isn't used to losing her footing, and she doesn't like it.

"I was not put on this earth to grovel for my granddaughter's love," Luba seethes.

"But your granddaughter was put on this earth to serve you, no matter what she's felt for you," I reply. "Well, Granny, all that's about to change."

Luba swallows hard, and her skinny throat engorges; the skin expands as if reluctantly allowing a tumor entry to the rest of her body. But it seems as if her body refuses to accept the offering, and the huge lump stays in her throat. Guess it's time to give it a little push.

"Worst of all, Nadine will never trust you again; she'll never follow your command," I say. "And you can't control Nadine like you controlled Napoleon."

The lump slides down a little farther and rests just at the bottom of Luba's throat.

"And without Nadine you will never, ever know your full potential," I add. "And you'll be showered in Orion's spit as he labels you a disgrace."

Finally the lump is gone.

"I suspect that you, wolf-girl, have a solution?" Luba asks, her words crawling out from behind gritted teeth.

My tongue glides across my lips, and I'm reminded that hunger doesn't always have to be satisfied with a meal; sometimes it merely needs agreement from an enemy to be satiated.

I explain my plan to Luba and learn that she can be a very obstinate opponent.

"Never!"

Her voice is so loud I wait a moment, expecting Elkie or Winston to barge into the room, but no one comes. Her anger is meant for me alone to hear.

"You want to work with me, Luba? You want to be my partner? Well, that's my plan," I announce. "Help me separate the children. Nadine keeps one, and one is handed over to Vera."

This time when Luba paces the room, I don't hear the clicking of her boots against the floor, because she's walking on clouds of her own dark black energy. Her hatred and fury and rage are transporting her around the room, and for the first time since I've known this woman, I'm not sure who's leading whom. I don't know if Luba has unleashed evil or if evil is dragging Luba around in its clutches.

"I will never give one of my own to Vera!" Luba roars. "She is undeserving; she is self-righteous. . . ."

"She is *Orion's* messenger."

My words stop Luba in her midair tracks, the black cloud underneath her bubbling restlessly, unsure if it should continue to travel or return to its source. Like most truths, my words create confusion.

"And let me remind you that if you refuse to offer one of your great-grandchildren to Vera, you are refusing an offering to Orion," I proclaim. "Why do you think your god sent Vera here in the first place? She's here to restore balance! Not to allow Nadine to gain control, not to kill one of his descendants, but to return things to the way they were, the way they were supposed to be!" The next words rush out of my mouth before I understand their true meaning. "The way it was when you avenged your husband's death."

I am just as shocked as Luba is by my statement, but it wasn't mine; no, it couldn't have been. It must have been this goddess, this Artemis speaking, not me. There's no way that I can understand what Luba did. And yet there's a part of me that does.

"So, child, we're finally standing on the same side of the line," Luba states. "On the side of rightful vengeance."

I wish I had a black cloud underneath my feet that would help me escape, but I can't; I have to stand firm. I have to see this through. I have to get Luba to agree to my plan.

"So are we a team?" I growl.

It doesn't take long for Luba to answer, but when she does it's as if a whole new brand of fury has been unleashed from the depths of whatever's left of her rotted soul, the fury born from defeat.

The roar that escapes Luba's mouth is so loud, so primal, that it's silent for a few seconds, as if the earth has to prepare itself for the sound. When the scream fills up the room, I can feel my body shake, but I refuse to run; I refuse to give in to it. If we're going to work together, Luba needs to know that I am just as strong as she is.

Black smoke bombards me, striking me in the face and the arms and my chest, but I don't flinch. I can feel the wolf's paws scraping against the underside of my skin, but I will it to remain docile, remain in its place. Luba cannot sense that I am struggling for control. Suddenly the smoke turns into a black serpent, burnt by an eternity spent slithering through the flames of hell, and it wraps itself around me until its grotesque face is inches from my own. A thin, blistered tongue extends from the snake's mouth and glides across my cheek, sealing my pact with Luba with a death kiss.

After the tongue recoils I can feel its foul saliva drip down my face and collect at my chin. I have never been more disgusted in my entire life, but I don't show it. I bottle it inside, keep it as a memory so I never forget that even though Luba and I have entered into a new relationship, she herself has not changed. In fact, I know exactly what words are about to spill out of her mouth, so I beat her to it.

"Do not betray me!" I command.

Running down The Hallway to Nowhere, I scrape the snake spittle from my face, surprised that my hands don't burn from the touch. I know that I've just made a pact with the devil, and yet I can't help feeling triumphant. I stood my ground against Luba, I showed her that I'm worthy, and more important I showed myself that I can control my fear and anger and confusion. Just as I get to the end of the hall, Elkie appears, and I have to stop short. Now face to face with someone who is supposed to be my friend, I feel anxiety latch onto my spine, and I know that today's lesson is about to be erased from my mind.

"This is for you."

The envelope Elkie is holding in her hands is thin, but I somehow know that it contains a powerful message.

"I found it in Essie's things," Elkie informs me. Her voice isn't a whisper, but she's speaking quietly so we won't be overheard.

"Essie left something for me?" I ask stupidly.

"Yes, there was a note attached that said you should read

this after her death," Elkie explains. "I was waiting for the right time, and I suspect that time has come."

The simple kindness and sincerity emanating from Elkie's face and voice remind me of her sister, one of the few people I could trust implicitly. I don't know what this offering means or what its significance might be, but my gut tells me that if it's linked to Essie, it has to be something good. So without hesitation I take the envelope from Elkie's hands.

When I see Winston and Melinda enter the hallway from his office, I just as instinctively hide the envelope behind my back.

"Tell me, Elkie, what are you doing out from behind your desk?" Winston asks in his usual arrogant tone. "Do you want to keep this job or wind up unemployed like your predecessor?"

An infuriated woman responds to Winston's heartless comment, but it isn't Elkie.

"Her predecessor was *murdered*, you idiot!"

Revulsion drips off of Melinda's tongue and splatters onto the linoleum. I half-expect Winston to jump up and down to avoid coming into contact with his girlfriend's venom. As usual Winston's true cowardice reveals itself as he awkwardly tries to regain control of the situation.

"Well, yes, Essie w-was mur-mur . . . ," he stutters. "But I w-was going to fire her. She was becoming . . . unnecessary."

"A feeling you must know very well, Mr. Lundgarden," Elkie replies.

Her voice is so calm and even friendly that I'm amazed that she's speaking to the man who indirectly caused her sister's death. I'm not sure if Elkie knows all the details surrounding Essie's murder, but she's smart and intuitive if not completely psychic, so she must know that Winston played a featured role. Is this what it means to be an adult? Being cold and heartless? Or is it all just an act?

"The world is filled with unnecessary men," Elkie continues. "And an even larger group of unnecessary women."

Immediately Melinda's smile fades when she realizes that Elkie addressed her last comment to her. Her face is a blank mask, completely empty; the only blemish is the small cleft in the center of her nose. No, Elkie is hardly heartless. She's just really good with words. Guess that's why I know I can trust anything she says. When she hugs me tight and whispers in my ear that I should open Essie's envelope alone, the thought to betray her instruction doesn't cross my mind.

Locked inside my bedroom I sit on my floor facing the window and stare at the envelope. My name has been written on it in red ink, but I don't know whose handwriting it is—could be Essie's, could be Elkie's, I have no idea because I never paid attention to the details of Essie's life. I have to pay attention now. Whatever's inside this envelope has got to be important or else Essie would have just shared the information with me; she would've just told me while she was flipping through a celebrity magazine; she wouldn't have hidden it to be revealed only after her death.

I dig a fingernail in between the top flaps and then run my finger slowly along the length of the envelope. I feel like a surgeon opening up a body, not certain if I'll uncover healthy organs or disease. But all I see is a photograph.

The two girls smiling back at me are about three years old, wearing colorful dresses and party hats, their arms around one another. The joy and happiness and possibility within their eyes leaps out of the photo, and I wish I could grab hold of it, but I see something else in the photo that frightens me. One of the girls is holding something in her hands. Peering closer at the photo with my wolf eyes I see that she's holding the Little Bo Peep compact, the same one that my mother has.

I look again at the two girls and focus on their noses. They each have a small line running down the center, a cleft just like . . . no! I can't see their faces anymore because the photo starts to shake in my hand.

Gripping it tighter I turn the picture around, and the writing on the back is blurry because there are tears forming in my eyes. I know the truth before I read it, and some truths are too heinous to accept.

M & S, 3rd Birthday

There's no doubt about it. I don't have to read any further to know that Melinda and Suzanne are sisters. But when I read the rest of the writing on the back, the same handwriting from the front of the envelope, I have confirmation that the world is a vile and unforgiving and unnecessary place.

Melinda is your aunt.

Chapter 21

Blindly I rummage through the contents of my closet until I find it. I slam the metal box onto my bed and try to lift the lid, but it's locked. I know the key is on my keychain tucked inside the pocket of my jeans, but I want it open now. One wolf-yank and the lock is broken. I dip my hand inside, and it's like I'm sticking my face into shark-infested waters; as careful as I try to be, I know I'm going to get bitten. When I touch the engraved inlay of the compact I expect to see blood gush from my fingers.

Comparing the compact I'm holding—the one my mother told me her mother gave to her on her third birthday—to the one the little girl is holding in the photograph, I can tell they're identical. Melinda Jaffe and my mother are not just sisters, but twins! That's not possible! That isn't fair! But deep down in both my guts I know that it's more than possible and that life is anything but fair.

From the first moment I met Melinda, she reminded me of my mother, due to her physical resemblance, especially the cleft in her nose, and some other intangible connection that I couldn't explain or describe. Afterward, however, when I found out her true character, all thoughts of a link were eradicated; there could be no way that someone as ugly and vicious and remorseless as Nadine's mother could be related to mine. Except I've forgotten one very important thing—the importance of maintaining balance. And what better way to do that than to make two children born from the same cell become the antitheses of each other. Nadine and Napoleon are twins, so why not Melinda and Suzanne?

But can this really be true? Can our families truly be bound together by more than just a curse? Are the fates crueler than Luba?

The last thing Essie said to me before she died was "Melinda is your . . ." I filled in the blank for her and thought the next word in that sentence was *enemy*. I assumed that Essie was trying to warn me about Melinda before crossing over, before she no longer had a chance, but no, she was trying to tell me that Melinda is my flesh and blood.

Essie has become so much more surprising to me in death than she ever was in life. She must have been way smarter than I ever thought she was to have uncovered this information. Maybe she was conducting her own private investigation into Winston to find out who his girlfriend was and stumbled upon the truth? I'll never know, because even though I hardly thought about Essie, she was always thinking about me. She spent her last moments on this earth trying to connect with me, while I spent almost my entire life ignoring her. How awful a person am I? I used to think my actions while under this curse were deplorable, but it's the things you don't do that are worse.

"Oh, Essie, I'm so sorry," I sob.

Please, God, let Essie hear my apology. Please let her know how terribly sorry I am that she had to die because she got mixed up with me and that it's taken me so long to see her for the truly wonderful woman she was. For someone who has such incredible vision, it takes me quite a while to see things the way they really are.

My hearing, thankfully, is much better.

Downstairs I hear Arla and Barnaby in the kitchen. In another moment they'll call out for me to find out if I'm home. I can't be here; I can't deal with them right now. Yes, they're my family, but some new relatives have just crashed the party, and I have to figure out what all this means.

When I stop running and see that I'm surrounded by dirt and sand and rocks, I know exactly where I am—at Dry Land, where all this started. The place where I first transformed, the place where I first was cursed, the place where I first killed.

"Why is this happening, Jess!?"

My cry is so fierce that I disrupt my surroundings. A small flock of birds flee the barren branches of a tree a few hundred yards away; the bushes in the distance shake as some creatures scramble to run from the noise. I don't care! I don't care who hears me!

"Why does it keep getting worse and worse and worse?!" I scream.

What is that noise? I'm so lost in my outrage that I don't even realize that it's coming from me; I'm the one howling. When I recognize the sound that usually doesn't appear unless a full moon is hanging in the sky, I'm not startled; it appears perfectly natural. I've had enough! Miss Ro's senseless death, having to team up with Luba to fight against Nadine, and now finding out that she's my cousin because one of the women I despise most in this world, Melinda Jaffe, shares DNA with my mother. How much more of this destiny garbage am I supposed to take?

"I don't want to be connected to Nadine's family by blood!"

My word-rage is swallowed up by a burst of golden light. But the sunshine that engulfs me isn't bright and filled with promise; it's blinding and filled with just as much anger as is spewing from my body. I'm not the only one who's had enough.

"SHUT! UP!!!"

Jess's voice hurls out of nowhere to slam into my chest and throw me several feet into the air. I linger, suspended, hanging by golden rays of light, and look down in fascination at the earth until the golden rays release me and I fall, not stopping until I land, incredibly hard, on the cold ground. Momentarily dazed, I don't regain complete consciousness for a few moments. When I do, I realize Jess hasn't stopped shouting.

"You are *not* the only one connected to Nadine and her family!" she screams. "You are NOT the only one who's cursed!"

Oh my God! Once again I was only thinking of myself. How stupid was I to think that Jess wouldn't find out about Jeremy?

"And how selfish could you be not to tell me?!"

For the second time Jess's supernaturally enhanced voice rams into me, making my body shake like I'm on some G-force roller coaster. I have never seen her this angry or this powerful. My best friend definitely is changing; she is almost all Omikami. I just hope there's enough human left in her to understand why I kept the fact that Jeremy is the father of Nadine's twins a secret.

"I've caused you enough harm and heartache, Jess," I explain. "I didn't want to add to it."

"I've told you a thousand times, Dominy, I do not blame you for killing me!" Jess rails. "Let go of the shame and guilt and remorse, because it's not doing either of us any good! What I'm having a hard time dealing with is the fact that you knew Nadine used my brother to father her children and you kept that from me!"

"Because I didn't want you to do anything that would get Jeremy in any more trouble!" I scream. "You know what Nadine's capable of! If she had any idea that you were seeking revenge against her for using your brother or that you were trying to tell Jeremy the truth, she'd kill him just to get him out of the way. Do you actually think she ever intended to share their children with him?!"

I still can't see Jess's face, but her sunlight isn't as blinding as it was a few moments earlier. The sunshadow is lifting.

"Is that what you want?" I ask. "For your brother to greet you on the other side?"

Still no sign of Jess's face, but I know that she's as shocked by the harshness of my words as I am. Shocked, but relieved.

"No, Dominy," she says. "I would never want that."

When Jess appears, she looks almost translucent, as if she's part of the sun and not just lit by it. I don't have the strength to get up, not because I'm physically wounded, but because the sight makes me terribly sad. So I sit back on the ground and grab on to a rock to steady myself. My friend, my dear sweet Jess, is almost entirely gone.

No! Don't dwell on that now. She's still here; she's still sitting on the dirt right in front of you, Dominy. Focus on that!

"As far as I can tell, Jeremy has no memory of sleeping with Nadine," I relay. "In fact, he's said that it's as if he's coming out of a fog, so whatever mind games she was playing with him seem to be over. He served his purpose, so she's moved on."

Jess turns away from me, and for a few seconds I'm plunged into darkness. Part of me wants to stay here forever, hidden from the world, but soon Jess turns back and I'm doused with light.

"She tricked me again," Jess states. "I don't know how she does it. Maybe I've helped her by clinging to my human emotions longer than I should have."

Oh, Jess, I don't ever want you to let go of them!

"She tricked me into believing she was going to use your brother to get pregnant to distract me so I didn't discover that she was using mine," Jess states. "She might be a witch, but she's a smart one."

I reach out my hand to Jess, and she stares at it as if she doesn't know what it is or what to do with it. Finally she grabs hold of me, and again I can feel my heart breaking because it's as if I'm clutching a cloud.

"I'm sorry, Jess," I blurt out. "I'm sorry I didn't tell you. I'm just . . . confused . . . and tired of all of this. One day I'm ecstatic and I'm making love to Caleb and the next I'm horrified and forced to watch Miss Ro die, and now this. . . . When, Jess, when will it end?"

For the first time Jess smiles. It isn't a big smile; it isn't going to turn into a belly laugh, but it's an anchor that I grasp onto. When she speaks, I feel like letting go.

"Dominy, our journey never ends," she says. "You're staring at proof of that."

"But does it get any better?" I ask cautiously.

Her smile grows. "Yes, it definitely gets better," she advises. "But even when it gets better, there are still frustrations."

Without mentioning it I know she's referring to her limitations, the rules that have been thrust upon her by some higher being. The rules that she has to live her new life by.

"It's almost as if life and death are the same," I ponder.

Jess cocks her head to the side, throwing a ball of sunlight into the air. "Ooh, Dominysan," she replies. "Little grasshopper is getting so wise and philosophical. Mr. Dice would be impressed."

"Mr. Dice would be impressed if I mastered my multiplication tables," I joke.

My comment makes me laugh out loud, and soon gigglaughs are penetrating Jess's sunlight. Jess doesn't join in; she just watches me, a happy smile fixed upon her face, but a part of me knows that she's watching me in curiosity, from a distance, and not as my best friend who used to laugh with me for hours on end about the most nonsensical things. Ignoring what I'm feeling in my heart, I listen to my brain.

"Remember, Jess," I declare, trying to sound like my mother. "We're smart too."

"Then don't be misled," she replies.

"By what?"

"Just because the Jaffes' blood is mixed in with Jeremy's and your mother's and even with Napoleon's, it's still poisonous," she proclaims.

It takes me a bit to understand the ramifications of her remark, but quickly I comprehend the Jesspeak. "So even though there's goodness in their history," I say, "there's still evil, in order to maintain the balance."

"Well done," Jess says, sounding more like a mentor than a friend. "And if you want to postpone your permanent relocation to my side of the universe's playground, don't ever forget that."

After the third bang on my bedroom door, I unlock it and let it swing open. Here I am, world, I've got nothing to hide. Yeah, even I don't believe that.

"Are you forgetting to tell me something, Dominy?"

Ever since I got home I've been trying to avoid Arla, but she's been circling me waiting for the right time to strike. Which is now. She's developed some pretty good tracking skills, and from one good hunter to another I respect that. Doesn't mean I'm going to answer her though.

"Nope."

She stands in the doorway of my bedroom and crosses her arms. I take a good look at her for the first time since I've come home, and I realize she probably just returned from a run since she's wigless, scrubbed of all her makeup, and sweaty. This is her no-nonsense look; she has questions, and she wants answers, and there's no way that she's going to let up on me until I supply them. Like any good hunter I know when I'm cornered.

I usher Arla into my bedroom and close the door behind us. Jumping on my bed, I hold a pillow in my lap in an effort to look as nonchalant as possible before speaking.

"I told Luba that Nadine is having twins and that we have to work together in order to stop her," I say.

Arla purses her lips together, mulling over my announcement. "Did Grandma agree?"

"It took me a bit of convincing to make her see that my plan is best, but yes, she ultimately agreed," I say.

"And?"

"And what?"

"And what else aren't you telling me?"

"Nothing!" I protest way too vehemently. "Why the third degree?"

"Because you're withholding information from me, Dominy, and the only way we're going to remain safe is if we stay one step ahead of the crazies," Arla states, grabbing the pillow from my hands and tossing it onto the floor. "So I'm prepared to give you the fourth, fifth, and if you're not careful, the sixth degree to find out what you're hiding from me. And word to the wise, Dom, the sixth degree is more unpleasant than your monthly curse."

Oh how I wish Arla were just talking about my period.

"Okay, fine!" I finally shout. "You want to know the whole truth?"

"Why else do you think I'm standing here smelling like something at the bottom of Barnaby's laundry basket?" Arla shouts.

"Melinda Jaffe is my aunt."

So few statements that come out of my mouth render my friends speechless these days that I'm always surprised—and I must admit to feeling a tad bit pompous—when something does. I give Arla a moment to digest this awful truth.

"Shut your wolf trap!"

Okay, that's a new one. I think I should be offended, but I kind of like it.

"Even if I never opened it again, it wouldn't change the facts," I say. "Somehow Melinda and my mother are sisters, more than sisters actually; they're twins."

"One good, one bad," Arla cries. "Just like Nadine and Napoleon!"

Exactly!

I watch Arla pace back and forth mumbling to herself, and I marvel at how, once again, she's diffused a foul situation. A few hours ago I was devastated by this news, and now, well, it's a lot more palatable. She really has become a worthy successor to Jess in the best friend department. Actually, she's much more than a best friend.

"Can you imagine if my father and Melinda had gotten married?" Arla states, her words shocking her into a standstill. "Dom, this is something he can never find out about! He might think that if she's related to your mother, she might be a good person and worthy of a second chance."

"My lips are sealed, Arla!" I say, pulling an imaginary zipper across my mouth.

"Be serious, Dominy!" she says, getting even more agitated. "Promise me that you won't tell my father about this!"

"Tell your father about what?"

Does everyone eavesdrop?!

Slowly, the blood drains from Arla's face until she looks like the feminine version of Archie. The two of us avoid looking at Louis, who's standing in my doorway, and stare at each other like two kids who just got their hands caught in the cookie jar, because that's basically what we did. Except we didn't get caught holding onto a cookie, but to a secret.

"I asked you a question, Arla," Louis says. "Which means I want an answer."

Like daughter, like father, I suppose.

A little more of the color drains from Arla's face, and I seriously think that she might faint if I don't do something. So
without the faintest idea of what to say, I start talking.

"Louis, I can explain everything," I start.

"So explain," he replies.

He crosses his arms in front of his chest, further proof that
these two other people in my room are related by blood.
Maybe it's a sign that I should tell Louis the truth about
Melinda and my mother. Maybe this is what Vera meant
when she said it's time Louis learned the truth. If all those
maybes are correct, then why is the inner lining of my stomach acting as if it's about to explode. My gut is doing its best
to grab my attention, so I need to listen.

"I bumped into Lars Svenson today," I lie.

"And?"

Oh my God! Will the similarities never end?

"And, well, you know how chatty he can get," I ramble.
"It's as if communicating with the entire town on a weekly
basis isn't enough for him; he has to engage in long-winded
conversations about things that he really shouldn't be talking
about."

"Like what?" Louis asks, interrupting me.

I say the first idiotic thing that comes to my mind. "Officer
Gallegos."

Excellent, Dominy! Lead the detective right to the scene of
the crime.

"What about Officer Gallegos?" Louis asks, and this time
in his cop voice.

"Well, Lars said . . . *insinuated* is more like it," I stammer,
"Lars *insinuated* that the medical examiner was mistaken
about the human blood that was found in Gallegos's system."

Once again Louis cuts me off. "That isn't true."

"Oh, but Lars . . ."

"Lars is an idiot who likes to spread gossip and rumor,"
Louis replies flatly. "I can't explain and neither can Quinlan,

the medical examiner, but there was wolf and human DNA found in Gallegos's body."

I've opened up this can of worms; I might as well continue.

"Any chance he got bit by a feisty felon?" I ask. "Or a frisky girlfriend?"

Crickets.

"No," Louis says. "They haven't been able to trace or identify the human DNA beyond the fact that it's female."

That would be correct.

"Well, there was a fifty-fifty chance of that, right?" I ask.

Ignoring my rhetorical question, Louis stares at Arla and then back at me. His eyes judging us the entire time. "Is there anything else you'd like to tell me?" he asks. "And before you answer me, there are two things you should know."

By now the color has returned to Arla's face, and she's actually found her voice again. "What would those, um, two things be?"

"First, regardless of what you tell me it will remain confidential, and if necessary I will do everything I can to protect you."

Once again I'm reminded why my father chose Louis to be our guardian.

"And the second?" Arla asks.

"I don't believe a word you just said, Dominy."

Ditto to what I just said before.

Before I realize it, the tears start to well up in my eyes, because I'm no longer looking at Louis or listening to him talk; I'm looking at my father and hearing his voice. I'm hearing him tell me that he will always protect me, that I will never have to be afraid as long as he's alive. Even in death, my father has kept his promise; he put my life in the hands of a man who has sworn to protect me as well, and how do I repay Louis? With constant lies and deception. Vera was right about having to work with Luba, and I think she's right about having to confess to Louis.

"There is something else that you should know," I say.

We'll never know what I was going to say because just then Barnaby starts screaming from somewhere downstairs.

"Barnaby!"

Scrambling, Arla and I follow Louis as he races downstairs to find Barnaby on the kitchen floor with blood pouring out of his thigh.

"What the hell!" he screams. "Barnaby, what happened?"

"I . . . I don't know," my brother replies. "But it hurts!"

"Stay with him!" Louis orders before racing back upstairs, presumably to get the first aid kit out of the bathroom.

Barnaby uncomfortably shifts his weight, and I see that he's sitting on a knife. Before he knows I've seen it, he sits back down and tries to cover the blade with his hand. Too late! I grab my brother's shoulder and practically lift him off of the floor so I can pull out the knife and wave it in his face.

"You did this to yourself," I state, then ask, "Why?"

"I don't know what's going on with you two," Barnaby spits. "But leave Louis out of it."

His voice is so forceful and protective that I can only stare at Barnaby and the man he's become. When Barnaby looks deep within my eyes, I realize he's not just growing up; he's aged well beyond his years. And it's all thanks to me.

"Whatever secrets you have, Dominy, keep them to yourself," Barnaby says. "Because I don't want Louis to end up like our father."

Chapter 22

Erase everything I previously said. Pregnancy does not become Nadine. When she opens the door I feel like I'm looking at a girl who's about to die instead of one who's about to give birth.

Her round face isn't rounder, but puffed up, swollen, and her skin is not beautiwhite like Archie's, but pale with whisks of gray on her cheeks, and underneath her eyes are blotches so dark they're black. A crumpled forehead and glassy eyes complete the picture of a girl caught in the throes of pain instead of one who should be expecting joy. I guess the intrusion of not one, but two foreign objects in her body has taken its toll.

Yet, beneath this soiled exterior, the real Nadine remains. When her eyes focus on me and she sees exactly who's standing on her front steps, I notice a change. Some of the darkness underneath her eyes slowly climbs up until it latches itself onto the bottom lid and hoists itself into the sockets. Like a chemical reaction, the glassiness disappears, disintegrates, and is replaced by clear-eyed malice. The rest of her body might be in agony and desperately in need of a rest, but her eyes look ready for a fight.

"What the hell are *you* doing here?"

Her voice isn't drastically distorted, but it's still alarming. It sounds old.

"I want to see Luba," I reply.

Nadine's eyes bore into me, scrutinize my intentions, but the rest of her can't remain motionless. She places one hand on her back, right above the hip bone, and twists her body, lengthening it, so the huge mound protruding from her belly seems to rise and float in the air. All attempts at being sinister and dangerous and strong have fled her body along with her innocence, and what remains is a tired crone. If I didn't know that Nadine had brought all of this on herself, I'd feel sorry for her, but this is her doing; it's what she's wanted, so she has no one to blame but herself.

"She isn't at The Retreat," I say. "So I know she's here."

"My grandmother doesn't accept callers without an invitation," Nadine snarls.

A hint of a smile appears on the corner of her mouth, but it doesn't have enough strength to claim ownership over her face, so it just hangs there like a lone bee clinging to a flower, defiantly sucking on a petal that contains no pollen. Finally the bee gives up and flies away, the small slice of a smile leaving with it, and she slams the door in my face.

Just as I raise my hand to knock on the door once more, it opens.

"Now that's no way to treat our visitors," Luba purrs. "I raised you better than that, Nadine."

Side by side the physical difference between Luba and Nadine is startling; it's like the demonic version of *Freaky Friday*. Luba looks youthful and refreshed, while Nadine's old and haggard.

"Come in, Dominy," Luba says. "I've been expecting you."

She waves her hand in front of her to welcome me into her home. It's a normal human gesture; I don't see any trail of black smoke emanating from her fingertips, but I still feel as if her stained fingernails have just reached inside of me to drag me into her house. I have to remain on guard not because I've entered enemy territory, but because I've entered my family's home.

Sitting on the couch, Melinda Jaffe is reading a book. Her eyes remain fixed on the page, and although I've never read Jackie Collins, I can't imagine her fiction could be more interesting to Melinda than the unexpected arrival of her niece. She's trying so hard to appear unaffected by my presence that she looks artificial. Legs tucked underneath her, her free hand clutching her ankle, her thumb absentmindedly tracing circles on the flesh around the bone, her overly glossed lips sometimes mouthing words like she's some oversized kindergartner just learning how to read. She looks positively disgusting.

Next to her is a china cup filled with tea that must have just been poured from the kettle because little whiffs of smoke are still rising from the liquid. The pattern on the cup is actually more disconcerting than Melinda herself. Along the front and curving around the side is a small collection of pink roses, robust and dew-kissed and the landing strip for a butterfly, whose unfurled orange wings look as if they're trying to flutter away, but have lost the power of flight. I can't help but think of poor Napoleon. He was stuck in this family, like the butterfly is stuck there on the roses in the pattern on this cup, both held captive, prisoners forever, unless the cup smashes to the ground and breaks into tiny little pieces or his sister covers his mouth with her hand to stop him from breathing. Either way Melinda would be so unbothered by the mess that she wouldn't look up from her book. Not even when her daughter asks her to intervene.

"Mother!" Nadine cries. "I don't want her here. Do something!"

I don't know where Nadine's been living these days, but action doesn't come quickly to her mother. Melinda may set things in motion, she may plant seeds, she may spend her day thinking terrible and horrible and homicidal thoughts, but rarely is she the one to act on those thoughts. It's always someone else, Winston, Luba, or even Nadine, while Melinda watches like a mildly interested spider as a ladybug wanders into its web. She knows that the end result will be the ladybug's death, but she's in no hurry to make that death speedy. And now she's in absolutely no rush to ease her daughter's discomfort from having me in her house.

"Quiet, darling," Melinda says, her eyes moving left to right reading what must be the scintillating prose on the page. "You'll trigger labor pains, and I'm not in the mood to be interrupted. This book is far too juicy to put down."

If I didn't despise this woman so much already, I'd force my fangs to appear so I could scoop out her eyes and spit them across the room. But a better fate for my aunt—oh, how I despise that word already!—is for me to ignore her so when the time comes she'll have her vision intact and have no excuse not to serve as her daughter's midwife.

Seriously, I can't believe the apathetic liquid masquerading within Melinda's veins is connected to the blood that's pumping through mine. This revelation that she is my mother's twin may be the sickest one of all. And one that demands further explanation.

"Don't stop reading on my part," I snark. "I've come here to talk to . . . Grand-mère."

Sorry, I couldn't help myself; the French version of the word just slipped out, two seconds before the book almost slips out of Melinda's hands.

"What did you say?" she asks.

Her voice is so low and the words spoken so slowly and deliberately that I know she heard what I said, and she knows why I chose that particular word. So does Luba.

"I was wondering how long it would take you to figure it all out," Luba interjects, her voice in stark contrast to her daughter-in-law's. She's practically giddy, her hands clasped in prayer motion, her long fingers bouncing joyfully against one another. A joy that lands like a thud in the laps of the others in the room.

"What are you talking about?" Nadine demands.

"Our little friend here is smarter than the average . . . *beast,*" Luba replies. "Or she simply stumbles upon information like a wolf stumbles upon unsuspecting prey."

Colorful imagery may be a bit much for Nadine at the moment.

"Stop speaking in riddles!!" she screams. "Tell me what you're talking about!!"

A flick of Luba's head sends streams of jet-black smoke in Nadine's direction. Either Nadine is too weakened by her pregnancy or Luba is too infuriated by how it's making her granddaughter act, but whatever the reason, Nadine can't duck in time, and the smoke slices across her cheek, leaving a trail of burned flesh behind it after it evaporates into the air.

Crying out in pain and shock, Nadine clutches her face and stumbles clumsily into the door. No one in the room rushes to her side, so she has to grab hold of the doorknob and a small table to stop from falling to the floor. The only response she gets from Luba is a warning.

"*Never* speak to me that way again."

As delusional as any petulant, self-entitled child can be, Nadine ignores the venomous sound of Luba's voice and asks her mother for help. She might as well direct her request to the couch her mother's sitting on; she'd get a more enthusiastic response.

"Mother!" Nadine shouts. "Did you see what that witch did to me?!"

"No, darling, I did not," Melinda replies. "I might have been momentarily distracted by our smooth-talking visitor, but I really am thoroughly engrossed in my book."

Once again, despite his unnecessary and untimely death, I can't help but feel Napoleon is the luckier twin.

"So if you will excuse me," Melinda says, rising from the couch, "I think I'll continue reading where I won't be disturbed."

Melinda doesn't bother to look at her daughter, still clutching her cheek in apparent pain, but she can't take her eyes off of me. I stare right back; there's no way I'm going to give her the pleasure of backing down. I have no desire to speak with her or have any sort of family reunion, but if that's what she wants, I will not run from it. Naturally, when faced with a far-superior opponent, Melinda reacts like her boyfriend, Winston, and cowardly slinks away from confrontation. But before she leaves the room, Melinda turns to her daughter and adds, "I really do want to finish this book, so please keep that unborn child you're carrying quiet until the morning."

Child? So Nadine hasn't even told her mother that she's expecting twins. Obviously she wants to keep it a secret until they arrive, kicking and screaming and hissing and bathed in their mother's foul witchblood. Fine with me. That's one secret that can remain unspoken. I've come to hear the details of another.

"Speaking of privacy, Luba," I announce. "Is there anywhere you and I can talk without this one overhearing?"

Even burdened by pain and the loss of physical strength, Nadine still manages to overpower the space with her voice. "This is my house! How dare you ask me to leave!"

Both annoyed and amused, Luba shakes her head. "No one is asking you to leave, Nadine."

"Good!" she shouts back. "Because I'm not going anywhere."

"Of course you aren't," Luba replies. "We are."

Luba raises her hand, and once again black smoke appears, this time rocketing to the floor and swirling around our feet. The smoke slowly starts to ascend, encircling our calves, our knees, then our thighs, as if mummifying us with its intangible presence. When it reaches our waists the color begins to shift from ebony to gray, but the change isn't coming from the source; it's coming from another visitor.

"Vera!" Luba cries. "Leave us alone!"

"How can I, Luba," Vera replies, her body still unseen, "when you know how much I love to get inside that demented brain of yours."

The last thing I hear before everything goes silent and black is Nadine's bloodcurdling scream. I think she actually hates Vera more than she hates me. That or she really just doesn't want to be left in the house alone with her mother, and for that I can't blame her. At the moment, however, I have more urgent matters to focus on, like how not to give in to the claustrophobia I'm starting to feel cramped inside Luba's memory alongside Vera.

With her disguise intact, Vera looks the same, but now her voice has taken on an eerie quality. Maybe it's because I know that she's part of the Original Hunter, but when she speaks it's like hearing a voice from another body escape her lips. She opens her mouth to form words, but I know the words are someone else's, so it's like watching a movie where the soundtrack is on a half-second delay. But Vera isn't the only one who sounds different.

Now that we have a companion, Luba's lost the little charm she had. Back in her living room it looked like she was relishing putting Nadine in her place and playing hostess to me. Now I get the sense that she'd rather be spending a quiet night at home with her back-stabbing family. Even when she speaks, the scowl refuses to release its grip upon her face.

"I'm afraid you're going to be bored, Vera," Luba grumbles. "This memory is coming alive for Dominy's entertainment only."

"This is about Melinda and my mother, isn't it?" I ask.

"Like I said, I'm not sure if you're clever or lucky, but yes, my daughter-in-law and your mother are twins," Luba replies.

Her words stab at me like a rusty knife. Hardly new, but the pain is even stronger now that I don't have shock and disbelief to cushion the blow of her words.

"How can that be?" I mumble. "How is that even possible?"

"Destiny and order and balance are such surprising playmates, aren't they?" Luba asks. Her question was clearly meant to be rhetorical, but Vera uses it as an opportunity to remind Luba just how right she is.

"And the outcome of their games is sometimes the most surprising of all," Vera states. "No matter how powerful you think you are, you never know how things are going to end."

Seething, Luba keeps her lips so tightly shut she can only breathe through her nose. Her chest rises up and down several times before she has calmed down enough to reply. "I think it's time you left us, Vera," Luba fumes. "I need to enlighten Dominy on an as-yet-unknown portion of her mother's past."

"Oh by all means, Luba, enlighten us," Vera replies, her bemused smile never leaving her face. "You know how Orion cherishes enlightenment."

The mention of Orion's name makes Luba shiver, and a wave of cold air rushes over my body as well. When I see my mother standing before me, I feel like I'm standing inside a cube of ice.

"Mama!"

Disgusted by my reaction, Luba waves a hand in front of my face. "Don't overexcite yourself, creature. It's merely a memory."

It can't be; I don't remember my mother ever looking so young. But wait, no, no! This isn't my memory; it's Luba's! Immediately I feel even sicker than before, sicker than when I uncovered that my mother shares blood with Melinda, because now that sick feeling is mixed in with fear. Somehow my mother also knew Luba, which means she also knew agony.

"How do you know my mother?" I demand.

"Watch," Luba replies. "And you will learn."

My mother looks impossibly young and beautiful standing alone in a field of wildflowers on a bright, sunny day. Her face is glistening in the sunshine, and I gasp because this is what I must look like when Jess is around. Only there's no way I can look as pretty as my mother; there's something incandescent about her, something unreal. The moment I see the other person standing just outside the memory, I know what it is; it's because she has everything she's ever wanted in life—a loving husband and two children whom she loves even more deeply—and they're all about to be torn away from her by one man.

"Thorne."

My mother's voice sounds as strange coming out of her body as Vera's voice sounds coming out of hers. Even though my mother is real and not some ethereal entity, right now she's nothing more than a hallucination. Plus, I have so few memories of my mother talking to me while she was alive that watching her now feels even less real than watching Vera prance around as a schoolgirl. My mind and my heart and my body are being assaulted by such a cavalcade of emotions that I have to push down hard on the ground not to fall over. Stay in control, Dominy! You have to see this; you must see this!

"Suzanne!" Thorne replies, more shocked to see my mother than I was. "I told you not to come here."

"I had to," she replies, her French accent strong and lush, presumably because she's as emotional as I'm feeling right now. "I've been so worried about you."

What?! Wait a second! My mother knew Thorne! And she's worried about him! What the hell is going on here? Am

I completely mistaken? Is this before my mother was married to my father?

"Shut up!" Luba cries out in response to my litany of silent questions. "You're just like my granddaughter! Your trouble is that you have no patience! Watch them, listen to them, and you'll learn everything you need to know."

Chastised into silence, I turn my attention back onto my mother and Luba's son, terrified of how this memory scene will unfold, but mesmerized by it at the same time.

"When you said you were leaving, I knew exactly where to find you," my mother says.

There's a shift in point-of-view, and it's as if the camera has panned out to the right so we can see more of the countryside. When I see the Jaffe family cabin, I know exactly where we are. In the center of hell.

"You need to go, Suzanne," Thorne instructs. "Please leave now and go back to your husband."

"Mason understands why I had to come," my mother replies. "He doesn't like it, but he understands."

"He doesn't like it because he knows it's dangerous for you to be here," Thorne claims. "Trust me, Suzanne. Just turn around and go; forget that you ever met me."

"How can I do that, Thorne, when you've been such a good friend to me?" my mother states. "Despite everything that my sister's done to you, despite the way Melinda's treated you."

With those words a little piece of my heart shrivels up and dies. Up until now there was still the smallest doubt, the smallest possibility that maybe I was wrong. Maybe Essie's message to me was misinformed. But no—now hearing the words uttered by my mother, there's no going back. Melinda Jaffe is my aunt, and her daughter Nadine is my cousin. We're all connected by cursed blood.

"That's why you have to leave," Thorne implores, stealing nervous glances back to the cabin. "If she finds out you've come, things will only get worse. I won't be able to protect you from her."

"I'm not afraid of my sister," my mother scoffs. "I've known what she is my entire life."

Suddenly Thorne's expression turns gravely serious, because he sees something before my mother does, even before I do. Not something, actually, but someone.

"He isn't talking about me, Suzanne. He's talking about my mother-in-law."

Melinda Jaffe is standing in the open doorway of the cabin, her arms crossed in front of her, leaning on the doorjamb. They're each wearing their hair differently and Melinda has on much more makeup than my mother, so they resemble each other, but they aren't identical. Physically they're different, and emotionally they couldn't be further apart.

"Hello, Melinda," my mother says. "I thought you liked to stay as far away from Thorne as possible."

"A wife has certain obligations to her husband, Suzanne," Melinda retorts. "Speaking of which, shouldn't you be home with yours? Or have you finally driven Mason psychotic with your fake French accent?"

Shaking her head, my mother replies, "Not all of us have turned our backs on our heritage to join a cult."

"We do not belong to a cult!"

Luba isn't visible, but her words from within the memory invade the scene. Her presence is felt, and I know that she's just on the other side of the front door.

"Oh, Suzie," Melinda scolds. "You've gone and pissed off Luba, such a stupid thing to do."

"Come here!" Luba cries.

Suddenly we're all whisked inside the cabin, and the claustrophobic feeling returns. There's more than enough room to house us all, but with Thorne, my mother, Melinda, two Lubas, Vera, and myself, things feel uncomfortably crowded.

"I want to go," I whimper.

"No, you need to see this."

When Luba doesn't acknowledge Vera's comment, I know that it was only meant for me to hear.

"Why?" I silently ask.

"It's all part of Orion's plan," she replies. "Trust Him."

Trust him?! Is she certifiably insane?! I hear the *B* word slam into my ears—balance. True, Orion may have empowered Luba with evil, but he's also saddled her with mercy to let me see my mother in a way that I've never seen her before. Like some beautiful and heroic and avenging angel.

Taking a few steps closer to Luba and the two streams of black smoke rising from her shoulders, which make her look like a three-headed serpent, my mother doesn't look at all afraid. I look closer with my wolf eyes, and all I can see is her fierce fury and loyalty.

"Thorne has told me all about you, you sick witch!" my mother cries. "I know all about your powers and this curse and your connection to your . . . *Orion!*"

My mother says his name with such unbridled contempt that both present-day Luba and Vera bristle, but there's nothing they can do; the verbal assault took place years ago. They just have to accept the fact that not everyone on this planet worships this particular spot in the heavens.

"Then you know what I'm capable of?" Memory Luba asks.

"I know that you, just like that bitch over there who calls herself my sister, *think* you can get away with murder and destroying people's lives!"

"We don't *think* we can, Suzanne; we *know* we can . . . BECAUSE WE HAVE!"

I'm not sure what's more shocking, my mother's courage face-to-face with such a demon or the tone of Luba's voice. I've only ever heard her sound this angry and uncontrolled once before, when she was screaming at me in her room at

The Retreat after being upstaged by Vera. Just as Vera acted that time, my mother doesn't back down in Luba's presence.

"And now that's all going to change!" my mother howls. "I will never allow you to hurt my family! Do you hear me, Luba?! You will not harm my children!"

More frightened than when I've previously seen him confronting his mother or his wife, Thorne is standing against the wall, his palms against the wood, bracing himself, forcing himself to remain upright. I think the only reason he's stayed inside the cabin is because he can't turn into a phantom and dematerialize to penetrate the walls and flee to the sunlight outside. He's stuck within the darkness, where my mother is about to enter.

"I have been blessed with the power of Orion!" Luba wails. "The curse has been set into motion, and there is nothing you can do to save your family."

My mother moves even closer to Luba, fear still incredibly not a part of her face or her body. She's like a warrior, with only one salvo: to protect those she loves.

"I will love and protect and defend my family with every breath I have!" my mother roars.

Then so does Luba.

The Luba in the memory extends her arms and rises from the floor like an eagle, her long black hair spreading out around her, her entire body lying horizontal, so my mother has to look up to see Luba's face. It's the first time I see terror start to creep into her expression. Perhaps it's because she knows what Luba is going to say before the words spill out of her mouth and soak my mother with their foul stench.

"And what will you do if I take all your breaths away?" Luba hisses. "How will you protect your family if you're dead?"

"That's a wonderful question, Luba," Melinda says. "Do you have an answer, Suzie? Or are you just going to stand there like my husband, mute and afraid?"

I notice my mother's left leg start to shake, just slightly, but enough to tell me that she understands Luba isn't issuing an idle threat; she's stating fact. All I want to do is close my eyes, render myself blind so I don't have to see what comes next, but I can't; I have to watch. I know my mother is feeling the same way; she wants to close her eyes, turn and run, but she's come too far now. She's standing on the edge of a cliff and she knows that whatever the outcome, she is going to have to take another step forward and plummet to the waiting ground below. Or she'll be lifted even higher.

Extending her arm, Luba clasps the air above my mother's head and lifts her arm higher. As if her clutch is connected to my mother, I watch horrified as she is lifted, reluctantly, off the ground.

"NO!!!"

The sound of my mother's voice echoes in the cabin and in my brain, and I know instinctively that it's the last sound she's going to utter for a very long time. How can she, when she no longer has control over her body; Luba does.

Once again I'm reminded of those stupid skew lines from math, two geometric shapes always separated, but never unconnected. Luba and my mother are both floating horizontally in the air, one on top of the other, their bodies twisting and turning and contorting in a silent, untethered battle. Finally, with both of them silent, Thorne finally finds the strength to speak.

"Please, Mother, no!" he cries, his voice cracking. "Hasn't there been enough destruction? Haven't you done enough killing?!"

Horrified that her son has found the courage to speak to her so harshly and directly, Luba momentarily loses control of my mother's body, and my mother plummets, only to be caught by Luba's invisible hold inches before crashing into the wooden planks.

"That's it, Mother, please!" Thorne begs. "Show some mercy."

Luba lifts her hand higher, and my mother starts the slow rise back to midair, while Luba inspects her son, intrigued. It's as if his words, his plea is something she had never contemplated before. If she's going to contemplate it now, there must be something in it for her.

"And if I do this thing that you ask, if I spare the life of this undeserving creature," Luba says, staring down at her son as she continues to float flat near the roof of the cabin, "what will you do for me?"

Relieved, but incredibly saddened, Thorne tells his mother the only thing that will make her give in to his demands, something so simple, but something that will seal the fates of so many.

"If you let Suzanne live," Thorne replies, "I will never interfere with your plans again."

"Don't trust him, Luba," Melinda interjects. "He'll find a way to squirm out of his promise."

I can't believe I'm hearing this! I knew Melinda was cold-hearted, but she'd rather watch her own sister be murdered than allow her husband the upper hand for once in his life. I can't believe Luba shows more compassion to my mother than her own sister.

Smiling triumphantly and devilishly, Luba lowers her arm, and my mother slowly descends until she stops moving about an inch from the floor. Thorne kneels underneath her and carefully cradles her body in his arms until my mother's arms and legs and head go completely limp. The only movement is the slight rising up and down of her chest. Luba's kept her promise. Sort of.

"Your friend is alive," Luba declares. "But she'll never live again."

Thorne's soft whimpering is quickly overshadowed by Luba's maniacal laughter. Soon the Luba standing near me joins in with the sound of her memory, and I feel like I'm about to be swallowed up by evil. I can't take it anymore. Not only did Luba put a curse on my head, but she cursed my mother too! Luba's the reason she's been in a coma all these years! Oh my God—that's wonderful news! If Luba is the reason for my mother's fate, she can also be my mother's salvation.

"You put my mother in a coma!" I scream. "You can take her out of it!"

Luba merely sneers at me, like my breath is as foul as hers. "My, my, Dominy, you really are making a lot of demands lately, aren't you?"

Trapped within the confines of Luba's mind and her memory, I decide to take advantage of the surroundings and tap into my inner beast. I can see small puffs of red dust sprinkle out of my mouth with every violent breath I take. I don't want to transform right here and now, but if I do, so be it!

"This is what you created, Luba!" I howl. "You want me to be an animal, then I'll act like one!"

Luba's laughter turns into a banshee cry, and the cabin and the memory and whatever space in time we're inhabiting is filled with her black, angry smoke. I feel fear scraping at my shins and my knees and my arms, but I ignore it, because I feel something even more powerful—a connection to my mother. The two of us, stupid as we may be, are not afraid of Luba. We will not allow her to watch us grovel at her feet anymore!

"I said bring my mother back to me!"

The smoke is gone; Luba is alone. The two of us stare at each other as Vera watches with interest from the sidelines. No one makes a sound until Luba makes a proposition.

"I will make you an offer, Dominy," Luba begins. "I will revive Suzanne, but . . ."

Like Archie once said, nothing good ever comes after a but. "But what?" I ask.

"There has to be something in it for me."

What more does this woman want? "What, Luba, what else could you possibly want from me?" I ask.

"Don't be so arrogant," Luba replies. "I don't want anything from you. I want something from Vera."

Vera?!

"And what would that be, Luba?" Vera asks, sounding much calmer than my thoughts.

"The child that is not taken away by Vera," Luba explains, "will be killed by me."

Bluffing! She must be bluffing! If she kills one of Nadine's kids and the other is taken away by Vera and Orion, then there will no longer be a triumvirate; Luba will never reach her full potential. There's no way that she'll let that happen.

"I know what you're thinking, that without the child the triangle will be broken," Luba says. "But what you might not realize is that I'm not as power-hungry as my granddaughter. I have enough magic in my bones to overcome even the bitterest of disappointments."

Is this what all you sick people call balance?! I turn to Vera, who is looking through us like she's no longer interested. *Help me! Help me figure out if Luba's telling the truth or bluffing.* The only thing I can hear is my mother's voice.

Remember, Dominy, you are blessed.

With a conscience! Which is something I don't need right now. How can I condemn an innocent child to death in order to bring my mother back to life? Even if Luba is bluffing, there's no way for me to know that until it's too late. The only thing I know for certain is that if she brings my mother back to life and a child dies as a result, I'll never forgive myself. I can hardly deal with the fact that I had to give in to Rayna's request and kill her and that I jump-started Miss Ro's death; I can't . . . No. No!! I simply cannot have another death on my head.

"Leave...my mother alone," I whisper. "Just let her sleep."

"As you wish," Luba replies, not even hiding the fact that she's incredibly satisfied.

"You just remember what you agreed to, Luba," Vera reminds her. "One of the children will be given to Orion."

"And both children will live," I add.

Luba bows theatrically, bending her head so far over her knees that her hair covers her face entirely. From behind the black curtain, she whispers, "And you should both remember that Luba always wins."

Before she even stands up, the moment has come for her to claim victory. A scream penetrates the memory with such ferocity that the past is obliterated and we're thrust back to the present, right in the middle of the Jaffe living room, right where Nadine has fallen to the floor in agony, kneeling in a pool of water, both hands clutched around her belly that is still swollen, but now appears to be vibrating.

"How opportune," Luba gushes. "It looks like my granddaughter is about to give birth."

Chapter 23

Sometimes being a witch has its benefits.

While Nadine was still in mid-scream, all of us—Luba, Vera, Nadine, me, and Melinda—joined hands and instantly vanished from the Jaffe house to take yet another journey. This trip was noisy, but thankfully, short, and no one except me was surprised by our final destination.

"Why did we come to The Retreat?" I ask. "Shouldn't we have gone to Memorial Hospital?"

Pushing Nadine through the front door that Winston is holding open, Luba snipes over her shoulder, "We have our own way of doing things."

Once inside I immediately look over to the receptionist's desk and see Elkie staring at us. She is hardly startled by the screaming pregnant girl and her motley entourage; if anything, she looks as if she's been expecting us.

"Get the operating room ready!" Winston bellows, trying to sound authoritative, but coming off as merely anxious.

"Already done, Mr. Lundgarden," Elkie replies, with an aura of efficiency. "And now that you're all here, I've set the alarm."

"Good, then you can go!"

This time the voice is much more authoritative because it doesn't belong to Winston, but to Melinda. Elkie pauses a moment just to prove that she isn't following orders, but is merely ready to leave now that she's performed all her duties. As she walks by me, she whispers in my ear, "Don't forget there's a full moon tonight."

When I pause before responding it's not because I want to make sure Elkie makes it safely outside; it's only because I had totally forgotten! After my fiasco last year with a BM—Blue Moon—and the calendar I made for Caleb and me before he went to college, I can't believe I still forgot. I know I have a lot on my mind and things have been moving at warp speed lately, but that's no excuse. How am I going to make sure Nadine's twins are safe if I transform? This better be the quickest delivery in reproductive history!

"Ahhhh!!!!!" Nadine shrieks. "Hurry up! They're coming!!"

Sounds like I may get my wish. Melinda, however, isn't quite sure what she heard.

"What do you mean *they're* coming?" she asks.

It's lucky for Melinda that Winston is holding Nadine on one side and Luba is holding her on the other, because Nadine lurches forward as if she'd like to strike her mother with the full force of her power. "I'm having twins, you idiot!"

"Twins?!" Melinda shouts.

Ten, nine, eight, by the time I count down to seven, surprise has turned to fear. "Luba, did you know about this?"

Snorting smugly, Luba replies, "Why do you think I'm allowing her to be here?"

Everyone's head snaps toward me. I guess they've all come to know me as Unwanted Guest #1. Group thought isn't always effective or correct.

"Not her!" Luba scolds. "The *other* intruder."

Turning around, I see Vera, who's appeared in physical form for the first time since we arrived at The Retreat, carrying two balloons, one blue, one pink.

"I don't know about y'all," she says, "but I'm hoping for one of each."

She may not be human, but she does have a sense of humor. Unfortunately, Nadine doesn't find Vera or her comment humorous. On the contrary, she knows that if Vera's around, that can only mean she's in trouble.

"Get . . . her . . . OUT OF HERE!!"

"Nadine, what are you getting so upset about?" her mother asks. "She's nothing."

Struggling violently to break free from Winston and Luba, Nadine is so terrified by the possibilities of what Vera's presence means that she's forgotten to use her powers. She's turned back into what she was when she entered this world, just another helpless child. Well, this child is about to bring two more into the world, and through the window I can see the sky starting to darken, so she better do it soon or else she's going to have a wolf next to the stargirl in the delivery room. I can't imagine that will sit well with Nadine.

"Don't be a fool, Mother!!" Nadine wails. "Don't you know what she is?!"

"No! No, I don't!" Melinda replies. "Luba, what the hell is going on?!"

Now Luba and Winston are practically dragging Nadine down The Hallway to Nowhere, with the rest of us following close behind. We turn the corner on the right, and I see a brightly lit room at the end of the corridor that must be the delivery room. Nadine comes to the same conclusion as I do.

"No!!! Don't let her in there with me!"

"Luba!" Melinda shouts over her daughter's continued screaming. "Who is she?!"

"Not who, Melinda, what!" Luba states. "Orion has sent one of His minions to check up on us."

Melinda literally does a double take, but still can't quite believe that the girl she's staring at is connected in any way to Orion, the god her family worships. Vera must sense Melinda's doubt, because the next thing she does is rip the flesh mask off her face to reveal a floating orb of starlight.

"Now do you believe it?" Vera asks.

Stumbling backward, Melinda slams into the open door to the delivery room and stares dumbfounded at the starlight where Vera's head used to be as the rest of us pile into the room. The light jutting out from Vera's body is blinding, and until she puts her face back on, no one can see a thing. Temporary blindness is doing nothing to calm Nadine's nerves, and the moment they try to strap her onto the operating table, she slaps Winston in the face with the back of her hand and runs for the door. Before she can reach it both Vera and Luba raise their hands, and the door to the room slams shut.

Sobbing, Nadine bangs on the door. "Let me out! Someone, please!! Let me out!!"

I have to look away because I don't want to feel pity for her. I know what she's capable of; I know what she's done. I know what they're doing to her now isn't right, but it is fair and just. And it's the only thing we can do to prevent her from becoming even more evil than she already is. When I look back I don't expect to actually want to help Nadine.

Obviously, Luba wants this delivery over as quickly as I do, but whereas I'm willing to let nature take its course, Luba has never been one to succumb to greater forces. She reaches out with her right fist and then pulls it close to her chest. With a thud Nadine falls to the ground.

"Let go of me!" she cries.

Luba repeats the movement with her left hand, and Nadine starts to slide across the floor, frantically grasping at the air and the linoleum to try to stop herself from moving, all the while flailing and kicking and digging the heels of her white sneakers into the floor, so the squeaking noise mixes in with her screams.

Another movement of Luba's hands brings Nadine closer to her fate, but she isn't about to stop trying to break free. I flinch when Nadine twists onto her stomach. I reel back when she stares at me and mouths the words, "Help me." It's exactly what I needed to be reminded that Nadine is getting exactly what she deserves; those are the exact same words Napoleon mouthed to me last year. I couldn't help him, but I can help the children who will never be able to call him uncle. Thanks to the girl standing next to me.

"Stop struggling, Nadine," Vera says. "You know it's futile to go against the Master's plan."

I don't have to look at Luba to know that she's raising her arms, because Nadine starts to rise off the ground and float toward the operating table.

"This isn't the Master's plan!" Nadine screams. "It's yours!"

"No, child," Luba corrects. "It's mine."

For the first time since we've arrived at The Retreat, Nadine is quiet, not because she's at peace, but because she's been stunned into silence. *Yes, Nadine, this is what it feels like to be betrayed; this is what it feels like to know that someone you thought loved you has turned against you; this is what it feels like to have your entire world destroyed. Enjoy the feeling!*

"After everything I've done for you, Grandmother," Nadine starts, "you're going to betray me?"

Luba opens her mouth to respond, but no words emerge, only four blasts of black smoke that whip out of her and around Nadine's wrists and ankles. Once her granddaughter is strapped to the table, Luba finally speaks.

"Isn't that what you were going to do to me?" Luba asks.

Nadine's defiant expression speaks louder than any reply, and we all know what her intentions were. Luba leans in close to Nadine and whispers, "Now, child, the time has come for you to learn your true place in this world."

Those are the last words Nadine hears before passing out.

Glancing outside, I see that the sky is becoming completely

dark; I don't have much more time left. I can see the full moon slightly visible in the dusk, and I can feel the wolf spirit begin to stir deep inside of me. Could it be possible that just for tonight I could keep the animal at bay? Why not! He's been brought out in the light before, which is against the rules, so why can't he stay hidden during a full moon?

"It's time," Vera announces.

No! I can't transform yet! The girl has to stay; the girl has to be the one to protect these children! I don't trust any of these people!

"The first child is coming!" Luba shouts.

Nadine might not be conscious, but she's clearly in pain. Her face is contorted into a grimace, and it's covered in sweat. Her chest is heaving up and down like she's having difficulty breathing, and her wrists and ankles are twisting and turning, trying to break free from Luba's smoke cuffs.

"Winston, hold her steady!" Luba commands.

The Cell Keeper tries, but it's as if he's afraid of touching Nadine, like he's finally realized that the Jaffes are contaminated, and he doesn't want to risk an infection. Too late, fool!

"I . . . I c-can't," he stammers. "She won't stop m-moving."

"My God, you are such an imbecile!" Melinda cries out in disgust.

Pushing her lover out of the way, Melinda positions herself behind Nadine and places Nadine's head in between her hands. Nadine must know that her mother is holding her because her movements become even more agitated.

As Melinda leans in close to her daughter, I have to turn on my wolf-hearing to eavesdrop. It serves me right to listen in on someone else's private conversation.

"Remember, Nadine," Melinda whispers, "you are blessed."

No! She's stealing my mother's words; she's trying to be like her! Melinda will never be like my mother! She'll never be anything like her!

I feel a warmth on my shoulder, and for a fleeting moment I think that Jess has arrived to help ease the pain, but the light burrowing into my skin is silver, not golden. Vera smiles at me, not like a mother, but like a friend. I don't know why, but I know that even though I may not be able to trust everyone in the room, I can trust her. Even though she's Orion's offspring, she has truly come here to help me.

"Soon it will all be over," Vera says, just before turning her attention to the patient. "I can see the baby's crown."

Then, at the same time, Vera and Luba whisper, "Push."

Two streams of smoke—one silver, one black—twirl together to combine, to become one, and grow so large that they practically consume Nadine's body. Slowly the smoke cloud begins to dissipate, and Nadine is reacting as if her body is on fire.

I'm so focused on watching Luba and Vera deliver Nadine's children that I don't feel my cell phone vibrating in my back pocket until the second time. Looking at my phone I see that Arla wants to know where I am and if I'm safe since the moon is about to make its monthly appearance.

Quickly, I text her that I'm at The Retreat and that Nadine is about to give birth. By the time I put the phone away, her first child is born.

"It's a boy," Luba pronounces proudly.

The newborn wails loudly, could be happy to be alive, could be furious to be part of this family, but he sounds healthy and strong and resilient. Luba places the child on a cloud of black smoke where he continues to gurgle and cry, but he's alive. So far Luba is holding to her promise.

The silver-black smoke thickens again, writhing and undulating all around Nadine's body until finally it disappears completely. Its job is done; the second child has been born.

"It's a girl," Vera announces, placing her on a cloud of smoke next to her brother.

I watch the two babies, only seconds old, coo and wiggle,

as they acclimate to their new surroundings. Instinctively, their tiny hands reach out to feel the other's fingers, reconnect, resume the connection that they had only moments ago in the womb. A connection that is about to be severed forever.

Without looking at the children or Vera, Luba states, "Take one of them and leave."

"No," Vera replies.

What do you mean "no"?! That's the whole reason you're here; that's the whole reason I'm here! I can feel the fire start to pulse through my veins and the pain begin to enter my limbs. Outside the full moon has risen; inside I'm faced with another turning point.

"I said choose one child and then leave here for good!" Luba cries.

"It isn't my decision," Vera replies. "It's Dominy's."

"What?!" I hear myself shriek in a voice that's dangerously close to a howl. "Why is it mine?"

"In order for true balance on earth to be restored, it must be maintained by one who was born here," Vera explains. "I was not, and Orion doesn't trust Luba to issue a mandate that she won't benefit from. Only you can make this decision, Dominy, because only you will decide what is best for the children."

If I had more time to dwell on the conflicting rush of emotions bouncing inside my head and my heart and my soul, I probably would, but I don't. The full moon is casting a glow on me that I can't ignore; I'll soon be under its command, and then I won't be able to make any decisions. I have to act, and I have to act now. And the only way to decide is to trust my instincts.

I look at the boy and then the girl, and both of them have the mark of Orion, three stars just above their hips. Except for their gender the children are identical, until I see another marking on the boy's foot. It's almost invisible, but my wolf's vision can see that he bears another birthmark, this one in the shape of a golden sun, this one a gift from my friend. This small imperfection on the boy's skin is a message from Jess showing me that he will remain protected by the spirit of the Omikami while being raised by Nadine. Once again and maybe for the last time, Jess has crossed dimensions to help me, to guide me when I need her most.

Crying for myself and for the baby girl that I'm holding, I offer the child to Vera. Just as she takes the girl, the transformation overwhelms me, and I crash to the floor. I can hear Winston screaming in the distance, so I know that I'm changing before their eyes. Despite the pain, I've got to reach out once more to Vera before she vanishes with Nadine's daughter! She must hear me.

"Please . . . protect . . . her!"

I don't know if I'm hearing Vera's words or if I'm listening to her thoughts, but she promises me that she will. She also promises me that I will be repaid for restoring balance and carrying out Orion's wishes. I don't care about any of that right now; I just want to get out of here. A hospital room is no place for a wolf.

Luba couldn't agree more.

"Listen to me, *animal*," she silently speaks. "Get out of here. Get out of here now before I forget that we have a truce!"

Trust me, Luba, you'll never forget! Just like Jess will never let that child be harmed!

Outside I gulp down the air, and it tastes as sweet as the freshest carcass. I'm about to run off to lose myself in Robin's Park when two smells wrap themselves around my snout; the scents are dissimilar, but both are familiar. One is alive and luscious and vigorous, and the other is decaying and bitter and harsh. I lift my head, and in the distance I see two humans whose faces I instantly recognize.

The girl with skin the color of mud speaks first.

"Dominy?" she asks. "It's me, Arla. Do you recognize me?"

It takes a moment for the memory to burrow its way through my fur, but yes, yes, I do. I breathe deeply and recognize her clean scent, pure and good. But I choke when the pale-skinned boy walks toward me, and my paws claw at the dirt; I want to dig a hole, cover my body with the cold earth to escape the foul odor that clings to his body. There's something wrong inside of him; I can smell it. He's like a diseased animal.

"Dom, it's me, Archie," he says.

No, it isn't! You're an imposter; you've become something different. You're trying to hide from it, you're trying to disguise yourself, but looking at you now with wolf eyes, I can see through you; I can see through the masquerade. My howl is plaintive and sad and a warning to this boy and those around him that everything is about to change, even more so than it already has. Not everyone pays attention to my message.

"I don't care if you run this facility, Winston. I want you gone!"

I know this woman too, the older one with the blond hair. There's a foul odor clinging to her too, but hers is stale; it's been a part of her since her birth. Not like Archie's; his scent is new, and he has chosen this repugnant fragrance.

"Melinda, p-please," Winston stutters. "N-not with that thing out there."

His cowardly voice is pathetic. I have to prevent myself from racing through the air and pouncing on his back, digging my claws into his flesh, and ripping out his throat so I don't have to hear his whining any longer.

"Oh sometimes you make me sick, Winston," Melinda replies. "Look at it; it's nothing more than a harmless girl playing dress up."

The immoral are always such idiots.

"I-I've seen what she c-can do," he continues. "L-let me protect you."

A bemused smirk lights up her face. "Do you actually think I need *your* protection?"

Winston takes a step closer to Melinda, but she moves away so her back is pressing against the front door. "B-but I l-love you," he says.

The sound of the woman's laughter is deafening; it roars through the air like a snowstorm, widespread and strong and touching everything in its path, the trees, the ground, the air, until there's nothing left to listen to.

"Are you that stupid to think that I care that you love me?" she asks. "Or that I could ever love you?"

"B-but you said . . ."

"I said I needed you, that we needed to work together," she clarifies. "In the beginning you were a diversion, but seriously, Winston, you disgust me. I had so hoped that after we got rid of Napoleon I would never have to see you again."

I can see the black roots grow slowly in Archie's hair, sucking away some of the pure white. A similar change takes place in his eyes, a black line runs the circumference of his violet irises, round and round until all the color is replaced with darkness. Arla can't see any of this; she can only see Archie's body bend forward like the weight of Melinda's words is resting on his back.

"Archie, what's wrong?" she asks. "Are you all right?"

Finally, Melinda notices that they have company.

"Oh dear God, you two again!" she exclaims. "Stop stalking us! Napoleon's dead. There's no reason for you to keep coming around!"

My growl is meant to be a warning, but all it does is get them angrier. Listen to me, you fools! I'm trying to save you! Get inside!

"Oh shut up!" Winston screams. "I've had enough of you!"

"Don't talk to my friend like that," Archie says.

His voice is like two pieces of rough sandpaper rubbing together. He doesn't sound anything like the Archie I remember.
"Now you're going to give me orders?" Winston asks.
He's trying to cover up his cowardice with bravado, and all
it's doing is getting Archie angrier. "Let's hope Nadine's boy
doesn't grow up to be like Napoleon, right, Melinda?"

The woman doesn't answer because she's ignoring him;
she's much more interested in watching Archie allow the
beast that's been hibernating within him become unleashed.
Just like her daughter moments earlier, Archie is about to
give birth to another living creature.

"I mean, let's be honest," Winston says. "We w-wouldn't
want the newest member of the family to be another f-faggot,
would we?"

Winston is still looking at Melinda for approval or positive reinforcement or just a glance, so he doesn't see Archie
leap through the air like a torpedo, but he definitely feels
Archie's fists slam into his chest. The impact is so strong it
hurtles Winston backwards onto the front steps of The Retreat.

"Archie, no!" Arla cries.

But Archie can't be stopped, not now that he's allowed the
evil within him to breathe, to come alive, to control him. It's
ironic that he's infused with Nadine's power, because the
same power that killed Napoleon is now the power that is
defending him. Life really is all about balance.

"Get . . . off . . . me!"

I can hear Winston's bones break every time Archie
punches him. I can hear the blood start to gurgle in his throat.
I can hear his spirit struggle to remain attached to his body.

Lunging forward, I clasp my mouth around Archie's ankle,
not too harshly, not even to draw blood, but enough to pull
him off of Winston. Archie, however, is determined to do
more damage, and he shakes his leg wildly until I lose my
grip. By the time I make contact with him again, he's grabbed

Winston, lifted him up, and thrown him several yards away so he lands headfirst into the sign in front of the facility.

I can hear a faint sigh coming from the man's unmoving body, but no one rushes to his side to try and bring him back to life, because another soul has returned from the grave.

"Archie."

The boy's voice is coming from the girl's body, but it seems completely natural to everyone except the boy's mother.

"Napoleon?" Melinda asks, stumbling backward and grabbing hold of the railing on the front steps. "Napoleon, is that you?"

"Does it matter?" the girl/boy asks.

Through the darkness the woman's face begins to shine as if whatever goodness is still lying stagnant in her soul has rushed to the surface, and for a moment it looks like she is going to run toward the girl and hug her, squeeze her so tight that the boy trapped inside of her pops out and joins the rest of us, but just as quickly the shadow returns; darkness has once again melded into the contours of the woman's face.

"No," she replies. "I guess it really doesn't matter any longer."

"Just as well," the boy says. "I've nothing to say to you, Mother. I've come to speak with Archie. And please don't act insulted; I know you're relieved."

Arla walks up to Archie and grabs him by the shoulders so he can't look away.

"Archie, look at me. Please walk back into the light."

"I can't see any light, Nap," Archie replies, shaking his head. "Only darkness."

"Because you're not trying hard enough," Napoleon replies. "You're giving in to what's easy, what makes the hurt go away."

Archie grabs the girl's face with his hands roughly, tenderly, but he's looking into the soul of Napoleon.

"It doesn't ever go away. Don't you understand?" he cries.

"The only time it gets better is when I give in and lose myself, when I let the blackness take over."

"But you can't do that, Archie! Please trust me, if you do give in, you'll lose yourself forever."

Suddenly Archie pushes the girl away from him.

"Maybe that's what I want," he says. "To lose myself and forget everything."

Arla reaches out and grabs Archie's hand; she lifts it to her lips and kisses his skin softly. "I can't forget the guy I fell in love with, and neither can you."

Holding onto Arla's hand desperately, like a lifeline, Archie begins to cry. "I'm afraid, Nap," he says through his tears. "Without you I'm so alone that sometimes I don't want to survive. I just want to lie down and fall asleep and never wake up."

"Oh, Archie, please don't talk like that," Nap begs. "You have so much life ahead of you, so much light and goodness and joy, but if you give in to this . . . if you give in to what my sister did to you, you'll be just like her."

But he already is. Winston's stopped breathing.

I don't know if Archie can see the man's spirit rise out of his body, but he suddenly turns away from Napoleon to stare at the fresh corpse. When Archie's expression changes from interest to fear to horror, I know that he is fully aware of what he's just done.

"Oh my God . . . no!" Archie cries. "I killed him! I killed Winston!"

The stillness in the air is interrupted by the odd, unnatural sound of applause.

"And finally," Melinda declares, "one of you children has done something that I can applaud."

And Archie has done something that he may never be able to forgive himself for.

Chapter 24

I can smell Archie, but I can't see him.

Turning left I follow the scent. My snout twitches uncomfortably because I want to push the odor away. I'd much rather bury my face in the snow patches that cover the ground and revel in their freshness, roll my body around in their unstained, clean scent, but I can't; I need to follow the other smell, the one that reminds me of fragrant violets that have begun to rot from being in the sun too long. The violets bend, giving in, letting decay take over because they don't realize salvation is only a rainstorm away. Archie needs to know that it's about to rain.

I know that he wants to be left alone, that he wants the entire world to forget that he exists, that even he wants to forget that he exists, but forgetting doesn't change anything; I know that all too well. Ignoring the past, wishing that it didn't exist, convincing yourself that it was nothing more than a dream doesn't erase it; it only delays the inevitable, the day when the memory returns and refuses to be pushed aside. I need to find my friend and make him understand that running is not a solution, it's just an interruption.

A gust of wind throws the foul stench into my face, and an

involuntary growl attacks the unseen assailant. My neck twists, cranes to the left, the right; my snout pushes against the offensive air before I can control my body, get it to stop and let the rancid smell wash over me, let it pass to reveal what it's covering, the fragrance of a blooming violet. Fresh and alive and hopeful. The scent is still there; it's just shrouded in noxious fumes.

The howl that pierces the cold night is not impulsive, it's deliberate. I want my voice to be heard not only by Archie, but by the moon and the stars that are shining madly in the sky as well. I want them all to know that they are not alone; there is someone here who will never give up fighting, who will no longer run out of fear, who refuses to remain silent. This creature, this wolf, this girl has had enough with destruction and havoc and death. It's time for the healing to begin.

I still can't see Archie, but I can hear him. His breathing sounds quicker than his movement, so his body may be trying to convince him to stop running, reminding him that the world is too vast a place to be outrun. *Listen to your body, Archie; let go of your fear and be still; let the world catch up to you so it can help you heal.*

Gracefully I step over a cluster of rocks and then sidestep the sharp edges of a hollowed out tree that must have fallen to its death decades ago. Injury will not prevent me from reaching Archie; nothing will, not even his desire to remain unfound.

"Leave me alone!"

The childlike fear in his voice makes me lose my footing, and I slip on a piece of ice, sliding to the right until the trunk of a particularly large tree stops me. I don't know if Archie is shouting at me or at the demons in his brain, the dark black energy that Nadine unleashed into his body, the energy that won't settle for anything less than total domination. But it doesn't matter why he's shouting. I have to reach him.

With renewed determination he's on the move again, and I hear the snow crunch underneath his footsteps and the snap of weak branches, but I have his scent in my nostrils and his sound in my ears, so it's only a matter of seconds before I will have his body in my sight. A few moments later when that finally happens, when Archie has finally given in and stopped moving, I'm not prepared for that sight. Even covered in fur, underneath the armor of a merciless hunter, I feel pity.

He is crouched on all fours, his hands and knees buried in snow, and I see his head dangling from his neck, a stream of sandy-colored vomit pouring from his mouth. When the foul-smelling liquid stops flowing from deep within Archie's gut, a tremor grips his body, making him shake so badly that his hands slide forward and his head dips closer to the vomit-stained ground. Whimpering and moaning, he swings his head from side to side like a pendulum, but the movement is interrupted when another wave of nausea rips through him. His neck bulges and widens; I can see the veins pop out on his flesh as his mouth opens as wide as it possibly can, as if he wants to scream so the entire universe will hear him, but no sound emerges, only another stream of vile-smelling liquid.

His chest heaving, Archie sits back on his haunches exhausted. I can see the sweat trickle down the side of his face, and a long string of bile that is latched onto the corner of his mouth rests on his chin until a sudden wind lifts it so it ripples in the air until it finally breaks free from its host and soars away on its own. Archie's tear-stained eyes watch it with envy as it rises higher and higher until it disappears from view. I know he wishes they could trade places; I know he wishes he could fly away and melt into the sky, become part of the unseen tapestry of the world. But he can't; he's still back here on earth with me.

I circle Archie, and he doesn't even notice me. His vision is too blurred by his tears, and I'm sure his mind is too confused by images of Winston's dead body. He's staring straight ahead, but seeing nothing, only the past, only the moment when he gave in and stepped over the line to join Nadine in her world. I have to connect with him; I have to let him know that he can still step back. But is it too late? Has his time finally run out? Has Nadine actually won in recruiting another member to join her army? It would be somehow poetic; on the same night that she lost one child to Orion, she's gained another. No! I can't accept that; I will not accept the fact that I've lost one of my best friends forever, not to her!

My growl sounds more menacing than I want it to be, but that's okay, if it'll just get Archie's attention. Make him turn and face me. But nothing; he's still watching the loop in his mind, how he sprang forward and attacked Winston, how he didn't let go until Winston's body went limp and fell to the ground, how we all watched the life seep out of Winston's body like air wheezing out of a balloon until it was a lifeless mass of flesh.

The third time I circle Archie, his eyes blink. I take it as a sign, and I stop in front of him; maybe my physical presence can block the mental images ravaging through his mind. Slowly, I see the haze lift, and Archie's eyes focus on mine. He's still confused and afraid and ashamed, but he's present. I'll accept it. I refuse, however, to accept his request.

"Kill me."

Never!

"Do it, Dominy," he pleads. "Please."

His voice is barely a whisper, but it's strong. Despite his weakened condition, despite the fact that he looks as if Winston was the victor in their deadly skirmish, Archie's voice is filled with conviction. I need to get him to reverse this power, make him use it for his survival, not his destruction.

Shaking my snout from side to side, I bump my head into his knees, just to make some sort of physical connection. He doesn't flinch; he doesn't reach out to touch my luxurious fur or strike me; he wants to die, but he doesn't want to be a willing participant. I take that as a good sign.

"Archie, I'm not sure if you can hear me," I say. "But you've got to fight."

Silence and wind rush into the space between us. I've got to fill the void with something more, something that Archie can hold on to. Something that he can grab on to that he'd never want to let go of. Found it!

"Napoleon!" I cry. "Remember how much Napoleon loves you, remember how much he believes in you!"

A frigid breeze passes through me, dancing on top of my fur. I know the same icy sensation is spreading itself over Archie's skin, but he doesn't move; he doesn't shiver; he doesn't feel anything.

"Archie! Try to hear me!" I cry from within the body of the wolf. "Napoleon wants you to live!"

The noisy cacophony of my growls and howls must be drowning out my words. Archie isn't responding to anything I'm saying, and no matter how despondent he may be, how deeply resolute in his determination to die, if he heard Napoleon's name, it would make some sort of a difference. But wait! If he can't hear Napoleon's name, he can still see it.

I drag my paw in the snow to create a vertical line, then a slash mark, and then another vertical line to create an *N*. I continue writing in the snow, another slash connected to another one pointing in the opposite direction and then a horizontal line in the middle of them to make an *A*. By the time I'm finished with the third letter, I can see the tears fall from Archie's eyes. He recognizes the name; he knows that I'm trying to tell him that Nap wouldn't want this.

"Nap."

Archie's voice is filled with bewilderment and wonder. When he speaks again his voice only contains shame.

"I'm so . . . sorry!"

There's nothing left for me to do except press my warm

body next to Archie's and let him hold on to me for support. His cold hands now tremble with freedom; he doesn't have to hide his fear and pain and sorrow; he can unleash it. I can feel his tears wet my fur, stinging my flesh with their scorching heat. When he presses his mouth into my back and screams, I camouflage the sound because he's not yet brave enough to share his agony and turmoil with the rest of the world. For now it's only ours. Two creatures who know what it's like to kill, and two creatures who have to deal with the pain of that everlasting memory.

The next morning in my bedroom the pain hasn't softened; it's still as strong as it was last night. But at least now I've transformed back, and Arla is with us, so Archie is surrounded by friends. Left to his own devices, I'm not sure what he would do. The only thing I'm sure that he wants to do is speak with Napoleon, but it doesn't sound like that's going to happen unless Nap also wants to have a conversation.

"I told you, Archie. It doesn't work that way," Arla says. "I have no control over when Nap uses me as a cross-dimensional microphone."

"But you're connected," he replies.

"Yes, we're connected," she confirms. "But that doesn't mean it's an equal partnership. Nap calls all the shots. I've just begged him not to take over my body when I'm at the wheel of a car or taking a test. I'd rather not crash on the road or academically, and thus far he seems to be holding up his end of the bargain."

Arla's presented her argument, but Archie won't take no for an answer.

"But if he's meeting your demands on those counts," he counters, "he must be listening to you. Please, Arla, ask him to talk to me."

"What do you think I've been doing all morning?!" she blurts out.

Sounds like sometimes Arla isn't in control of her own voice even when Nap isn't taking over.

"So he just doesn't want to speak with me," Archie declares.

"I don't know, Arch," Arla explains. "I honestly don't know how our connection works. You guys hear his voice; I don't. In fact, I don't remember anything about the conversations he has with you, so I'm just guessing that he's heard my request. It could be nothing more than dumb luck."

"Or it could be that he's disgusted with me for killing Lundgarden," Archie states.

I may not know anything about psychic connections, but I do know a thing or two about killing. It's my turn to interject.

"First thing that you have to remember, Archie," I say, "is that you didn't *kill* anyone."

Jumping off of my bed, Archie grabs Jess's old Hello Kitty pillow and squeezes it so tight that I'm afraid she's going to start screaming a string of Japanese obscenities.

"I know you were in wolf form last night, Dom, but I also know that you were witness to everything," he states. "I most certainly *killed* Winston Lundgarden."

"No, you didn't!"

Arla's and my voices conjoin to create one outraged sound.

"Then who did?" Archie asks.

Once again, Arla and I reply in unison. "Nadine!"

Archie slams the pillow onto the floor with such force that Kitty rocks back and forth a few times before stopping, her impish smile never leaving her face.

"Nadine might have started all of this, but I'm the one who gave in," Archie begins. "I'm the one who attacked an innocent man and didn't stop punching and clawing at him until he was dead!"

He turns away from us so he doesn't have to look at our faces any longer and winds up facing his own reflection in the mirror. Wolflexes take over, and I leap off of the bed to grab Archie's fist before he smashes it into the mirror, saving Kitty and the rest of us from being showered by flying fragments of glass.

"You didn't give in, Archie; you didn't *want* to kill," I explain. "Nadine's black energy took over. It's the same exact thing that happened to me . . . when I . . ."

After all this time it's still hard for me to just say the words. I take a deep breath and try again.

"When I . . . when I killed Jess."

There, I've said it, but the problem is I don't one hundred percent believe in the comparison. I was cursed; I still am cursed, but in the beginning I had absolutely no idea what was happening to me. I wasn't really even aware that anything was happening to me. Archie, however, has had warnings. He's known that he has both Jess's golden light and Nadine's dark energy flowing through his veins in equal measure. He's known for quite some time now that all he has to do is make a choice, decide to fight against the darkness that has unnaturally been placed within him. He did make a choice, but unfortunately, it was the wrong one.

I don't want to bring all this up now. I don't want to discuss it because it's only going to appear as if I'm judging him. I mean, it took me a while to corral my primal instincts; it took my almost blinding Arla for me to truly understand that I had to somehow find the strength to fight back and take control of who I am away from the devilish forces living inside of me. Guess I should cut Archie some slack since he's on a similar journey. But looking into his eyes now, my instinct is telling me that our journeys are going to be completely different.

"The Archie I know is not a killer, but he is a fighter," I declare. "He wouldn't let schoolyard bullies pick on him; he wouldn't let society convince him that he was born unworthy of love or respect; he fought back, and that's what you have to do now."

"But how can I, Dom?" he asks. "I took a life."

He says this to me as if it's something I know nothing about.

"And so did I, Archie. You know that!" I shout. "All this time you've been standing beside me, telling me that I was not responsible, that I'm a good person and I only acted barbarically because someone had taken possession of my body. I think it's time you started listening to your own words."

"She's right, Arch," Arla adds. "Take your own advice."

Archie covers his face with the palms of his hands to hide from us, but he can't hide from the horror that's still so pure and ripe. His hands turn into fists and then into weapons, and his face becomes prey. Bam, bam, bam, he slams his fists into his face until Arla and I each grab one hand to prevent him from doing any permanent damage.

"Stop it!" I cry.

"Let go of me!"

"Archie, c'mon, you have to stop," Arla pleads.

"God forgive me, I liked it!!"

He liked hitting himself in the face? He needs forgiveness for that. No, oh no, it's much worse.

"You don't understand! I liked killing Lundgarden," he confesses. "I *enjoyed* it!"

His startling admission produces no rebuttal, no response, no remonstration. How can we answer or argue against something we can't fathom?

"You don't know what you're saying, Arch. You . . . you can't mean that."

Poor Arla. She has absolutely no idea how wrong she is. It takes me a moment, but finally I understand Archie's comment.

"I think I did too," I say. "I think I must have enjoyed killing Jess."

The thought of it makes me gasp even louder than Arla. It's the first time I've ever thought about how I must have felt as a wolf during her death. I've been so preoccupied with blaming myself for her murder and then forgiving myself, or trying the best that I could to forgive myself. I even thought about what must have been going through Jess's mind when I was killing her, the terror, the panic, the sheer un-understanding of the entire situation. I mean she was the first person ever to watch me transform. I know that she was horrified, but then to be killed by this thing that she thought was her friend—it's un-fathomable. But I never, not for one second, thought about how I must have felt while I was taking her body and her life and her soul from her. I must have been joyful.

"It makes sense that I would have, right?" I say, not both-ering to wipe the tears from my cheeks. "A wolf likes to kill, it's in its nature, so why wouldn't I have enjoyed killing Jess?"

I feel like I've just taken two giant steps backward in my Wolfaholic Anonymous treatment, but I pray that my admis-sion is helpful to Archie.

"So you . . . you understand?" he asks. "You get how I en-joyed it?"

I nod my head a few times first, because the sobs are pre-venting me from speaking. "Yes, Archie, I do."

We hug each other tightly, and when my mouth is pressed against his ear I whisper, "But you have to fight against it, Archie. You have got to fight with every ounce of strength you have. You cannot let Nadine win."

When we pull away from each other, I see that she may be winning already. His eyes are brimming with tears, but they're also brimming with blackness.

*　*　*

A few days later at Winston's funeral mass, St. Edmund's Church is packed to the rafters. Who knew The Cell Keeper would have so many mourners? Of course Lars Svenson is in attendance; he's got to be the first one to get the scoop on all the local gossip. And Elkie is here wearing a gorgeous black satin pantsuit with a red rose in her lapel for a splash of color and defiance. Since she has arrived in the dual capacity of employee and almost-a-relative, thanks to Essie's once-romantic relationship with the deceased, Elkie has VIP seating. I see Officer Gallegos just in the nick of time before he walks past me. He's out of his uniform, wearing civilian clothes, so I almost didn't recognize him, but luckily I had enough time to turn away before he looked into my eyes and recognized me. But the most surprising pew member of all is Melinda Jaffe.

Unlike at Napoleon's funeral where I could tell that she was acting the role of grieving mother, she now wears her sadness as if it's her own and not borrowed off some rack that specializes in mournwear. Perhaps it's because she's alone this time—Nadine is home resting after her traumatic childbirth with Luba as protective guardian and watchdog—but Melinda looks as if she's truly affected by Winston's death. I'm still convinced that her heart is made of stone, but there might be the smallest crack on the surface.

I'm not the only one who's noticed.

Arla reaches over and grabs my arm when Louis walks up to Melinda, and, after exchanging a few words, sits in the pew next to her.

"Wolf up, Dominy," Arla commands. "I want to know what he's saying to her."

Reluctantly, I switch over to wolf-hearing to eavesdrop from the other side of the church, certain that I'll hear something incredibly private that will destroy whatever lingering innocence I still might own, but I'm wrong. I don't know if hearing her son's voice rebuff her from beyond the grave or witnessing her ex-lover's death has changed her, but the inappropriate response she displayed after Winston died might have just been bravado. I can't detect a false note in her voice.

"Thank you, Louis," she says. "That's very sweet of you to say after . . . well, after everything that I've done to you."

Melinda may not be able to look at Louis, but he can't take his eyes off of her.

"That's in the past," he says. "What's done is done."

As she turns to face Louis, I can't see Melinda's expression, but the way that she's touching his face, I imagine it must be tender. She's tracing his cheek with her finger, and I recall the time she did the same thing to Winston and ended up digging her fingernails into him and ripping off some flesh. Now she simply holds Louis's chin in her hand.

"You are the sweetest man I've ever known, Louis Bergeron," she states.

What?! I'm thrilled to hear that Melinda is retreating, scaling back her bitchery, but deep down she couldn't possibly have changed that much in just a few short days, could she? Arla grabs my arm tighter, and I know that she's thinking what I'm thinking: We have to interrupt this scene before it escalates and Melinda and Louis reunite in the shadow of Winston's casket. Once again while we deliberate, my brother jumps to action.

"Louis," Barnaby says, standing behind him. "Could I see you for a moment?"

"Uh . . . uh, sure," Louis stammers. "Is, um, everything okay?"

Playing his role as interloper with conviction, Barnaby nods reassuringly. "Everything's fine. You just need to speak with Lars Svenson before he prints more lies in the *Three W* about Mr. Lundgarden's death. I know none of us would want any falsehoods printed."

Turning back to Melinda, Louis still looks empathetic, but

the allure of a possible re-romance has been broken. "I have to take care of something," he says.

"Of course," Melinda replies, a bit crestfallen.

Standing up, Louis turns to follow Barnaby, but turns back at the last moment to say one more thing to Melinda.

"But I meant what I said," Louis adds. "If you ever need me, just call."

Again, I can't see Melinda's face, but I know her expression has to be happier than the one Barnaby's wearing. And definitely more joyful than the scowl that appears on Arla's face once I present her with a verbal transcript of their conversation.

During the rest of the mass I try to zero in on Archie, make sure that he doesn't freak out and throw himself on the coffin while giving some eleventh-hour confession, or worse, that he doesn't break down if he begins to relive the tragic event that ended Winston's life. He remains quiet throughout the mass though, sitting with his family, who must have known Lundgarden in some capacity. Archie's expression is sometimes dour, but always respectful and appropriate for the setting.

I'm a different story. By the end of the funeral my gigglaughs threaten to destroy the serenity of the proceedings, because it dawns on me just as they lower Winston's casket into the cold ground that this is the first unexplained death in this town that I really had nothing to do with. I look over at Melinda and even Archie, and I know it isn't right, but I feel a little relief. I hated the man, but I didn't want him dead, and I did try to prevent his death from happening.

Right or wrong, I whisper out loud three words that I never thought I'd hear myself say. "Thanks, Cell Keeper."

Chapter 25

Thin Nadine doesn't look right.

I guess I got so used to seeing her fat and swollen and pregnant that now with a flatter stomach she looks somehow wrong. Her transformation isn't as impressive as mine, or even Gwen's when she went from hog to hog-wild, but there's something physically different about her. I look at her from the waist up and find the culprit: The change isn't in her waistline, it's in her face. During her pregnancy she was all smiles; now she's wearing a permascowl. Is it possible for witches to suffer from postpartum depression?

The one thing that remains the same is her signature sound. I'd know that squeak anywhere. Even if I didn't know she was returning to school today, nobody makes that noise walking down the hallway except Nadine. Today, however, her tempo's a bit more rushed than usual.

"Hey, Speed Demon, accent on the demon, catching up on lost time?" I ask.

"Where's my daughter?" Nadine asks back.

Okay, number one: That was a funny joke that deserved some kind of reaction. And number two: It's taken her almost a month to figure out that she only has one kid around the house when she was supposed to deliver twins? I know the first few weeks of motherhood can be a difficult time, a whirlwind of epic proportions, but she couldn't find a spare moment in between nursing and changing diapers to pose this question to her mother or Luba?

"Why don't you ask your grandmother?" I reply.

As I start to walk toward my locker to retrieve my physics book, which is too big to carry around unless I'm heading directly to class, Nadine grabs my arm. And by grab I mean latches onto me as if her hand is hermetically sealed to my body.

Wolf-sneer to witch-scowl, I bark, "Get your hand off of me!"

"Not until you tell me where my daughter is," she demands. "I know you had something to do with her disappearance."

Glancing around the near-empty hallway, I don't see anyone staring at me, so I use my full strength to pry Nadine off of me with my free hand and shove her across the hall. She squeaks to a halt just before crashing into a row of lockers.

"And I told you if you want to know anything about your daughter you should ask that psycho you call grandma!" I shout.

When I turn around to face my locker, I face Nadine instead. She's witchraveled in public to move from one side of the hallway to the other in the blink of an eye. Really fun way to move from point A to point B, but not a smart idea if you want to appear completely human to your fellow classmates. Nadine's always been a risk taker, but now she doesn't care if she gets caught, which means she's upped the risquotient to certifiably insane.

"I'm asking *you!*" she screams.

If her flash drive didn't attract attention, her screech has, and now several of the kids in the hallway have stopped moving and rummaging through their lockers and are staring at us. They're not even pretending not to listen; they've gone from apathetic students to interested audience, and now they're waiting for my next move. So is Nadine.

"Are you going to answer me?" she screamasks. "You know how I get when I'm ignored."

Unfortunately, I do. And one false move and several unlucky members of Two W are going to find out as well. Where is Vera Bailey-Clarke when you need her?! Whenever Nadine would see Vera walking toward her, she would run the other way; if only Vera would show up now, maybe the twinemy would flee the spotlight. But ever since stargirl left with Nadine's daughter, Vera gave up the charade of playing high schooler, which means she isn't around to scare off the teenaged motherwitch.

Taking a deep breath more for a chance to collect my thoughts than out of necessity, I stare at Nadine, and surprisingly I don't see her black light trickle out of her body like usual. But in the silence while everyone waits for me to speak, I do hear her squeaking again. How can that be? She's not even walking. Wait a second! I have no idea if a witch can suffer from postpartum depression, but she clearly can suffer from an old-fashioned case of the nerves. Nadine's light isn't making an entrance because she's nervous and therefore not completely in control of herself. Motherhood really does change some people.

Using my newfound knowledge to my advantage, I decide to toy with Nadine's fragile emotional state.

"Are you talking about the baby girl with the thick mop of brown hair?" I ask.

"Tell me!"

"I'm so sorry if you misplaced your daughter, Nadine, but are you sure you were having twins?" I ask. "I mean, maybe you just gained a ton of weight during your pregnancy and were carrying really, really big, so it looked like you were expecting twins."

Between the shrieks of laughter from the kids and the shrill ringing of the class bell, I can't hear Nadine's reply even with wolf ears. Still, I'm pretty sure her comments wouldn't get anything lower than an R rating, and that's if the ratings people were in a super-magnanimous mood.

By the time the bell stops ringing, it's only Nadine and me left in the hallway; the rest of the kids have run off to class. So much for my perfect attendance record. And so much for trying to avoid a confrontation on public turf.

"You may think you're funny, Dominy," Nadine remarks. "But you have no idea how powerful I've become now that I'm a mother."

Hmm, maybe I have competition for worst math student of the century.

"Really? I thought the triumvirate needed three participants," I reply. "If you can't find your daughter, that just leaves you plus your son, which equals two."

"Where is she?!" she screams, ignoring my mathematical formula.

"And with only two of you, you really have no ammunition to make Luba step down from her throne," I state. "Which means you don't have as much power as you would like me to think. In fact, with Luba still in charge, you don't have any power at all."

Enraged by the truth, Nadine raises her hand, and I instinctively brace myself for some sort of attack. But instead of seeing beams of energy shooting out of the palm of her hand, I watch in fascination as her entire arm becomes wrapped in golden sunshine. I turn to my left, expecting to see Jess floating in the middle of the hallway having come to my rescue once again, but it looks like a supernatural upgrade has taken place.

"Mr. Dice?" I ask.

Actually, he's dropped his professor shtick and is floating in the center of the hallway in full Okami garb. Physically, he

looks basically the same as he always does, except that his
hair is longer and pulled back in a ponytail, but he's wearing
the most gorgeous kimono that's about twenty-five different
shades of yellow. I haven't seen him wear this before, so
maybe this is some special occasion, but regardless, the robe
hangs to the floor and then sweeps back in a train that continues for as far as my wolf eyes can see. It's stunning, and
I'm sure Jess has done her best to coax Dice to let her try it
on, though I'm not sure if clothes swapping is allowed in
their dimension. Speaking of what's allowed, I didn't think
Okamis could interfere with mere witch 'n' were fights. Has
someone thrown out the supernatural rulebook?

"You've caused enough death and damage within these
walls, Nadine," Dice declares. "I will not let you bring any
more pain into this school."

His voice is so deep and baritoney that it slams into the
lockers and echoes down the hall. If I didn't know he was on
my side, I'd be as nervous as Nadine looks.

Her shoes squeak loudly as she shifts her body, trying to
break free from Dice's Okamihold, but he's too strong for
her. It's intriguing to see Nadine look frustrated. She's not exactly afraid like she was around Vera; she almost looks like a
little girl who can't understand why her mother won't let her
have a third slice of cake. If only Nadine had had a mother
who didn't indulge Nadine in her every whim or let her do
whatever she wished or encourage her to treat people despi-
cably, maybe she would've turned out differently. But I witnessed a flicker of change in Melinda, so perhaps there's hope
for her daughter.

"By the power of Orion, I compel you to let go of me!" she
screams. "Or I'll have the Hunter unleash a thousand horrors
in your realm!"

And then again maybe not.

Dice laughs so uncontrollably at Nadine's feeble threat
that his body starts to shake, the train of his robe rippling

like a golden dragon behind him. Nadine is so infuriated that she isn't being taken seriously that she can't enjoy the sheer beauty of the image; then again, I have a feeling this visual display wouldn't be considered beautiful in the eye of this bee-holder. She's more about making things die than having things come alive.

"You have so much to learn, Nadine," Dice replies, still laughing. "Orion is powerful, but even His regime has boundaries."

"His power knows no limits!" Nadine retaliates. "It's as vast as the universe."

And sometimes you have to choose your words carefully because your opponent can use them against you.

"And in the universe, my friend," Dice says, in full patronizing teacher-voice, "a cluster of stars is no match for the power of the sun."

To prove his point, Mr. Dice rips off the sash holding his robe together, an action that frees Nadine's arm, but before she can retaliate in any way, he opens his robe to unleash the full force of his Okami sun god power into the small space of the hallway. Once again, Nadine and I view this revelation in completely different ways.

Wave after wave of glorious sunlight passes over me. I should be blinded by it, I should be burnt to a crisp, but instead it feels like I'm being transported inside a new world, a place I never had the mental capacity to imagine. I think I'm getting another small taste of where Jess lives.

Nadine, however, is reacting as if she's suddenly been thrust into the fiery pits of hell. Screaming and shielding her eyes, she cowers on the floor and is literally trying to crawl away from the sun slaughter. Every time she crawls a foot away, she's dragged back by golden ropes wrapped around her legs, only to attempt escape again with the same results.

Like any good teacher, Mr. Dice recognizes when a student is unwilling to learn or just incapable of comprehending previously unknown concepts and ideas, so he closes his robe to extinguish the extreme sun display from the hallway. But like the good teacher he is, he never gives up on a student.

"Learn from this, Nadine," he says kindly. "Power comes in many forms, so be careful what you wish for."

Ooh, an ominous Okami! With that final word, Dice disappears, taking the sunshine with him. I wish I could go with him, even if it means spending an hour in calculus. It would be better than being stuck here with Nadine.

Awkwardly standing over her still crouched body, I know I should help her up, but I'm relishing this vision of her. It's sort of the flipside of when she watches me as a wolf.

"If you don't want to answer my questions here," she hisses, "then we'll do it at my cabin."

She always wants to play on home turf.

"Fine," I reply. "If that's what you want. But I'm telling you right now, I have nothing to say to you."

As she finally stands up, I have to hold back a loud string of gigglaughs, Nadine tries to strike a menacing pose, but she's barely able to gather her dignity.

"We'll see about that," she announces. "I want to know what role you played in my daughter's kidnapping."

Like Mr. Dice said, be careful what you wish for, Nadine.

"I'll see you there tonight," I say.

"No," Nadine replies. "Tomorrow night will be much better for my schedule."

Before I can disagree, Nadine disappears in a flash as quickly, but not nearly as flamboyantly, as Mr. Dice did.

"But tomorrow night is a full moon!" I shout.

"Do you have something against full moons?"

Twisting around, I see someone who fills me with more happy sunshine than Mr. Dice and all his Okami magic could ever produce.

"Caleb!" I squeal. "What are you doing here?"

"I have two words for you, Domgirl: 'spring break,' " he replies. "Where else would I be but next to my girl?"

All thoughts of Nadine and Mr. Dice are yanked out of my brain and in their place are images of Caleb and me naked, kissing and holding each other and whispering the most heartfelt words we can think of in each other's ears. I run toward him and throw my arms around him in a full girlie-girl, big-screen, end-of-a-rom-com moment and give him the kind of welcoming he deserves.

I can feel his body come alive in our embrace, and when we finally stop kissing I look up into his face as if I'm seeing him for the first time. Brown eyes, blond curls, smooth complexion with just the smallest amounts of stubble on his chin and upper lip—once again Prince Caleb has come to the rescue.

"I've missed you so much," I confess.

"We just chatted last night on the phone," he says with a laugh.

"In my world that feels like years ago!" I reply. "You have no idea how much can happen in a day around here."

"I haven't been gone for that long," he says. "And I caught a little bit of the tail end of your confro with the bee. She wants to meet tomorrow night?"

"Yes, in order for me to tell her all the details surrounding the birth of the twins," I convey. "And what happened to her daughter."

"Then you have no choice," Caleb says. "You'll have to meet her."

"But it's a full moon tomorrow night," I remind him. "Don't you think that's a bad omen?"

"It would be if you were going alone," he replies. "But you'll have your Wolf Pack as backup. Me, Arla, and, of course, Winter."

And here's the part of the reunion where I get to break my boyfriend's heart.

"There's something I have to tell you about Archie."

* * *

As we sit on some rocks outside Nadine's cabin, the air feels chilly, but not freezing. March can be so unpredictable, like friendships. Caleb thought he was coming home for a couple of weeks of lighthearted fun; he had no idea he was walking into an emotional minefield. Well, that may not be entirely true. As my boyfriend, he's learned to expect the un-expected. But things have been much more easygoing for him in the role of Archie's best friend. Until now.

"What did it feel like?"

Archie doesn't look up from the ground when he answers Caleb's question; he keeps staring at the snow circles he's drawing with a twig.

"Exciting," he replies. His voice part ashamed and part re-lieved at the chance to explain himself. "Invigorating, com-pletely natural."

If he were describing his first date with Napoleon, I would be thrilled, but he's not; he's describing Winston's death. Thankfully, I filled Caleb in on what's been going on with Archie—physically and mentally—so Caleb isn't blindsided; he was prepared to hear this news. Still, I can tell, by the way his hands remain shoved in his jacket pockets and his eyes re-main glued to Archie's face, that he's both mesmerized and disgusted by our friend's comments.

"Had you thought about killing Winston or anyone before he started badmouthing Napoleon?" Caleb asks.

His twig stops moving, but Archie keeps staring at his art-work. "No."

"Then it sounds like Arla and Domgirl are right," Caleb de-duces. "When you heard Lundgarden disparaging Napoleon, it triggered something inside of you, and some other force took control of your body."

Finally, Archie drops the twig and turns to face Caleb. "But I didn't stop it. I never even thought about reeling it in. I just wanted to kill."

"Because it was the first time," Caleb replies. "Just like with Domgirl. But now that you know, now that you're aware of what this energy inside of you is capable of, you can prevent it from ever taking control of you again."

Archie is smiling and shaking his head at the same time. I'm not sure if he's amused or annoyed by Caleb's questioning. "You make it sound so simple," he says.

"Winter, it is simple," Caleb affirms. "If you want it to be."

"And what's that supposed to mean?"

Caleb takes his hands out of his pockets and grabs Archie by the neck. It's an old-man gesture, and in an instant Caleb ages before my eyes. His words and his actions possess a maturity I've never seen before.

"You're the strongest guy I know, Winter," Caleb says, his voice soft and direct. "And if you make the choice to beat this thing, to overcome it the next time it wants to control you, you'll succeed. It's your call."

A gust of wind blows Archie's hair around to reveal that the black roots still haven't gone away. Despite Archie's protestations, Nadine's evil presence is alive and well and living inside of him. And the problem is, I don't know if Archie wants to rid himself of the intruder.

I look up and see the moon rising in the sky. For the first time in months I actually wish the moon were already full and reigning so I could escape all of this. When Nadine opens the cabin door, I hesitate before following my friends inside. A part of me just wants to run through the woods and lose myself in the forest, but Archie isn't the only one who has to make a choice. Besides, there's no way I'm leaving Caleb and my friends at the mercy of Nadine, since when it comes to mercy, the girl is bankrupt.

"We need to make this fast, Nadine," I announce once inside her cabin. "The moon is almost full, and we all know what that means."

"Then tell me where my daughter is," Nadine replies.

"Don't you find it the least bit odd that your grandmother didn't tell you?" Arla asks. "Or that woman who calls herself your mother?"

"And what would you know about the relationship between a mother and a daughter?" Nadine retorts. "Chat with lesbmom lately?"

"Leave her out of this, Nadine," I say. "This is between you and me. Vera took your daughter."

A black silhouette appears around Nadine's body. She's angry, but in control.

"I knew it!" she shouts. "How? How did she do it?"

"With my help," I admit.

The silhouette grows a few inches, so she looks like the depiction of a revered saint.

"Tell me what you did!"

"I worked with your grandmother," I say. "If it weren't for Luba, I could never have done it."

The silhouette is gone, and the midnight-black snakes are back. They're writhing and flailing about Nadine's body. It's a wonder she isn't having a seizure from all their activity.

"Explain it to me!" she screams. "How exactly did you do it?"

"You mean *we*, how exactly did *we* do it," I say, correcting her. "I found out you were having twins, and I shared your secret with Luba. She wasn't thrilled to find out that you were lying to her, but she had suspected you were plotting something."

"You had no right!"

"I had every right!" I roar. "Because if you had both your children now, you would be in the position of ultimate power. There would be no need for Luba, and you'd have killed her just as easily as you killed your brother! I may not be valedictorian, but I'm not stupid!"

Nadine starts to pace the room like a wild animal, black streaks and curlicues traveling behind her. "I knew my grandmother was too stupid to figure it out on her own," Nadine rails. "She thinks she's so untouchable. She thinks that no one could be as smart or powerful or cunning as her. She's always underestimated me, but no more. Where is my daughter!?"

"I told you, she's with Vera!" I shout. "She and Orion will raise your daughter and keep her far away from you. Forever."

"She should be with me!" Nadine screams. "I'm her mother! How dare you intervene?!"

"You should be thanking me!" I cry. "If it were up to Luba, your daughter would be dead!"

"That isn't true!"

"You don't believe me, ask her yourself!"

"Tell me the truth, Dominy," Nadine seethes. "Or I swear on my brother's life I'll kill whatever's left of your family and all of your friends!"

"Haven't you killed enough already?!"

When Nadine hears her brother's voice, I expect her to react the way her mother did, but I couldn't be more wrong.

"Shut up, you fool!"

"What more do you have to prove?" Napoleon asks.

"I told you to shut up!" Nadine cries. "I don't want to hear another word out of you."

No, Nap's vocal appearance isn't going to make Nadine show remorse or reflect upon her actions; it's going to make her take action. All the tendrils of black light floating around her body fuse into one long stream and shoot out from Nadine's body directly into Arla's mouth. If it weren't for Caleb's grabbing hold of Arla just as she starts to collapse, she would be on the floor.

"Napoleon!" Archie cries, rushing to Arla's side. "Please don't go."

"Stop whimpering, you idiot," Nadine chastises. "My brother's dead."

He may be dead, but he isn't taking things lying down.

Just as Arla wakes up, the fireplace erupts; flames burst in every direction almost as wildly as Nadine's energy. After the initial explosion, the flames begin to shrink, and puffs of black smoke appear in between the red and orange fire. Napoleon is not happy with his sister's threats.

"And when I get through with all of you," Nadine declares, "my grandmother's going to join him for betraying me!"

Suddenly the flames lose all their color, and a huge chunk of black smoke fills the fireplace. It levitates and frees itself from the confines of the hearth to move into the center of the cabin, filling the room with the smell of rotting eggs. I can't believe Nadine's words are getting her brother so angry; he's never reacted like this before. When the black smoke disappears, my confusion is justified. The smoke wasn't housing Napoleon; it was Luba.

"It's time for you to find out *exactly* what I'm capable of!" Luba shrieks, wisps of charred smoke tumbling out of her mouth when she speaks. "And if you think you're any match for my power, child . . . *think again!*"

Clearly frightened, Nadine holds her ground and lashes back at Luba with the same rage. "You plotted against me! How dare you?!"

"How dare you think you're worthy of taking my place!" Luba wails. "You want to defy me? You want to steal my power from me? Perhaps it's time that you suffered for your hubris!"

Nadine takes a step closer to Luba, all fear gone from her eyes. "You would *never* hurt me!"

"No, child, I wouldn't," Luba replies.

A triumphant smile spreads across Nadine's thin lips. But her victory is short-lived and over by the time Luba finishes her sentence.

"But Dominy would."

Chapter 26

Unwolf me!

I can feel the moon's grip latch into my bones, digging deep into my soul to claim ownership, temporarily, but completely, and as much as I want to give in and become the moon's slave yet again, as much as I want to lose myself within a cloak of glorious red fur, it's too soon. No! I can't transform now, not after an announcement like that. Luba has a plan. I don't know what it is, but it involves me. As always she wants to use me, make me her pawn, her wolf-puppet, make me do the things that she's too cowardly to do herself. She wants to recline on her black throne and do her best imitation of her own disgusting god—Orion. *Well, guess what, Luba? Game time is over. I know too much now; I have too much knowledge; I know all about how balance works in this world, and I refuse to let someone as pathetic as you use me again!*

You're not the only one with a plan.

"Is that right, Luba?" I ask, fully aware that I only have control over my voice for about another minute. "You believe I'll hurt Nadine because you're afraid of her?"

Luba's body doesn't move; she appears to be frozen in a

black cloud of smoke, like an immaculately preserved fossil from a lost era. But then slowly the petrified surface begins to thaw, and her thin lips elongate to form a smile that has never known a moment of pure joy.

Making the sign of Orion with her left hand—her pinky and thumb touching, while her three remaining fingers point at me—Luba acknowledges that she understands I want to play a game. She also knows my playtime is running out.

"Are you that foolish, wolf-child, to accuse me of knowing fear?" she asks.

"I've seen your eyes when you look at Vera," I reply. "It's the same look you had in your eyes when I told you about Nadine's plot to get rid of you."

"That's a lie!" Nadine protests. "Don't listen to her!"

"Quiet!"

The sound of Luba's voice reaches Nadine a few seconds after the blast of black smoke slams into her face.

Caleb moves in front of Arla, who is standing now, once again in control of her body, in a feeble attempt to protect her. I wish they would leave, take Archie with them, but I know they won't; they're going to see this out to the end. Maybe it's time to push things along. Luba wants to use me; well, it's time I used her.

I look outside and see that the moonglow is blinding; it's pulsing with life, *my* life! It wants me, and it doesn't want to wait any longer for its prize.

"What are you so afraid of, Luba?" I ask, trying to ignore the blood starting to boil underneath my flesh. "Why are you so afraid to be the one to show Nadine exactly how furious you are? Exactly who has more power!"

Silence is her reaction! Well, I don't have *time* for silence!!

"Are you that *stupid*, Luba?!" I shout. "Your granddaughter wanted you dead!"

"She *still* wants her dead!" Nadine screams.

Her voice sounds more ferocious and wild and primitive

than any sound that has ever emerged from my wolf lips. Nadine's eyes are mad, her neck thickened and reddened by the angry, blood-soaked veins trying to escape their fleshy host, her entire body tilting forward, kept in place only by Luba's black smoke.

"You ... stole ... my ... child!"

The heat spreading throughout my body is too much to ignore, and I gasp as I fall forward and my hands slam into the wooden floor. *Fight this, Dominy; fight it for as long as you can!*

"Luba wanted to kill your daughter!" I scream, the last word sounding more like some horrific, guttural cry.

I shake my head futilely, trying to ward off the onslaught of pain and change. Even through my blurred vision I can see Caleb and my friends shudder and press their backs into the walls of the cabin, desperately trying to escape what they know they'll witness once again.

"If it weren't for me, Nadine, your daughter would be dead!"

"No!" Nadine cries.

That one sound contains such innocence and horror and shame that it's almost pitiable. Nadine is fully aware of what her grandmother is capable of; she can testify to Luba's maliciousness; she has carried out Luba's sinister plots and championed her evil—but there was always a speck in Nadine's soiled soul that was pure. It was alive with the knowledge that her grandmother was her ally.

Every familial relationship is complex; it's filled with love and hate, compassion and vengeance, pride and envy. Nadine and Luba's relationship is really no different than my relationship with Barnaby. No matter how dire the circumstances between us may seem, I would stand beside my brother and protect him with my dying breath. Nadine thought she could expect the same from Luba. She was wrong.

"You were going to kill my daughter?" she asks.

Gone is fury; in its place, meek wonder. And as a reply, brutal honesty.

"Of course I was going to kill her," Luba replies, her voice clear and unfettered by a conscience. "Do you truly think I was going to allow you to replace me without taking action?"

The clouds surrounding the moon depart, allowing it to hang in the sky in all its silver glory. A huge burst of moonlight engulfs the room and shines on Nadine's face, making her look younger and more fragile than she's ever appeared.

"I thought..." she says. "I thought you would understand."

Instantly the black smoke swirls around Nadine's body and then retreats into Luba's waiting, hungry mouth. Once Luba's swallowed, once she's consumed whatever disgust is contained within that blackness, she flies through the air, only stopping when her face is an inch from Nadine's. Completely horizontal, completely mesmerizing, Luba finally replies.

"You...thought...*wrong!*"

When my bones begin to break I know my time is up; I've stayed on this side of humanhood as long as possible. I don't know if it's because I fought the transformation this time or if it's because I'm terrified of being in this cursed state while in Luba's presence, but the pain is excruciating.

Each snap feels like it's in slow motion, the pain lingering within me, making my body shake violently. I bang my fist so hard into the ground that I break a floorboard in two. I'm gripping it so tightly with my fingers that for a second I think I'm looking at my reddened flesh and not my fur-covered paw.

In mid-change, I raise my neck and catch Arla staring at me, her eyes fascinated and frightened. She tries valiantly, but she can only hold my gaze for a few seconds before closing her eyes and moving her lips frantically in prayer. There is no way I can hold her instinct against her; she knows what I'm capable of. Caleb's quite a different story.

His eyes never wander; they never falter; they consume me just as the moon and the curse and the wolf devour my body. His eyes look the same as they did the first time he kissed me, the first time he made love to me, the way they're always going to look at me for the rest of our lives, no matter if we stay together or if we part tomorrow. They're filled with unconditional love. And I stare back at him with the same look in my eyes.

Even when the girl is buried deep within the wolf's soul, unseen by the rest of the world, I stare at him, tug on our invisible thread, and maintain my connection to the real world. Unfortunately, Luba has a way of making me question which world—the wolf's or the girl's—is the most real.

"You shouldn't have lied to me, child," Luba tells Nadine. "You shouldn't have concealed the truth about your pregnancy."

Lowering her chin and lengthening her back, Nadine tries to compose herself; she tries to exude her usual arrogance, but only succeeds in looking childishly defiant. "I know you would've done the same thing if you were in my place," Nadine retorts.

"If our roles had been reversed, child," Luba whispers, "you would already be dead."

"Then how can you hold my actions against me?" Nadine asks. "You *do* understand. You would've done the same thing!"

"Because I am Luba! And you are nothing more than my subject!"

Her voice is so loud and thunderous, I can feel the fur all over my body sway in the breeze. I'm not sure what's more grotesque, her words or their impact. She's rationalizing her own despicable actions; she's rationalizing plotting to kill her own great-granddaughter.

"I thought I was your heir!" Nadine rails back. "I thought I was being groomed to inherit your power."

"Again, you thought wrong!" Luba cries. "Had you not been so selfish and greedy and impatient, my power would have come to you naturally, but you have defiled Orion's spirit!"

"How?!" Nadine asks. "By wanting to be filled with more of His glory?"

"By thinking you were ready to defeat His most sacred pupil!" Luba replies. "But if it's a fight you want, perhaps we can find you a worthy opponent."

Still floating in the air, Luba twists her neck so all her hair falls from the left side of her face like an onyx dagger. Smiling at me and then at Nadine, she roars, "My two most prized possessions! The wolf and the witch."

I drag my nails across the floor, disgusted by the comparison.

"Shall we see which one is stronger?"

Howling furiously, I try to convey to the others that I understand Luba's plan. She wants Nadine and me to fight to the death. Either she'll be rid of her nemesis, her wayward creation, and move on to another prey, or she'll be rid of her granddaughter, her unscrupulous sycophant, and be able to reclaim the child Vera took and raise Nadine's twins as her own, once again the head of the triumvirate, administering power instead of sharing it. It's a foolproof plan; either way Luba ends up victorious.

There's only one problem. There's no way I'm going to fight; there's no way I'm going to allow Luba to curse me with causing another death. That's brave talk for a wolf, but a girl is much weaker.

In an instant Luba is standing in front of me, unfazed by my open mouth, my saliva-glistened fangs. That's because she can see beyond the exterior and peer deep within the wolf. To stare into the soul of the girl.

"Come out, Dominy," she taunts. "Come out, come out, wherever you are."

"Leave her alone!" Caleb shouts.

Luba doesn't look away; she merely raises her arm, and I don't have to turn my head to know that Caleb and Arla have been attacked, because I hear them crash into the floor. There is silence on my other side. Archie hasn't moved, not to run away, nor to try and protect me. He's merely watching.

"We're waiting!"

Glaring at me, Luba once again makes the sign of Orion and extends her arm. Is she insane? She's going to shove her hand in my mouth. Do it! Do it so I can bite it off and swallow it! I'll digest every disgusting piece of your flesh if it'll stop you! But Luba isn't that careless; she's putting on a show.

Three streams of black smoke spring out from her fingers, twist around each other like a long, ebony braid, and hover in the air for just a second before plunging straight down my throat. I bite down hard, but it's too late; my body's being invaded by this foreign force, and I'm defenseless against its attack.

"Dominy!"

Caleb's voice crashes against my ears as Luba's smoke burns into my stomach and spreads out like wind, unstoppable, deep within me.

"What are you doing to her?" Caleb cries.

"Making her reveal her true self," Luba replies.

Something tells me to keep my mouth clenched, to not allow the smoke to free itself from this wolf prison. Whimpering sounds trickle out of me as my body bangs into the floor; my paws try to grip into the wood, but my legs can hardly remain straight. There's a war going on inside of me, and regardless of who wins, I lose.

"Open wide, Dominy," Luba commands.

For the first time that I can remember, Luba uses her own

two hands to do battle. She grabs my snout, one hand on top, the other on the bottom, and tries to open my mouth. Clenching down tight against her assault, I can hear my teeth gnash against each other; I can feel my fangs pierce the skin of my lip; I can taste my own sweet, sweet blood. It reminds me of how hungry I am, and it gives Luba that tiny piece of leverage she needs.

She yanks open my mouth with such force that I expect her to rip my jaw from my body and raise it over her head as her trophy. But Luba isn't interested in fleshly prizes. She's come for my soul.

Smoke pours out of my mouth, but it isn't black; it's red. It isn't Luba's spirit that's leaving my body; it's Dominy's.

Like an illusionist pulling a long red scarf from his mouth, Luba pulls a long stream of red smoke from mine. Inch by inch the smoke emerges, making me gag and retch and choke. Tears sputter from my eyes, moistening my fur, making my vision as blurry as it is during a transformation, which makes sense, because right now I'm going through another change. I blink my eyes because I can't believe what I'm seeing. The red smoke is taking shape, the shape of a girl, the girl who lives deep inside of me.

"Dominy!"

The people around me shout the same name practically in unison. They're as shocked as I am to see this girl emerge, to see her shape become molded by the smoke, to see her come alive bathed in the color of blood right before their eyes. But this is no frightened newborn; this girl has been waiting to be freed.

Inhaling sharply, Dominy's body floats a few feet higher off the floor. Her head tilts back so her long, incredibly long, red hair, a wild tangled mane, hangs behind her. Her lithe body is covered in a long slip, almost a membrane that barely covers her sinewy, muscled body. Every feature of her is glorious; every inch of her body is alive.

Face-to-face we stand, wolf and girl, for the first time since our cursed birth, separated, tentative, and unsure of our new surroundings, these new sensations, but desperate to experience them. We look deeply into each other's eyes, and we see ourselves, and we smile. For all the horror we have witnessed, we always know we'll have each other.

But right now Dominy doesn't want anyone. All she wants is vengeance.

"Nadine!"

Dominy's voice bellows through the cabin, making the walls vibrate as if in a dream.

"It's time you found out what it's like to be me!"

Consumed by years of anger and pain and suffering, Dominy grabs Nadine by the throat and lifts her over her head. The other girl twists in her grip, claws at her hands, but there's no escape, not even when Caleb begs Dominy to let go.

"Dominy, no!" Caleb cries. "Don't do this!"

Swinging around to face her boyfriend, Dominy doesn't let go of Nadine; she keeps her raised in the air.

"This is part of me, Caleb," she replies. "If you love me, you have to accept all of me, the good . . . and the bad."

Her words strike against him like razors, but he's a strong one; it will take a lot more than that to push him away. "Just remember who you really are," he pleads.

Pausing only momentarily to reflect upon his request, Dominy smiles. "That's exactly what I'm going to have Nadine do."

Turning back around to face the open window, Dominy positions Nadine so she faces the full moon.

"Look at the moon, Nadine!" Dominy cries. "And tell me how it feels!"

Suddenly Dominy lets go of Nadine, but instead of crashing onto the floor, the terrified girl is blasted with silver moonlight that lifts her even higher, until she almost touches

the ceiling. Screaming wildly, her back arched, hands gripping the air, Nadine looks like she's being electrocuted. Nothing so pleasurable, however. She's being transformed.

The blaze of silver light disappears, and Nadine falls to the
floor with such force that her hand slices through an end
table. Instead of passing out from the pain, she scrambles to
her knees, but before she can get upright she clutches her
stomach in agony and lurches forward, her face slamming
into some broken shards of wood.

"What are you doing to me?!" she wails.

"The same thing that you and your grandmother have done
to me!" Dominy cries. "Month after month after month!!"

Nadine's eyes widen, and the realization hits her that Dominy
has reversed the curse; she's forcing Nadine to undergo the same
cruel and painful and incessant transformation that Dominy has
had to experience since her sixteenth birthday.

"Help me!!"

Even if anyone wanted to help Nadine, they couldn't.
Once such power is unleashed, it can't be squashed until it's
finished its journey. And Nadine's transformation is just beginning.

"I'm on fire!!"

"How does it feel, Nadine?" Dominy asks. "Like lava
rushing through your veins?"

I turn my head and see Arla's face buried in Caleb's shoulder, his own face turned away from the scene, neither of them
wishing to bear witness to the ugliness. But Archie's eyes are
wide open; he's consuming every second of Nadine's torture.
He could be repelled by it or relishing it; I can't tell. Whatever the reason, he cannot or will not look away. Neither will
Dominy. She wants to see Nadine suffer like she must every
month; she wants her to know what she has to go through
because of Nadine's family's curse.

"This is what you've done to me!" Dominy cries. "Do you
understand what you people are putting me through?!"

"Stop it!!" Nadine begs. "Please st . . . ahhh!"

Her plea turns into a shriek as she watches her legs break in the wrong direction, and then she screams maniacally as she watches her arms and her flesh begin to be covered with foul black fur. All remnants of the light that often accompanies her are gone, vanished from sight so as not to partake in their host's gruesome metamorphosis.

"I'm dying!" she manages to scream. "Help me!"

Words are completely lost as her face disappears underneath a mask of fur and fangs and fear. Exhausted, Nadine's body slumps onto the floor until it can find the strength to rise. Panting wildly, the black wolf stands up; the transformation is complete.

"Now you know what it's like to be me," Dominy says.

Cowering in Dominy's presence, Nadine backs up, one shaky paw after another trying to lead the way to escape, but there is none. Not in Luba's presence.

"Now fight!"

"No!!"

All heads turn to see Arla, her eyes rolled back in her head so only the whites remain, her mouth opening, Napoleon's voice speaking.

"Enough fighting!" Nap cries. "This is our chance for peace."

"Napoleon?"

Archie's voice is ignored. Napoleon only wants to speak to his sister.

"Nadine," he continues. "This is your chance! Let your daughter be free. Raise your son to love and not to hate."

His message may be for his sister, but his grandmother has heard every word, and she is not pleased. Flying through the air, she grabs Arla by the throat and squeezes her thin, ivory fingers around the girl's dark skin.

"This isn't about love or hate, you stupid, *stupid* idiot!!" Luba screams. "It is about power!"

A wave of blackness flies out of Luba's mouth and into Arla's, and just as Dominy was pulled from deep within the bowels of the wolf, Napoleon is severed from Arla's body.

"Napoleon!!"

This time Archie races toward his boyfriend's resurrected body and tries to grab hold of him, but before he can reach him, before he can make contact with the person he desperately wants to touch, Luba flings her grandson into the air.

"BEGONE!"

"Nooo!!" Archie cries.

Napoleon's body disintegrates before our eyes, splintering like cracked glass, but leaving behind no remnants, no physical reminder that he was once here, that he was once a very important part of our lives. There is nothing left behind, nothing except for Archie's rage.

"Damn you!" Archie cries, racing toward Luba.

"No," Luba spits. "You, white one, are the one who is damned!"

Luba's scream turns into a dark cloud that passes through Archie and rips his pure white flesh from his body to reveal a maze of bone underneath, the color of untouched coal, brilliantly black.

"No one can hide from who he truly is!" Luba cries. "And you, child, are nothing but pure evil!"

Archie's skin returns, covering his ebony bones like a horde of savage white worms. Horrified by the vision of his soul, Archie turns to Dominy, tears pouring from his violet eyes.

"I'm sorry," he says. "I'm not as strong as you."

"No, Archie!" Dominy cries, flying toward him and grabbing his hands. "Don't give in. Remember what Napoleon said: You have to fight."

"It's no use," Archie replies. "Look at what you've just done. I know I'm capable of much worse."

Confused, Dominy turns to see the black wolf crouched low to the ground, not ready to attack, but hoping to disappear.

"Oh my God," Dominy gasps. "What have I done?"

"Helped show me exactly who I am," Archie replies.

Pushing Dominy away, Archie starts to run out of the room and is about to burst open the door when Caleb grabs his arm.

"Winter, stop!" he begs. "This isn't you!"

"No, Caleb," he says. "This is exactly who I've become."

Slowly the darkness creeps back into his eyes, and the beautiful shade of violet is gone, irreversibly replaced by two black orbs. The darkened roots staining his hair begin to spread out like hundreds of tiny black spiders, until his white hair drowns in a sea of oil. Just as Dominy has had to do, Archie has had to make a choice. He's given in.

"Archie, no!" Caleb cries.

I don't know if it's involuntary or deliberate, but Caleb lets go of Archie's arm, and it's with that one gesture from his dearest friend that the last reason for Archie to stay is taken away from him.

Archie flings open the door so furiously that it almost rips free of its hinges, and we watch him run into the woods, having no idea if he's running toward something or away from what he's become.

A gust of cold air invades the room, but it's no match for the chill residing inside. The game is over, and Luba has won.

Luba spreads her arms out to the sides, and the red cloud is hurtled back into my mouth—Dominy and I are one again. Once we are reconnected, the black wolf disappears, and Nadine is standing in its place, white-faced, sweat-soaked, and shaken.

I shake my snout and howl angrily. I can't stay here any longer; I have to chase after Archie, prevent him from doing anything foolish. But the door is blocked. Vera has returned and is standing there, holding Nadine's sleeping babies, one in each arm.

"You have made Orion very unhappy," she says.

Chapter 27

And how happy do you think Orion has made me?!

Vera smiles in my direction, but I can't let her disarm me; I can't be fooled by her relaxed demeanor. Moving to my right I stand in front of Caleb and Arla, a low growl coming out of my mouth. I don't want to attack, but I will protect.

Her smile grows wider, but I'm not sure if it's out of respect or if it's patronizing. Like always Vera confuses me. I should know better than anyone—human, animal, or spirit—not to be fooled by a disguise, but I thought Vera was different. Yes, I know that she is simply a fragment of Orion's constellation in human form, a fallen star, but I thought we had an understanding. How dare she burst in here and tell me that I've made Orion unhappy! Despite everything that *he* has allowed to happen to me, I've done everything in my power to help *him*. If it weren't for me, Luba might be dead and Nadine might be cradling her kids in some new town as the head of an even more malicious coven. He should be thanking me instead of chastising me.

And perhaps I should listen better.

"Sorry, Artemis, I wasn't talking to you," Vera clarifies. "I was talking to them."

"*Artemis?*" Luba asks. "What in the world are you talking about?"

"Private joke, Luba," Vera says, smiling rascally. "Nothing to worry your newly pretty head about."

One thing's for sure: Vera has a sense of humor. That's more than can be said about Luba and Nadine. I twist my neck to look behind me, and, swathed in the glow of the full moon, those two are staring at Vera as if she's some foul, repugnant thing instead of a messenger of their god. Such hypocrites! They love Orion, but they disrespect him; they worship at his altar of starlight and accept the gift of being infused with his glory, yet all the while what they really crave is unbridled power. They want to live their lives according to their own rules, ignoring that their strengths come from a source independent of them. They are nothing without Orion, and yet they refuse to bow to him.

But now it appears as if Vera is going to force them to genuflect, at least symbolically.

"Luba and Nadine, the Original Hunter is not amused by your behavior," Vera asserts. "While He does find a certain amount of . . . *moxie* . . . admirable and a hint of the spirited rogue to be whimsical, the two of you have crossed the line into insolence and sacrilege, and therefore must be punished."

When Nadine speaks it's evident she hasn't listened to a word Vera has said.

"Give me my children!" she wails.

"You haven't proven you are *worthy* of children!"

The sound that comes out of Vera's mouth is so earsplitting I'm more amazed that the babies haven't stirred in her arms than I am at the intensity of her outburst.

"First, Nadine, you must prove you are still worthy to be a child of Orion," Vera continues, her voice now much, much calmer.

"I have spent a *lifetime* proving my worth!" Nadine states, her voice anything but calm.

"And it only took nine short months to destroy the foundation you had created," Vera claims.

Angrily waving her hand in the air, Luba interrupts their debate. "Enough talk of these children! Get on with this unjust trial!"

Delighted by watching Nadine and Luba squirm, Vera pauses to bounce the children in her arms. She lifts the boy to her face and, smiling at him as if he were her own child, she inhales deeply, breathing in his fresh, newborn scent.

"Very well," Vera says. "Luba and Nadine, how do you plead?"

I'm not sure if a silent reply constitutes a formal response, but Vera accepts their silence as an admission of guilt.

"Guilty as charged," she affirms.

Regardless of who Vera is or what she represents, Luba cannot stand to be insulted by anyone.

"This is an outrage!" Luba shouts. "A mockery of the life I have given to Orion! Of the sacrifices I have made and the magic that I have created in His name!"

While defending herself, Luba walks toward Vera, seemingly unafraid, urged on by her own passionate desire to preserve her dignity and stature as Orion's most beloved offspring.

"You have absolutely no idea who I am, do you?!" Luba rails.

Once again Vera proves that while Luba may be strong and close to invincible, Vera is of an altogether higher order. She softly blows in Luba's face and sends the woman flying through the air until her back crashes into the wall on the other side of the cabin. When Luba doesn't give in to gravity and slide down to the floor, I think for a moment that she's been impaled by a hook or a stray nail, but it's clear that Vera is just putting on a show for everyone, and she's the one keeping Luba suspended a few feet off the ground.

"I know *exactly* who you are, Luba," Vera replies, her voice as cheery as Luba's was threatening. "You are an ignorant child in the body of an old woman. A creature who has acquired corpses instead of knowledge, a being who has studied improperly and still has so much more to learn."

Vera pauses to glance over at me. "I thought by now Dominy would have taught you some important lessons," she adds.

"Dominy?!" Luba blurts, her body still looking as if it's nailed to the wall and her face looking as if she has just devoured sour flesh.

"Yes, the one you cursed," Vera replies. "She is also the one who shall lead."

The mere mention of being my supplicant enrages Luba so utterly that she finally frees herself from Vera's hold. Stumbling to the floor, her hands and knees hitting the wooden planks with a thud, she lifts her head and then her body and then her voice.

"I will *NEVER* follow that . . . *THING!*" she declares.

Just as Luba raises her hand to point it in my direction, Vera's eyes disappear, and two rays of light zoom out from the sockets to burn a hole through Luba's palm. Clutching her wrist and violently screaming in agony, Luba falls to her knees, half-horrified and half-amazed that she can see right through her flesh.

After only a slight hesitation, Nadine rushes to Luba's side and clasps her grandmother's wounded hand in hers. A swirl of black energy surrounds their interlocked hands, and when Nadine releases her hold on her grandmother, the laceration begins to heal. New flesh forms along the circumference of the open hole in Luba's hand, weaving a black lattice of skin and muscle and veins until the wound is healed and only a gnarled black scar remains that will serve as a reminder to Luba of her true place in this world.

How interesting that it has taken a common enemy for Nadine and Luba to once again work alongside each other. Vera shares my opinion.

"What a beautiful sight to behold," Vera cheers. "Different generations working together to solve a problem. Teamwork does make Orion happy."

"If you want to make *me* happy, Vera," Nadine says, "give me my children."

Vera's hearty laughter smothers the cabin.

"I have no desire or need to make you happy, Nadine," she replies. "You are an abomination, a blight."

Before Nadine can protest, Vera continues.

"However, you are also a descendant of the Hunter," she states. "So He has decided to show mercy . . . if you comply."

"Does He consider it merciful to allow you to steal my daughter?" Nadine asks.

Every trace of laughter evacuates from the cabin and from Vera's expression. It looks as if the girl doesn't even comprehend the meaning of the word.

"You may want to rephrase that," Vera corrects. "Both He and Dominy have shown mercy by allowing your daughter to *live*. If it were not for them both, you know Luba would have killed her; she would never have allowed you to raise two children, knowing that you would be plotting her death along with their future."

Vera hugs Nadine's children closer to her body. "Orion believes in the holiness of His lineage, and so He had to do everything in His power to prevent your babies' deaths."

"Give them to me, and I will protect them," Nadine pleads. "I'll protect them both, I swear!"

"Are you ignorant, or do you take me for a fool?" Vera asks. "If both your babies remain here on earth, Luba will not rest until one of them is dead, so unless you're finally ready to kill your dear, sweet grandmother right here and right now, you can only have one child. There can only be three of you because of . . . Oh what word does Jess always use?"

"Lim . . . limitations?" Caleb answers.

Vera looks at Caleb as if she's noticing him for the first time. She's pleased by what she sees. "Ah, yes," she confirms. "Limitations."

Nadine shifts her weight from one foot to the other, squeaking loudly. "This isn't fair!" she squeals. "She's my child."

"Not anymore," Vera replies, firmly. "You forfeited your right to claim ownership when you sought to overturn the balance of your triangle—Luba, Nadine, and Napoleon. That was the way Orion wanted it to be."

"The boy was unworthy!" Luba exclaims.

"According to whom, Luba?" Vera asks. "You?"

"He was a disgrace!" Luba screams. "He was just like his father!"

"And yet in Orion's eyes he played an important role," Vera states. "A role that Nadine extinguished prematurely. Such behavior shall not be rewarded."

"But they are my children!"

"SILENCE!!" Vera exclaims.

Once again her shriek is so volatile it's amazing that the babies in her arms don't cry in utter fear, but they remain silent, sleeping comfortably in her arms. Orion must be protecting them from the commotion, or Vera's words are only meant for us to hear.

"It is done, and it *will* be obeyed," Vera instructs. "The boy shall be raised by you, Nadine, and I shall find a home for the girl in some part of the universe. Do not waste your time trying to locate her, because every attempt will end in failure."

Vera drops her arm, and miraculously the baby boy rests in the air. She blows him a gentle kiss, and the child floats from one side of the room to the other, landing in Nadine's waiting arms. Despite her past actions, despite the malice that clings to her like flesh, she holds her son tenderly and astoundingly appears to be grateful for their reunion. Luba, however, still hasn't wiped the contempt off of her face. Vera may have to do it for her.

"And you, Luba!" Vera screams. "Remember to honor your truce with Dominy."

Luba lowers her head, and her lips form into a sneer. "I have no intention of going against my word," she says.

"Swear to it," Vera commands.

Reluctantly Luba raises her hand in the sign of Orion, and Vera matches her gesture. "I swear," Luba replies.

"Good," Vera says. "And because we don't trust you, we will be watching to make sure you keep your promise. You have created and caused enough damage. It's time to let both the wolf and the girl live in peace."

Thank you.

"Remember, Luba, you are powerful," Vera adds. "But not nearly as powerful as you think."

It's clear from her clenched fists that Luba is infuriated by Vera's comments, but she stands motionless, reluctantly wearing a mask of cordiality. The only other sign giving away that she is enraged is the quick rise and fall of her chest. The two slivers of flesh that constitute her lips remain clamped so she doesn't say anything to unleash Vera's full fury. Perhaps Vera's wrong; perhaps Luba does know herself and her own limitations as well.

Heaven only knows what lies within Luba's heart and mind and soul, but I know what lies within mine. Even hidden by fur, I know exactly what I am: a girl who has made a choice to protect my family and my friends and not allow this curse that has been placed upon my head to destroy me. I'm better than that.

"Yes, you are, Dominy," Vera replies to my silent musing.

The rest of what Vera tells me is in silence—star to wolf—
so it can't be overheard.

"You have served Orion and your friends well," she states.
"You have overcome insurmountable odds and understood
the need for balance and how to maintain it. But most of all
you have served *yourself* well."

A few short years ago I wouldn't have believed any of
those words. Now I do.

"Thank you."

"There will be more battles for you to face," Vera cau-
tions. "But remember, Dominy, you are strong, you are
courageous, and above all else, you are blessed."

"This sounds like a farewell," I reply.

"Oh no," she corrects. "You'll definitely be seeing me
again, sooner than you think. We aren't done with you yet."

Abruptly, a glorious display of starlight fills the room, and
I watch with gratitude and hope as Vera along with Nadine's
daughter disappear. *Please God let that child have a good
life.* Looking across the cabin I pray the same thing for Nadine's other child. He may, but it won't be in Weeping Water.

"I'm taking my family away from here," Luba announces.

"That sounds like it's for the best," Caleb replies. His
comment is much more diplomatic than the thoughts bouncing around my head.

"But don't shed too many tears," Nadine adds, her sarcasm having resurfaced since Vera's departure. "Rest assured
we will return."

"And we'll be waiting for you," Arla interjects.

"How wonderful! My son and I will be counting the days
until we're all reunited," Nadine replies. "Oh, don't you
want to know his name?"

Sarcasm meet sarcasm.

"Not really, but I'm sure you're going to tell us anyway,"
Caleb replies.

"Hunter," Nadine offers. "So you'll never forget who . . . and what he is."

Looking at the golden birthmark on the boy's foot, I'm reassured that even though he's going to be raised by someone with, at best, questionable mothering skills, he will be protected by Jess's light. Who knows how the boy will turn out; he may overcome the odds and be as defiant as Napoleon tried to be, or he may choose to follow in the footsteps of the Jaffe women. I would like to say that I'm optimistic that he'll choose to rebel against Nadine and her vile nature, but that would be a foolish thought; there are too many factors at play. I just hope he is strong enough to know his life is filled with options. For now, however, he is his mother's child, for better and worse.

Smug and noisy, Nadine starts to leave the cabin, her son in her arms. She is headed toward a future that I have no doubt is warily waiting for her next move. Before she greets the future, however, she has to say good-bye to the past.

"Good-bye . . . cousin," she says.

That's a fact I plan to quickly forget.

"Enjoy your peace while it lasts," Nadine adds. "I know I will."

I pant louder as I watch Nadine leave the cabin and enter into the waiting night, not because I'm anxious, but because I want to drown out the sound of her incessant squeaking. I hope I never have to hear that sound again. The other sound I never want to hear again is this hiss that masquerades as Luba's voice. Unfortunately, she has a few more things left to say.

Turning around I see Luba frozen in her spot, staring at me. Her eyes don't leave mine even when she addresses Caleb and Arla.

"Would you two . . . *children* give us a moment alone?" she asks.

I can feel Caleb's hesitation; he doesn't want to leave me

alone in Luba's presence even if she did swear to a truce in front of Vera and under the watchful eye of Orion. Normally, I'd agree with him—Luba cannot be trusted—but now, I get the sense that all she wants is closure.

Howling softly, I then tilt my head to the front door, letting them both know it's okay to leave us alone.

"We'll be right outside," Arla announces.

The moment they step outside I can feel Luba's hot breath on my snout. She's kneeling down on all fours, staring me in the face, creature to creature.

"Remember, Dominy, I created you," Luba reminds me. "And some day, I *will* destroy you."

I've heard this before, and I know that Luba means it now, but I'm not afraid. One day, whether it be next week, a year from now, twenty years from now, Luba will come looking for me with or without Nadine and her child in tow, but wherever I am and whatever I'm doing in my life, I'll be prepared. Because not only did Luba create me, she's also taught me very well. I know how to fight against evil. And I know how to win.

"Until we meet again, Dominy," Luba whispers.

"Good-bye, Psycho Squaw," I silently reply.

And for once I'm thrilled that she can read my mind.

Chapter 28

It's been three weeks, and still no sign of Archie.

After everything that's happened to and around me, his disappearance is probably one of the most difficult things to rebound from because, ultimately, when I think about what he's done, I can't escape feeling disappointed in him.

No one completely understands the desire, the utmost need to vanish, to want to be classified as extinct, more than I do. Many times since this curse began I have wanted to hit a button or flip a switch and be non-Dom, nevermore, escape from myself and from everything and everyone around me, but what would that solve? Wherever I wound up and whenever I opened my eyes, the curse would still be with me and, worse, I would be part of nothingness. I would be alone without my friends and family, and so I made the only choice I could: I chose to stay and fight back. Knowing that Archie didn't make the same decision, I can't help but be filled with disappointment and anger and sorrow.

But even as I allow these feelings to fester inside of me, I know my father would not approve. I remember he said to me once not to judge another person, because you never know the truth of their situation, nor can you expect someone else to respond to a problem the way you would. I try to cling to that fatherly bon mot now, but it's hard. Archie was a witness to what I've gone through, and he knows that without my Wolf Pack, I would not have been able to survive. I just don't understand why he ignored the example of my life, why he felt the need to leave, why he couldn't even say a proper good-bye!

Selfish, yes, that's exactly what I am, and I'm not going to apologize for it. I wanted to share a lifetime with Archie by my side as my friend, not only to lean on him for support, but to offer him my hand and heart and knowledge. In so many ways I could have helped him; I could still help him, but in order to do that I first have to find him.

I know exactly what he's going through; I know exactly what it's like to be split in two and have to share your body and mind and soul with another creature. I could have guided him in ways to corral Bad Archie, taught him how to keep all the unhealthy urges at bay and let Good Archie, the Archie that I know and love, thrive and grow and live a wonderful life. The same kind of life that I'm determined to live.

I guess I'm so angry because there are too many unanswered questions. If he had only said "help me" instead of "good-bye," those questions could have been resolved. And maybe it's as simple as that: I'm really just pissed off because Archie never said good-bye to me.

When I open my locker, I realize that I'm wrong.

The letter is taped to the inside of the metal door, and I don't have to open it up to know that it's from Archie; I recognize his handwriting. There's no dot over the *i* in my name; he's topped that letter off with the bottom part of the *y*, which ends in a little circle, so it looks like a lasso or even a shooting star. I start to cry at the sight of it.

"Dom, are you okay?"

No, I'm not.

Gwen's hand feels so soft on my arm, like a bird perched

on a branch. But our roles are reversed; she's as poised and strong as a tree, and I'm the one who feels like she could be carried off to parts unknown if the wind changed its pattern. I look into the dark center of her eyes, and I understand why my brother is dating her. Whether she's zaftig or svelte, whether she looks like a model train or just a model, she has inner strength that she's willing to share.

It's time for me to understand that I don't have to keep everything tucked away; I don't have to carry a lock with me to make sure that no one knows what's going on inside of me, because those ugly parts are going to spill over anyway.

"No, Gwen, I'm not."

"Are you thinking about Archie?" she asks.

Her fingers slide down my arm to hold my hand, and the urge to flee doesn't come; I actually welcome this intrusion.

"Yes," I answer. "He left me a letter."

With my free hand I swing open my locker to reveal the envelope bearing my name. Gwen doesn't appear to be shocked; in fact, she appears to be delighted.

"He always had such girlie handwriting," she comments.

Now I'm laughing.

"Why don't you go read it in private," Gwen suggests. "The music room should be empty for another hour or so."

This girl never ceases to impress me.

"Gwenevere," I say, "that's a brilliant idea."

Inside the soundproof closet off of the music room, I sit on the floor and lean back against the cushioned wall. I grip the envelope from both ends and wish that if only I could pull, tear the paper in two, Archie would pop out and sit next to me, just so I could see his face one more time. His words will have to do.

> Dear Dominy,
> I'm not sure where I'll be when you read
> this. Truth is, I really have no idea where I'm

going. I only know that I can't stay here any longer. I don't belong here, not in the way that you and Caleb and Arla do, so I need to find a place where I do belong, a place that I can call my home.

I'm different now. I haven't been the same person for quite a while, ever since the night I fought with Nadine, the same night that Napoleon died. Everything changed for me then, and I think you've always known that it didn't change for the better. How I wish I were as strong as you are; how I wish I could fight the changes and the urges and these unnamed demons living inside of me, but I can't. I've tried and failed, and there's a reason for that. After I killed Winston I realized I didn't want to defeat those demons; I didn't want to reverse the changes that have been happening to me; I only want them to grow.

I know it's wrong. I know I should fight harder to keep them buried, but I like the way they make me feel, reckless and wild and free. Maybe if Napoleon were still alive or if he could speak to me or even through me, I would have the strength to fight back. Then again, it might only prolong the inevitable.

When I look in the mirror I feel so proud and magnificent, but when I look at you I only feel ashamed and disgusted with myself. And no one should feel that way about himself. That's why I can't stay here; it's because of you.

I'm not blaming you for making me run away; that's not what I mean. But it's because you have always fought; you've never given in to the curse or to Luba or Nadine. You've risen above all of this, Dom, instead of giving in to it. You've been the perfect example of how I should lead my life, and yet I just can't do it! I just can't be like you. And even if you and the others don't hold that against me, I hold it against myself.

It would be so easy for me to blame this all on Nadine and say that she turned me into this evil thing, but that wouldn't be the whole truth. I've made a choice. Someday I may choose to fight back and let Jess's light take over and be stronger, but for now that isn't what I want. So for now I have to leave.

I am going to try very hard to push you from my mind so I'm not constantly reminded that there are other choices I could have made, and I hope you can do the same about me.

But until you do forget about me, please forgive me.

Your friend,
Archie

All the anger I was feeling before I opened the letter is gone. How could it remain? In its place I feel such aching grief, like I'm mourning, but even more than when Jess died, because Archie could've been saved.

The letter in my hand feels so heavy I let it fall into my lap and let my hands fall to my sides. *Oh, Archie, how could I ever forget you? If it weren't for your helping me, standing beside me, believing in me, I don't know where I would be right now. But forgive you? No, I can't do that either, not right now anyway. I will always love you, but the next time I see you—and I won't rest until I do see you again—I will slap you so hard across your face, the sting marks won't fade away for weeks.*

And then I will hug you so tight that you'll never be able to leave me again.

When the door opens I see that it's time for me to leave.

"Dominy?"

I shove the letter into its envelope, fold the envelope roughly in two, and look up.

"Mr. Dice?"

What is he doing here? Spying on me? Oh no, that's right, he's also choir master as well as faux math teacher and Okamilord.

"Sorry, I didn't think you guys had class for a few more hours," I explain. "I'll vacate the premises."

He opens the door, and a shadow of sunlight fills the room.

"Band isn't for a while yet. I followed you here," he replies. "I wish I didn't have to intrude, but this can't wait any longer."

So, um, he was spying on me.

"What can't wait?" I ask.

"Jess."

Our hands touch, and it's as if Two W is thrown into the incinerator; we're engulfed in the most outrageously vivid sunshine I've ever experienced. Despite the yelloverdose, the air is cool and fresh and fragrant with the smell of cherry blossoms. I feel like I could grab on to the air and hold it in my hands, but the thickness isn't oppressive; just the opposite, it's light and buoyant and soothing.

We're not quite walking and not quite floating over the lush landscape, more like skimming, our bodies rising and falling instinctively according to the rolling terrain below our feet. Just below my toes the acres of grass and immense trees and plump bushes that populate the land are all in shades of yellow, a thousand different hues of the same color. The overall effect should be unreal and blinding, but it's the most natural sight in the world.

A golden bird as big as a parrot flies from one yellow tree to another, singing a bright, happy melody, its wings stretched out in mid-flight, creating a breeze that ripples through the air until the wave caresses my face and rustles my hair. To my left, I hear a splash and realize what I thought was an extension of a curved hill is actually a stream filled with golden water. A fish breaks through the surface, its face and tail such a deep shade of yellow it tinges on orange, while its body is the pale color of a faded, old-fashioned photograph. It creates a perfect arc in the air and then dives back down into the water.

Mr. Dice doesn't have to tell me where I am. I already know that this is Jess's new home.

"We thought it was time for you to see how the other half lives," he says.

"Because it's time for us to say good-bye, isn't it?" I reply.

"And everybody used to call me the drama queen!"

I grip Mr. Dice's hand tighter when I see Jess standing in front of us, and my feet circle the air like I'm riding a bike, in search of something firm to stand on because I'm shocked by the sight. Understanding my need to feel grounded, Mr. Dice slowly descends until we touch down and I'm standing in a foot of golden grass. I can feel the blades through my pants, and they're as soft as cotton. I don't even wonder how I can feel them because I can't believe how beautiful Jess looks.

It's like she's airbrushed, but instead of turning into some gross reflection of perfection, of what someone would want to look like, she's been turned into what she truly is. An image of Archie's blackened bones comes into my mind, but I shake it away. I'll have time to relive that memory and ponder that evolution; now I want to give my entire self, my eyes, my mind, my heart, to Jess.

Her hair is long and straight, but completely blond like her natural color, a nice compromise between Japanese and Caucasian aesthetics that looks perfect on her. Her skin glows from within, her eyes are twinkling in the light, and her smile is at once all-knowing and impish.

"Yellow, Dom!" she cries. "Welcome to Omikamiland."

Jess grabs the sides of her kimono, not as elaborate as Mr. Dice's, but still made of some crazy luxuriant silk-like fabric with long-flowing sleeves and a stiff upturned collar that makes Jess's face look even more eternally youthful, and she bows to me.

I don't know what it is about the gesture, the subservience, the humility, the joy contained in the movement, but it makes me cry. I do my best to mimic her motion, but I feel awkward and hardly graceful, so with my head still looking down at the yellow land I start to gigglaugh. And I hear Jess's cackle join in with me.

We might be in some other dimension, we might be an Omikami and a werewolf, but right here, right now, and forever, we are friends.

"It's pretty *subarashi,* don't you think?" Jess asks.

"Super *subarashi,*" I reply.

"I'll leave the two of you alone," Mr. Dice interjects. "I'll be waiting near the stream when you're done."

When we're done. I don't want to ever be done with Jess, but I think our time is coming to an end. I've known this would have to happen; Jess has been preparing me for it. But now that it's arrived, I don't think I'm ready.

Scouring my mind for an alternative, a solution, some sort of extension, I'm jolted out of my thoughts by a rustling in the grass near me. Looking down I see a rabbit, its fur fluffy, its body perfectly rounded, nibbling on a long yellow-orange carrot, and it almost looks like the animal version of Jess's precious Hello Kitty, who herself is an animal, but more like a girl. After a moment it scampers away, and I'm struck with an interesting thought. I almost missed this sight because I was trying to figure out a way to change my life. How much more of life have I missed trying to alter my fate? How enjoyable can life be if you just accept that it's yours to live and not yours to waste?

"Sorry, Dom, I can't waste any more time," Jess says. "And my to-do list is jammed today."

"Oh really," I reply. "And what's first on your list?"

Without hesitation she grabs my hand.

"I'd like to see my family once more."

In an instant we've left paradise and are in Jess's family's kitchen. She looks exactly the same except that her expression is a bit harder. She's not trying to hide her feelings from me; it's just that she's a different person now, and she understands she's here as a visitor.

When Jess's mother enters the kitchen, Jess sits in a chair in the corner of the room and watches her mother go through her routine. Even though neither of us can be seen, I stand in a corner of the kitchen and try to disappear into the wall to lessen the feeling I have of being a voyeur. We both watch enraptured as Mrs. Wyatt takes groceries out from a shopping bag adorned with Japanese characters that spell out words Jess's mother never bothered to decipher. She doesn't care what the words are; she only knows her daughter gave her that bag, and that's good enough for her.

Jess watches her mother fold up the bag slowly and neatly and slip it in between some cookbooks in the baker's rack from which she'll retrieve it the next time she has to go food shopping.

Mrs. Wyatt takes the teakettle off of the stove, fills it with water, lights the flame, and places the kettle back to its original position. Then she sits at the kitchen table, her legs to the side, not underneath the table, in case she has to get up quickly to answer the phone or rush out of the room to take care of some forgotten chore. And then suddenly Jess gets up and kneels on the floor next to her mother and lays her head on her mother's lap.

I have a vague memory of doing the same thing to my

mother—I guess every child has the same memory if he or she is lucky—and I don't know if Mrs. Wyatt can feel her daughter's presence, but she closes her eyes and lets the tears fall uninterrupted down her cheeks.

When the teardrops fall through Jess, they turn into tiny golden balls of water that explode like little fireworks when they touch the floor.

Without wiping away her tears, Mrs. Wyatt smiles, and I'm certain that she knows Jess is next to her. She will carry the memory of her daughter's death with her for the rest of her life; she has learned to handle the pain; she has learned to allow the joy of what it was like to know and raise Jess to touch her heart; she has learned how to maintain balance.

Misutakiti clearly needs a lesson.

Barking madly when he sees Jess, Misu jumps on top of her with such gusto that if she weren't some supernatural deity, she would've fallen over onto the floor. Mrs. Wyatt watches in amazement at the sight of her dog jumping and frolicking and rolling on the ground, yelping, his tail wagging out of control. She looks over at Jess. I have no idea if she's looking at her daughter or through her, but she smiles; it isn't wistful or forced, but genuine. Jess's mother is forever changed by what life has thrown at her, but she's going to be okay.

The shrill whistle of the teakettle pulls her from her reverie, and she gets up, steps over the still-animated Misu, and pours herself a cup of tea. She lingers in front of the window, the teacup in her hand, and lets the sunshine pour over her. This time she's pulled from her thoughts by a different, even more surprising, sound.

"Amelia."

Jess's father is standing in the archway that separates the living room from the kitchen. He looks tired, but not as worn out as he did the last time I saw him. Jess stops playing with

Misu in order to look up into her father's face. She is as startled to see him as her mother is.

"Henry," Mrs. Wyatt says. "What are you doing here? Is everything all right?"

He smiles at her awkwardly, like he must have the first time he asked her out on a date. "I thought," he starts, before clearing his throat. "I thought we could have lunch together."

Jess's parents stare at each other, and I believe it's the first time they're truly seeing each other since Jess's death.

"That would be very nice."

Without speaking another word, Mrs. Wyatt opens up the refrigerator, and Mr. Wyatt sits at the kitchen table. When they find their voices again, they chat about the choices they have for food, though neither cares at all what they will eat, as long as they sit at the same table and face each other.

"I just have one more stop to make," Jess says.

She grabs my hand, and we're whisked away to her brother's dorm room, the one he shares with Caleb at Big Red. It's empty, and I do my best not to look around to visually eavesdrop on Caleb's side of the room, though I do steal a glance at his bed, where he and I first made love, and despite the golden glow that's surrounding me, I feel my cheeks redden.

Jess sits at her brother's desk and pulls open a drawer on the left. I step a little closer and see that, among some papers and pens and even some stray beer bottle caps, is a photograph of Jess and Jeremy. It was taken when Jeremy was probably thirteen and Jess eleven, on Halloween, when Jess begged her brother to dress up as a Japanese samurai warrior and she went as Mulan. I remember how they fought about it and how he refused for weeks, saying that he wanted to dress up as the killer from the movie *Scream* or some wrestler, but Jess wouldn't relent. She pestered and begged and finally told him that he had to honor her request because she was an ancient Japanese princess, and ancient Japanese princesses always get their way.

The look on Jeremy's face was priceless. He wanted to tell her that she was crazy, but at the same time he loved her more than ever before for exactly that reason. He had a crazy sister, and instead of pushing her away, he embraced her. And that year he dressed up as a samurai warrior and later told me, in complete confidence, that it was the best Halloween ever. I swore I would keep his secret, and I did for about fifteen minutes, and then I told Jess exactly what he said.

She pulls a yellow rose out of the pocket of her robe and places it next to the photograph, next to the smiling faces of a brother and a sister, who will never forget one another even if they never see each other again.

When Jess turns to me, I know it's my turn to feel the same exact way.

"This is our good-bye too, isn't it?" I ask.

We're back in Omikamiland or wherever this yellow Eden exists, and I know that we're now moments away from being separated once and for all.

"It is, Dominysan," Jess replies. "I wish it weren't so, but this is the way it has to be."

I don't waste the few precious moments we have left questioning or debating. I reach out and grab my friend's hands and look her in her eyes.

"I love you, Jess," I say. "You have been like a sister to me my entire life."

"I feel the same way about you, Dom," she replies.

Before I can continue on, Jess beats me to the punch.

"And I don't want to hear another word about guilt or shame or remorse over my death," she insists. "Things happen, and we have to move on. And if you haven't noticed, this is a pretty amazing place to move on to."

Gigglaughing, I reply, "It's a place built for an Amaterasu Omikami, which is what you are."

"Right now I just feel like a girl saying good-bye to her friend," Jess says.

We hug each other tightly, and it's as if our memories merge. Images of our life together pass through our minds, the two of us playing dress up, riding the bus to school, poring through fashion magazines, chatting in the dark lying side by side in my bed, sharing clothes and bras and gossip, all the simple things that make up a lifetime and a friendship. These things will never leave me; they'll never leave either of us, even if we have to leave each other.

"It's time, girls."

Very reluctantly, I pull away from Jess, and when I look behind her, I gasp. It can't be! I blink my eyes and I was wrong; Mr. Dice is standing in front of me, but a second ago I could have sworn my father was gazing at me from over Jess's shoulder. His handsome, kind face, looking at me like he used to when he would have to wake me up for school on those days I just wanted to sleep for a few minutes longer. Could this man before me be my father? Could he and Mr. Dice be one and the same?

"Jess?" I start to ask.

Shrugging her shoulders, Jess replies, *"Seigen."*

"What?"

"Oh come on!" she cries. "Do you seriously not know the Japanese word for limitations?"

Smiling, I take one last look at Jess. My heart is so filled with emotion that it's hard not to cry, but I don't want to; I don't want to cloud my vision with tears; I just want to look at her.

"I have never . . . *ever* known a friendship like yours," I say.

"And you never will again," Jess replies.

More gigglaughs and cackles invade the serenity, and Mr. Dice or my father, whoever this man is, patiently stands by us, his hands folded behind his back, rolling his eyes. But the smile never leaves his face.

"Good-bye, Jess."

"Good-bye, Dominy."

Just before Jess fades away into the golden sunlight, she turns to me one last time.

"I have one more surprise for you," she announces.

"What?!"

"Turn around."

When I do, all the golden light has disappeared, and in its place everything has turned silver.

"Hello, Dominy," Vera says. "I told you we weren't done with you just yet."

Chapter 29

I want to trust Vera; I really do. But it amazes me that a simple change in pronoun causes me such concern. Sure, I'm a logophile, someone who loves words, so the inclusion of "we" shouldn't freak me out. Unless that "we" includes Orion.

"Does it matter that I'd like to be done with you?" I say. "No offense."

Smiling at me and looking way older than her fauxteen years, she says, "None taken."

When we land in front of The Retreat, my instincts—the wolf's and the girl's—react, and not in a happy, optimistic way. My stomach churns, fueled by a feeling of dread.

"This is payback time, Dominy," Vera states.

Payback? I know Vera isn't from this earth, but she must know that payback is not generally a good thing! Especially here, on this semi-possessed spot that houses The Retreat. This place was Luba's home-away-from-home for years; it's where both Essie and Winston were killed; it's where I almost got locked in The Dungeon, and it's where Nadine used to work. All of that adds up to not great odds in favor of payback's being any kind of gift that I'd like to receive.

"Trust me."

Vera smiles and then walks toward the front entrance. She never looks back because she knows I'm going to follow her. Am I that obvious? Maybe. Then again, maybe I'm just curious. Like Elkie.

"Vera," Essie's twin calls out from behind her receptionist's desk. "I never expected to see you again."

Without breaking her stride, Vera replies, "Then what a lucky day it is for you, Elkie."

I hesitate for a moment watching Vera walk down The Hallway to Nowhere and stare at Elkie. What is she? Is she a witch too? Or some other unidentified supernatural species? Could she just be possessed by Essie's spirit? I have no idea, but there's something not quite right about her. The good news is that she's on my side.

"It's a lucky day for you too, Dominy," Elkie says.

Hmm, what does she know that I don't know?

"Why do you say that?" I ask.

She folds her hands primly and places them on top of her desk. "Rumor has it that Melinda and her brood left town," she announces. "Scurried away in the middle of the night like freeloaders who could no longer afford to pay their rent."

I employ shocked-face to make it appear as if this is the first I'm hearing this news. "Really!" I fake-gasp. "That means the entire town got lucky!"

Duly convinced that she's told me the best news of the century, Elkie beams, "And I have a feeling that your luck is going to continue."

Entering Room 19, I expect to see Vera standing next to my mother. I never expect to see my mother standing next to Vera.

"*Kishi kaisei,*" Vera says.

Wake from death and return to life! In the past I've found those words to be inspirational, but I never took them literally, I never thought those words would come true, especially not in connection with my mother.

"Mom?!"

Her tears come first and then her words.

"Oh, Dominy!"

My mother's voice sounds a bit different now; it's not so ethereal; it doesn't sound as if it's calling out to me from another dimension, and that's because she's merely calling out to me from the other side of the room.

"My baby," my mother cries.

Her knees buckle, but she wills herself to stand strong. Her arms reach out to me, her hands wide open, so anxious to touch something rather than to be touched. "Please . . . please come to me."

The walk toward my mother seems to take hours only because I'm so frightened that when I reach my destination I'm going to find out that Vera is playing a cruel hoax on me and my mother is just a hologram, a phantom. I'm terrified that I'm going to wrap my arms around empty air, embrace an image of my mother, nothing more. But I'm wrong. My arms press against her warm back, and I feel her hands wrap themselves around me and pull me closer to her.

"Oh, Mom," I sob. "I can't believe this!"

"Oh, my baby, it's real," she replies. "I'm here, I'm right here, and I'm never leaving you again."

I'm overcome by the scent of Guerlinade, lilacs and powder and love smothering me and yet making it easier for me to breathe than it has been in years. Neither of us wants to let go and so we don't; we hold on to each other, thrilled that our touch elicits a response. No more one-sided conversations, no more embraces that have to be filled in with imagination. My mother is no longer in a coma, no longer unconscious. She's alive, but how?

"Payback," Vera replies.

Pulling away from my mother is agony, but I must. I have

to find out how this has happened. And above all else, I have to make sure that this is permanent.

"I don't understand," I say. "Payback for what?"

"For maintaining balance, Dominy," Vera answers. "Orion has unlocked Luba's spell and brought Suzanne back to life. He felt it was only proper, the only way for Him to follow your lead and maintain balance as well."

"Follow *my* lead?" I ask.

Vera nods her head. "Luba isn't the only one who has learned from you."

What do you know? I struggle for years in math and yet I've taught a star god a thing or two.

"Thank you, Vera," my mother says.

It's such a simple comment for such an extraordinary act.

"Yes . . . thank you," I add.

After everything I've been through, however, I'm not as simple or trusting as I used to be. "And this can't be changed, right?" I ask. "Luba can't come back at some point and return things to the way they were?"

"No, because this is the way things should be," Vera replies. "And that's all that matters."

I stare again at my mother and realize that I could stay in this spot forever without ever growing weary.

"How do you feel?" I ask.

She smiles at me, and I know exactly what she's going to say.

"Blessed," she replies. "I know about everything you've had to go through. I've been a silent witness to all your pain, and, *ma chère,* I am so *very* proud of you."

Instead of crying, I smile, and I say the first thing that comes to my mind.

"I'm proud of myself too."

"And you should be, Dominy," Vera says. "Remember, like it or not, you are Orion's child too."

After she leaves, my mother and I are alone. Despite the fact that the both of us are awake at the same time in over a decade, the space between us isn't awkward; it's filled with joy. Incredibly, the joy explodes when my brother walks into the room.

"Mom."

His voice is soft and unsure; he can't quite understand what he's seeing. But quickly belief takes over, and he doesn't waste another second trying to comprehend the implausibility of the situation; he rushes into my mother's arms. They're both so overcome with emotion; I'm not sure who's holding the other up.

"Barnaby," my mother whispers. "My little boy."

Finally they unhug, but refuse to fully separate and keep holding hands as they stare at one another.

"My little boy," my mother says, "is now a little man."

"And my mom is alive."

Leave it to Barnaby to be blunt.

"When Vera told me to meet her here," he continues, "I thought she wanted to give me a brush-up lesson before my exams next week."

So that's why he showed up.

"Nope," I say. "She had a much better surprise for you."

Barnaby looks at me with a knowing stare. I'm not sure what knowledge is percolating behind his eyes, but he's much smarter than I give him credit for.

"Looks like you and Vera are alike," he comments.

"In what way?" I ask warily.

"You're both full of surprises," he says.

Before I can think of some way to answer my brother, his attention turns back to my mother, where it should be. "But your resurrection, Mom," he claims, "trumps any surprise Dominy could ever come up with."

For the briefest instant my mother and I catch each other's eye, and we smile conspiratorially; it's like our mother-daughter relationship was never interrupted. Well, no more interruptions. I can't wait to fill her in on all the details of my life, formally introduce her to Caleb, reunite her with Louis, have her meet the now-grown Arla, whom she hasn't seen since she was a little girl. First, however, I need to take her home.

As luck would have it, the people who bought my old house have fallen onto hard times. Not that that's lucky for them, but it is lucky for us. With Louis's help, we were able to buy back our house with the money my father put aside for Barnaby's and my future, and the new owners even made a small profit, enough to help them become hopeful that their future would be brighter.

Moving back into our old home is definitely bittersweet. Louis has truly come to cherish his role as my and my brother's guardian, and he was looking forward to helping us navigate life's twists and turns. Thanks to Barnaby, Louis won't get off the hook just because my mother is now the head of our family.

"It's okay if I still come to you if I have any questions about, you know, *stuff*, right?"

Barnaby's question leaves Louis speechless. He has to focus on the sidewalk outside of his house and then glance over to the moving van that houses our bedroom furniture before answering.

"Barnaby," Louis says, his voice now strong and certain, "you have an open invitation."

"Cool," Barnaby replies. "I may not listen to you, but it's good to know you'll be there in case I need to ask."

"Thank you, Louis," my mother says, making his name sound Frencher than ever before. She holds his hand tenderly. "I don't think I can ever repay you for loving my children."

Louis swallows hard before answering. "It was the easiest job I've ever had."

Laughter and hugs and a few tears come next, which is normal when people enter new phases of their lives. Louis and Arla gave us a home when we didn't have one, and I will be eternally grateful to them for their kindness.

But now it's time for us to build a home together—Barnaby, our mother, and me—in the home we shared all too briefly and the home that I'm now reluctant to leave.

"I've made a decision, Caleb," I say. "And don't yell at me."

We're sitting on my bed, a fresh coat of pink paint on the wall facing it, so I can wake up every morning and see my favorite color.

"Do I ever yell?" he asks. "What've you decided?"

"I'm putting off college for a year," I announce.

I scrunch up my face, waiting for the yell to come from Mr. Academician. It never does.

"I think that's a great idea," he says, fiddling with the string bracelet he still wears around his wrist. "You need time to reconnect with your mom."

"How'd you know that was the reason?" I ask.

He stops playing with the string and looks at me quizzically, his hands folded in his lap. "Because I never stop thinking about you, Domgirl."

He hasn't touched me, and yet I still feel myself blush.

"Before I open my eyes, you're the first face I see," he says without a hint of embarrassment. "And when I go to bed at night, you're the last image I see before I fall off to sleep. You're with me, Dominy, always."

I feel the same way about Caleb. It came over me unexpectedly, a bit sneakily, but lately, maybe since my life is much calmer than it's been in years, only the good stuff rises to the surface. And there's nothing gooder than Caleb.

"And if I have anything to say about it, Domgirl," he states, "that's the way it's going to be for the rest of my life."

Did he just propose? He isn't even out of college yet. And then there's med school. Or maybe I'm just getting ahead of myself.

"But for right now you just enjoy a year of reconnecting with your mother and Barnaby," he says, throwing his arm around my shoulder. "Relearn what it's like to be a family."

I plan on doing just that.

Most girls can't wait to graduate high school and go off to college to get away from their mother and little brother. But not me. I guess it really is true what they say: One person's curse is another person's blessing.

Epilogue

Ten Years Later

"Winter!"

When my shriek doesn't garner a reply, I walk into the living room.

"Winter, didn't I tell you not to color on the floor?"

My son looks up at me, his three-year-old eyes lacking a hint of shame or guilt or remorse. Only logic.

"But I ran out of paper, Mommy."

"There are five coloring books right there in the corner."

"But I wanted to draw a picture of a horse," he replies. "And none of them have horse pictures."

"What do they have pictures of?" I ask.

"Dinosaurs and cars and flowers," he replies.

"Do you think you could color one of those until I can find some paper for you?"

He tilts his head to the side, his long black bangs falling into his eyes, to ponder my request. "Okay, I think I can do that for you."

"You're too good to me, Mr. Winter Bettany."

My son skips to the other side of the living room to collect a coloring book, and in a voice too old for his body replies, "That's what I've always told ya."

"Mommy!"

This voice comes from the kitchen, but I'm not alarmed at the shriek. After three years I know how to separate my kids' cries into categories, and this one is definitely excited.

"Yes, Jessica," I reply. "I'm right here."

"Is Grand-mère coming over tonight to babysit?" my daughter asks.

"Yes, she is," I answer, scooping her up in my arms. I swing her around, and she does what she always does when we're this close; she grabs my hair and connects it to hers so it's one super-long strand of red meeting jet-black.

"It's yours and Daddy's 'versary?" she asks.

"Yes, sweetie," I reply, turning the swing into a bounce. "Your daddy and I have been married five years today, and we're going away for the night to celebrate."

"That's not fair," Winter proclaims.

"Why?" I ask. "Can't we celebrate a happy occasion?"

"Of course," he replies. "But you have to swing me too!"

Luckily, my wolf-strength hasn't abandoned me after all these years, and I lift my son up in my other arm like he is a half-full bag of groceries. The three of us bounce and swing and jump around the room, gigglaughs and cackles filling it.

I stare at my twins, the children Caleb and I adopted in order to create the family we always dreamed about having, and I marvel at how lucky I am. Although I have my lycanthropy under control—as much as a wild beast can be controlled—neither Caleb nor I felt comfortable taking the chance on my giving birth to a child who might inherit my mutation. We almost gave up during the lengthy adoption process, but persevered, and when I held Winter and Jessica in my arms the first time, I knew we had made the right decision.

In a few hours, my mother will come over and spend a

couple days with my twins, coloring with them, teaching them how to make croissants, introducing them to some new French words, so Caleb and I can have a romantic dinner and then spend the night at one of the new casinos in Lincoln. Neither of us likes to gamble, but the place is half casino and half resort, so we can get massages and I can treat myself to a facial while he beats some stranger at racquetball. It's only an overnight trip since he can't take that much time away from his practice. Since he is Weeping Water's resident general practitioner, the town relies on his services.

As for me, my job can wait a day or two until I get back. As editor-in-chief of *The Weeping Water Weekly,* I can make my own hours. Plus, now that the Jaffes are no longer in town and the Full Moon Killer is part of town folklore, I doubt there's going to be a newsworthy event while I'm away.

When I was younger I always assumed I would stay close to Weeping Water, but, when Lars Svenson's will was read and he left me his paper, that cinched it. A lot of people in town questioned why I became heir to the town's long-running paper, and I simply assumed it was because I graduated with degrees in English and journalism and had written a few articles for the paper while studying at Big Red. Turns out I was wrong. Mr. Svenson left me an envelope to be opened a year after he died, which contained the most infamous issue of the *Three W* ever published, the one with the one-word headline: WEREWOLF? I will never know if he knew the truth about me or somehow had his suspicions. If he did, it wouldn't surprise me. Nothing ever does.

Not even when I turned on the TV a few years ago and saw Gwenevere Schültzenhoggen, rechristened Gwen Hogen, starring in her own sitcom. She plays a recently jilted lesbian woman, who is forced to move back home and live with her divorced mother and her widowed grandmother. It's called *The Lesbian, the Divorcee, and the Widow,* shortened, of course, to *LDW.*

Right after high school she broke up with Barnaby and stunned everyone by declaring that she was moving to Hollywood to become an actress. Sure, she had glammed up, but no one expected her to turn her dream into a career. She proved us wrong.

The only time I was really surprised was when Barnaby asked to have dinner with Caleb and me one night after we first got married. He said he wanted to introduce us to his new girlfriend, who I was sure would be the latest in a line of interchangeable faces belonging to an endless stream of girlfriends he introduced us to all throughout college and the years after. When Arla walked through the door I almost fainted.

She was beaming and shy at the same time. Even though she often worked with Caleb when they were both surgical interns at Memorial Hospital, he knew nothing about Barnaby and Arla's courtship, so Caleb was just as shocked as I was. Naturally, shock quickly segued to thrill, and they were married a year later. Louis may have lost a stepson, but he gained a son-in-law. As well as a lovely girlfriend named Darlene, whom he brought to the wedding and who, incidentally, just moved in with him.

Despite my curse, my life has turned out pretty darn *subarashi*. There've been a few low points, like when we heard that Archie had moved to Alaska after spending several years in New York. The town gossip has him working on the pipeline up there, but I can't be sure. I think of my friend every day. The letter he left for me after he ran away is in my green metal box with my other precious mementos, and I pray that he knows he is loved and can one day find his own inner strength to return home. After I pray, I remind myself, however, that everyone has their own journey, and it can't be steered by anyone else but them. No matter how powerful those people think they may be.

I know that Luba and Nadine and her son, Hunter, are out

there somewhere, probably watching me and waiting for the perfect moment to strike again. But I refuse to live my life thinking about them and dwelling on this curse. It's my lot in life, end of story. Yes, at one time they had power over me, but I took that power back to make it my own, and I will never relinquish it again.

Standing on my front porch, I see Caleb pull into the driveway, and I can hear my kids laughing in the background. Golden sunshine is pouring down on my face, and I open my eyes to it; I see Jess's face before me, and I capture the moment. Something flies by me then, and the idyllic scene is disrupted. Hovering in the space between me and all that's good in my life is a bee, buzzing quietly, wondering which way to fly. Involuntarily, I think of Nadine, of all she's done to me, and all she can still do.

Then Caleb swats the air, and the bee flies away. My husband kisses me hello, but I keep my eyes open and see the bee has returned and is watching me from a distance. No, I won't give in to those thoughts; I will not give energy to those fears. Instead, I will cling to what I've always known and what helped me survive during the worst of it all.

I will remember that I am, and always will be, blessed.